WE ALL HAVE A
STORY

by Tiffanye R. Paige

Lightning Fast Book Publishing, LLC
P.O. Box 441328
Fort Washington, MD 20744

www.lfbookpublishing.com

The author of this book tells a fictional story of a relatable family, with a theme of anything being possible with the support of family. The literary offering provided is fictional and derived from the imagination of the author. The intent is to give readers an entertaining read with life lessons interspersed throughout this literary work. In the event that you use or enact any of the material in this book, the author and publisher assume no responsibility for your actions.

This is a work of fiction. All characters and events are fictional.

The publisher, Lightning Fast Book Publishing, assumes no responsibility for any content presented in this book.

ISBN-10: 0-9974925-8-9
ISBN-13: 978-0-9974925-8-3

TABLE OF CONTENTS

DEDICATION

To Tylan, you are and always will be my driving force. Thank you for loving me and being my reason to always want to be better than I was the day before. I was able to finish this book because I wanted you to be proud. To my mom and dad, thank you for your love and always having my back. Chris, my big brother, I will always love you. Thank you for stepping up and being there for me when I needed someone the most. You always told me that I could do better and be better than I even knew myself. Nicole and Maurice, I love you, thank you for being my flashlight. You helped guide me out of the darkness. You all are, and always will be the wind beneath my wings.

INTRODUCTION

I t was a sunny day in June of 1992. I remember it well because it was the day of my mother's bridal shower (yes, my mother's bridal shower) and everyone seemed happy and excited. My mother's best friends and bridesmaids, Little Bits and her sister Candy, were throwing the shower. They lived across the street from us, so we didn't have to travel far. The grown folks were downstairs while we (the children) were hidden in a room upstairs. We were supposed to be watching a movie but we found ourselves watching the strippers instead while they undressed and got ready to perform. Life seemed so full and complete. We were all happy and all together, and for our family that was truly rare. I couldn't remember the last time all of us were together in the same room. I'm speaking of the women in my immediate family. I'm talking about grandma, my mother, my aunt Elsa, my aunt Whitney, my cousin Daphne, and me. The six of us together have a lifetime worth of stories. And now it's time the world hears them.

At first things were really quiet down there. They were all laughing and joking. Then all of a sudden the music began to blast and the strippers went down the stairs to perform. The next thing we knew things really started to liven up and Lola (my mother), being her normal self, ran like hell and tried to hide in a corner. She asked them not to hurt her. She is scared of strippers. Well, really, she is scared of anything that moves, and she hates being the center of attention. She has never been the type of person to like this sort of thing, but everyone thought it would be a good idea to have the bridal shower with strippers. Most of them are really freaks behind closed doors, but not sweet Lola. She is as green as they come. They wanted to see her reaction. And boy was it one to remember.

Everyone else enjoyed the party more than she did, and after the first guy let her go she ran as fast as she could out the front door. She let everyone else enjoy the festivities, because she was out of there. And she didn't come back until the coast was clear and the strippers were fully dressed and in their cars. Grandma, on the other hand, loved it. She was sitting in the corner enjoying the excitement. You see, Mrs. Mary Magdalene Carson Lawson Turner Hayes Turner (She married my grandfather twice) is a jazz/blues singer and this sort of thing is right up her alley. This is a regular night for her. And she is really into this today. She thought she was going to a party for easy church-going women, which means she thought she would be bored out of her mind. But when those strippers came out, so did the freak in a lot of those women. And Mary loved every minute of it and was right there in the midst of all the excitement, laughing and carrying on while sister so-and-so cut loose and screamed for more as the stripper stuck his stuff all up in her face. Child, Mary was in the center of all the action, telling one of the Deaconesses of the church she better move out of the way because she needed to see what this young man was dragging around in his pants. She was telling them to shake what their mamas gave them. My grandmother is not a normal grandmother. Where others were baking cookies and going on fun outings with their grandmothers, mine was teaching me and Daphne about sex and where babies truly came from, with all of the gruesome details. She didn't think this would traumatize us and have us (well, mainly me) not wanting to ever have sex or children. But then again, maybe that was her point.

Oh, and did I forget to mention the crazy thing about my grandmother? She smokes weed. Yes, that is just what I said, weed, Mary Jane, marijuana or whatever you want to call it. She is a pro at smoking. Her motto is as long as God grows it, it gives her the right to smoke it. Grandma really is a trip. Whitney, my aunt, Mary's favorite child, and the baby girl of the family, at the time was eight months pregnant with her sixth child. She was dancing up a storm with the strippers. We (the children) could hear the commotion upstairs. I still can't believe my aunt was carrying on the way she was with a big belly. The stripper was rubbing his private areas all on her belly. We thought this was the nastiest thing we had ever seen. But she let him and she was fine. I know that the baby got a good work out that day. And then there is Elsa, my favorite aunt and my mother's older sister, who just recently came home from prison. She is basically the comedian in the family. She did her own dance routine over top of the dancers and when they told her she was showing her underwear she said she wasn't wearing any and she didn't care. It was just like her because she was and has always been the life of the party. I believe it was the highlight of the night because Elsa gave the strippers a nice show. Even they laughed about it. They said no one had ever given them a tease at a party they were working. I always thought they should've turned over the money they collected to her because she was doing her own rendition of a strip tease for them.

After the performance was over they allowed us children to come downstairs. We saw half of what was going on anyway because we snuck to the middle of the stairs and watched it all unfold. Daphne (Elsa's daughter and my older cousin, but were raised more like sisters) was the ring leader.

She was trying to get us to watch these men undress and trying to get us to sneak down to watch the show. Then she saw her mother performing and said we should go back upstairs. She was embarrassed. But I followed her down and when she decided to go back I up I went right along with it. I didn't want the adults to see us because we would've been in for some real trouble due to the x-rated things that were going on.

Daphne was always trying to talk me into something. And for some stupid crazy reason, even when I knew it was wrong, I still went along with it. I think I was addicted to the excitement. But the adults were so into what was going on they were none the wiser. To this day they don't know we saw what was going on. We enjoyed seeing them like that, though, because they were always so serious. And for once we could see the real people. They were always acting civilized in front of us, so this was a drastic change for them. Well, all of them except for Elsa, that is. They were all laughing and joking. These were fun times. We really saw how nasty some of these women really were. I'm talking about church women, praising the Lord on Sunday morning but that Saturday night they all were sinners. Some were telling the strippers to shake their asses and putting more money down their pants than they could afford. But it was alright; they could pray to God and ask for forgiveness the next morning.

Then they gave some of the nastiest gifts. It was funny seeing how nervous my mother was. She gets embarrassed really easily and her face was pink from blushing at some of the gifts. She got lacy see-through negligees and a lot of thong underwear. She was very uncomfortable with these gifts, but she was also appreciative. She didn't let on that she didn't like the stuff that much. Then one of my older aunts gave her a used night gown. That was hilarious. Everyone noticed it but no one was bold enough to say anything about it.

As I said, these were happy times for us. My mother was getting married, I had just graduated from elementary school, Lawrence had just come home after completing his first year at Morehouse College, and our family was all together. It was just two years ago we were thanking God we were alive. My mother was in a singing group and they were invited to perform at the director's church in Florida. Well, on our way there we were in a terrible accident. The guy wasn't paying attention and the van went off the road into an embankment. My mother had to get 37 stitches in her face and I had a collapsed lung, so we have a lot to be thankful for and God was truly blessing us.

Then the 80's weren't good for our family at all. Big Mama died, the family collapsed, and Granddaddy died of a cerebral hemorrhage. As in many cases in black communities, drugs nearly tore our family apart. Elsa had an addiction, but thank God when she came home, she really wanted to get her life on track. But Whitney is still on drugs. However, we weren't focusing on that today. Today was different. We didn't have to worry today. We didn't have any cares today because things were looking up, or so we thought. We were all here today, and that was a miracle all by itself. We were thankful just for that.

They told my mother she was drinking an exotic drink called a fuzzy navel, but it was actually vodka and orange juice, and before it was over we had to get Lawrence (my older brother and the neighborhood sweetheart, everyone wanted to be around him and everyone wanted their daughters to fall in love with him. Why? I don't know) to carry her across the street to our house. Oh, did I forget to mention where we live? The corner house at 1600 Sixth Street. Everyone knows that house. That address was so infamous it was mentioned in a local band's song. It was known back in the day as the real BIG MAMA's house, where she sold liquor, wrote numbers and ran a tourist home for the elderly. It was the hot spot and the place everyone wanted to be. Even the preachers would leave church to come over to have a drink with Ms. Tootie. Sixth Street was family. Everyone knew everybody and took care of everybody, and as families go, everybody was always in your damn business. Because our families grew up together (they went back for generations), we were always there for each other, and in today's time that is very rare.

But anyway, back to the story. He had to carry her across the street. She stayed in bed for two days. My mother can get tipsy just smelling liquor. So just imagine what four or five cups of that stuff did to her. It was a cruel joke for them to play, but I tell you one thing – it was funny. Everything was looking up. A wedding! What a reason for us to celebrate.

Oh, did I forget to introduce myself? I'm Lana, known in the family to everyone as the mean one, the all-around smartass, the crazy one and the one you don't mess with because I will chase you out of the house with a knife or even boiling hot water. I don't play. But I'm still everyone's baby girl. They all feel the need to protect me. But back to the story because you will see how we all will go through some things, but one thing about us is we always come out better people for what we have just gone through. And I believe you have the power to overcome anything. We used the wrongs in our lives to make some type of right. Maybe you can use these tools in your own life. We've all lived through something, whether it is good or bad. This is our life. This is our story.

THE WEDDING

On June 13, 1992, Lola and Twinkie (my father, and yes, his name really is Twinkie) are finally going to jump the broom after 18 years of tears, fussing and fighting, breakups and makeups. There have been quite a few ups and downs. You see for starters, there's a major age difference. He is 16 years older, but he tries to dress young so people won't notice it, but even a blind man could see the age difference. Believe me there was a struggle trying to get them together, and it has not been because of my mother, either. It's because he is a low-down no good dirty dog. He met Lola when she was 19 years old and there has been nothing but drama between them ever since.

Big Mama called him Jesus because Lola loved him so much. Do you recall the song "Olivia" by the Whispers? Everyone in the family called Lola "Olivia," and Twinkie was the Big Bad Wolf that distracted her on her way to grandma's house. And what do you think he was driving? A Cadillac Seville. In her eyes, he was her knight in shining armor, but she was the only one who saw him that way. Everyone else saw him for the dirty rotten scoundrel he really is. They met in a strange way. Lola, Elsa, and our cousin Ella had a singing group; these three sisters could really blow. Well, Twinkie had a record label so he wanted to meet with their singing group, and from what I hear my father wanted my mother because she had a hell of a shape. She had a tiny waist and a big butt. She was shaped something like a coca cola bottle.

At the time, though, my mother wasn't at all interested in him because he came in wearing a sage green suit with beige socks and brown shoes, not to mention he was no Chucky Booker. He was wearing bifocals and had a grill that would make a dentist rich. She laughed at him mostly, and she always said that for laughing at him she was cursed, and that's why she fell so hard for him. He hawked her until he got her, but at the time he didn't show his true colors. He was like a predator going after its prey.

Twinkie treated her like a man should treat a woman. And she wasn't used to this type of attention. He would call every night and he would always end each call by saying, "God bless you." She thought she had really found a good, decent guy. That is, until she fell for him, and then his colors started to show; very bright colors. He was no longer that sweet man, he no longer spoke of God blessing anything, and now every other word was a curse word. He truly became the Big Bad Wolf. But at this point my mother really loved him. And he was showing her attention she never received anywhere else. And you know what they say, some attention is better than none at all.

Oh, and did I forget to mention he has other children? Eight, to be exact, which is a story all by itself. He has enough to start a damn basketball team. You see, papa was a rolling stone. Therefore, you know the baby mommas were in the picture as well as another woman he was seeing. Everyone always wondered how in the hell this nice girl could wind up with such a devil. Even the people in his family wondered how and why. They always thought she was too good for him. But to her he was her prince charming and there was nothing anyone could say that would make her see otherwise. After all the years of heartache, Lola still wanted to marry him, even though the year before Lawrence caught him with another woman, and his lame excuse was he was helping his niece move. And since she had never met his niece, she believed him.

The day before the wedding, Granddaddy Oliver (Twinkie's father and my grandfather) got really sick and had to be rushed to the hospital, and the lady who made the dress did not finish it until the morning of the wedding, and she still hadn't finished the bouquet. And he couldn't even show up for the rehearsal. My uncle had to stand in for him. He said, "I'm not coming up to that church until tomorrow. I have something to do. I'll be there when I'm supposed to be there." Talk about an omen. But they still went through with it.

The time went by really slow leading up to the day, which was good because we (Lawrence and me) thought it was a blessing and maybe they wouldn't go through with it, but the day was finally here and everything was going to happen, whether we wanted it to or not. Everyone was all dressed up and looking sharp. We (my mother and me) were over at Aunt Betsy's and Uncle John's (not really related, just good friends of the family) house getting ready just before the limo driver got there.

The next thing I knew, my mother broke down. She said she didn't want to do it. She told Aunt Betsy, "This is a mistake and now I realize it. I've got to get out of this." Aunt Betsy told her it was just cold feet. I could have kicked the holy shit out of her. My mother knew it wasn't cold feet. Her life with Twinkie flashed before her eyes and she did not want to do it. She knew it was wrong. It wasn't cold feet. It was God giving her one more chance to get it together. It was the fact that for 18 years this man had only brought hurt into her life, with the exception of me being born, and that was drama with him too. GOD was telling her not to go through with it, and she knew up until this point she was being disobedient to His word, but she loved Twinkie so much. As always, she wouldn't listen to anyone's advice, not even God's. She gave Lawrence (my older brother) and me a sign, though. She said, "If I run out of the church during my vows, I want the two of you to meet me in the back where the limos are and we are going to Atlantic City to celebrate." But the feelings passed and the day went on as planned.

Grandma was to walk down the aisle first; she was so pretty that day. She was the prettiest I'd ever seen her look in my 12 years, and believe me she knew it. She had on a fuchsia laced dress and a head piece to match; you couldn't tell her a thing today. She said, "I'm the mother of the bride and I look better than most of the bridesmaids." The time leading up to the wedding was hilarious. Grandma was looking sharp at my mother's expense. It's funny, I always heard growing up that the wedding is supposed to be paid for by the parents of the bride, although my mother was 37 when she got married. I never heard of any age limitations. Well, Mary must have had the meaning confused because whenever we went to a store to pick up something for the wedding she would pick out her items (this included her dress, underwear, shoes, stockings and even her hair) and she would go to the counter and stand in line, but when she got to the front she would put her things up and then she would walk away and my mother would have to pay the bill. And when her things were paid for then she would come back over and pick up her bag as if an imaginary person paid the tab. And she wouldn't say a thing, as if it didn't happen. It was really funny. Mary Magdalene is a card. But my mother didn't mind. It was one of the happiest times in her life. And she knew it was just typical Mary. She said what she always says when it comes to grandma, "It's my mother."

None of my mother's sisters were in the wedding because she made a pact with her friends that if any of them were to marry, they would all have to be bridesmaids and they all were in each other's weddings, so the running was out for her sisters, but they were still there to support her. Aunt Drusilla (Granddaddy's daughter by another woman) was even there, and so were her two daughters, Ronnie and Shanisha, all gussied up. Whitney used this opportunity to return to her modeling days; she changed clothes like three different times. You would have thought she was doing a concert with different sets; she had on one outfit when she got there, then she changed before the wedding, then at the reception she changed again. Elsa was quiet today. She acted like someone other than herself. She composed herself and really behaved, which was not at all normal for my aunt. I asked her was she feeling alright, because it wasn't like her to be this quiet. She said, "Today is not a day for any foolishness. I am behaving myself for my sister." I understood and left her alone.

It's really funny, this was one of the only times all our family had all gathered together for a joyous event since 1982. After Big Mama died, our family hasn't quite been a family. We rarely support each other. So today was really nice seeing everyone. I know today Big Mama smiled on us. I know she wouldn't be happy about the blessed event, but she would be happy to see us all together. Daphne was a junior bridesmaid, I was the maid of honor, because my mother couldn't pick one friend over another. She looks at them all as equals, so I was given that honor. Lawrence was a groomsman, and Tico (Elsa's oldest son, my partner in crime, and the baddest child in the world) was the ring bearer. They had a huge wedding party: Eight bridesmaids, eight groomsmen, two flower girls, one ring bearer, one bible bearer, two flower girls, two junior bridesmaids, one maid of honor and one best man.

The wedding was really beautiful; it was just the bride and groom that made me sick. I just didn't think they belonged together. Twinkie got his hair died so their age difference wouldn't be so obvious. But please, everyone there knew of their rocky past and the age difference. So really, who was he fooling? His hair was mixed grey the day before, then the next day his hair was jet black. This is the biggest thing to happen for us in a long time. Everyone was in a different place today, all smiles, and happiness filled the church. And everyone came out, because everyone loves Lola and wants what's best for her, even though no one thought this is what was best, they just wanted her to be happy. If Twinkie made her happy, then they would be happy for her.

Uncle Fester gave her away, because my granddaddy (the coolest man you would ever want to meet) died in 1987. Uncle Fester was always like a father to her, so he took time out of his busy schedule (because he still writes numbers) to come and give her away. But she had to change the time of the wedding from 2:00 p.m. to 12:00 p.m. so it would not interfere with his business.

When we got to the church, everyone was already there. Kathy (our Assistant Pastor's wife) stood in the capacity of the wedding coordinator, and she wanted my mother to be in a room by herself. She didn't even want me in there with her, which to this day I still cannot understand the reason why. When we go to the church, she sent me downstairs with the rest of the bridal party. She said, "The bride needs to be alone. No one is allowed in this room." I had a few choice words for her, but my mother didn't want any confusion, so I agreed and did as I was told.

The first person I ran into was my stupid brother Lawrence. He really looked handsome today and when I told him so, he was his arrogant self. He told me, "Look, you don't have to tell me something I already know. I am the man, and it shows in the way I walk. Just watch me walk away." He wanted to know where our mother was. I told him, "You are supposed to be the man, so you can find her yourself." He threatened me, so I finally told him. I let him know he wasn't allowed in the room with her. The orders came down from Kathy. He said, "Didn't I tell you who I was? If she says something to me I'm going to have to knock her ass out, because I'm going in there to see my mother." He found her and he could not believe how beautiful she looked. I think he even cried, but blamed it on his allergies. He is such a wimp.

Then I saw Dwight, our cousin who lives with us. He cleaned up nice, and people are still talking about how they couldn't believe it was him. He didn't even stink today. And that was a blessing all by itself. So, there we were downstairs in the choir room bored out of our minds. Then they finally sent for us. It was time to line up. All I could think about was how my mother was really going to go through with this. She is really going to marry this nut.

One of my mother's friends was singing "I Believe in You and Me," long before Whitney Houston, but the funny thing was that he was singing the wrong words. I was sidetracked by my thoughts. He was really messing up. And since no one had heard the song before, they were all talking about how good he sounded. I just laughed because I knew different. He really chopped that song up and made it his own. Then he finished singing and the feelings of doubt came back. I know he is my father, but I couldn't understand why she wanted to marry him.

Maybe I lived the last twelve years in a dream and how he treated all of us wasn't real. Maybe I really didn't see my mother crying all those time. Maybe she laughing when they argued. Maybe they never really argued at all; it was just loving discussions between a man and a woman. And maybe I just made up all the bad things in my mind. I couldn't figure it out. I couldn't see what she saw and I don't think I ever would.

The music started to play and one by one we went down the aisle. Everyone was mismatched and no one wanted to go down the aisle with their partner. My brother Raymond (of course, one of Twinkie's other children) was a no-show, so Little Bits had to walk down the aisle by herself. There I was standing there by myself, with a knot in the pit of my stomach. As I walked down the aisle, I saw my father standing there and the feelings only intensified. But everyone was there smiling and they seemed so happy for my mother, so I faked a smile, closed my eyes, and kept going down the aisle.

Then the doors closed and the music changed. The doors reopened and there she was, my mother. This beautiful creature wanted to be with this man. It was really crazy. There were a lot of mixed emotions going on. Reverend Wally Turnblad officiated and the ceremony started. I thought the whole thing was ridiculous as I looked around the church to see people's reactions. Everyone seemed cheerful. And that disgusted me to no end. They knew the hell he put her through. But they all just smiled and cried.

Reverend Turnblad was going on and on about to love and to cherish and I was ready to run out of there myself. When they exchanged vows, my father frowned when he said to love and honor. It was like he knew even then he wasn't going to take his vows seriously. Then it happened: Bertha Simmons (one of my mother's good friends and the church soloist) got up to sing her selection and the people really started to get into it. They actually started to shout up in the church during the middle of the ceremony and Gertrude (one of the bridesmaids) got the Holy Ghost. She hit Fred (one of the groomsmen) in the face. He didn't like her because at the rehearsal she wanted to be a dictator. She wanted to tell people where to stand and how to stand. She really got on everybody's nerves. So, he faked the Holy Ghost just to get his licks in. He had to have slapped her at least five times. She thought that this man was turning his life over to God, that he really had the spirit in him, so she encouraged him to keep up the shouting. She did not know how much of a prankster he was. I looked up at my brother and all he could do was laugh. Fred was one of his best friends, so he knew what he was doing. His laughing made me laugh. In my opinion, it was the highlight of the entire day. It took away most of the stress I felt.

Then Rev. Turnblad made the announcement they were Mr. and Mrs. Gavin Felder. There she was – my mother, the ecstatic bride standing next to him, the heartless groom and now they were finally married. When they kissed it made me sick and my stomach turned upside down. But all in all, it really turned out to be fabulous affair. They seemed so happy, but somewhere deep inside I knew it wasn't going to last. I wasn't being negative, I was just being real. So, I just stared at Lawrence while everyone cheered as they walked down the aisle as Mr. and Mrs. Felder, and he gave me that look. It was the look an older brother gives to his baby sister as if to say, "Let our mother have her day. Be happy for her." So, I was and I did.

After the wedding was over, we had to take our pictures. Then my mother and father got into their ride and headed to the reception. My mother said he was the sweetest to her at that moment because he told her she looked like a million bucks. She wasn't used to this sort of thing from him. This was one of the only compliments he had ever given her in all the years they were together. He didn't give compliments; it's always more like complaints. So, they had a nice ride. All her doubts from the morning all went away during that ride because he seemed so sincere.

We rode in a limo. That was different for Elsa, Daphne, Tico, Grandma and me. Elsa was trying to get me to sing and I didn't want to, at that time I was really shy and I didn't like for people to know I could sing. So, I was ready to get to the reception. I was tired of being put on the spot. And Daphne kept on pushing, but I wouldn't budge.

Well, after a nice ride through the city we arrived at the reception hall. They took us in a waiting area for the bridal party. We were there for a while only to find out from a family member walking by that a bunch of people from our neighborhood as well as people that we didn't know had crashed the reception. There we were waiting and the adult members of the bridal party had eaten all of the food that had been laid out for us. They told us we were young so we could wait a little while longer to eat. So, after being tired of sitting in that room with all of my mother's friends, because they didn't want the children to make any noise, I snuck out. I had to walk around the reception hall to find the room, and when I did that's when I saw it, the neighborhood drug dealers and a bunch of no-class folks sitting around in seats that were reserved for family members only.

You see, the reception hall was supposed to have a guest list and someone sitting at the table to check off each guest upon their entrance to the banquet hall. But these people at the reception hall obviously did not know they were dealing with people from the hood, and my mother, being who she was, did not want to ask them to leave because she knew it would only cause a scene. And she didn't want to hurt anybody's feelings. So, of course, Twinkie blamed her for the whole fiasco. If they didn't know about the wedding then they would not have shown up. Without even listening to the entire story right there in the lobby of the place he acted like a fool. And there she was in her wedding dress crying her eyes out.

In the end, the plush Aqua Room had to incur the cost because they were in fact the ones in the wrong. And all was well again. Except he never apologized for making such an ass of himself and embarrassing my mother in front of total strangers on their wedding day.

Our family got their tables and the unwanted guests got a free meal and all the liquor they could drink. It was funny, a man was sitting at the table with some of our family and when they asked if he knew the bride or the groom, he said, "I don't know either. Someone asked me did I want a free meal and free drinks. And I was hungry and thirsty, so I am going to eat my food and drink my liquor and when I finish they can have their damn seat back." They couldn't believe it but with all of the chaos going on they didn't want to add more fuel to the fire.

After this matter was finally cleared up, they allowed the wedding party to come in. One after the other the bridal party was announced and entered the banquet hall. Then the lights went out and smoke filled the air (Twinkie being as grandioso as he is rented a smoke machine and a spotlight just to show off) and the music started for their first dance as man and wife. My mother was so embarrassed. I thought it was a damn fire and was heading for the door until my uncle (who was the best man and people thought he was my grandfather) grabbed my arm and told me what was going on. Then the bridal party joined in while they danced. I was so embarrassed to be dancing with this old man. But I did it for my mother's sake. She had already been through enough today. You would have never known that just minutes before he had cursed her out. He must have forgotten they had that nice ride over there and the beautiful ceremony. He was going to be Twinkie even on their wedding day. But no one knew a thing.

I should have been happy, seeing them up there dancing, but I knew it was only a front on his part. But they danced and everyone thought it was just the sweetest thing. After all these years they were finally married. When they finished the dance we all sat down and waited for the best man to toast. It was really funny, the waiter actually thought I was an adult and poured me a glass of champagne. Hey, who was I to tell him he had made a mistake. I kept my mouth shut. I drank my glass of champagne, but it was the nastiest thing I had ever tasted.

When my uncle got up to toast, no one knew what the hell he was saying. My grandmother said, "Is he drunk?" People were all sitting around trying to figure it out what he was saying, so they just nodded their heads and raised their glasses to toast the happy couple. Then they laughed after the toast was over. Finally, they began to serve the food, but as luck would have it, it was the nastiest food I had ever tasted in my life. I couldn't even get a good meal out of the deal. At this point I knew I had to leave. For me this was the tip of the iceberg. I ducked out of a side door and went to the ladies' room.

But when I got there I found half of my family had the same idea. They all felt the same way; there was too much going on. Whitney was in there for her third wardrobe change. Aunt Drusilla was in there talking about how good she looked, if only you could see her. But they say beauty is in the eye of the beholder. And where Aunt Drusilla is concerned, that's a lot to behold. Daphne and Aunt Drusilla's daughter Shanisha were gossiping and laughing at Whitney.

I could not take it in there for long either so it was back to the reception to see what the lovely couple were up to. And as luck would have it, they were not together. Twinkie was sitting at the table taking all of the credit for a wedding he had nothing to do with. He was going around telling the guests he planned everything and my mother did nothing. And my mother was out mingling with the guests.

Elsa was sitting at the table and grandma was going around eating people's food. She had the nerve to say she was starving, and I actually saw her eating five different times at five different plates. My cousin Knuckles went to the restroom and when he got back his food was gone. To this day he doesn't know it was grandma who took his plate. I guess she had to stay busy to keep her mind off of not singing. My mother would not allow her to sing. She did give permission for one of grandma's jazz bands to get in there and do a set, but the compromise was that grandma had to sit and watch and not get up there and perform some of her blues numbers. It was killing her but she went along with it.

Then it was time to get into the festivities: The bouquet toss, the garter belt toss, and the cutting of the cake. All of the single desperate women lined up to catch a bunch of flowers as if this would actually bring them luck to get married. My mother's co-worker caught it. None of the men lined up for the garter belt. My brother Lawrence had three-year-olds running around playing with it and then finally a friend of his picked it up. Because the guy was so young, my mother's friend didn't want him to slide it up her leg.

When they cut the cake, I had to excuse myself. He pushed the cake in my mother's face but didn't want her to push it in his. He has to always be the one in control.

After all of this we left the reception hall and went out into the foyer to take more pictures. We were all smiles, but I don't think any of us were truly happy. My mother had the warning signs that morning, I was feeling emotional all day and Lawrence just went along with the flow. He is never one for conflict. Then before we knew it the reception was over. We never even went back into the banquet hall. Everyone claims they had a wonderful time. They danced and ate and drank until they couldn't do a thing but lay back and enjoy themselves. The day was over and they were finally married. It was funny, the people started leaving with all the decorations. Someone even tried to leave with the arch of balloons. It was hilarious.

Then the bride and groom got into separate cars and went on to their respective households. Yes, you heard it right, they hadn't moved in with each other. They had to postpone their honeymoon until they heard from the doctors about Grandad's condition. I thought at least maybe they would ride home together, but they went on their way like this was a normal thing. There were no hugs and kisses. He looked over at her and said, "So I guess I'll see you later." She said, "Yeah, I'm going home to change my clothes. Just call me." No one could believe it. I just laughed it off and got in the car.

When we got home, would you believe who was standing at our front door? Lawrence's father was waiting for us. Now believe it or not, they hadn't been together in almost 20 years. But he was still hurt by the fact that she married Twinkie. He actually said, "You know that you married him out of spite so you could get back at me for breaking up with you." My mother thought he was crazy. So, she laughed it off and he left.

Lawrence brought in all of the wedding gifts and boy was there a lot. My mother is really loved and it showed with the outpouring of gifts. Twinkie was only interested in the monetary gifts. But he still wanted an accounting of what gifts were there so he could find out how much each gift cost, so he could decide if it should go back to the store.

After we got home we changed out of our clothes. Dwight wouldn't take off his tuxedo. He said he had paid good money to rent it and he was going to get his money's worth. He wore it for three days. I know those people burned that suit when they got it back.

It was time for us to wind down. The day was finally over and they were married. But really nothing had changed as they still lived in separate households and he still wanted to be in control of both. He had a key to ours, but when we went to his we still had to knock on the door. It's funny how no matter how much things change they still remain the same. Then he came over and he wasn't even acting like they were just married. He wanted to sit and talk about all the negatives as always. And at that moment I knew this was never going to work. They say children always want to see their parents together but I am an exception to that rule because I never wanted to see them together. I always felt my mother would be better off without him. But I was only twelve years old at the time, so who would listen to me? They would only say I am standing in the way of my mother's happiness with the man she loves. But it's more like I'm standing in the way of her sadness. No one knows what happens except the people who live in that house. They expect me to just forget about all the years of heartache. Just put it out of my head and everything will be alright. But believe me, that's a damn lie.

MS. MARY MAGDALENE

Well how and where do I begin? What can I tell you about Ms. Mary Magdalene Carson? And yes, that is her real name. She is the matriarch of the family, having inherited that title from Big Mama. If she never existed then we wouldn't either. She was named by her grandfather (her mother's father). He wanted to give her name that meant something in the bible. Why in the hell he named her that is a mystery. She was one of two children. She has an older brother named Andy, who we fondly call Uncle Pappy.

The funny thing is that her mother and father were married but they didn't raise their children. Her mother was from a well-to-do family. However, she was considered to be an outcast because she married a very black man (Mary and Andy's father) and he was deemed to be beneath her. But she still married him and she was very much in love with him.

And then Mary's father was one of ten children. There were six boys and four girls. His sisters were unable to have children, so they went around taking their brother's children to raise as their own. And Mary just happened to be one of the children that was taken from their birth mothers. I never understood how a mother could allow someone to take their children away. But these were some big sisters and most women were scared to stand up to them.

Mary was taken care of by her Aunt Elsa. She was fondly called Aunt El. She was brought up with five cousins and her brother. She was the only girl. So of course, she was the center of attention. She grew up in an era where life was carefree. Yes, there was racism, but it never affected them. She lived on Sixth Street, where the load of chaos in the world didn't seem to matter so much.

She knew that she wanted to sing at an early age. Her father worked in one of the local theaters, along side her grandfather, so she was around the famous entertainers of that time. Everyone loved the little pintsized diva. She was truly a work of art. Then things started to change. She started to grow up and everything turned upside down. She was raped by a close family member at age eleven. And when she told Aunt El, she wouldn't believe her, because the family member was an older cousin and they didn't believe he was capable of doing something like that to her. And she told her if he did do it then she was probably the one to blame.

Then to top it off, she got pregnant when she was thirteen years old. She was going steady with a neighborhood boy named Levi Wallace and he was the father. The family was horrified, but what could they do? She had to have the baby. She gave birth to a baby girl. They named her Noel Casey, but she died shortly after she was born. After she lost the baby, Aunt El and Big Mama made sure that Levi Wallace kept his distance. They were all very upset about the baby dying, but they thought that it was a blessing in disguise. She was too young to have a baby.

The next couple of years were tough for her. She started to spiral down a roller coaster. The family couldn't believe she was turning into this person they didn't recognize. She graduated from high school and shortly after was married to her first husband. His name was Donald Lawson. She met him at the theater one night. He was visiting family. He was from out of town. She was there visiting her father and this guy came from behind and covered her eyes. He said, "Guess who?" She said, "I will do no such thing. Daddy is that you?" He said, "I'm not your daddy, but I could be if you want me to." She pulled his hands off of her eyes and when she turned around and saw him it was love at first sight. She had met her prince charming to take her away from all of the chaos that was starting to fill her life. She knew she wanted to marry this man. They didn't have a long courtship. After three weeks, he proposed. The family was furious. She didn't know anything about him and already she wanted to marry him.

Big Mama said, "Well at least she is doing the right thing. The last time she just went out and got pregnant." After she said that, the family agreed and they gave her their blessing. But the day of the wedding, she was getting dressed and got cold feet, and proceeded to walk out of the back door. She couldn't go through with it. She did not really know this man. But her cousin Shorty calmed her nerves and the wedding went on as planned.

During her marriage to Donald, who was a womanizer, Mary encountered many women; one in particular was Ida May Freeman. Mary could take a lot of things from her man, but the women were not one of the things she was going to allow. Ms. Ida May was something. She had really nappy hair and she was as black as tar. And she was after Mary's man. But you can not necessarily put all of the blame on her. Donald played a major part in it all.

Mary received good news – she was expecting their first child, and when she got home to tell him the news, she found him in her bed with that slut, Ida May. She whipped the hell out of the both of them. She forgot about being pregnant and when she finally came to her senses, it was too late. The excitement from that day was too stressful on her body. She lost the baby. It was devastating for her. Following these incidents, she decided that she was through with Donald. He was not ready to give up Ida May. And she could no longer put up with his womanizing, so they divorced.

Life for her was a bit shaky after her first marriage ended. Her father suddenly passed away. He was in the theater working. He had a heart attack and died right there on the stage, where she used to play and perform. The news shattered her whole existence. She fell into a deep state of depression. She suddenly had to deal with three of the worst things imaginable. The ending of her marriage, losing her baby and her father dying all at the same time. But luckily, she was still young. She had her whole life a head of her.

She decided to move back home with Big Mama and Aunt El. She never stopped singing. After she got over Donald, things started to pick up for her. She was singing in the posh night clubs of her time. She had a nice following. People were coming from all over the city to hear her raspy vocals. And boy could she sing the blues. She surely had lived through them.

Then one night she was having a drink before she got up to sing. Suddenly it happened – she met the man she had been wishing for in her dreams. A smooth-talking, good looking drummer named Duke Turner walked through the doors. She didn't want him to see how she was checking him out. She asked a couple of people if they knew who he was, but everyone told her the same thing: They didn't know too much about him.

He noticed her sitting there and he asked a friend who she was. His friend said, "Oh, that's Ms. Mary Mag. She is the blues singer everyone has been talking about." He said, "Well I want to meet Ms. Mary Mag."

She noticed he was looking over at her but she didn't want him to know she was looking at him. But he knew it. He could feel the attraction. One of the bartenders told him that she was asking about him. He walked over to meet her, but before he sat down he whispered in her ear, "Are you looking for someone?"

Mary played it cool. She turned around and said, "Do I look like I'm looking for someone?"

He said, "Yes, I thought I overheard someone saying you were looking for me."

She laughed and told him, "Look you need to get out of my way. I have a job to do and you are holding me up."

He laughed and said, "Well wherever you go I'm going to follow. Baby you lead the way."

She said, "Listen, I don't know who you are, but whatever you are selling I am not buying." She went up to do her set.

The announcer called out her name and asked for the band members to get ready. She didn't know this guy was the drummer. When she started to walk toward the stage to sing, he followed. That's when Mary got raunchy. She turned around and told him, "Look, mister, I don't know who you are and I don't want to know you. You need to get off this stage before I kick your natural black ass right out of this club."

Then her piano player ran over to intervene. He said, "Hey, Mary, hold on a minute. This is Duke Turner, our new drummer." She looked over at him and laughed. She couldn't believe she treated him this way before she even knew who he was.

He turned to her and said, "Hey, I was trying to tell you who I was but you didn't want to know, remember?" Then the both of them smiled and went to the stage to do their business. That was always an inside joke between them.

After the set, they went out to an after-hours spot and got to know each other better. After that night, they were inseparable. Mary was quite smitten with the gentleman who played the drums. But she didn't let on. She played hard to get for a while. They took the time to court each other. But before you knew it they were engaged and then for the second time Mary was getting married. Everyone in the family was outraged. Aunt Elsa wasn't at all pleased by her decision to marry this man. They knew very little about him. They didn't want a repeat of her marriage to Donald Lawson. But Mary could do no wrong in their eyes. She was their baby girl, so they sucked it up and welcomed Duke into the family with open arms. They didn't have a wedding this time though. They went to a judge and said there I do's.

They started out doing very well. They moved clear across town into their own apartment. And they were making their own way. The family was pleased with the way things were going. They were out every night singing or playing somewhere. Mary was truly making a name for herself in the jazz and blues circuit. Then the next thing you know, Mary was pregnant. This time she took all of the right precautions. Everyone was so excited, with all that she had been through, she finally found happiness. But during her pregnancy, the worst thing happened. Aunt Elsa got really sick. This was hard for Mary to deal with. This was the woman who raised her as her own. This was her mother. Then out of the blue, she died. It was really unexpected. It was devastating for Mary. The one person that she adored was gone. She felt the pain of a motherless child, even though her birth mother was very much alive. But she had to take it easy as she was far along in her pregnancy and she had to at least try to be calm. As heartbroken as she was, she had to take her focus and put it on her baby.

She was very uncertain about her pregnancy, because she was unlucky in her previous pregnancies. But she prayed about it and let God take control of the situation. Then a couple months later, Elsa Marlene Turner was born. She was the most beautiful baby girl in the world. She was everything to her parents. They took her everywhere. Everyone in the family was so proud of this bundle of joy. She was Mary's little princess. She was starting to get over all of the hurt and pain from her past. Things were finally looking up.

Then suddenly, marital bliss turned into a nightmare when Duke was arrested for drugs. He was sent to Ashland, Kentucky, to serve his time. Mary was taking care of a toddler and now the news came that she was expecting her second child. She did not want any handouts, so she didn't tell her family everything that was going on. She told Big Mama that Duke was on the road with his band. But somehow, they knew it was all a lie. They wanted her to come back home, but she wouldn't listen. She didn't want them throwing in her face how they were right about Duke, especially since she had two children to worry about. She didn't want her children growing up hearing bad things about their father. A good friend of hers named Marlene moved in so she would have someone there to take care of Elsa while she was out singing.

She sang up to a couple of days before the baby was born. She told everyone she was hoping for a little boy to make her little family complete. And when Duke came home they would have the perfect life. But out popped Lola Natasha Turner. She was just as beautiful as Elsa.

Things were as good as they could be under the circumstance. She really missed having Duke around. They were always together and now they were so far apart. She missed him so much that she took a cab from DC to Ashland, Kentucky. Marlene thought she had lost her mind. She left her babies behind because the ride was to long. When she finally returned home she was feeling really bad. She didn't know what direction her life was heading in. She had surrounded herself with the wrong crowd and they started to have negative influence over her.

Marlene told her that if she kept up this sort of behavior, she was going to leave. She said she couldn't tolerate her outlandish behavior anymore. And she was tired of taking care of the children while she was out all night. Mary was gone so often that the children thought Marlene was their mother. Mary wouldn't get into the house until very late. And then she would leave early in the morning. The landlord wanted his rent, the babies needed to eat. But Mary's main concern was herself. To bring her back to reality, Marlene packed up and left. She told Mary she needed to be there for these two helpless children. But even that didn't stop her. She started having wild parties while the children were in the bedroom. She was using drugs and the situation was only getting worse.

Marlene went over to visit and when she got there Mary was nowhere to be found. She heard little Lola crying and when she walked back to the bedroom, there they were, all alone. Elsa was taking care of her baby sister. Mary had really hit her lowest point. She left her two-year-old and five-month-old all alone. Marlene didn't know how long they had been by themselves. She did the only thing she could do. She called Big Mama and told her she needed to come and get Mary's babies. She said, "Ms. Tootie, Mary has hit rock bottom. And these poor little girls shouldn't have to suffer from their mother's bad decisions."

Big Mama agreed. She got someone to take her to Mary's place and she picked those babies up. When Mary returned home a couple days later, it took her a few hours to realize her children were gone. She was that high. She instantly called home and told them someone took the children, and Big Mama informed her she had them and there was no chance in hell she was going to give them back. She asked her, "Mary, what is your problem? You can't sit and let your life go down the toilet because your man is in the slammer."

Mary jumped in and said, "Now wait just one minute. He is on the road playing with Jimmy's band. I told you all that before. I wish that you would stop assuming that because he's been gone for a while he must be in prison."

Big Mama told her, "Listen, that friend of yours already told me the truth. You don't have to lie. But that's your husband; you feel you have to protect him. That's your priority. Well let me tell you something, these children are mine. So, until you can get your act together, don't even think that you are getting them back. Do I make myself clear?"

Mary said, "Yes ma'am." Everyone thought this would help Mary to get herself together, but she didn't. She started hanging out even more. Then it happened. She received a letter from Duke. He told her he couldn't be the man she needed him to be and the father their daughters needed. He was asking for a divorce. She deserved so much better and he couldn't give it to her.

This almost killed her. She had lost everything. Her husband no longer wanted her and Big Mama had her girls. She began using drugs more frequently. The next thing you know, she found herself in the slammer. Aunt Elsa was turning over in her grave. No one ever imagined Mary would end up like this. Here she has two beautiful children and she wasn't taking care of them and now she couldn't.

While she was in prison, Big Mama and Aunt Gertrude made sure the girls spent enough time with their mother. They would visit her at least once a month. Mary enjoyed the time with her girls and she promised that when she got home things would be different. While she was in prison she met a well-known jazz singer and they became really close. She told her that when she got out she should look her up. The singer was Ms. Billie Holliday.

Mary spent nearly five years in prison. When she came home, things had changed. Her babies weren't babies anymore. They were now of school age. Her little babies were now little girls. Elsa was six years old and Lola was four. They knew she was their mother, but it was hard for them to interact with her because they were little girls and she had been gone for so long. They only knew of Big Mama being their mother. Mary moved back home because she wanted to be close to them. She would sing to them and tell them stories. She had missed so much of their young lives. She didn't want to miss another moment.

She had no idea where Duke was. They lost contact once she was arrested. But somehow, he found out what happened to Mary. He wanted to have a relationship with his girls, but that was made hard by Big Mama. She wanted the girls to have nothing to do with Mr. Duke Turner. Big Mama and Aunt Gertrude couldn't stand him, but they never let on to the children. But they told Mary every chance that they got. She told them that she no longer wanted to hear it, and if they didn't have anything nice to say about him then they shouldn't say anything at all. And if they didn't stop, then she would take the girls away. It was really nerve-racking for her to constantly hear the I-told-you-so's over and over again. She would give them the evil eye but they wouldn't pay her any mind. They just kept right on along preaching, but it didn't matter because Mary was always high-strung. The things they said rolled off of her back.

She was trying her hardest to stay away from the music scene because she wanted a better life for her children. And she didn't want to fall back into the life that took her away from them. She was tired of hearing the bashing from Big Mama, so she went to her cousin to see if he could help her get a job, but he told her she could either put out or get out of his office. She looked at him and said, "You no good dirty rotten son of a bitch. How could you even dare to say something like that to me?"

He put his hand on her leg and said, "I know we are family, but you are a woman and I am a man. If you give me what I want then I will give you what you want."

She spat in his face, and then told him to kiss her natural black ass. She went home to tell Big Mama and Aunt Gertrude, but because it was their beloved Fred they didn't want to believe her.

Even through her trials and tribulations she always knew she would succeed. Coming home from prison on Good Friday was a sign her life could be resurrected. Things started to get a little too crowded inside Big Mama's house, so she and a friend, May Templeton, took an apartment together. That is when she met Winston Hayes.

Winston Hayes was younger than she was but it never stopped him from pursuing her. He was six-foot-four and always smelling of Jade East and looking like he stepped out of GQ magazine. Winston was an only child and was raised by his three aunts and grandmother. His mother died when he was very young. He thought he was all that and then some. But he wanted Mary and eventually he wore her down. During this time Mary started hanging with a lady named Big Betsy. She was a nationally known jazz vocalist who had personal ties with Ella Fitzgerald, Ray Charles, Billy Eckstein, and Sarah Vaughn, just to name a few. It was then that she came into contact with her buddy from prison, Billie Holliday. Her passion for music never died and she was finally back in her world.

Winston was satisfied as long as he was by her side, but he longed for a simpler life. He convinced Mary to move into an apartment around the corner from Big Mama, so she could be closer to her girls. During this time, Winston had met and become very fond of Elsa and Lola. And they would spend weekends over at their place. Her house became the model for all the latest technology. She was the first person in the area to have a floor model color television, air conditioning, and a floor model stereo.

Winston wanted to marry Mary, but she said no. She told him, "I have been down this road two times before and I am not ready to make the same mistake a third time." He told her, "The third time will be a charm."

She didn't want to ruin their relationship, but Winston would not take no for an answer. Mary constantly told him that she was not ready to be someone else's wife. She said, "Look, we need to let things stay the way they are. We love each other and we live together. What will change if we get married? Nothing. If we get married, we will end up breaking up."

Winston didn't want to hear it. He wanted her to be his wife. And then fate stepped in. Mary found out she was pregnant with Winston's baby. Winston would finally have his way. She was still fighting it all the way until three days before she gave birth. She became Mrs. Winston Hayes. Then out popped Whitney Inez Hayes. Winston finally made her an honest woman and now he wanted to make them all a family.

Mary hunted down Duke. And since he wasn't in a position to take care of them because he was still on drugs, he felt the best gift he could give his little girls would be to sign over his parental rights. And Winston adopted them. Elsa and Lola Turner became Elsa and Lola Hayes. Mary didn't want to admit it, but she was happy with her decision. She finally had a real man who loved her unconditionally, and he loved her children too. The family loved him too. You couldn't help but love him. He was a fun-loving type of guy.

Mary wanted the girls to move in with her. Elsa was happy, but Lola wanted no part of it. Elsa moved in and Lola stayed with Big Mama. Mary was hurt that she didn't have her whole family, but she understood that too much time had passed and Lola was still a little girl.

Despite the fact that Lola didn't live with her, Mary's life was still looking up. She got a job as an administrative assistant at a law firm, Hoodwinked and Bamboozled attorneys at law. She and Winston moved next door to Big Mama's house. She now had a three-bedroom house and things were only getting better. She still had an itch she couldn't quite get rid of. She still loved the night life, so Winston gave in and allowed her to start gigging again on the DC club scene. Even though this was not his natural habitat, he let Mary do her thing, and in the process he started to lose himself. He was a family man and now he finally saw that as much as she wanted her family, music came before anything else in her life. When Mary saw the distress Winston was in, she decided she would pacify him and stop singing for awhile until she could figure out what to do with him or until she had the urge again.

During this time, Mary became very involved in the PTA, and that is where she met Lucy Proctor. Her children had been friends with Elsa, Lola and Whitney for years but the two of them had never met. They formed a strong and fast friendship. They would visit each other on the weekend, playing cards and just enjoying each other's company.

But little did Mary know Lucy was serving more than Kool-Aid to Winston. They say you never trust your friends around your man or woman. Well in Mary's case this proved to be the truth. He began having an affair and Mary was none the wiser about it. She was too caught up in her own world to see how her man was getting loving from someone she considered to be a really close friend. He began to spend a lot of quality time with Lucy and when her husband questioned him about it, Lucy jumped in and told him it was none of his business. She said Mary and Winston were going through a very rough time and he needed them to help him through the hard times.

But her husband wasn't stupid. He picked up on the chemistry between them and when he told her to choose, she picked Winston. Even then, Mary didn't wise up and take notice how her friend was trying to get her husband and how her husband was following her lead. One day Whitney and Ms. Lucy's daughter Charlene were out playing. Charlene asked Whitney, "How is Daddy Winston doing?" Whitney was stunned; she wanted to know why this girl was referring to her father as daddy.

She said, "Charlene that is my father, why did you call him Daddy Winston? You either call him Mr. Winston or Mr. Hayes. But don't ever refer to him as Daddy again. That is me and my sister's father, not yours. And don't ever let me hear you calling him that again."

Charlene couldn't believe she didn't know. She said, "Whitney I am sorry, but that is what he told us to call him. He has been seeing my mother for almost two years. He is our daddy, too."

Whitney smacked the girl in the face and ran home to tell Mary. When she got in the house she told her everything that had just went on. And Mary rushed around the corner to approach Lucy. But when she got there Winston was coming out of the bedroom. She looked over at him and said, "So it is true. The entire time that I was walking around here I was praying it was all just a misunderstanding. But it is the truth. You are a rotten son of a bitch. For two years you allowed this to go on right under my nose and you never let on that anything was going on.

He said, "Mary, I am glad the cat is finally out of the bag. I am with Lucy now. I am sorry but now I realize I am not the man for you. We want different things out of life and you deserve much more."

Mary was flabbergasted. She couldn't believe her ears. She said, "Winston, Get your shit because we are going home. And Lucy, you no-class vagabond, you were supposed to be my friend and you have been sleeping with my husband. You low-down dirty slut bitch dog. You are lower than low."

Lucy said, "Well if you would have stayed home and worried about your family more than you worry about going out every night to the clubs then you wouldn't have to worry about your man now would you."

Before she knew it, Mary was beating her in the head with a rolling pin and Winston was pulling her off. He dragged her out of there and took her home and when they got there she told him he had to leave. She said, "I knew that eventually this was going to happen, I just didn't know when. I guess our relationship has just run its course. Why couldn't you just tell me? You have been sleeping with someone I allowed into our house and around our children. Someone I considered to be a friend and you knew what was going on all of the time. That's why Ralph left, isn't it?"

He nodded his head yes. Mary was devastated. He didn't say a word, he just packed up his things and left. There was no explanation. He went into the room got a suitcase and before she knew it, he was out of the door and back into Lucy's arms. Elsa and Whitney were distraught. For years they played with Lucy's children and looked at Lucy as an honorary aunt, and now this woman was going to be their stepmother.

It was hard for Mary, living in that house without Winston, so she packed up and moved around the corner. Whitney was eight years old at the time and Elsa was seventeen. Elsa wanted to go around to Ms. Lucy's house and kick some asses, but she didn't. Mary told her that the best thing to do was to make sure Whitney was okay. She didn't know what kind of effect this was all having on Whitney, to have her father living with her mother's best friend, the woman she called Aunt Lucy. She started taking Whitney with her to all of the hot spots. Big Mama and Aunt Gertrude didn't think that it was a good idea to have a young impressionable mind in the places where Mary was hanging, but Mary told them they needed to mind their business. She said, "Listen, you all may have had your say in Elsa and Lola's life, but I have been there for Whitney since the day she was born and there is nothing you can say to me about the way I am raising my daughter."

Aunt Gertrude said, "Mary you are making a big mistake and it will only cause you heartache in the end. The things that she sees are going to take their toll and it's going to come back to haunt you. I only pray I am alive when that dog comes back to bite you on the ass."

Mary didn't want to hear it. She stormed out. It was like the whole world was against her. Her husband was living a life of sin with her friend and instead of her family being supportive of her they were talking about her parenting. They didn't see how all of this was really hurting this poor little girl. She idolized her father and now he was gone. But Mary still had to press on. She had to do what was best for her and her girls.

In the process, she didn't see how Elsa was really following in her footsteps. She was headed down the same road as her mother, and Mary was so involved in the Winston storyline that she wasn't conscious of Elsa's problems. She had dropped out of school and she was gone for days and weeks at a time without anyone knowing where she was or who she was with. Big Mama and Aunt Gertrude swore it was the roosters coming home to nest.

At this time in her life, Mary was truly batting a thousand. But she had to press on and try to make her wrong situation right. She allowed Elsa to move in with this guy that was twice her age. His name was Olden. Of course, Big Mama had a fit, but once she met him she fell in love with him. He was a really nice guy. He was just too old for Elsa but it was a means to an end. If Mary allowed them to move in, then she knew where Elsa was. And now finally, she was putting the needs of her daughters in front of her own.

LEESBURG

Things did not change much after the wedding. Of course, we did not move in with my father. They had decided they would live in separate houses for the time being since granddad was still so sick. And the house was still under construction. Twinkie didn't come over as much anymore. That was excellent for us. He wasn't dictating to us about every little thing, or trying to control our every move.

We were on our summer vacation. Daphne and I would be going to the same school. I was going to Junior High this year. Lawrence was going back to Morehouse in the fall. He was going to be a sophomore. Grandma is still singing at her night club. She is 65 years old and still singing the same old blues she sang at 20. But she loves it and it keeps her young. Elsa was really trying to get herself together. She had even got into contact with grandma's casting agency and had gotten a job as an extra.

Whitney was going to pop any day. That baby was ready to make an entrance. But she still won't leave the streets and drugs alone. Everyone is praying the baby is born healthy without any complications. And it's really killing grandma day by day seeing her this way. At this point it seemed this was how things were going to be. It was okay for us. And for a moment we thought that nothing would change, unless it was for the better, that is. The wedding was just the beginning.

But then we were hit with a blow. Grandma's foster son, Bobby, thought Elsa needed to get away, so he begged and begged until she agreed to come and visit him in Leesburg, Virginia. She went away just before the Fourth of July weekend. We all stayed home to enjoy the yearly festivities on our block. Lawrence is a big kid, so he always puts on a show, buying lots of fireworks. At the time, Daphne and Tico were living with Grandma, so they had very little supervision. Grandma isn't a disciplinarian, so they were allowed to stay out all hours of the night. It was after 10:00 p.m. and they were still out with their friends, running the streets. Grandma was probably out somewhere and Whitney was out on the streets again. She had been gone for days, and this time Grandma did not feel like going out to find her.

So, there we were all on our block watching the fireworks. It was a ritual we all loved and enjoyed. Elsa was in Virginia and she met a friend of Bobby's. He seemed to be a very nice man. They both had similar backgrounds and the both of them were trying to get their lives on track. They talked and talked and talked and finally decided they had too much in common; they had to do something about it. Well back at home, we were going on doing our day-to-day routine and we got a call. Elsa was moving to Leesburg, and she was going to marry a man she met. And since it was Elsa, no one took the call seriously. We thought that it was a joke. Then we got a call from Mary. "This guy is loaded," she said. "He owns a night club and I'm going to be the featured act!"

Everyone was so happy for Elsa, and not because Mary said all the stuff about the money, either. It was the fact she was moving away from all the chaos. You see, it would have been easy for her to fall back into that same lifestyle. But she didn't want it anymore and she meant it. We knew if she moved away from all she knew then she really never would go back to the life she was leading, because living in a house with Whitney and Mary is enough to drive anyone insane, because they were all on drugs.

So here it is three weeks later and another wedding. Not the extravagant event like Lola and Twinkie. They were going to the Justice of the Peace. Grandma went up for the event. She wanted to check this guy out, so she could come back and give a report. Everything was going fine. We just wanted the low-down on this mystery man. And here is when the confusion started. Grandma had told all these stories about Elsa's new husband. We didn't know anything about him. Therefore, we could not judge him. We could only go by what Mary was saying. And Grandma being her normal self stretched the truth a lot. Everything she told us was a lie.

When Elsa finally returned home so she could pack up Daphne and Tico, she brought her new husband with her to meet everybody. His name is Mr. Eugene Parker. He seemed to be a very nice man. He was someone that would be able to fit in very well with the family. But after talking to him, it was obvious how somewhere, someone had lied. He did not own a club. He was speaking about his job and how he had to go to work and about his supervisor possibly getting Elsa a job. So that's how we knew Mary had lied. She always asks, "Who would tell you all a thing like that?" And me being the big mouth that I am, I tell her, "It was you grandma. We didn't know Uncle Eugene from Adam. Where would we get it from? You were the one reporting false information."

Daphne and Tico weren't pleased by this news either. They were thinking they were moving away from poverty into a lavish life out into the country to live in this big beautiful home. Then they come to find out all of the stories were false. Don't get me wrong, he was willing to provide everything they needed, but they were expecting one thing and got another altogether different thing. It wasn't his fault grandma lied on him. So that's when things turned ugly. Daphne and Tico truly became rebels without a cause.

Then on top of that, Aunt Drusilla was having trouble with Ronnie at the time, so Elsa willingly took Ronnie along to live with her as well. Though things were changing, it was truly for the best. They would all finally be together as a family. Elsa had been away from them for a long time during her addiction. She was giving them their mother back and it is a beautiful thing.

Whitney was about to go into labor and she had already decided she didn't want this baby. She isn't taking care of the others either. Her oldest kids were sent away to live with their grandparents in Denver, the two in the middle lived on and off in a foster home, and the one before this one, she left in the hospital. So, she talked it over with Aunt Drusilla and she agreed to take the baby. She had a little girl. They named her Vonisha, after Vick, Ronnie, and Shanisha. She was so pretty. She looked just like Whitney. The funny part about it is, Whitney always wanted a beauty mark above her left cheek and guess what? This little baby girl got her beauty mark. We always tease her about it.

All of a sudden, our lives were turning upside down. I am not saying that it's a bad thing. It is just funny because you truly never know from one day to the next what's going to happen and what could change your life. Well, they packed up and moved. I can still remember the day after they left I felt lonely. You are with someone your whole life and then in the next instant they are gone. But the feelings of loneliness did not last for long.

Lawrence got news from Morehouse. He had lost his scholarship because he and our cousin Brandon wanted to entertain more than they wanted to study. Our mother had already put out enough money that year, while he was gone. He came home at least once a month and when he did she would end up spending a good thousand dollars on him each time. So, she did not think that it was a good idea, especially since she worked at Maryland University and he could go there for free. And furthermore, Twinkie was not having it; "Lawrence was in her pockets enough," he said. You see, she had just settled our case from the accident and she got a nice bulk of money.

It's a funny concept; we were the ones in the accident. She had thirty-seven stitches in her face. She actually had to have plastic surgery to cover up the scars. But you would have thought Twinkie was the one who got hurt, the way that he was spending the money. He needed major reconstruction to his house. He needed this, he needed that. He never thought about what we needed or even what she wanted. But nevertheless, after hearing the news from Morehouse, it was off to good old Maryland University for Lawrence. He did not like it at first, but got used to the idea, once he started getting the attention of the ladies. Lawrence is staying home and going to Maryland. It should have been on the front cover of the newspaper. It was like women were coming out of the woodwork. I was happy, though. As much as we argued, I hated the fact we were away from each other that year. Lawrence is my idol.

Well, the time was moving by fast for us, but up in Leesburg it was a totally different story. Elsa was having her fair share of drama. She was trying to lay down ground rules for Daphne, Tico, and Ronnie. Tico and Ronnie weren't the problem. It was Daphne; she felt her mother had let her down for all the years she had been away. She did not want to forgive her mother and she let her know every moment she could, in some way or another.

Tico was just glad to be with her; he loved his mother unconditionally. I believe his love is so deep that if he had to live in a mud hole he woul,d as long as they were together. Everyone told Elsa to just give it time and Daphne would come around. She had to get over years of hurt. But how long would it take? They would be starting school soon and how would she react being in this new environment? Daphne just didn't want to be there and there was nothing any of us could say to make her change her mind.

Back at home we got a call. It had to have been about 2:00 a.m. We were not used to getting calls like this and with all that was going on in Leesburg with Elsa; my mother feared something was terribly wrong. It was grandma, she had a job that morning and Whitney had been gone for days and no one would be home to watch the children. So, my mother woke me up and we picked grandma up and went on an escapade. We drove down more alleys and side streets looking for my crazy aunt. Grandma went knocking on crack house doors, but there was no sign of Whitney anywhere. Drug Addicts must have a code of silence or something, because when grandma would ask had anyone seen her, they would not answer. It was like grandma was standing there speaking a foreign language.

Then after a couple of hours of searching for her we were ready to give up. We were at a stoplight and heard some one screaming. Grandma said, "It sounds like it's coming from the alley." We turned up the street and who do we see? Whitney was throwing rocks up at the window trying to get some man named Melvin to pay her some money she claimed he owed her. Grandma jumped out of the car and they fussed for a while. Grandma was throwing her usual lines at Whitney. Finally, after going through the motions, my mother convinced them to get into the car. Whitney is so dramatic. She got in and as usual my mother began to pray for her. When she finished her prayer, as always, the routine is to ask Whitney, what makes her do these things? Why won't she go into a program? We would all support her. Elsa got herself together and so should she. Our family needs her to be with us. She cried and cried and then she admits she does have a problem and she needs and wants the help and then she would cry some more.

This time is different, though, she said she wants to go to a program now. "I need to go right now," she said. The hospital has a program; all you have to do is drop the patient off when they feel the need to go in. As we were on our way there, we were right around the corner from the hospital. We were caught by the light and, Whitney kept on crying, "I want to get my self together, I am so tired," she said. All this time she had her head down, the car was moving but as soon as she realized that we had come to a stop she said, "I want to get my self together, and I'm going to get myself together, but not today." She jumped out the car so fast, I don't even remember her opening the door. I swear she jumped out the window. So, of course, grandma had to take off from work that day. Whitney came home three days later.

Well our summer days are winding down. I am going to junior high school. I decided I wanted to go to school with my friends instead of going to the school where Daphne went. It wouldn't be the same going there without her. Lawrence was used to the fact he wasn't going back to Atlanta. He still walked around the house moping, but he was seeing a new girl named Tamika. She is a real bitch, if you ask me, but he was falling for this one, and hard. She was Little Bits's niece and my mother's goddaughter. But no one really liked her, not even her own family. And she had him wrapped around her finger like a little puppy dog.

Things between Lola and Twinkie were okay, too. She would go there on the weekends and as long as she was there, we did not have to be bothered with him. Things were perfect in that aspect. My mother was also starting a new job. She would still be working at Maryland University, but in another department.

The summer was rushing by really fast and before I knew it, September had rolled around. My first day of school was a living hell. My mother let me go to school with my friends, even though she thought it was a bad idea. It was a living nightmare. The kids were jumping on the desks, fighting, and cursing the teachers out. It was a zoo. And I had to get out of there. Luckily, my mom understood about it all. She called the school I was originally supposed to go to and the assistant principal never sent my transcripts. At this point I did not care that Daphne wasn't there. I just had to get out of the hell hole I was in. I was ecstatic when I heard the news. My mother always takes care of me.

Things were going good in Leesburg too. Daphne and Ronnie were adjusting well at their school and Tico was behaving himself at his new school. And that was rare for Tico because he always gave the teachers a fit at our elementary school. He was known as the terror. All of the teachers feared having him as a student. One of his teachers wouldn't let him go to the restroom one day, because he wanted to go when his friends went and she knew it would only cause friction, having them out of the classroom at the same time. So, she told him he would have to wait. He asked three or four more times and she said NO every time. He pulled his pants down in front of the whole entire class and peed right there in his chair. And another teacher said she wished she could catch him in a dark alley because she wanted to whip the hell out of him. This crazy boy would take his shoes off, stand on top of the desk, and then slide back and forth across the desk. So, believe me it was a miracle he was behaving himself.

Elsa got a job working at the restaurant with Uncle Eugene. It was really good having my aunt back. I can remember when we were little children how she would dress up like a clown and do shows for us. She was always the fun one. I really missed having her around and now that she is back I am eternally grateful to God. Things seemed great for them.

Our cousin Elmo (his mother died when he was really young and he was raised by my mother and Elsa) even moved up there to be close to Elsa. Our family was separated by the move but at the same time it brought us closer together. Our phone bills were extremely high. I would wait until I went to the hospital to call them from my grandfather's phone. I often wondered what the people in the hospital thought. Here is this man knocking on death's door, but he always had these long distance phone calls on his phone bill.

The phone calls weren't enough. We hadn't seen each other since they left that summer, so we all decided we would get together for Thanksgiving. I was so excited. It seemed like Thanksgiving would never come. My mother had a fear of highways (that would be thanks to Twinkie), and Lawrence decided not to accompany us. He would rather stay home to be with that slut. Dwight was going, though. He and Elmo are brothers, so it was only right that he come up with us. He was especially looking forward to going. He could eat and drink as much as he wanted and did not have to worry about going to work for a couple days. It was just like heaven to him.

Elmo drove down to pick us up. At the time, he was living right down the street, so we stayed with him. There was too much going on at Elsa's place. Grandma was going to be there and I could not deal with her stories and singing. It seemed like we weren't ever going to get there. It was only a two-hour drive, but it seemed more like forever. We got there late that night and it was like we were long lost relatives, as if we didn't talk every day. There were a lot of tears and hugs and kisses. Uncle Eugene welcomed everyone with open arms. And that had to be hard, because if they weren't all my family, I'm not sure if I could do the same.

Elsa was emotional because everyone came up to support her. And this was the first time in years we all would be together for a holiday. Daphne wanted to immediately know what was going on and who was dating who back at school. Tico was interested in money or what my mother brought him. He has always been my mother's favorite. He could milk her out of anything with his smile. It was good being with our family.

Grandma and her crew came up in Bobby's van. Boy I still can't imagine how that went. It was Grandma, Whitney, Aunt Drusilla, the twins (Whitney's of course), the new baby Vonisha, Shanisha, and Aunt Drusilla's boyfriend Vick. It was like they were driving a clown car. We could believe how many people were in that van. I know that there was a lot of fussing and fighting going on driving up the road that night. And poor Bobby, he had to endure that for two hours. But they survived the ride and there weren't any casualties.

After we settled in, we talked and talked and talked, and suddenly realized the sun was coming up. It was Thanksgiving and boy did we have a lot to be thankful for this year. My mother was a little upset because it was her first holiday as a married woman and she wasn't with her husband, and it was her first Thanksgiving without Lawrence.

Lawrence was at home doing God knows what with that whore of his, and there is no telling what Twinkie was into. But she wasn't down for long. She would have a Thanksgiving dinner for our house on Sunday. She always cooked for Twinkie and Uncle Fester. And Lawrence would sell what was left over to people in our neighborhood.

Whitney came strolling out to the kitchen and boy did she have on one of her famous getups. She had on a scarf, so her weave wouldn't come out, a multi-colored nightgown and some stockings that made her feet look like she was an elf. It was early in the morning and she was talking out of her head. Boy does she have some weird conversations sometimes, and she always smacks her lips when she talks, so it's really hard to understand her when she starts going on and on.

Then shortly after, Aunt Drusilla came staggering in. She and Vick were up all night as well. But they weren't up talking, they had been doing grown-up business and you could hear every moan and groan. It was quite disgusting, if you ask me. My mother and Elsa didn't believe us when we told them. They sent us outside so we could stay out of the way.

Elsa cooked a huge feast. It was her first in a long time and we all were amazed. Dinnertime slowly came around and we were ready to say grace, but some of the family members were missing: Grandma, Aunt Drusilla, Vick, and Whitney. Of course, you should know they were out smoking weed. Elsa was livid, that they would bring this to her house, knowing she was in recovery. But they did and it was typical of them to do something like this. Then after each of us went around one by one giving thanks for something, Aunt Drusilla and Vick excused themselves again, and again you could hear the moaning and groaning because this time they were in Elsa's bathroom. We all couldn't help but laugh. I can remember Elmo almost falling out of his chair from laughing so hard. When they finished they came out as if nothing had happened. They sat down and Aunt Drusilla said, "Where's the food? I'm hungry!" Elmo mumbled, "Yeah, I know you want something to eat after that workout." We all laughed and laughed. The adults had no idea what we were talking about.

It was nice to be sitting around the table with our loved ones. Then after dinner we got the big news. Elsa was expecting a baby, so you see this really was thanksgiving now. We wished that night would never end, because we knew in the morning we would be going home. Ronnie told Aunt Drusilla she wasn't happy with the living arrangements and she was ready to come home. Shanisha had the nerve to write Uncle Eugene a love letter and had the nerve to put for your eyes only on it. Things were starting to really get crazy so we knew that it was time to leave. We left feeling a sense of peace. It was really true, Elsa was the old Elsa. She made believers out of everyone; she made the naysayers look like fools. And everyone was proud to see her progression.

We got home that afternoon, and things were back to business as usual. Twinkie was being his normal pushy self. He wanted his Thanksgiving meal. Lawrence was with that slut. My mother was getting ready for her dinner and I was soaking it all up.

Christmas came and Lawrence proposed to that slut bitch. We heard it through the grapevine. He didn't tell us a word. And when my mother inquired, he evaded the question. Little Bits called and told her what happened. She had Christmas breakfast and he did it right there in front of their whole family. He didn't even respect us enough to let us know. I told him that as long as I lived, I would never accept him or their marriage if he went through with it. My mother felt the same way. She washed her hands of the situation. Everyone in the family was hurt by the fact he didn't give us forewarning.

Then on top of that grandma had to be rushed to the hospital a couple of days after Christmas. Whitney took that time and used it to her advantage. While Mary was away, Whitney played. She went through all of grandma's things and then went out on the streets to sell the valuable items she came up with. It just so happened that Elsa's mink coat was in the merchandise she had acquired. Well, grandma called to tell my mother that Whitney had went out and sold a lot of her jewelry, but what she didn't know was that the jewelry was just plain costume jewelry. What got my mother's attention was when she said she had sold the extravagant coat for only fifteen dollars. My mother went to the man but he wouldn't give her the coat back. He said it was a no-refund deal. The coat cost at least five thousand dollars and he got it for fifteen dollars. He took that coat home to his mother, wife, or girlfriend. My mother did not press the issue. She walked away.

We went back to grandma's house and when we got there, she went to approach Whitney. But Whitney didn't want to hear what my mother was saying. She wanted to get smart out of the mouth. The next thing I knew they were fighting. Well it was more like a parent whipping on a child. My mother tore her up. When Mary found out about the fight, she was outraged, and asked my mother to leave the house. She told my mother she didn't appreciate her disrespecting her house. My mother couldn't believe it. She told her, "Mama, as long as you live don't ever call me and ask me to get involved when Whitney does something to you. From now on I'm out of it." My mother was so hurt but she considered the source. No matter what Whitney does, grandma will always be on her side.

A few days later we were ringing in the New Year, but it wasn't good. Things were just starting to heat up. Granddaddy Oliver's condition worsened and the doctors were only giving him six months to live. Lola and Twinkie weren't exactly on good terms either. My mother and I were sitting in the hospital room with granddad and my father walked in. They had very few words for each other. Then my father told me he needed to talk to me. He told me he wanted me to meet my new stepmother. My mother jumped up and said, "You rotten son of a bitch. After all this bullshit I have put up with, you have the nerve to come in this hospital and say something like that to our daughter?"

He said, "You don't have a damn thing to do with it. I'm talking to my child." Then right there at the hospital they began to fight. They fought from my grandfather's room all the way to the parking lot. Then he asked her to get into his car with him. She goes in and they started to fight again. The van was rocking back and forth from the vibration. My mother may be a lot of things, but she is not the type that will put up with a man's shit. After all that she was doing for him and his father. She would leave work every day, then go and sit at the hospital for about two hours. Then come home and cook dinner. She had no time for herself. But he wasn't appreciative of that. As always, Twinkie only cared about Twinkie.

This was the last straw for her. She was tired of him and she wanted to make a drastic change. She woke me and Lawrence up on a Saturday morning and told us that she was going to buy a new car. We didn't believe her, because she never did this sort of thing without my father. We went anyway and when we got there, she did in fact purchase a new car. It truly shocked the hell out of us. Lawrence and I couldn't believe it. This was the first time she'd ever done something on her own. When we got home, Twinkie was waiting for us in the driveway. It was like he knew. He hadn't been up to the house in months and all of a sudden, he was there. It was weird. He made a big deal about the car; he couldn't believe she would go out and do this without consulting him first. He is very narcissistic. He said he would never ride in the car because that is what broke up their marriage. He made no mention about this mystery woman he told me about just a couple of weeks ago. And furthermore, why should she consult him? He never consulted her in the past when he went out and bought cars and she had to help pay for them. They argued and argued and as normal, he stormed out. They didn't speak for days.

Then it happened. Granddaddy Oliver was tired of fighting and died. The doctor's prognosis was wrong. He didn't last a month. Twinkie was emotionless when he called. When he spoke to my mother, he said, "Daddy died this morning." He wasn't sympathetic about it at all. He was just Twinkie. My mother, being who she is, dropped everything to be with him. She immediately called Lawrence and told him to come and pick her up from work. I was at school at the time. Lawrence took it exceptionally hard. Granddaddy never knew Lawrence wasn't his biological grandson. But it never mattered, blood was never a factor. Lawrence loved him as if he was his real grandfather.

I found out in a most unique way. My mother told Lawrence and Dwight not to tell me a thing. Everyone knew how close I was to Granddaddy Oliver and they wanted to sit me down to break it to me gently. But Lawrence did not listen. I was walking home from school and Lawrence saw me. He walked over and said, "Granddaddy's gone." My question was, "Gone where? Did the doctors let him go home?" Then he proceeded to tell me that he was dead. I instantly flipped out. My first instinct was to run. Lawrence caught me and put me over his shoulders. It was one of the saddest moments of my entire life. My mother was upset with Lawrence because he actually told me when she insisted he shouldn't. But that was our bond. He wanted to be the one to tell me so he could be there for me, and he was. He pushed his pain aside and took me out. He wasn't being a jerk (since we really hadn't spoken in a few days because of his damn girlfriend).

My mother and father were still on the outs but she still was there with him every step of the way. She went with him to pick out the casket, and to make all of the funeral arrangements. She thought this would maybe change him, and he seemed softer. He was mellow. It wasn't the Twinkie that was treating her like dirt weeks before. He held her hand and told her she was the only family he had left. This made her forget all of the bad stuff.

The funeral was hard to deal with. It was a very somber day. Elsa came down with Uncle Eugene. And grandma came straggling along behind them. They just wanted to show support. Elsa and Mary were always fond of my grandfather. Whitney was out on the streets doing her thing. Lawrence was really affected. He really broke down. This was only the second time I had ever seen my brother cry. My mother sat with Lawrence, so she could console him.

But then *she* walked in. Ernestine. She's the woman that was seeing my father before and during the beginning of my parent's relationship.

She came in looking like a Thanksgiving day float. How dare she stroll in there like she was the wife? And to top it off, this BITCH had the nerve to sit on the row that was reserved for family members only. My mother kindly walked over to her and quietly asked her if she wouldn't mind sitting with the guests. As she got up to find another seat, Daisy walked in. This is Veronica's mother (One of Twinkie's daughters). This is the woman that called my mother a bitch because my mother answered my father's telephone. My mother's response was, "When I see you, I am going to show you how much of a bitch I truly am." This was the first time they'd ever laid eyes on each other in almost twenty years. But it was neither the time nor place for such animosity.

It was like Twinkie's women were coming out of the woodwork. Lola was ready for them, though. She served every last one of them something that day. And they couldn't take it one bit. That is, all except Ernestine. She stayed, because she is really close to my Aunt Fran, Uncle Rob's wife. Daisy left after my father introduced her to my mother. My mother gave her that look of death and she hurried up and got the hell out of there. The service was short and sweet. It was just the way granddaddy wanted. He was brief and to the point.

When the services were over, we went to the cemetery. I rode with two of my other brothers, Eric and Randy. I didn't know them very well, so I figured this time with them would help us to bond with each other. When we got to the cemetery, the preacher finished his prayer, and everyone grabbed their flowers and started to walk towards their cars. My father then made an announcement that no one was allowed to leave until Granddaddy was in the ground. I said to him, "Look, Daddy, I am cold." He told me, "If you get into one of those cars, you won't be able to go out or use the phone for months. Have some respect for your grandfather. We are going to watch them put his body in the ground.

Then you can get into the car and warm yourself. It's not going to hurt to stay in the cold for a few minutes."

He actually made everyone stand there. It was freezing below zero, and it had just snowed days before. I can still remember my brothers, Eric and Randy, saying how crazy he was. Randy said, "Man, forget this. I am going over there." He said, "Look, Dad, I have somewhere to be. I can't stand out here. I'm leaving. I will be over to the house when I finish." He told Randy he would whip his ass. So out of respect, Randy stayed.

After the diggers were finished, everyone was allowed to get back into their cars and leave. Twinkie did not want a repast at the church, but Aunt Ester from Florida talked him into having one at his house. To this day she is the only person I have ever met that my father fears. He was actually a normal, decent man while he was in her presence. You would have thought he and my mother were the happiest couple in the world, and that we were the happiest family. There was a lot of lying going on. He was calling my mother honey and baby. And he was saying what wonderful kids Lawrence and I were, and how happy he was with all of us living there. If only she knew the truth. We weren't the happy family and weren't living under the same roof.

My father's children and I went into the family room. We all sat around and talked and got to know each other better. It was the first time some of my brothers and sisters had ever met. We all tried to get to know each other the best we could. After the repast was over and everyone had gone, we had to clean up. Twinkie looked over at my mother while she was washing dishes and said, "Don't think that this changes anything."

She was devastated. She actually thought that through all of this they had a fighting chance. But even in the midst of all that was going on, hee was still going to be an ass. I was hurt seeing my mother like this. I also felt happy, because I got a chance to spend some time with my other brothers and my sisters. I knew it was going to be hard without granddaddy, but he was really sick for a long time and I know he was tired of suffering. He was 83 at the time of his death, so he lived a very full life.

These were rough times for us down here after granddad's death. My mother and father were on the outs now more than ever before. He was such a mean person and he was being mean to the person he vowed to love the most. Lawrence started treating us like dirt because of his girlfriend. She was his top priority. He actually got mad at my mother because she said, "That girl is something," instead of using her name. I told him he should be happy it wasn't me because I wouldn't have been that nice. She didn't deserve to be called by her first name. She was a bitch and I let him know it. And I told him that if she needed clarity I would tell her, too.

My mother was falling into a depression because of how things were turning out with my father (to be married for almost a year and you spend more time apart than you do together). I was lashing out because Lawrence was putting someone in front of me. We constantly fought all of the time. And that was taking its toll on my mother, too. She hated seeing us at odds. But until he would realize this girl was no good for him, I couldn't be bothered.

Grandma was being her normal self. She is a weed-smoking crazy nut case. Whitney is out on the streets, and she and my mother still aren't speaking after the fight. Elsa is getting bigger and bigger. Things in Leesburg are really good. They were finally beginning to adjust to their new surroundings.

Then one Sunday morning, while we were dressing for Sunday school, the phone started to ring. It was Elsa saying Daphne had run away, so we were on our way to Leesburg. This time Lawrence would be going. He had to drive. The ride didn't seem as long, maybe because Lawrence drives like a bat out of hell. We were there in no time. Once we got there we heard of all the particulars. Lawrence, Tico and I drove around for hours but there was no trace of Daphne. She got into an argument with Aunt Elsa and Uncle Eugene over her curfew. She wanted to stay out all hours of the night. And Elsa wasn't having it. So, Daphne stormed out and had been gone all night.

My mother was steaming mad; she was concerned about Elsa's pregnancy. You see, Elsa isn't a spring chicken. She was 40 years old and she was about to have a baby. Daphne was taking her rebellious attitude to the extreme. No one knew where she was. We went to her friends' houses, and either they were lying or they really didn't know where she was. After a couple of hours of searching, Uncle Eugene called the police. The town is so small, this was considered headline news. Eventually her anger wore off and before we left, Daphne came home. We were all so grateful that nothing had happen to her. After my mother sat down with her and discussed the situation with Daphne, it was time for us to leave.

We packed up for the nice ride home. Then things really got wild. Grandma and Whitney were having major issues. As always, it was concerning her welfare check. Grandma wouldn't hand it over to her. She knew if she did the children wouldn't have any food. So, Whitney called Elsa. When Elsa answered the phone, she could hardly understand her because she was talking so fast. She said, "Elsa mama is stealing your money and you need to come down here, get it and then whip her ass." She had to repeat herself a couple more times before Elsa finally understood what she was saying. When she finally heard her, she wanted to know what she was talking about. She said, "Whitney, what are you talking about? What money?"

She said, "Daphne's real father, Big Boy, has been paying child support for her since she was five years old and mama has been taking the money. She never said anything to you because she figured you didn't need the money." Elsa dropped the phone. She couldn't believe her own mother would do this. She told Whitney that she was the scum of the earth. She said, "You knew this all along. That's the problem with you and mama. You all are probably mad at each other and that's probably the only reason you are telling me this now."

Whitney said, "The hell with you, see if ever I look out for you again." Elsa called my mother and asked her what she should do. My mother was amazed. They never thought grandma was this low. Well, they found out different. Elsa called the courts first; she didn't want to accuse grandma of something that wasn't true, because Whitney lies a lot. Low and behold the clerk gave her all of the information she needed. It was all true. Then she called grandma. There was very little she could say. Elsa said, "You old bag, you had better be happy I am not pressing charges against you for fraud, or have the courts make you pay restitution for all of the money you have taken over the course of the last 10 years. And I know the last check was mailed out a couple of days ago. I know you better have the money and if you don't, you had better get it or I will call the police."

Grandma was scared to death. She said, "Elsa, I know I was wrong and I'm sorry. Is there anyway you would be able to forgive me?" Elsa hung up on her. One thing about grandma, she is a true actress. Elsa didn't want to hear the nonsense she was talking. The next day, Elsa and Uncle Eugene came down so they could get the money. Elsa told Uncle Eugene to go in. She didn't want to look grandma in the face. When he walked through the door, grandma tried to explain her self. But he told her, "Ma, I don't want to get involved in the situation. I will say this, though. You are totally wrong. And your daughter is really hurt." Then he walked out.

Elsa didn't speak to grandma for weeks after the situation. Mary tried to get my mother to intervene, but my mother told her she had her own problems she was dealing with. Lawrence was getting closer and closer with his girlfriend, Tamika. Her mother had a drug problem and couldn't take care of her younger siblings, so Lawrence took on the role as a father figure to these children. He would bring them over and they would eat my mother's food even though none of the little bitches had manners. They would walk into the house and wouldn't speak. I hated every minute of it. I told him I didn't care if they did or did not speak to me, but they were not going to disrespect my mother. I said, "Either you handle it or I will." He just looked at me and walked away. But he made sure they spoke to my mother from that moment on.

I clung to my other brothers and my nephew Martin. He was a lot older so he took on the role of my mentor, since Lawrence was so preoccupied being a so-called father. My mother was disgusted with Lawrence; his nose was wide open for this girl and everyone could see she was no good for him. It was like history was repeating itself. Lola and Twinkie all over again, except this time Twinkie was in the form of a no good dirty tramping woman.

Then one night the shit hit the fan. I mean it really got crazy. My mother was over at my father's house and Lawrence wouldn't allow me to get on the phone. He knew I had a curfew for the phone. But he wouldn't allow me to get on the phone. He was talking to that trollop. I picked up the phone without him knowing and I overheard her calling me a bitch. I didn't go looking for this trouble but since it's coming to me I had no other choice but to handle my business. And I handled it right then and there. I kindly walked into his room and I told him and that piece of gutter trash that she was no longer welcome in my house and that if she tried to walk her slut ass in there I would try my best to kill her. She was nothing but a low down dirty bitch, and Lawrence was a bitch for talking to her and allowing her to disrespect me. Then I told her that when she came around I was going to show her how much of a bitch I could be. They were both scared at this point; they didn't know what I was capable of. So, Lawrence hung up with her and called my mother and she rushed home. But once she got there the entire story changed. They said I called her mother a bitch and told her mother I was going to kill her. I didn't even know this lady. And even if I did I wouldn't disrespect her, unless she disrespected me, that is. So, I was grounded and my phone privileges were taken away from me for a while. I had to actually apologize to this bitch. Then they told her mother what was going on and this crack-head actually took part in what was going on and I had to apologize to that bitch, too.

I was so angry. But I tell you one thing – she didn't come around for about a month after that. Because if she did, I was going to give her something she would have never forgotten. I put together a concoction and when she walked in the door, I was going to dump it all over her. My mother found the stuff and my punishment was extended. All because Lawrence's hormones were out of whack and this girl was doing some extremely nasty things to him. He was alienating himself from everyone.

Before I knew it, summertime had rolled around again. A whole year had passed. We were still living on Sixth Street, Twinkie couldn't blame it on granddaddy anymore and the house was complete. It was obvious to everyone except my mother that we weren't ever going to move. They were just married on paper. They played house every other weekend, when she would go over there. Lawrence was involved in his life with that slut. Whitney was being Whitney. We all still prayed every night for her, but I don't think it's doing any good. Grandma is excited; she is going to be a grandmother again. I don't know why, though, seeing as she has 12 grandchildren already and she doesn't play a major role in any of our lives. This baby is going to be just another number once he gets here. Well, except Whitney's two children that live with them. But she is more like a mother to them since Whitney is always gone.

Daphne and Tico were looking forward to the summer, because they were spending it with us. We are going to be together. Time really flew by. Then things got worse. Our Aunt Lillie (not really related) had been very sick and she had to be rushed to the hospital. They were not sure what was wrong. So, they kept her there to monitor her. Everyone on the block was worried. She was the only one left from the old days. One night, my cousin Smokey (Aunt Lillie's grandson) was over at the house. We were watching a movie and it got really late. For some reason, we started talking about death and burials. He said he would bury his family members like the Vikings did. He said that If Aunt Lillie died, he was going to put her body on a boat and push her into the river and set the boat on fire. We laughed and laughed, and then he left.

Minutes later we heard gunshots. It had to have been at least 20 shots that were fired, and then we heard someone screaming. We thought that Smokey had gotten shot, so we were hysterical. A couple seconds later, Smokey ran back over to the house and we found out it that it was Stanley. He was killed instantly. He had been outside with some friends and someone came through and sprayed the entire block with bullets. After someone called the police, we all just gathered outside and waited. One of the guys that was out there that night was a real jerk. He wanted to mouth off to the police and curse out the people from the medical examiner's office. Lawrence stepped in and told him he would appreciate it if he toned it down. He was being very disrespectful to the older women that were out there. The guy proceeded to get even louder. He was really trying to provoke Lawrence, because they didn't like each other anyway. At this point Lawrence jumped up in his face and told him if he did not stop, he would really hurt him because he would not disrespect his mother, his little sister or any of the women in his family that were out there that night.

The next morning every one just walked around in a daze. It was a very sad day on Sixth Street. No one could believe this happened. Then the next day someone went up to the hospital and told Aunt Lillie someone had killed Stanley, her favorite grandchild. She had a heart attack and died. Now they were planning two funerals instead of one. I can still remember the somber look on everybody's faces. No one knew the exact words to say, because no one had lived through anything quite like this. Even Grandma was speechless.

Aunt Lillie had been in our family since Grandma was a child. Aunt Lillie was one of Big Mama's dear friends. Elsa came down, and she was huge. We couldn't believe how big she was. It looked like the baby was going to come at any minute. Daphne and Tico came down with Elsa and Uncle Eugene, but they were staying for the rest of the summer. Everyone was walking around like zombies. It was really terrible. The funeral was very sad. A grandmother and her grandson. She loved him more than she loved her own children, and now the both of them were gone forever. A few days later, Amad Duke (after my grandfather) Parker was born. A new life has just begun. This is a beautiful new start. Life is funny. We had lost so much, but gained more with the soul of a precious baby boy.

LOLA'S SONG

L ittle Lola, she was so small for her age. Her earliest memories would not include her mother or father. The both of them were in jail or "gone away to college" as it was referred to back then. But she has Big Mama and Daddy Ritchie (that's Big Mama's husband). He loved the idea of having two little ones (Elsa and Lola) in the house since they were never blessed with children of their own. And Lola is his child. She is the responsible one, the one that even as a little girl wouldn't take any mess off of you.

There she was, a little over eight years old, raising babies, cooking, cleaning, grocery shopping, and paying bills. It was obvious that though she was just a baby, Big Mama was grooming her to one day become the family matriarch. Big Mama must have known she was the only one to handle the job, because there were so many others in or around that house, but still she put her trust in this tiny little girl. Little Lola, she was very short for her age, but what she lacked in stature she gained in courage and compassion.

The local crowd that hung in the house on Sixth Street all called her Grandma. These old ass men that were clearly old enough to be her grandfather, but still all of them had a respect for her even though she was that young. But even with all of Big Mama's attention and the love and admiration of the fellow drunks in or around the house, Lola's self-esteem was still broken while growing up. She was considered the ugly duckling with raccoon eyes, while Elsa was the flourishing beautiful swan. That's how it was to everyone except Aunt Mattie, her kindred spirit. Aunt Mattie always felt she was a beautiful child inside and out. And she made sure that she let her know whenever she could. Lola was the only child in that house Aunt Mattie loved; she could care less about the rest of them. But no matter what people said about her, to her face or behind her back, she hid her insecurities and continued to go unnoticed because she was always looked at as Elsa's little sister and she always lurked in her shadows.

Because both of her parents were paying their debts to society while the girls were in their formative years, people automatically assumed that Ms. Tootie and Mr. Ritchie were their biological parents. Even though they were old as dirt, you couldn't tell if Ms. Tootie had been pregnant or not because her fifty-two dress size never changed. It didn't bother Lola much, though, because she never had a bond with her mother. Big Mama always said it was because Mary left them alone so often when she was an infant that Lola never had the time to connect with Mary.

Big Mama and Aunt Gertrude were the mother figures this little girl had come to know and love. They would take Elsa and Lola to visit Mary while she was away in prison. Elsa was always really needy and clingy to their mother, whereas Lola would go to the other end of the long visiting table and just stare at her mother and in a very mean, condescending tone ask, "Why don't you have any shoestrings in your shoes?" And though she didn't feel anything for her mother, Mary never did anything to make the child feel as if she was wanted. She would always hug and kiss on Elsa, but Lola wasn't affectionate and Mary never pressed the issue.

When she came home she lived in the family house with them for awhile and she would sing her little darlings to sleep, but even then there was always a difference between her two girls. Big Mama always joked around and said Mary felt intimidated by this little girl and that she could see straight through her mother, that's why Mary wanted no part of her. Mary would just brush it off and said Big Mama didn't know what she was talking about.

Once Mary got on her feet, she moved out. And when she finally had it all together, she decided it was time for her and her little girls to be together. Lola had just turned nine years old and Elsa was almost eleven. Little Lola couldn't imagine her world without Big Mama, Daddy Ritchie, and not living in "the house" as family members referred to the family home. Mary was just her birth mother, but deep down inside she never truly felt her mother's love and Mary never showed it.

One day out of the blue, Mary stormed into the house. She went to Big Mama and told her now was the time for her little girls to come home. Big Mama said, "Have you lost your damn mind? These girls aren't going anywhere. They are home. You can't just come in after all these years and uproot these children."

Mary said, "Now look, you are forgetting one thing, these are my children and now I am stable and I want them back."

Big Mama said, "You are right, they are your children because you gave birth to them, but I am their mother. You ask them if they want to come home with you and see what they say." So, they waited until the children got out of school. "Here they come now," Big Mama said.

Mary called them into the house. "Elsa! Lola! Come in this house right now. No time for chit chatting with your friends, you can do that later." They rushed into the house. They didn't know what was going on. Lola was scared that someone had died. "Where is my Big Mama?" she said nervously.

"I am right here baby, everything is alright. Your mother has something to say to the two of you. So, take off your jackets and come sit down at the table." They put down their things and took a seat to see what was going on.

Mary slowly started explaining to them what she was planning on doing. "You both know your mother loves you dearly. I have been away from you long enough and now that I have my life in order, I am ready for the both of you to come home." Lola couldn't believe her ears as her mother was talking. "You will now have your own rooms and beautiful things to play with. And we will all be together like families should be. And you can come and spend time with Big Mama whenever you want. She is just around the corner."

Elsa was all smiles. She was so happy; she ran and hugged her mother. She was always the gleam in her mother's eyes. But Lola, on the other hand, was just about ready to explode. Her little face began to turn as red as the tablecloth covering the dining room table.

"Lola, aren't you happy, too? You are finally going to live with your mother," Big Mama asked, even though she didn't agree with what Mary was doing. The truth is, Mary was right. They were her daughters. She just wanted what was best for them. Lola didn't answer; she just sat there staring into space, similar to the way she would stare at Mary on those visits to the jail. "Lola did you hear me? I just asked you a question," Big Mama said now in a very demanding tone. "Yes ma'am," Lola muttered under her breath.

Now Mary jumped in, "Aren't you happy, baby?" Big Mama saw it in her eyes as the tears began to roll down her face. She could no longer hold it in. Her little body was about to burst. Suddenly she began screaming at the top of her lungs, and usually she was so soft spoken that she even scared herself. "NO! I AM NOT HAPPY! I DON'T WANT TO LIVE ANYWHERE WITH HER! I DON'T CARE ABOUT THE ROOMS

OR THE TOYS! SHE IS NOT MY MOTHER. BIG MAMA, YOU ARE MY MOTHER AND I ONLY WANT TO LIVE HERE. IF YOU MAKE ME LEAVE THEN I WILL KILL MYSELF."

The tears were uncontrollable at this point. When she finished, Mary leaped across the table, she was trying to grab her so she could whip her ass. But Lola, though she was a little girl, she was as fast as lightning and she was too quick for Mary. She hopped up from the table and then went flying up the stairs. She ran straight into the bathroom and locked the door. Mary went charging up the stairs after her. She began pounding on the door. The more Mary pounded on the door, the more Lola screamed. Finally, Big Mama interceded and put an end to the whole ordeal. "MARY!" she yelled at the top of her lungs, "Let that girl alone. If she doesn't want to go then fine, let her stay here. I told you I didn't think this was a good idea, you coming in here trying to uproot them from the only home they have ever known."

Mary said in response, "Well, Elsa is ok with the idea, so Lola will just have to learn to adjust."

Big Mama went on, "Lola and Elsa are two different people and you will not treat her like she doesn't matter just because Elsa is okay with the idea of all this. You have always treated them differently. They are both your daughters."

"Well, I am her mother and I make the decisions. She is a child, she doesn't have a say in all of this. She will not control me," Mary said.

Big Mama was worked up now. "Well, I said leave her alone. I can still knock your damn teeth down your throat. I don't care how old you are and how many other children you have, that little girl is staying here and there is nothing you or anyone else can do about it."

Mary finally agreed, "Alright, I will allow her to stay for now until the idea of it all settles in her head, then she has to come live with me."

Big Mama looked at her and said firmly, "She is home now. She will come to live with you if and when SHE is ready and not one minute sooner." And that was Big Mama's final say and Mary knew not to utter another word.

Mary walked over to Elsa and told her to pack her things. When Elsa was done, the two of them went storming out of the house. A few minutes later after the smoke cleared, Lola came creeping out of the bathroom. When she turned the corner there was Big Mama sitting on the bed waiting for her. Lola stood there for a minute. She had a puzzled but startled look on her face. She didn't know whether to run back to the bathroom or to run straight into Big Mama's arms. But Big Mama reached out for her and instantly she knew that as mothers do, she had made everything alright. She ran and jumped into her arms. The feelings of emptiness were mutual. Big Mama never wanted to be separated from those girls. She had been the one that loved and nurtured them all of that time while Mary was out doing whatever her heart desired. But she didn't want to keep them away from their mother if they wanted to be with her.

Mary stayed away for quite a while. She wouldn't even allow Elsa to venture around the corner, making her walk all the way around the block in order to get to school in the morning. She was trying to punish Lola for not wanting to live with her and she knew the only way to do that would be through the absence of her sister. Lola and Elsa were inseparable; she even went to the extreme of telling her not to even speak to the little girl while they were in school. And this was killing Lola. She went home from school every day in tears.

Finally, Big Mama came to the rescue and put and end to it. She called Mary and lit into her, telling her that enough was enough. She said, "What you don't seem to understand is what you are doing is making Lola never want to live with you at all. It is only making her resent you even more."

Mary didn't want to give in, but soon after the conversation, she knew it was time to let go of her bitterness and anger towards the pint-sized child. Minutes later, Elsa came running around the corner and the sisters were reunited. It was like it had been years the way the little girls were behaving, but only a few days had passed. Lola loved her sister and she missed her dearly, but after a couple weeks had passed she realized she kind of liked the idea of the new arrangement. She didn't need to live with Mary because she had her own room now anyway. Elsa and other cousins would come over and visit, but they would go home and she was the only one that lived there and the only one soaking up all of Big Mama's attention.

The two of them were sort of kindred spirits. They would wake up early in the morning while everyone was sleeping and sit in the window watching the old men in the alley behind the house. Some would be creeping into their houses after a late night, some would be sleeping on the cold hard concrete because they got put out the night before, and some with their nasty asses would be pissing in the bushes. Lola and Big Mama would yell crazy and obscene things at them and then they would duck back out of the window so that no one would know who it was. And they wouldn't know what direction it was coming from so they would be looking from side to side to see if they could catch the person bold enough to say whatever to them.

"Don't you know what time it is? You can't creep into the house this time, and I hope she beats the hell out of you," to the one sneaking in the house. "Wake your ass up! Don't you have a home to go to?" to the one sleeping on the ground. And to that nasty ass pissing in the trees, "You nasty sick bastard, if my roses die, I am going to kick your ass. You should be ashamed of yourself. You can't even wash your damn hands." Then they would fall back laughing and throughout the day either of them would look at the other and the both of them would get the giggles and no one else knew what was so funny and didn't understand it was a joke only shared between the two of them. And that's how it always was.

Because of their relationship, she became the only child allowed in the house while "grown folks" talked about family issues and business. And that's how she got the nickname grandma. She was an old soul and for that reason Big Mama chose her over any of the others.

The years ahead would turn into devastation for her and the rest of the family. Aunt Mattie suddenly died; Lola was away at summer camp and on the day she returned the ambulance was their taking her beloved aunt away and she never came home again. She was the first one other than Big Mama and Daddy Ritchie that paid any real attention to her. Aunt Mattie wasn't too fond of children, but she loved little Lola. Lola was around twelve when she passed on. It didn't seem to them that the age difference was that much. Aunt Mattie was close to seventy when she died, but didn't act a day over thirty. Lola never did handle death too well. But Big Mama helped her through it.

She was growing so fast. Though she was still the runt of the bunch, she was still the tallest in Big Mama's eyes. By this time, she was starting seventh grade. And for the first time, living with Big Mama and Daddy Ritchie became a problem. Older people could care less about the latest fashions. And living with them was hard when she had to wear the most hideous ensembles. She went to Mary to see if she could take her shopping and finally Mary knew she had her moment to get the little girl back for turning her down all of those many years ago. "Go look in your sister's closet. You want clothes like that, right?" Mary asked.

"Yes, Mama. How did you know?" Lola said back excited and anxious.

"Because I am your mother. Now, didn't I tell you there was going to be a time when you would regret not coming home to live with me?

Well, that time has come sweetheart, and now you have to suffer the consequences," Mary said back to the devastated little girl.

She ran all of the way home crying her poor little eyes out. The nerve of her mother, to do something like that. To add insult to injury, a few minutes after she got home, Mary drove up and picked up all of the neighborhood kids to take them shopping and left Lola at home sitting on the porch to think about the day she turned her mother down.

But just as Mary thought she had been vindicated, fate stepped in and Uncle Rusty and a few older cousins took control and became Lola's fairy godparents. Little Lola got her pass to the ball after all. Mary was furious to know that anyone stepped in when she was trying to teach her daughter a lesson. But Big Mama had to let her know just how wrong she was. Lola went from fashion misfit to one of the best dressed girls in the school. Even Elsa had to admit that her little sister could rag. And even though Mary made sure Elsa stayed up on all of the latest fashion trends, Elsa would still sneak into the house and steal her sister's clothes. And one day Lola got tired of it and they fought in the middle of French class at school. The teachers broke it up and sent the two girls to the principal's office.

No one in the office knew the two of them were sisters because their records had two different names for their guardians. When Mary got word, she went to the school to see about her children. The principal made her wait because they were still waiting on Lola's mother. Elsa had a name for being a bully and because of that, Mary became quite familiar with the principal's office, where on the other hand Big Mama had only been there once to enroll Lola. Mary went to the secretary to see what the holdup was. "Ms. Matthews, I am here to see about my two daughters, Elsa and Lola Hayes. I have been sitting her waiting long enough. Is there someone that can tell me something, because I have to get back to work?" The secretary looked startled, as if Mary was talking in a foreign language.

She told Mary she would be with her in a minute. She went inside the principal's office and told him Mrs. Hayes was the mother of both Elsa and Lola and that she was tired of waiting in the office.

Mrs. Lombardi couldn't believe her ears. "You mean to tell me that the two of you are sisters?"

"Yes ma'am," the two of them said back as if they were ashamed. She called for Mary to come into the office. Mary asked why they were fighting and Lola told her about Elsa stealing her clothes and instead of Mary getting on Elsa she told Lola she was selfish and stingy. The principal held Lola back and told her she was sorry for the way her mother had just behaved. Elsa was in the wrong, but it was clear that Mary being their mother could care less about what she had done. All she cared about was chastising Lola. But Lola didn't care. Mary was only the woman that brought her into the world. Big Mama was her mother. That whole ordeal didn't phase her one bit.

Things were going so well for Lola. But as life had always been for her when things seemed to be at their peak in her life, something had to come and turn things around and the bad would rear its ugly head. Daddy Ritchie had just turned sixty-five years old and his job was making him retire. The night before, he cried to Lola, "I don't want to leave my job. I don't know what I am going to do if I am not working." Lola just brushed his head and told him everything was going to be alright. The next day when he got home from work, Lola went to check on him and he was slumped over in his favorite chair. Lola called out to him a few times but he didn't answer. Then she ran over to him and hit him but he didn't budge. She just hit him a few times, saying to one of her little cousins she was going to get all of her licks back for the spankings that she got over the years. But she was joking and it never crossed her mind that her daddy was laying there dead.

After a few minutes passed she told Big Mama he wasn't breathing and Big Mama flew out of the house like someone was chasing her. Big Mama could tolerate a lot of things, but the sick and the dead was unfortunately not her cup of tea. And she vowed that unless Ritchie got up she was not coming back into that house. Lola ran across the street to get help. Her best friend's mother was a nurse and she knew she would be able to help.

But when Myrtle got there, too much time had passed and he was already gone. Lola's world sadly started tumbling down. This was her father. He was the only consistent male presence in her life since birth and now he was gone. Lola's heart began to break and the next thing that you know, she suffered a nervous breakdown. But just like with every obstacle she had faced since birth, she overcame that, too.

After all of the heartache she had faced at such a young age, she still continued to be the most compassionate person. By the time she reached high school, Elsa had dropped out and was living the life, doing as she pleased. Big Mama was so happy because she knew all of those years ago that Lola's good heart and spirit would have been ruined if she ever lived in the same house as her mother.

Lola was devastated that her sister was going down the road that she was, but what could she do? Elsa was her older sister. And Elsa was the type that never let anyone stop her from doing what she wanted to do.

Elsa had been gone for a long time and then all of a sudden, Lola was called to the front office and when she got there, there was Elsa swinging a pocketbook, chewing gum, looking like a bag lady. She wanted Lola to meet her new boyfriend. This guy looked as old as Mary, but Lola didn't judge. She went and met him. She spent a few minutes with Elsa, but she had to get back to class. She asked if Elsa coming home and Elsa's response was, "I'll be home when I get some time." And she kept on swinging that purse and chewing that gum as if she was a cow. It was good for Lola just to see her sister and know she was alright.

When she got home that evening she let everyone know she saw Elsa and that she seemed to be doing alright for herself. Mary was angered by the fact that she didn't call to let them know Elsa was up at the school. But she told them, "No one can make Elsa come home. She will come back when she is ready. If I would have called, then she would have been mad at me. And then no one would know how she was doing." Big Mama agreed and told Mary to stop worrying about the child. Elsa was almost eighteen. And when she was ready to come back home then she would. Lola had more important things to worry about like making good grades. But to Mary none of that ever mattered to her. As much as Lola studied, as popular as she became and as much as everyone loved her, Mary always felt it should have been Elsa. Lola and Mary's relationship was never the best and because of Mary it would never be what it should have been for a mother and daughter. Mary always had a problem with her daughter and she always showed it.

After the breakup with Winston, she rekindled an old flame with one of her high school boyfriends, Billy Buckner, who had found Allah and changed his name to Bilal. And one day out of the blue she called Lola to her house. When Lola got there Mary informed her that the man she thought to be her father all of her life, Duke Turner, was not her father, and that in fact this total stranger, Bilal, was her father. Instantly Lola began screaming at the top of her lungs, "HOW COULD YOU DO SOMETHING LIKE THIS? THIS MAN IS NOT MY FATHER. DUKE TURNER IS MY FATHER AND YOU KNOW IT."

Mary just gazed out of the window. "I have wanted to tell you this for years now, but I just didn't know how to, and when Bilal came back into our lives I realized I had to tell you. I could no longer walk around with this secret. You have to know that this has been a burden on me all of these years. But your father is here now and he is ready to be a father and to make up for all of the time that he has missed in your life."

Lola went flying out of the house. She raced home to tell Big Mama. She was so upset she could hardly get the words out. No one could believe what was coming out of her mouth. Big Mama and Aunt Gertrude had a thing or two to tell Mary. The two of them wanted to kill her for putting Lola through all of this crap. Big Mama wanted answers. She called for Mary to meet her at the house. And when she got there, she got down to the bottom of the story. Bilal had come from a very rich family and they needed an heir. Elsa was in and out of trouble and the time didn't match up with Whitney and that left Lola the good girl. The one that any old lady would be proud to have for her grandchild, Mary and Bilal had received word that his mother was coming to town specifically for the purpose of meeting her long lost grandchild, to make up for the time that she had been apart from her because of her son's irresponsible behaviors over the years.

When Big Mama and Aunt Gertrude finished with Mary, she apologized for hurting Lola but she said that the woman had too much money to tell her it was all a lie. She told Lola that Duke was her father but begged for her to keep up the act for this woman. Lola wanted no part of Mary, Bilal, or their plot to manipulate this innocent old woman. It was sad. All for the love of money, Mary was willing to sell her precious daughter to the highest bidder.

The episode finally blew over and Lola was starting a new phase in her life. She was just about ready to complete high school. The only thing she wanted for her graduation was to see her father. She wanted her biological father to be there for her graduation. Of course, Daddy Ritchie was the best father that a child could have, and Winston Hayes gave her his name and his heart, but she still longed for her dad. He was the missing piece in her life and she wanted to see him.

Mary wanted to make up for the pain she had inflicted on her so she gave Lola his last known address and Lola went on a scavenger hunt trying to find him. And when she found him, he wasn't in his best condition. When he saw her, he knew who she was instantly and he began to cry. And at that moment she knew where she had come from. This compassionate man sat on the curb and cried like a baby, because the only thing she wanted was for her daddy to be there at her graduation. He apologized over and over for the time they had lost, but she had forgiven him the moment the first tear fell from his eyes.

He told her that he wasn't in the position to make it to the graduation, but would be there for her from that moment on, and he was. He began to tease her by saying that at the moment when she found him he was as greasy as a pork chop, but she didn't care because all she wanted was her daddy. On the day of her graduation, Big Mama felt her own sense of accomplishment because she knew she had made the right decision for her little girl all those years ago. She was a very popular girl in her high school; she was even voted class president. She only wanted the position so she could get free tickets to the prom and the honor of introducing the speaker at their graduation with a seat right on the stage at her ceremony.

At that moment, Big Mama's chest puffed out with pride. She was so proud seeing her baby girl sitting there on that stage. Even Mary, with all of her issues with her daughter, had to admit she was proud, too.

Lola had blossomed into such an eloquent speaker, and on this evening she had finally taken her place, she had finally arrived, she was the belle of the ball. And in the fall, she would attend college to pursue her dream of becoming a teacher. Life was going so well for Lola; Elsa had resurfaced and was back at home, and she and her sister were closer than ever.

Everything had finally been put back in its place. She was in school and working in the government.

Elsa was allowing her to hang out on some evenings with her and her friends. One evening she was relaxing after a long week of work and school and Elsa persuaded her to hang out at this club, and while she was sitting there at the bar in walked the finest, smoothest cat Lola ever had the privilege of seeing in her life. She called for Elsa to come over. "Who is that?" Lola asked her sister.

"Oh, that is Lance, but get it out of your head. He is a nut." was Elsa's response.

"Well I don't care what you say he is, please introduce us," Lola said now in a very demanding way.

"Alright, but don't say that I didn't warn you," Elsa said before calling him over.

When he walked over, she introduced the two but he didn't seem that interested until he saw her leave the bar to go to the ladies' room. When he saw that eighteen-inch waist and apple bottom, he shortly changed his tune and wanted to know everything about her. Little Lola was a brick house. She was teased so often, people said she had a body like a coca cola bottle, small at the top but fat at the bottom. Lance was twenty-three, fine as wine, and crazy as a damn bed bug, but once they hooked up that didn't stop Lola from falling in love with him. He was a true ladies' man and everyone thought he was a little out of Lola's league. She was such a nice girl and undoubtedly, he was a very bad boy. But Lola wanted him and as the song says, what Lola wants, Lola gets. And after she got him she got a lot of heartache, and little Lawrence came shortly after.

Over the course of the next couple years, so much changed for Lola. She had a baby boy. She and Lance split because he realized she was too good for him. She dropped out of school to raise her son, and then she met the devil incarnate: Twinkie. But even with all of the changes, her heart still remained the same. And no matter how much her self-esteem seemed broken, she flourished into a beautiful swan on the inside and out.

THE WHIRLWIND

Well, summer was winding down and Elsa was coming down soon to pick up Daphne and Tico. We were all very eager to meet the new addition to the family. However, Daphne and Tico did not want to go back. The time down here made them realize just how much they really missed being home. Yes, they were adjusting in their new environment, but there is no place like home. And no matter how cozy things were in Leesburg, there was a major difference. And they did not want to go back.

For a week we all came up with plans so that they wouldn't have to go back to Leesburg, even Lawrence was apart of the conspiracy. He and Tamika were on the outs, so he had time to lend his assistance. And his mind was more powerful than anyone we knew. He sometimes had a devious way of thinking. We just couldn't tell anyone he was involved if we got caught. We plotted day and night, until finally someone said they should run away. Maybe if they were gone long enough, their mother would leave and then things would go back to the way they used to be. That was the best plan we could think of.

Elsa was coming down on Sunday, so Saturday night we synchronized our watches and set the plan in motion. When they got there, Elsa came in and brought one of the cutest babies I'd ever seen. He was a chubby little thing and I fell in love with him instantly. I took him upstairs to see Daphne and she did not want to see him. She said she could care less about that baby. I was so angry at her, but I knew that she was going off of emotion. Once she got over her anger about them coming, she would fall in love with him, too.

Then I noticed something. Everyone was there except Tico. He was gone. We didn't even know he had left the house. No one knew where he was and Daphne did not follow through with the plan. For the first time, they thought it was Tico that was being the problem. But they had no idea we put the idea in his head to run away. We looked high and low. We went to all of his friends' houses. We went to the playgrounds and to places he would never be, but there was still no trace of Tico anywhere. No one knew where he was. Elsa was hysterical and my mother was a nervous wreck. None of us dared to say it was our plan to do this. We just prayed he would come to his senses and come home.

After hours of torture, who comes walking around the corner? Tico! He was on the roof of the store, behind the house. He was watching everything going on, the entire time. The adults were outraged, but they were happy he was alright, so he didn't get into any trouble.

Shortly after he came back they all packed up for the ride home. They had to go back. The feelings of loneliness came back for me. A part of me thought the plan would work, and that part of me would have been happy if it did. But I know it was wrong.

The rest of the summer went by really fast. Nothing was really going on. We still weren't moving and my father was in no rush to change that. My mother just dealt with it and continued to pray for the success of her marriage. One day they would get it right. She was really going through something regarding her situation, but she left it in the hands of the Lord. We woke up one Saturday morning and she wanted to go out because the walls were closing in and the situation was starting to seem unbearable. We told Lawrence we were leaving. When we drove off, we saw Denise and Aunt Joanne (She is Aunt Lillie's daughter) and they had this baby. My mother parked and went over to see the cute little girl. Aunt Joanne was hitting on the baby because she wouldn't stop crying. My mother asked, "Who does this child belong to?" They told her she belonged to this crack-head they knew who asked if they could hold the baby and then she ran off and had been gone for a few days. Then Aunt Joanne smacked the baby again.

My mother said, "You don't hit on that baby. Give her to me and if and when her mother comes back tell her I have the baby." We went to the drugstore and bought the baby formula, diapers, t-shirts, and baby food, because she was filthy and they had been feeding her food from the carryout. When we got that baby home, we gave her a bath and fed her. She slept for about eight hours. My mother kept going into the room to make sure she was alright. My mother felt this was God's way of taking her mind off of my father, so she was going to do everything in her power to make sure this little girl was alright.

Later on that night, Lawrence went out with a friend of his and we got the call. Lawrence asked, "Where is Ma?" I told him she was on the front porch. He said for me to tell her he was in a really bad accident but he was alright. The car ,on the other hand, was a different story. He was driving and a drunk driver came out of nowhere and smashed the passenger side of the car in. He was so scared. But my mother was thankful he and his friend were alright. Just as the commotion with Lawrence and the car started, there was a knock at the door. It was the baby's mother.

She wanted her baby back. She was a very nice woman, but my mother told her if she didn't want her, she could leave her with us. She took the baby and we thought we would never see her again.

My mother felt a sense of peace because she had helped someone. And even though Lawrence was in an accident, she thanked God he was alright. She couldn't do anything but give thanks.

Grandma was just being herself. Early one morning, my mother got a call that grandma had fallen down the stairs at the club. As I said before, grandma is a blues singer. She sings on the weekends at Club Nuvo. My mother panicked. She immediately called Elsa and they prayed everything was alright. My mother told her she would call once she got word from the doctor. We rushed out of the house in the middle of the night to go to the hospital. The people said they weren't sure what happened. She was walking down the steps and her balance gave way under her. My mother immediately thought of the worst thing. Could it be an aneurism like granddaddy had? Is there swelling on her brain? She was so upset thinking about what the outcome of it all would be.

Then the doctor came out of the emergency room. She was so deep in thought that she didn't hear the doctor calling her name. Come to find out grandma was blatantly drunk and very high off of a joint she smoked before she came down. My mother thanked God first. Then she was ready to kill grandma. We took her home and when we got into the house, my mother called Elsa and told her what had happened so she could get on grandma, too. Safe to say after this episode grandma didn't drink anymore. But no one was going to stop her from smoking weed — she needs it to survive.

After we found out she was alright, the story somehow seemed funny. Even grandma joked about it. She said, "I can put down the glass, but I'll keep my joint raised up."

Things were getting back to normal. But then my mother was hit with a devastating blow. Little Bits got really sick. The doctors did not know what was wrong with her. They kept giving her medicine and sending her home. But then her condition worsened and she went into a coma. My mother was frantic. This has been one of her best friends since she was nine years old. The doctors finally thought they knew what the problem was. She came out of the coma. She said the only voice that she heard was my mother's. It was very touching and my mother was honored. She went home and she seemed to be doing better.

My mother went down to visit her on her lunch break and they prayed God would heal Little Bits and they reminisced about the good old days. They laughed and laughed. And everything seemed like it was going to be alright. But all of a sudden, she took a turn for the worst and died shortly after that. My mother was devastated. One of her dearest friends was gone. And again, we had to deal with another hard blow on Sixth Street.

It was just a couple months later. Things were constantly changing around us. School started back up, Lawrence was back to being himself. He had a job working at a law firm. He really enjoyed working in that type of environment since he wanted to be a lawyer. He and Tamika were together, but things started to get ugly between them. He found out she had been secretly sending money he was giving her to one of her ex-boyfriends who was in jail. He was so hurt. He just walked away. He actually cried over this piece of trash. I wanted to beat the hell out of her for hurting my brother. But they wouldn't let me.

He started to see other girls but the longing for her was still there. He went back but shortly after they got back together, he found a pair of sneakers in a box addressed to the same guy. He stormed out of there and this time it was final. She couldn't be trusted. He was helping support her and her convict. When he left, he took her keys and threw them into her front yard. She chased after him but it was too late. He was gone and this time he wasn't coming back.

She walked over to our house thinking he was there and it happened. My mother opened the door. She was on her lunch break. She didn't have any knowledge of the incident that had just occurred, so she let her in. She asked could she get some of her things out of Lawrence's room. My mother said yes. After a while, my mother noticed she had not come down, so she went up to see what she was doing. She had a lot of my brother's things and when my mother approached her. She said told my mother what happened. Then she said that until Lawrence gave back her keys she was taking all of his things. Lola wasn't having it. That's when the motherly instincts kicked in. She asked Tamika nicely not to involve her in their business, but this slut proceeded to push her way out of Lawrence's room and she told my mother she was not putting his things down. He had something of hers, so she was taking something of his. That's when crazy Annie came out. My mother taxed that ass. All of the animosity and emotions from putting up with her for two years came out. And when she finished, she threw her down the steps. My mother said it looked like she was a mouse scrounging around on the floor trying to get out of there.

Afterwards, my mother went back to work. Her coworker told her she should go home, because she had a feeling Tamika had called the police. My mother didn't think she was capable of something like that, but she agreed and went home. When she pulled up, low and behold the police were parked in front of Tamika's house. My mother called Lawrence and told him what happened. He came flying home. They walked over to the police and in fact, she and her grandmother had called the police on the both of them. She wanted to press charges for assault and theft. But what the dumb bitch didn't know was they couldn't press charges, because she was in my mother's house and there weren't any witnesses that saw my mother assaulting her. And you can't say someone stole your property, especially if it's sitting on your lawn. Where is the crime in that? The funny thing is, my mother could have pressed charges on her because she was in our house. But she didn't because she knew it would hurt her family and she thought about the memory of her friend.

The police left. My mother and Lawrence were free to go. Lawrence saw what a bitch she really was. And she lost the best thing that had ever happened to her and in turn got a pretty good ass whipping in the process. It was a beautiful situation all around, with one exception: My brother was really hurting. I hated to see him like that, but I was happy he finally saw her for the slut she was. People always say every no-good woman was made by a no-good man. Well, if that's the case my brother was made a no-good man by a no-good woman. He never cheated or abused her in anyway. He loved that trick unconditionally, and she used it to her advantage. But in the end, she got just what she deserved.

The year flew by and things were going well. Daphne was getting along very well with Uncle Eugene and Elsa. She was working in the food court at the mall. Everyone was proud of her. Tico was being Tico. He also has a job, working a paper route. Elsa was just happy things were finally working out. Leesburg was the best thing that could've happened to them.

Back at home things were just about the same. Whitney would get herself together for awhile. Then she would fall back into the same pattern. It was really sad seeing her like this, and no matter how much we want it for her, she has to want it for herself.

Grandma is never going to change, she is still smoking weed, and using her herbs. She thinks these herbs are the cure for anything. Lawrence had a cold and grandma called, he answered the phone. He said, "Hello," but his voice was really raspy. Grandma said, "Boy, what is wrong with you? You sound terrible. What are you taking for it?"

He said, "Grandma, I have a cold. The doctor called in a prescription. I am not sure of the name."

She said, "Boy, that medicine is no good. Those doctors don't know what they are doing. I'm going to tell you what to do. Send your sister around here and I am going to send you something that will knock it right out." Lawrence thought it was a joke. I couldn't help but laugh, because whatever it was, it wasn't going to be good. Grandma can't cook at all. And Lawrence didn't want anything she was cooking up. I went around there though because I didn't want to hurt her feelings.

She always says, "You all don't take me serious. I've been on this earth far longer than you. I think I know what I'm doing." When I got there, she gave me a ziplock bag and told me to put it under my shirt. She said, "You don't want the police to stop you, do you?" I just couldn't stop laughing because I didn't know what she was giving me. Then she said, "Tell Lawrence to take a teaspoon and dump it into some hot water. It will knock whatever he has right out. He will probably be out of it for a few hours, depending on how much he uses. The best thing for him to do is sleep it off. And he will probably be hungry when he wakes up."

When I got to my house, I gave Lawrence this homemade remedy she came up with. He said, "Well, where in the hell is it?" I told him she made me put it in a paper bag and put it under my shirt. He was ticked off. He knew what it was. He couldn't believe grandma would make me bring weed around the corner. And furthermore ask him to take it. He threw that shit down the toilet. He said, "That old woman is crazy as shit." He called and told my mother after the fact. My mother wanted to know was there anything else in the bad. Because grandma wasn't the best housekeeper and sometimes her company followed you back home, when you left her house. Lawrence told her he flushed the stuff. She was ok with it. She wanted to call grandma and get on her, but she didn't because Lawrence told her that she was only trying to help.

Things in our house were running smoothly. My mother asked Dwight to leave because he started using drugs and was stealing her wedding gifts out of the house and selling them to our neighbors. A friend of hers brought her carving knife down to our house and asked did it look familiar. My mother looked twice and realized it was her knife. She had to buy it back from him. Then he owed some drug dealers some money and they came to our door, looking for him. My mother had too much to lose, so he was out of there.

Twinkie wasn't around that much. He wasn't missed either. He is so conniving that he told my mother these lies about my brothers. He just didn't want me to get close to them. How selfish is that? A father not wanting his own children to have relationships with each other. But that is the type of person he is. My mother loved him, and she will always protect him. She still won't listen to what anyone has to say about him. They still argued and they still lived separate lives. The more things change, the more they remain the same. She's interested in church activities, work and life at home, while his main goals for living are, and always will be sex and money.

I was getting ready to turn fourteen. Boy did time fly. I was just standing at the altar watching in total disgust as my mother and father got married. Now I am more interested in counting the days until I am eighteen, when I could be free to do what I want to do. And my father can't add his two cents in. And my mother can't take his side, even if she knows he is wrong.

Things on Sixth Street were changing, too. There were people from other neighborhoods moving in and the family atmosphere was leaving. And drugs and violence were taking over. We were all sitting on the porch and one of my mother's distant cousins stopped by. My mother was standing at the car door and all of a sudden, these two guys started fighting. My cousin, Monica, said, "That's a change. You don't see people fighting anymore." And before she could finish her statement the bullets started to fly. My mother is so slow. She thought it was the neighborhood kids shooting off firecrackers. Lawrence kept hollering for her to duck. But she kept right on talking. Then my cousin said, "You damn fool duck, they are shooting!" She looked up and saw the bullets firing from the gun. I thought my mother ran track that day. She didn't duck. She flew past us and ran into the house. I don't even think she knew she could run that fast.

Then a couple of weeks later Lawrence went to take the trash out. He was gone for quite some time, then he came back in and his leather jacket had rocks and scratches on it. I thought that maybe he was outside playing games with someone. My mother said, "What took you so long to take the trash out? And what in the hell happened to you?"

Then he told us, "Man, someone came by shooting and I had to jump under a car so I wouldn't get hit." My mother was tired of waiting on my father at this point because things were getting out of hand around there.

There was a lot going on, but for me things were going great. Then Elsa called. "Daphne was driving around town. She and some girlfriends were in a terrible accident." My mother couldn't make out everything she was saying because she was hysterical, so she said, "Elsa calm down, I can hardly hear what you are saying."

Then Elsa repeated herself. "Daphne was driving with a group of her friends and they were in a terrible car accident. She flew out of the car. She had to be rushed to Children's Hospital by a helicopter." My mother dropped the phone and called out to the name of Jesus. Lawrence and I knew whatever it was, it wasn't good. Elsa said she was on her way and she would meet us at the hospital. Lawrence, my mother and I rushed out of the house to make it up there. We prayed the entire way.

The doctors couldn't tell my mother anything because she is a minor and my mother wasn't her guardian, so we had to wait. When Elsa and Uncle Eugene got there, Lawrence took Tico and Ahmad and went back to the house. I stayed with my mother, while Elsa and Uncle Eugene went back to speak to the doctors. She was bruised up pretty bad, but she was going to be alright. One of her friends on the other hand wasn't as lucky. She would have to have a series of tests to make sure there was no internal bleeding. After an entire night at the hospital we went home. Elsa and the gang slept for awhile then loaded up for the ride back home. We were pleased with the outcome.

Everything was back to being okay. I met my first boyfriend a couple days later. My father couldn't have any knowledge of it, though. He felt I should be at least eighteen when I start to date. Talk about becoming a social outcast. A few weeks later, a friend of my mother's wanted my mother and me to sing for a mother-daughter banquet her church was having for Mother's Day. She wanted my mother to bring grandma with her too. We symbolized what three generations of women were. Well, my mother agreed to do it, but I wasn't singing. I don't like singing in front of people, so they told us to just stand behind my mother while she sang. When my mother finished her selection, we were supposed to go back to our seats. Well, Mary wasn't having it. She didn't want someone to take her spotlight. She has to be seen. When my mother finished singing, she and I walked back over to the table. My mother turned around and there she was: Mary was still standing there at the podium.

My mother was trying to signal to her to come and sit down, but she wasn't having it. She picked up the microphone and introduced herself. She said, "Good morning ladies and gentlemen. My name is Mary

Magdalene Hayes. I am here with my daughter and granddaughter. We were invited by Jeanine Favors. I am not a church-going woman. I do my singing in the night club. But I do believe in God. He put a song on my heart today and I want to sing it for you all this morning." Then she broke out and began to sing, Somebody Prayed for Me. Then she started walking through the aisles and pointing out the people and saying their names. We were so embarrassed. My mother was almost under the table and I couldn't stop laughing. When she finally finished after about ten minutes, my mother told her, "You pick up your things and let's go."

Grandma said, "I'm not going anywhere. I want my food."

My mother told her, "Look, I will take you to McDonalds." We left and I just couldn't stop laughing. My mother and grandma didn't think it was funny. She took grandma to McDonalds and then we dropped her off. My mother was so embarrassed.

Finally, things were starting to really change for the better in our lives. I was starting my first summer job. I was excited. I would have my own money to buy whatever I wanted. And I wouldn't have to worry about my father chastising me about the cost of everything. I could buy my own school clothes and money was no object. Summertime came strolling around and things were going great, until my mother fell down the steps on her job and had to be rushed to the hospital.

She tore a ligament in her knee. The doctor gave us the bad news. She would have to have surgery. Then Uncle Ted, (Elmo and Dwight's grandfather) got really sick. He died suddenly. Everyone in the family was shocked. He was a sweet man. He never bothered anyone. But if you needed him he would be there. My mother was unable to go to the funeral. It was the day of her surgery. That morning, Lawrence and I took her to the hospital. Twinkie didn't even show up. I hated him for that. Lawrence was so upset. He left the waiting area. At first, I thought he was going to get something from the car. But he was gone for too long. I went out after him and there he was my older brother crying his eyes out. I had to console him for once. He got it together because he didn't want me to see him like that.

My mother wanted us to go home and at least try to pay our respects for her at Uncle Ted's funeral. And to be there for Elmo, Dwight, and Denise. Grandma was there in true form. The diva came out. She was, is and always will be the best that ever did it. She was strutting her stuff, meeting and greeting folks as they came into the funeral home. It was like she was at her club and she was finishing a set.

Of course, Whitney was missing in action. She is never around when things happen. Elsa came down. She and Uncle Eugene brought the baby. They were going to let me watch him while they went to the funeral. I just had to meet them so I could ride with them to the cemetery. When they dropped him off it was the first time I'd seen him since he was a little baby. He didn't know me, so he cried and cried and cried. Lawrence couldn't even get him to stop. He wanted his mother and father, so I put on my clothes and took him around to the funeral home. I asked Lawrence to drive me around there but he looked at me and said, "That's the problem with your damn generation. You are too damn lazy. You need the exercise. Walk your ass around that corner. The air will do you some good."

So, I got his things together and took the stroll. The funeral was still going on, so I waited outside. I don't like to be around that atmosphere. I have always been fearful of dead people. Lawrence always teased me after someone died. He would be lurking behind walls and standing over top of you while you slept, so I don't like to look at dead people. After the services were over, we went to Ted Jr.'s house for the repast. It was a mess. People were acting real standoffish I was ready to leave. It was like we all weren't family. I can't stand it when people act uppity. Grandma was as always giving a show, telling people about her gig at the club, and going around hitting people up for five dollars. It was quite embarrassing, but that was Mary and she was going to be herself. No matter what the setting may be. Elsa went over to her and whispered in grandma's ear, "This is a repast. Uncle Ted died. You shouldn't be in here begging people. Get your purse, we are leaving. It is a damn shame. We can't take you anywhere." Grandma didn't care one bit. She cleared close to a hundred bucks. I just laughed. I couldn't believe she was doing it. And I couldn't wait to get home to tell my mother and Lawrence.

When I got home my mother was there. She came through the surgery with flying colors. She would have to be off for about a month, though. She hated that. My mother gets restless really fast. But it was for the best. Her knee had to heal. We were sure having our fair share of grief. Lawrence started to have picnics at a water park every other weekend. He wanted to lighten the mood and take everyone's minds off of all that happened, and what was going on. My mother would do all of the cooking, and the entire neighborhood would show up. He would pay for everything. He was just interested in everybody having a good time. It was one of the best summers of my life. It also made Lawrence infamous. He started to hang with a different crowd. My mother didn't like it, though. He has too much going for him. But he just wants to be accepted by everyone. He thinks everybody is his friend and he can trust everyone.

One Saturday, I was preparing to get my things together for the picnic and I noticed my money was missing. I knew someone took it because it was in my special hiding place. I instantly started to blame people that were in the house. Because on Sixth Street we always had an open-door policy, whether it was day or night. People were always knocking on our door. Anyway, I went off. Someone had taken two hundred and fifty dollars and I wanted answers. I went to my mother and I asked did she know anything about my money. She pointed outside and said I needed to talk to my brother. I went outside and asked him first. Did he know anything about my money? He said, "Man, I took it to add to the money for the cook out." I let him have it right there in the middle of the street. I did not mind him borrowing the money, but damn he could have told me. It was the principle. He was big on that, but when it comes to your things, he has no problem claiming ownership. He apologized and said he would do something really nice for me when school started. I was cool after that. He is my brother. I couldn't disown him over two-fifty. It's small compared to our new-found love since Tamika was out of the picture.

Summertime soon faded and it was time to head back to school. Things in Leesburg were going great. The family moved into a house and little Ahmad is my heart. He just turned a year old. They had a birthday party for him. My mother couldn't get off, so we didn't make it up. Grandma, Whitney and the kids went. But then Whitney was missing in action. She said that she was going to the restroom, but she was gone for about a half an hour. Elsa got suspicious. She wanted to make sure the house was still standing so she went in after her. She looked in the bathroom first, but there was no Whitney. She went in the living room, no Whitney. Then she went upstairs and there she was. Whitney was sitting on the edge of Elsa's bed putting on a pair of socks. But when Elsa looked at the socks she noticed that they were a little small. Then she noticed the intricate detail. The socks belonged to little Ahmad. Whitney had stolen Ahmad's socks. Elsa told her to pack up her things because she didn't want her in their house. She was hitting rock bottom. She was stealing socks from her one-year-old nephew.

Time was surely flying by. I am starting ninth grade this year. I was able to purchase whatever I wanted for school this year. My brother taught me that money is no object when it is something that you want. When he paid me the money back and threw in a little extra so he could help me out. My mother gave me extra, too. Of course, Twinkie knew nothing about it. Things seemed wonderful. Everybody was happy and we were all thinking positive about the future.

Lawrence's birthday came. He is turning twenty-one. He thought he was really the man. He didn't want anything special for his birthday. He was just happy being the man on Sixth Street now. After this summer, he became notorious. Even the police knew who he was. He was known to them as the curbside attorney. He started hanging with a new crowd and the police didn't like any of them hanging on the corner. So, when the police would pull up, Lawrence would say, "You can't tell me to move. I own property around here. This is my neighborhood. I know my rights. As a matter of fact, what is your name and badge number? I am going to report your ass, because you are harassing me." So, the police wanted to get him.

And then it happened. The night of his birthday he went outside to get a gift from one of his many new girlfriends. He didn't have on clothes. He was wearing a pair of shorts and a wife-beater tank top. He was sitting in her car and the police pulled up. They arrested him. We were sleeping, so we didn't have any knowledge of what was going on. The girl was banging on our door and screaming for my mother. Finally, my mother woke up. The girl told her what happened. She said, "Lawrence said please come and get him out of jail. He didn't do anything. We were sitting in the car. He didn't even have shoes or clothes on." My mother thanked the girl but told her she had to go and bail her baby out of jail. His twenty first birthday was truly a memorable one.

When we got to the precinct the officers knew who we were instantly. My mother asked, "Where is my son and why was he arrested tonight?" The officer then told my mother he was arrested for sitting improperly in a parked car. And for being disruptive. Then another officer came up and told my mother, "Your son is a very bright young man but his mouth is going to get him in serious trouble."

A few minutes later Lawrence came strolling out, and the officers were just laughing. They said Lawrence was one of the funniest people they'd ever met. He started screaming when they put him in a cell with male prostitutes and then he began to recite the scene from the movie 48 Hours, when Eddie Murphy was singing Roxanne. He is a nut and that night the police saw another side of him. And after that night they didn't bother him anymore. After all of the hoopla about Lawrence's arrest, everybody decided we would go up to Leesburg again for the holiday. Even Lawrence was going up this year. And this year we were all going to be under the same roof. Elsa did not want any confusion, so she told grandma she wanted her to come up by herself. She was tired of seeing grandma take on Whitney's responsibility. So, this year Whitney stayed home with her own children. That was going to be a trip, because those children were never without grandma and Whitney is never really alone with them.

When we got there, Grandma was already there and she did one of the cruelest things you could do to a child, and to one of your grandchildren at that. She pulled out her wallet and called Daphne and Tico over to the couch. She hugged the both of them and told them how much she loved them and then gave them twenty dollars a piece. It was like it was intentional. Then she looked over at me and said, "You don't need anything from me, you have your mother." It crushed my feelings, but I played it off and told her, "You know what, you are right. I don't need you; I've never needed anything from you. My mother gives me everything I want and need."

Lawrence knew I was upset so he wanted to take me out. He said, "The hell with that old bitch. I don't care if she is our grandmother. She doesn't act like it." I laughed because he was right. Then he said, "Let's get the hell out of here, before I say something to her ass."

He took Daphne, Tico and me to the movies. We all hadn't been out together alone in a while. It was really great having the old Lawrence back. I was glad he was my brother. When we got back to the house, Elmo and his girlfriend were there. We all just sat around playing games and having fun. Tico told Lawrence he needed to talk him. He said, "Man, Lawrence, please. It's an emergency. I really need to speak to you right now." Lawrence stepped into the kitchen with him and asked him what his problem was. Tico said, "Lawrence, why won't my penis grow?" Lawrence had to step out into the hallway because he didn't want to laugh in his face. He then walked back into the kitchen and told him, "Look if you really want it to grow, I know a secret." He looked at him really serious and said, "Do you have any Blue Star ointment?" Tico said, "I am not sure what that is." Lawrence told him to go into the bathroom and check the medicine cabinet and then he described it to him. Tico went and checked and low and behold there it was. Lawrence told him to go into the bathroom and put some down there and he said, "I guarantee that when you wake up in the morning, you will have some changes."

This damn fool went into the bathroom and put some down there. All of a sudden, we heard someone screaming. Tico ran out of the bathroom screaming and patting his private area. Elsa said, "Boy, what is wrong with you?"

He said, "I wanted my penis to grow. Lawrence told me this stuff would work. He was jumping around holding himself with the bottle of Blue Star Ointment in his hand. He said, "Lawrence, it's not growing, it's burning really bad. I feel like I am on fire." He handed her the bottle of Blue Star Ointment and she fell out laughing. Lawrence looked and said, "Boy, I didn't think you were actually going to put it down there. Are you crazy. Your body will grow and you will change as you get older." We all laughed. It was the highlight of the evening. Tico sat in the corner for the rest of the night with a bag of ice in between his legs. Things seemed like they couldn't get any better. My mother was getting ready for bed. She had her laugh for the night.

We were all (the children, Lawrence, Tico, Daphne, Elmo, and me) in the living room watching TV. Then all of a sudden, we heard this loud boom. We all ran to the kitchen, we thought that it was my mother. She had just left the living room, so we assumed she had fallen down the stairs or something. But it wasn't her, it was Mary. Grandma had fallen down. I don't know how she fell. She was getting something to drink and suddenly fell back. She was alright though. I tried to lighten the mood. I said, "Grandma, have you been drinking again?" Everybody turned around and looked at me in total disgust. They were concerned, but I wasn't. She had made it obvious for so long that she didn't give a damn about me or my mother and Lawrence. So why should I care about her? She didn't break anything, so I was not going to sit here and rant and rave over her. She loves to be the center of attention.

Lawrence and I went back into the living room. My mother came in and got on us. She said, "No matter what that is still my mother and it's still your grandmother." But she treated us like garbage. So why should I give a damn about her? She was alright. If it was something serious we would have been more concerned.

The next morning came and we were blessed to see another Thanksgiving morning. We were all together. The ritual in our family is to play cards, whenever we are all under the same roof, so the games began. Elsa and Lawrence were teammates in every game – Spades, Bidwiss, and Pinochle. And they cheated every chance they got. They beat everyone, it was terrible. Grandma was so mad because she knew they were cheating, but she didn't have any proof. She kept on saying, "This shit is not funny. I've been playing these games for years. Why are you all beating everyone in the house? Something just ain't right." Then Lawrence told her, "Listen, grandma, if you can't stand the heat then get out of the kitchen. We can't help it if we're good." They had a system. They would pass hints across the table and every person that sat down got up with an attitude. And to top it all they were sitting there talking shit the whole night. And their excuse for winning was that the cards were floating in their direction. I'm just glad we didn't play for money, because that night they would have made a killing.

It was one of the best Thanksgivings that I have ever had. And I think everyone feels that way. After the butt-whipping from Elsa and Lawrence, we all turned in. We were leaving in the morning. Things were really great for a change. Everyone was happy and smiling. At this point we thought we could only rise higher and that things would only get better. Little did we know it was only the beginning of a spiral staircase going down.

My father had a knock at the door. It was about three in the morning. He was alarmed. It was a couple of agents from the FBI, and they were looking for my brother, Eric. He was on the run for killing a guy. It was supposedly in self defense, but no one knows what really happened. He got advice from someone in the streets and he went on the run. He didn't think the police would believe his story. The agents searched my father's house, but they didn't find anything. Eric hadn't been there since granddaddy died. The female agent told my father, "Sir your son is in real serious trouble and he is running out of time. We are trying to help him. He needs to turn himself in. If you know where he is, the best way to help him is to let us know where. and if he tries to contact you, let us know."

My father told her, "Listen, lady, I don't know where he is and if I did I wouldn't tell you a damn thing. You don't have a warrant so get the hell out of my house before I report you. And I wouldn't tell you shit. If I knew where he was and if he tried to contact me I'm going to tell him to keep on running. And furthermore, don't come around here anymore." They left. He was so disturbed he called my mother. And of course, she went running to his side.

A couple days after that, they caught Eric at his girlfriend's house. He was charged with murder and is now facing fifteen years to life.

It seemed like things would get worse before they got any better. A few days later Aunt Gertrude took ill. She was ninety-four years old. They rushed her to the hospital and the doctor couldn't find anything wrong. He said she was just tired and she was dying of old age. He said her bodily functions were shutting down. We went to the hospital to see her and she was still in her right state of mind.

Then it happened. I was in school and I got really sick. I was having hot and cold flashes and my temperature was up really high. They finally called my mother to come and get me. By the time we got home, there was a call from the hospital. Aunt Gertrude had passed away. I really don't remember any tears of sorrow, because she wanted to go. She was tired of living her life alone. No one in the family (other than my mother) would go and visit her. She would always say, "They have their own lives to live and I can't impose on their lives," so she was really at peace. Her funeral was funny, though. Aunt Judy came in wearing black and white striped socks and a green hat. Whitney talked about her the whole time. She kept on calling her Santa's helper. She said the only thing missing was a candy cane.

Then after the service, we thought we were taking a shortcut to the cemetery. Once we got there, my mother said we should wait at the gates so we could follow them in. After we sat there for a while Denise said, "Something is not right. They should have been here by now." The next thing we knew the funeral procession drove out of the cemetery. My mother stopped Lawrence and he said, "Man, where were you all? Aunt Gertrude has already been buried." My mother was really hurt, but we all laughed about it.

A couple of weeks passed by and my mother was at home on her lunch break and she heard someone in the house. She called out names but no one answered. She was in the bathroom. When she finished, she went out to see who it was. Elmo then yelled, "It's me, Lola." He was down for the day. He had a nice conversation with my mother. He told her he was thinking about moving back home. My mother was excited and happy to hear the news. He also said he and his kid's mother were getting back together. She was very please to hear this, because everyone in the family was always fond of her. After the conversation was over, Elmo left and my mother went back to work. She was happy about their conversation because she hadn't had a serious conversation with Elmo in a very long time.

Then it happened. It was the Friday night before Christmas. My mother called Lawrence and me and said that Elsa got a call from the hospital. Elmo was in a bad car accident. Elsa was driving to Winchester to see what was going on. They wouldn't tell her anything, she just had to get to the hospital and soon. We prayed and we just knew Elmo was alright. Everyone was in good spirits. We never thought of the worst. Then hours later the phone started to ring. It was the hospital. A man was on the phone and he asked for my mother. My cousin Monica was over at the house waiting to hear how he was doing. And then all of a sudden, my mother started to scream. "NO, NO, NO, NO!" I immediately ran up the stairs to see what was going on. But for some reason I already knew. Monica was hysterical, she and Elmo grew up like brother and sister, and she just fell to the floor. The man said, "Your sister Elsa asked me to make the phone call because she was not up to doing it. I am sorry to be the one to give you this news but your nephew Elmo expired tonight." He said it like he was a piece of food that had gone bad. I still can't get over that. My mother was overwhelmed with sorrow. I tried to be strong for her but I couldn't for long because it hit me.

I had to find Lawrence to give him the news. I wanted to be there for him, because I knew he would take this extremely hard. I tried to run out of the house, but my shirt got caught in the screen door. Then I tripped on the steps and rolled down the sidewalk, then to top it off I ripped my favorite shirt, but I didn't care. My mother flew past me and she got to Lawrence first. She fell in his arms and he knew. Elmo was gone. That was his older brother in a sense. The one that taught him about women and gave him tips on sex. All of that was gone. But he had to put his emotions aside and be strong for our mother and for me, as he always did.

After we got ourselves together it was now our turn to get the news out to everybody else. We first called Dwight but he wasn't at home. He was living with his boss at the time on the other side of town. In the process of my mother falling into Lawrence's arms, Denise (Big Girl) wanted to know what all of the commotion was about. She was hysterical, her baby brother gone and she didn't have the chance to say goodbye. She wanted to go and find Dwight. She got a friend of hers to take her over to his house and she waited until he got there. She walked up to the door and rang the doorbell. When he came out of the house she said, "Dwight, Elmo is dead." He couldn't believe what she was saying. And furthermore he couldn't believe how she told him. So, he walked back into the house and slammed the door in her face.

Then we had to get in contact with his children. They were so young and innocent, and they loved their father. He loved those kids to death too. He was one of the best fathers I've ever seen. We were gathering numbers and by this time Elsa was back at home and she was able to talk to us. She said he got into a confrontation with a so-called friend. He never thought this guy would do anything to him. The next day he was out and the people told him to be careful because this guy was outside waiting for him, with a gun. He didn't take the warning seriously. He walked out to his car and the guy started to shoot. It didn't seem real. Not Elmo. He wasn't the type, he was quiet and he would walk away from confrontation. I never even heard him yell. And now he is gone. Then finally, we got in contact with Dwight. He was on his way over to the house. By then his disbelief turned into anger. He was upset with Denise and he wanted to know who would do this to his brother and why. When he got to the house he was with his boss, Mr. Biggons. He was a so-called preacher and a crook all rolled into one. He said he wanted to pray for the family. My mother looked at Lawrence and me but out of respect we joined hands and closed our eyes. Then all of a sudden, he started babbling as if he was speaking in tongues. My mother couldn't hold it in any longer she burst into laughter. He was so angry he dropped Dwight's hand and stormed out of the house. But that was exactly what we all needed because the air was getting too thick in there, you could hardly breathe because of the overwhelming feelings we all had.

My mother and Elsa called Carla, the kids' mother and broke the news. She came flying over to the house. There they were, three innocent children and they were fatherless. It was funny, how children are resilient. They just stood there, with no emotion. Their older cousin was with them and this poor little guy was really hurting. He laid on his mother's chest and cried. One of Elmo's kids looked over and said, "Hey punk, why are you crying? He wasn't your father." I couldn't believe it. Then to top it all off, Elmo didn't have any insurance, so we were hit with two blows.

Christmas was just another day this year. We had to come up with the money and we had no idea how we were going to get it. Elsa and Uncle Eugene handled their part. They went and gathered up his things and sold the valuables. And we had to beg. Monica did most of the legwork. She and I went to the grocery store and stood with a bucket and a picture taped on the bucket. I only went for a couple of hours. Then we went door to door. It was the holiday season so people were caring and God really blessed us. Monica raised ninety percent of the money for his burial. And thank God for her because all of the monies were in on time. No one could believe we pulled it off.

The days leading up to the funeral were really hard for us to deal with. None of us wanted to accept the fact it was true. We didn't see Elmo that often, but we knew he would be around. He would just pop up, out of the blue. We didn't want to deal with it. It was just too much to fathom at once. The day they viewed the body was exceptionally hard. I didn't go. Sometimes it's best to remember people for who they were. And I wanted to remember Elmo as my easy-going, fun-loving older cousin. And the last time we were together we had a really nice time. I can still feel what I was feeling the day of the funeral. There were no smiles, just solemn looks on everybody's faces. I couldn't make anyone smile. There were no jokes that would change anyone's facial expressions. I couldn't even pump myself up.

I walked out of the house so I could take a breather and there was this guy parked out in front of the house. He looked very, very suspicious. Then it hit me. Lawrence was carrying around this picture all week of Elmo and this guy. I kept on asking who the guy was and Elsa finally told me. It was the so-called friend that killed him. Well anyway, that same guy was parked in front of my house. I began to scream at the top of my lungs. I didn't know what he was capable of. Then I ran to get

Lawrence. Lawrence came back out with a couple of his friends and the guy seemed worried and drove away. The nerve of this guy. It was like he wanted to make sure he was really dead. And he was getting satisfaction out of seeing us grieve. Lawrence made sure that someone stood guard at the church because he was unsure of his motives and if he would try to come back. Lawrence made me promise I would never tell my mother and Elsa because they had enough to deal with. To this day it still puzzles me why he was there.

That morning it seemed like time just flew by. We went to the church. Rev. Jenkins was doing the service. He was always fond of Elmo. Carla's great grandmother was there and she made my day. She thought it was a party. She had about five disposable cameras. And during the wake, she snapped a picture of everyone that went up to the casket. She was taking pictures like she was at a cabaret, even going to the extent of making people pose as they stood next to the casket. Then the services started and she was still snapping pictures. You couldn't even hear Rev. Jenkins at first because she kept on taking picture after picture. Then finally her daughter turned around and told her, "Granny, put those damn cameras up." She sucked he teeth and said, "I need to take these pictures for the children." Her daughter said, "They don't need any damn pictures of their father lying in a damn casket. Put the damn cameras up and now. Don't you take another picture in here today!"

Rev. Jenkins began his eulogy with a scripture. He started with the twenty-third Psalm. "The Lord is my Shepard I shall not want." He spoke about Elmo being a good, decent young man. And everyone in the church felt a sense of sadness. He talked about Elmo getting shot over a girl, and when Carla stabbed him. But then he began to get the stories confused with someone else. He said he got a call that Elmo was arrested, and then the time that he got shot in the foot. The tears began to stop. Everyone started to look around and whispers began to fill the air. "When did he get arrested? Who shot him in the foot? And when did it happen? And why didn't any of us know anything about it?" These were just a few. Lawrence said, "Elmo must have just called Rev. Jenkins on those days." And everyone started to laugh. And that really broke the ice. So, in the midst of our sorrow, we still found some reasons to smile. That's how Elmo would have wanted it.

After the service we took the long ride to the cemetery. Elsa and my mother were still distraught and Lawrence just stayed by the casket. He couldn't believe he was really gone. Daphne and Tico were really shaken by it all. He was with them on a regular basis. I just wanted to be there for everybody. I was trying to give them all reasons to smile. Twinkie was no where to be found. Don't ask about Whitney because you know she wasn't there. Grandma was going around scaring the children. They thought she was a witch. Monica and I were standing around the cars at the cemetery and all of a sudden, Elmo's daughter yelled, "The witch is coming!" Monica got scared because they say that children see spirits and she thought Jayla was seeing one. Well, when we turned around it was grandma walking up to meet us. It changed the serious tone and everyone laughed.

We went back to the church for the repast and we all just sat around and remembered Elmo. We all had so many good memories to warm our hearts. Shortly after the services, Elsa and the gang packed up to go home. It was going to be hard for her, because he was there everyday almost.

A couple days later the New Year rolled in but there wasn't much to celebrate. We found ourselves repeating the same conversation over and over again. We were all still in shock. We talked about the last time we were all together and how much fun we had. That record got old really fast. We tried not to focus on it. He didn't like people to fuss over him and that is exactly what we were doing. We tried to put our hurt in the back of our minds and put that energy to something else. Lawrence went back to school. My mother was focusing on her spirituality. Elsa was taking care of her family. Whitney's situation never changes. Sometimes she's off, sometimes she's on. Grandma is just plain old Mary. Still smoking weed, even though she was almost arrested. Daphne is starting to be rebellious. Losing Elmo was hard and instead of her releasing her feelings, she bottled them up and started to act out. Tico has changed. He is a country boy.

And me? I am boy crazy. I am starting to learn who I am. Over the course of the last couple of years, we all have been forced to grow up before our time. But we have to keep moving forward. Things couldn't go back to normal. They were different. I was focused on my fifteenth birthday. Lawrence was hanging out with the boys in the hood. My mother was fed up with Twinkie at this point. There were no excuses he could use anymore. They have been married for almost three years. All of his excuses have been used and his time is about up.

Daphne has been lying to everyone in Leesburg. She has been going around telling people she had this rough life. She was homeless; she has been shot and stabbed. And people have been snubbing Elsa. Elsa is tired of Daphne's girlfriends rolling their eyes and half-way speaking so she asked one of them, "What in the hell is your problem? I am tired of you all coming in here and disrespecting me." The girl said, "Ms. Elsa, I'm sorry, it's just we're so upset with you about the life that Daphne had to lead, because of your past." At this point, Elsa was beyond angry. She told the girl to tell her the whole story. Then the girl went on to tell her about Daphne's horrible child hood. Then Elsa let the girl have it. Then she gave Daphne a piece of her mind. Tico has really changed; he is turning into a responsible young man.

Grandma is going around begging anyone that will give her the time. She called my mother and when my mother heard her voice, she knew she wanted something. She said, "Hey baby, how are you doing today?" My mother said, "Oh hey mama, I'm good." Then grandma said, "I have run into a little trouble and I wanted to know if you could help me out of it." My mother said, "Help you how?" Grandma said, "Oh I need about two-thousand dollars to pay my mortgage." My mother went off. She said, "Mama what do you do with your money?" Grandma said, "Look, do you have the money or not?" My mother said, "I have to talk to Twinkie about it." Grandma was highly upset. She told my mother that she needs the money as soon as possible and she would appreciate it if she would call her back, after she spoke to my father.

My mother didn't even tell him, because she knew it would only start something between them. So, we went on about our day. We were going shopping and we drove past my father's house. The closer we got I noticed a car very similar to my grandmother's. I said, "Ma, doesn't that look like grandma's car?" My mother looked at the tags and it was in fact grandma's car. She quickly made a u-turn and when we got to the door and rang the doorbell, my father came and started to whisper, "Shhhh, be quiet, your mother is in there. She said she needs two-thousand dollars. And she told me not to tell you she was in there." My mother couldn't believe she had the nerve to drive all the way to his house. Then to top it off, she told him not to tell her she was here. When we walked into the family room where she was, her face turned purple. She began to talk really funny. My mother just gave her the look and she started to tell her story. My father said, "Now look, Mary, I would love to help you but I don't have that kind of money." She said, "Well, look what do you have." My grandmother is not a humble person. So, they gave her nine-hundred dollars. She wasn't pleased, but she took it. It was better than nothing.

Grandma has a serious problem. She is always begging but never pays people the money back. That's not a good combination. But, she's just Mary Magdalene, and who's going to tell her that she needs to change? Not me! And neither are any of the rest of them.

THE BABYGIRL

Isn't she lovely; made from love. Yeah, right, more like made from a bottle of Hennessey or some other brown liquor my father and mother were drinking on the night I was conceived. Well, after six years and two failed pregnancies, here I come into the world. December 24th. The day before Christmas, the most important holiday in the world, but more important to me was how I was born on my grandfather's birthday. My mother was so excited, she thought finally everything would come together and Twinkie would act like he had sense. But she was only fooling herself. He had already been down this road a few times before. And you best believe it was nothing but drama from start to finish. Twinkie was not the doting father-to-be. Hey, he had already been through this *eight times* already.

During most of my mother's pregnancy they were at odds. I don't think he ever wanted another child. However, my mother did and nothing could stop her from bringing me into the world. He told her if I was born I would have a rare blood disease. She knew by this time he was nothing but a liar, so she paid no attention. He wasn't even there when she went into labor. But for this I can't put the blame on him. He called looking for her and Denise said she had stepped out. After a day of him calling the house and no one told him a thing, he decided to call the hospital and low and behold, I was already here.

He raced to the hospital but visiting hours were over. He made up this story about him being in the army. He told the nurse he was being deployed the next morning and his only Christmas wish was to see his brand-new baby girl. They always told me he knew exactly who I was instantly. But for some reason I have always felt he paid that nurse just so he could get into my mother's good graces. He knows her so well, it worked.

Things between them were good for the first few months of my life. Even Big Mama started to accept him. She saw he was trying to be a good father. He brought duffle bags full of clothes for me and she thought he was out of his mind because of the rate babies grow. But through this she found a new respect for him. My mother and I lived back and forth between his house and back at home on Sixth Street. But Big Mama would not dare let Lawrence come along with us. She couldn't stop her from taking me because he was my father, but she did have a certain amount of say with Lawrence and he was staying right there in that house with her and the rest of the family.

Things were starting to get cramped in the house. We moved out when I was two years old. My mother didn't want to raise us in our family's home. It was too cluttered and the more she cleaned the filthier it got. Big Mama was old and sick by this time and she was still trying to take care of everything and everybody and that meant my mother leaving. Big Mama was devastated, but in her own way she never showed it. She understood and she was proud. A few months after we moved in, Big Mama's condition worsened and she died in the spring. Her body was old and tired. She had taken care of five generations and now finally she could have peace and get some rest.

My mother was overwhelmed with sorrow. Her mother, the woman who loved and nurtured her from the time she was five months old, was gone. But she knew Big Mama taught her well. She left some very big shoes to fill but she knew Lola was the one. While I was growing up, I was looked at as the tom boy. I was around my brother all day and he wanted someone to play with, and though I always had my dolls and I loved playing with them on my own time, it was out of the question for him to play with them, so I did whatever he told me to do. He was my big brother and I wanted to be just like him. I just wanted to be the female version.

It was crazy. He never wanted his friends to know he played with his little sister. But when he was punished, I was his best friend. He would sleep in the bed with me and play whatever games I wanted to play. But as soon as his punishment was over, out of the door he went and I became his little sister that got on his nerves all over again. But I didn't mind it much because he was my hero.

Growing up on Sixth Street was the best. Everything was right there that we needed. Our church was right across the street, so were our schools and our family house. On many days, whenever we wanted to find someone all we had to do was open the window and begin hollering out the person's name. Elsa lived in the house with her children, Denise, Dwight, and Elmo. We lived directly across the street in a new apartment complex.

It seemed as though life was one big party at that time, playing cards on Friday, shopping on Saturday, and going to church and selling dinners on Sunday. Well, Lawrence was the only one selling the dinners. We never thought about what tomorrow was going to bring. The guys would stand out on the corner and wrestle and act like fools until the wee hours of the morning. Everything about our childhood was peaceful and oh so mellow.

But just as the seasons change so did the peace in our lives. Tranquility went one way and drugs came the other. Before you knew it everyone except Lola became addicted in some way or the other to some drug and our lives were turned upside down.

The guys started to grow up and hustling became the new dodge ball or tag. I was so young it was hard to understand, but I did see how much money flowed in and around our family house. What was the family home where everyone would meet up to have fun, was now the neighborhood crack-house where the fun was shooting up or smoking the new high in everyone's life. The next thing we knew, Lawrence and I weren't allowed in there any more. Lola came home one day and out of the blue she told us, "I don't know what diseases may be flying in or around that house. I don't want the two of you in there anymore and if I catch you I am going to whip your ever-loving asses. Do you all understand?"

"Yes," we said back, nervous and scared. At this time, I was no more than five years old. There was nothing I could do but listen to my mother. And then worse came to worse. Lola got a call at her job. "Department of Anthropology," she said as she answered the phone. "Yes, may I speak to Ms. Lola Hayes please," a gentleman said back.

"Yes, this is she," Lola answered, not knowing who or what this strange voice could possibly want.

"Yes, ma'am, I am calling from L&V Mortgage and I am calling in regards to your property located at 1600 Sixth Street," the voice said.

"Ok, what is the problem?" Lola now asked in a disgruntled voice.

"Ma'am, we are starting the foreclosure process on said property because the payments are four months in arrears."

Her heart dropped, all she could do was envision Big Mama's face and remembering all of the things that had transpired in the house. "Sir, that is my family home. I don't live there. My grandmother passed away a few years back and I was still allowing my family to live there. Is there anything I can do to stop this process?"

"Yes there is. You can pay us the money that is owed," the man said, laughing. Lola laughed back because she knew it was a crazy question. He allowed her to wait a couple more days so she could get the money together. She immediately called Twinkie and then after their conversation she got in contact with Uncle Phil. And when they spoke he told her he had been giving Elsa the money to pay the mortgage but unfortunately her habit had taken control of her common sense and she was smoking the money up as fast as he was giving it to her. So, Lola had to be a grownup and, as much as it hurt, she had to evict Elsa and the rest of the family. It killed her to do it but she had to or she would end up losing everything Big Mama had worked for all of those years.

A few days later Lawrence and I were walking home from school and it was told to us we could not speak to Daphne and Tico anymore. My mother had given them a date to get out of the house and they were angered by it and they decided to take it out on Lawrence and me. Lawrence wiped the tears from my eyes and walked me across the street back to our apartment. He sat me down on the couch and told me, "I don't care who it is and what they have. You had better not ever let me see you crying for someone again. So what if you can't play with them? No matter what we still have each other. Do you understand me?"

"Yes," I replied to him, and from that moment on I never let anything they said affect me in any way. He was right. As long as we had each other everything else seemed pointless. Twinkie went to work on the house immediately. It was hard for us seeing Elsa and her crew and none of them saying a word to us as if we were strangers, but what I didn't understand was why in the world they were so upset with my mother. But I learned at a very young age that people get mad at you because they have done you wrong and expect you to just grin and bear it. It was a long road to completing that house, but by the time they did, everything was beautiful. Lola maxed out her credit cards but it was worth it. 1600 Sixth Street had never looked that good before. Reverend Turnblad turned our house into a showcase, even putting us on the news and in all of the papers, "From Crack House to the Front Cover of Modern Day Homes" read one of the articles. One of the reporters almost shoved her microphone down my throat trying to ask me how it felt to be living in such a beautiful home. I was only seven years old at the time what did I know about crack or modern-day homes?

My brother answered the question for me and when he finished he whispered for her to leave his little sister alone. "She is just a little kid she doesn't understand any of this" he told the very persistent lady. Though Elsa and Lola still hadn't mumbled even a hello to one another, things were as well as could be expected, until we were all in church and an usher ran to the choir loft to get my mother's attention. Someone had come into the church with a message from Grandma. My mother set aside her issues with Elsa and let her know what was going on. When we saw them hurrying out of the church in the middle of the service we knew something was terribly wrong. Denise grabbed us all and took us across the street. And when we got there we heard that something was wrong with granddaddy. We flew around the corner to grandma and when we got there we heard the story. He had a stroke out on the street and the hospital couldn't give out any information over the phone.

Grandma was scared to hear what happened so she decided to send my mother and Elsa so the two of them would have to talk. We just ran around playing. Daphne, Tico, and I were just excited to be playing with each other again. My mother and Elsa reached the hospital doors, then immediately went to the desk to see about their father and they were escorted into a room where they were met by a priest and another doctor. They assumed the worst had happened and they grabbed hands and tried to prepare themselves for the worst.

The doctor closed the door and asked were they the daughters of Mr. Duke Turner. "Yes," the both of them said as they held on tightly one to the other. "Doctor, is our father alive>" Lola said.

"Well, how can I say this without laughing," the doctor said back to her. My mother didn't know how to take it. She and Elsa were fearful for their father's life and this doctor talked about laughing. Elsa said, "Sir, I'm not sure what kind of sense of humor you have, but this is not a joking matter. You have some nerve. My sister and I just want to know how our father is doing."

The doctor said, "Miss I don't mean any harm, but your father is fine." Now Lola jumps in, "Fine? When in the hell has a stroke been categorized as fine? I want to see another doctor because obviously you don't know what you are doing."

"Ma'am can I finish before either of you cut me off again? Thank you. What I was trying to say is that your father didn't have a stroke." The two of them looked as pale as the softly driven snow. "He didn't?" they said, shocked from the news. "No, he didn't. I am sorry to be the one to tell you this, but your father is intoxicated, inebriated, or just to be frank, flat out drunk. He was sitting in front of the hospital foaming at the mouth and slurring his words. Unfortunately, these are the same symptoms as a person that's just had a stroke, so they brought him in. He is fine. They gave him some coffee to sober him up and he will be ready to go home in a bit."

Lola and Elsa were so embarrassed and when they let Granddaddy out of that room they let him have it. His response to them was at least they were talking again. They all laughed and when they got back to grandma's they realized just how petty the whole situation was. A few weeks later granddaddy was gone. I was too young to understand it all. I just knew my granddaddy was in heaven. I thought he was going to be at the funeral with us all, making us all laugh the way he had all of those years. As usual, I clung to my brother and let everything happen the way it was supposed to. Lawrence is my protector.

While we were sitting at the wake there was this woman there. She was pacing the floors. No one had enough nerve to walk over to her to see where she came from until she smacked my grandfather in the face. Then instantly Mary knew who she was. "She is one of Duke's women and he probably forgot to mention to her he was married." Grandma said, sort of tickled. My mother was outraged and she wanted to smack the lady. Time and time again this mysterious woman would walk over to the casket and cry over him and then in the same breath she would slap the shit out of him again. Lawrence, Daphne and I laughed and laughed. We were children and we didn't know any better. The third time Mary walked over and grabbed the woman's arm. "If you hit him one more time I am going to kick your ass. Do I make myself clear? Whatever you thought the two of you shared it doesn't matter now. He is gone. Therefore, you need to leave." And before Mary could finish her last line, Elsa, Lola, Whitney, and Aunt Drusilla walked up behind Grandma ready for whatever action this lady wanted to bring their way. But the woman didn't want any confusion. She was very respectful and walked out of the funeral home. I didn't understand any of it at that point. My granddaddy was laying there sleeping and this lady wanted to wake him up. Lawrence kept telling me death was when you sleep for a few days and when you wake up everyone is there to have a party. And that's exactly what I believed. I kept going around to people asking when granddaddy would waking up so we could have his party. Now I know why they stared at me and began to cry. When I realized the next day he was never waking up and that death was final, it was a terrible lesson for a seven-year-old to face. But little did I know as the years went on the lessons would only get harder and harder to deal with.

CHANGES

W ell, we were getting used to the way our lives were. This
is the new normal for us. Things were the best they could
be at this point. The wounds from Elmo's death are still
very fresh. Lawrence decided school was the best thing for him. It would
keep his mind off losing Elmo. Grandma was getting a string of jobs and
she might be in line for a sitcom. She was so excited her ship was finally
coming in. Unfortunately, none of us were in her plans, if in fact her ship
did come in. Mary only thinks of two things: Whitney and herself. We
are just the ones who pick up the pieces when they fall whenever Whitney
acts a fool. Other than that, grandma has no room for us.

Elsa was doing great. She has become very active in the school system.
Everyone is so proud of her; my mother especially. She always rants and
raves about her sister's accomplishments. It was really hard all of those
years seeing her fight her addiction. And now my mother is one of her
biggest fans. Daphne is still acting up. She is really hurting, and no one
is really taking the time to get down to the core of her problem. Tico is
interested in crazy things. He is turning more and more into a goofball. He
is slowly losing all of his street credibility. Once upon a time he had more

street sense than older men that had been on the streets for years. And now all he wants to talk about is skateboarding and trading basketball cards.

My mother is trying to figure things out. She wants to get off of Sixth Street. But Twinkie is still fighting it. He wants all the luxuries of being married as long as my mother lives in a separate house. They have decided to plan a Housewarming/Blessing sometime in the summer. But for whatever reason we haven't moved in yet. And the way that Lawrence and I see it, we are never moving. He took most of our furniture. He lives in a fully furnished home, but if we have company, we have to sit on the floor. Then he brought the seat out of his truck, because my mother had a few words with him.

My mother is planning to go to Chicago for a wedding. Our cousin Albert is getting married. This will give her time to regroup and think about the decisions she has to make about my father. Twinkie is happy the police finally found Eric, because he couldn't get over the fact that those agents came to his house. He tries to play hard, but deep down he is afraid of a lot of things. He makes me so sick. He told my mother all of these horror stories about Randy and Eric. But we never believed any of them because he is such a big liar. He said, "Randy and Eric are ruthless. You all shouldn't get close to them. They might come around here and shoot up the neighborhood for no reason." He told my mother she had better not have me around Randy, because he is a murderer and a drug dealer and people were looking for him. And if I was riding with him they would kill me too. He always tells my mother these types of things so she will be fearful of people and wouldn't allow them to come around us. Then he even went to the extent of saying they didn't want me to call them because I was being a pest and I called too much. But Randy told me he was lying. They very much wanted to be a part of all of our lives.

My brother Randy fascinated me. I am mesmerized by him, and so is Lawrence. I am unsure of his lifestyle, but it doesn't matter because there is just something about him. He recently came home from prison for something involving a shooting. The details were undisclosed and none of us wanted to just come out and ask him. We could only assume. It was more important he was home. But Twinkie made up all these elaborate stories about the incident. And he didn't have a clue what he was talking about. It's funny because my father glorifies Randy. I always felt he lived vicariously through Randy's antics. We never found out what happened, because they closed the case. And Randy didn't talk about it.

Since Eric's arrest, Randy started to come around more often. Lawrence resented them at first because I talked about them all of the time. But the more Randy came over the closer they got. I was starting to get angry because he wouldn't even come around to see me anymore. He would come over to be with Lawrence and I was just the pesky little sister getting in their way.

Then tragedy struck in Randy's life. His mother passed away. Randy was devastated. He is the type of person that is good at inflicting pain but he can't take it when it comes his way. He went berserk. He went to his mother's funeral wearing overalls and a straw hat. Then on top of that he got there late. The preacher was up delivering the eulogy when he walked in. He walked down the center aisle and told the preacher, "Excuse me sir, but you need to take your seat." The preacher couldn't believe it. He just stood there in shock. But Randy looked really scary, so the preacher took his seat. Then he told the undertaker he wanted the casket reopened. The undertaker said to him, "Sir the services have started; we can't open the casket. We have never opened a casket once it has been closed."

He told the man, "Listen, mister, do you see what I have?" The man looked down and saw that Randy had his gun out. He said, "Now look, I'm only going to ask you one more time. Can you please open this mother fucking casket right now or someone else is dying in here today. You make the decision." My father walked up to the casket at this point. He wanted to console him. And possibly talk him out of what he was doing. He said, "Look, Randy, the man can't open the casket. He is scared and they are going to call the police if you don't stop this mess. Put the gun away and come sit down. You know your mother wouldn't want you in here acting like this. You are scaring everybody."

He told him, "Dad, I know that you are trying to be here for me but if you don't get out of my way I'm going to shoot you too. I want to say goodbye to my mother and they are going to open this casket or somebody else is going to die." Safe to say Twinkie sat his ass down. He asked the undertaker to please open the casket because he was serious. The man understood his grief, so he reopened the casket. Then Randy called his four-year-old son, our brother Lamar and my father up so they could sing a selection. My father and brother were scared. They didn't know what Randy was doing. And they didn't know what he was capable of. He started to sing Kumbaya. Then he made everyone join in.

When my father got home, he called my mother and said, "Randy has lost his damn mind." He went on to tell her what happened. Then he told her not to let him in our house if he came around. But my mother is not the type to turn her back on anyone. She never turned her back on him when he acted like a damn fool and treated her like shit. He actually told her he loved Randy's mother more than he loved anyone, and this included her. She was crushed. But as always, she forgave and forgot. I didn't, though. I wanted to whip the hell out of him. But she said, "That's your father. You can't be that way towards him because God will punish you." So, I left it alone.

A couple weeks later, Randy came by the house. I was with my boyfriend Walter. We were sitting in the living room and there was a knock on the door. I looked through the peep hole and there he was. I walked away and tried to be as quiet as I could. But he knew I was home. He hollered, "Lana I know you are in there. Come and open this damn door right now." I told Walter to be quiet, because my crazy older brother was out there. He started to pound on the door. I was afraid, so I finally opened it. He walked in and said, "Girl, what took you so long? I've been out there for about five minutes calling out your name." I told him I didn't hear the door because I had the music up loud. But there wasn't a radio anywhere in sight. Then he looked over at Walter. He said, "Who in the hell are you?"

I said, "Randy, let me introduce you to my boyfriend." He was talking on the phone and then it hit him what I said. He turned around and said, "What did you say?"

I said, "My boyfriend." Then I tried to introduce them to each other but it was too late. Randy walked up to him and said, "That is my baby sister and if you ever put your hands anywhere on her body, I'm going to kill you. If you ever hurt her in any way, I'm going to kill you. You are walking on very thin ice, so you need to be careful." Then he pulled his shirt up and showed Walter his gun. By this time Lawrence ran into the house and grabbed Randy and told him what a decent young man Walter was. He felt comfortable with what Lawrence told him. But it was too late, Walter was scared to death. As soon as Randy was out of sight, Walter got the hell out of there. He stayed his distance for a while after that.

A couple days later, there was another knock at the door. And again, it was Randy. He wanted to talk to my mother. Since his mother's death, he has become attached to her. He comes around to talk or just to see her. I guess it gives him a sense of having his mother back. But this night in particular he looked at her as his priest, because all he wanted to do was confess all of his sins.

He started telling us how he had done wrong to people. And I mean he had some horror stories. He is this little guy. He stands about five feet tall. But his heart stands at least seven feet tall. He has been in the streets since he was a young boy. He has been involved in drive-by shootings, he's beat people up, sold drugs, and done a lot of other things that are better left unsaid. He talked for at least two hours, about all of the things he has done over the course of his life. When he left, my mother cried and cried. I was horrified. I couldn't sleep for days. For once, Twinkie didn't lie. But he didn't even know all of the things Randy had done. He was even shocked by all the things that we told him.

I told Lawrence and he said, "Damn, I knew he was crazy, but shit, I didn't know he was a lunatic." It's sad to say this, but after that conversation, I was no longer mesmerized by him. Now I feared him. The phone calls stopped. However, he still came around but I stayed my distance. He asked, "What's your problem? You don't love your big brother anymore?" I told him I had been really busy with school. Then it happened. I was leaving school. Usually I would leave through the loading docks. But today was a nice sunny day and I wanted to talk to my friends, so I went out through the front doors. I heard someone calling my name. I didn't see anyone, though, so I kept on talking. Then they got louder. One of my friends said they saw my brother, but I didn't believe them. I looked around and there was Lawrence. I started to scream, "My brother, my brother." But he was in a car I didn't recognize. Then I saw Randy in the driver's seat. I tried to run in the other direction, but they saw me and Randy yelled out the window, "Girl, we've been out here waiting for you, don't make me come and get you." I was thinking, how in the hell can I get away from them. But I knew he would get out and get me, so I did the only thing I could do. I got in the car with them. Once I got in, Lawrence put out his hand behind him and grabbed me. He was looking at me through the window. I asked him what he was doing in the car with him. He shrugged his shoulders as if to say he didn't know. I asked him if was he afraid. He nodded his head, as if to say yes. Then Randy told us that he had to make a stop. He was going to the market a couple of blocks from our house to meet someone. When we got there, we got out of the car, too. I told Lawrence we should split up. We could run home and he couldn't catch the both of us. But Lawrence said no because we couldn't turn our back on him. Plus, he would be at the house waiting for us when we got there. He got inside the market and acted a fool. He finally took us home and I thanked God. He has really gone crazy. I love him, but I'm afraid of his actions. But he is my brother and I was starting to feel bad for feeling this way. Twinkie was angry at us when my mother told him. But Randy really needed someone to be there for him. I told my father he should call him. He wouldn't listen. He still only thinks about himself. He doesn't realize the pain he is going through.

Everyone else in the family was adjusting very well though. Elsa and Uncle Eugene are doing well. They are taking care of their family and handling their business. Elsa is a stay-at-home mom. Little Ahmad is her job. And believe me, that is enough. Daphne has started to hang with an older crowd. She has a friend that's a little out of it. Her ticker does not tock. She is on the slow side. She brought her down to our house and she went off because Lawrence wouldn't get her a cigarette. He kept on trying to tell her he didn't smoke, but she just wouldn't listen. She yelled, kicked and cried. It was like she needed an exorcism. I fell out laughing. Lawrence told Daphne, "I don't care what's going on, don't you ever bring that crazy bitch down here any more. She is a damn nut." She didn't calm down until she got that nicotine in her system. Lawrence got them out of there fast.

Grandma is working. She's been in some local commercials, she still has her gig at the club, and she has been doing print ads. She dropped Magdalene out of her name. She is just Mary Hayes, the diva of all divas.

Whitney, what more can you say about Whitney. She is never going to change. She always talks about what she used to be. And grandma always reminds her that those days are long gone. The both of them are truly basket cases.

We thought that the sad days were over for us. But tragedy came, rearing its evil head around that corner. It was the Saturday before my fifteenth birthday. My mother was putting me in an enrichment program. I hated the idea, but I didn't want to hurt her feelings so I went along with it. As I was getting dressed, the phone began to ring. Lawrence had just walked in from going on a breakfast run. He threw me my sandwich and my mother began to scream. We ran into her room and there she was crying her eyes out. It was Twinkie on the other end. We didn't know what could possibly be wrong. Then she turned around and told us. "Randy shot himself this morning. He just died at the hospital," she said. I dropped my sandwich and I took off running. I couldn't believe it. When Lawrence caught me, I was half-way across the street. I wasn't even fully dressed; I was wearing a shirt and a pair of shorts. It was freezing outside, but I didn't feel it. I could only feel pain. I couldn't believe my brother was gone. We went back in the house to be with my mother. She was very emotional. We all were. We never thought he would do something to himself. My mother thought it was best for me to go to this program to take my mind off the situation. I went, but shortly after I got there, Lawrence had to come back to get me, because I broke down. It was really hitting me hard, because I truly loved him. We had just started to get close and now he was gone. My mother took me out and bought me some things. She was hoping the thought of my birthday would make me feel better, but I didn't care about anything at this point. I just wanted to see Randy again. But I couldn't. Then I told her I wanted to be with my father. I thought maybe he would need some comforting. After all, this was his son. So, after we left the mall we went over to his house. When we got there, he was emotionless. I wanted him to see a tape my mother bought and he looked over at me and said, "Is that all you can think about? You are more selfish than I thought. Your brother killed himself this morning and you are worried about a fucking tape." I couldn't believe he would say something like that to me. I have been going through it all day. I wanted to come to his house to be with him and he's flicking off on me. Randy didn't even like him. And I told him, "I have been upset all day. I loved my brother. And I was there for my brother. I don't have anything to be ashamed of when it comes to Randy. You, on the other hand, could have reached out a helping hand to him but you didn't. And now it's too late and now you have to deal with it." My mother had to pull us apart. He never called him or showed him he loved or cared about him. And now he was trying to take his guilt out on me. And I was not going to have it.

I left out of there because I felt myself about to go into attack mode. And this was definitely not the time for all of that. Then they got the call the insurance agency would not honor the policy because Randy committed suicide. This was really bad news. But Twinkie had just finished a big job and he agreed to pay the funeral expenses. He should have, he never did anything for him in life.

Things were crazy, my birthday came and I didn't feel like doing anything. Lawrence went out and bought me a big cake, but none of that mattered. He kept doing special things for me, but I was just out of it. I didn't want anything but Randy, but that was one wish that wouldn't come true.

The days leading up to Randy's funeral were all a blur. We went to the funeral home so they could view his body and so my father could pay off the balance. This is what brought me back down to reality. Randy's stepfather was there. This man was shorter than Randy and now he wanted to call some shots. He and Randy didn't get along, but he had been with his mother for so long, I think that he was there out of loyalty to her. He came in there and tried to start something with my father. Lamar pulled him away and told him, "Now is not the time for all of this. Any ill feelings that you might feel toward him, take that up after the funeral."

My father said, "No, if the little midget man has something to say let him say it now." The man agreed with Lamar and left it alone. We left the funeral home so my mother could go and finish the obituary. That was a hard task but we did it. After she finished, we had to go back to my father's house so he could look them over. But on our way there, we were side swiped and the person that hit us kept going. My mother called my father from the police station and this bastard wouldn't even come and pick us up. It was obvious my mother was shaken by all of this. He didn't care. He flicked off on us because someone hit us and took off. He wasn't even concerned. My mother said it was just his nerves. Now I know better. He is the most selfish person I have ever seen. When we finally got to his house, he cursed my mother out because Randy's picture wasn't in color. I wanted to kick him in his nuts. My mother was doing the best she could, but it wasn't good enough for him. Truthfully, it's never good enough. My mother was so hurt he was acting this way. But she put his feelings before her own, and left it alone. So, we left and he kept his stinking attitude.

The funeral was funny. There were people coming in off the streets that were there just to see him lying in the casket. I overheard one guy saying, "I just want to see if that nigga is really dead." I couldn't believe people could be so heartless. I didn't say anything to these guys, though, because I knew the type of life Randy lived and I didn't want anyone doing anything to me, so I walked in the other direction. My older sister Tracy looks a lot like Randy, so this guy approached her and said, "You must be some kin to Randy." The guy looked like he came in straight from the gutter. She told him, "No, I didn't know the guy. I'm here with my sister, she used to date him." Then to top all of that off, Randy's stepfather came into the church with a pistol in his pants. He was going to actually shoot at my father. Or maybe he needed it for protection. I don't know, but it was funny to me. He looked over at my father during the entire service. I couldn't help but laugh. My father didn't care, though. He pulled him to the side at the cemetery and told him, "I will kick your ass if you try something. And if you shoot me you had better kill me because if you don't when I get better I'm going to kick your ass again."

Things were crazy. I was just having the hardest time dealing with Randy's death. I couldn't understand why he would take his own life. Then I was feeling a sense of guilt for not calling like I was because I found out about the life he was leading. And I feared him. But Lawrence sat me down and told me I was a good little sister and he knew Randy really loved me. And I had nothing to be guilty about. Then he went on to say that depression is a sickness and Randy was really sick. I began to understand, and the load seemed a little lighter. Then I felt bad because Randy left behind two children and now they are growing up fatherless. But Lawrence promised he would do what he could to step in.

Right now, things in the family aren't going well at all. My mother and father are constantly fighting and she is miserable. Lawrence and I, on the other hand, are getting by quite well. He is my best friend again. I never thought things would ever be like this between us again. Daphne and Tico have a longing in their hearts for Sixth Street, so Elsa agreed that during spring break they can come down. Grandma has been gone a lot. She is the movie star in the family. She has five films under her belt now. You can't tell her anything. She is Ms. Glamour Girl. Whitney hasn't been home. She leaves the kids in the house with Uncle Earl. He lives there with them. He takes on the responsibility for the children when grandma isn't home. He knows Whitney will leave them at the drop of a dime.

We have truly been on a roller coaster ride and just when we think we've mastered a new normal something else happens. A month had gone by and things on Sixth Street were about the same. Lola and Twinkie are still going back and forth. I don't know why she keeps pressing the issue. We are not moving over there. He doesn't want us. And now Lawrence and I are to the point that we don't want to be there either. Why should we be somewhere we're not welcome? We're better off on Sixth Street. Grandma is going to North Carolina. She is going down for the pilot of a new sitcom. They had to begin taping. She called home to tell Whitney what was going on. Whitney called Elsa and my mother to let them know that grandma made it there safely and that she got the role. Everyone was excited for her. But that didn't last. We got the call the next morning. It was a hospital in Wilmington, North Carolina. The doctor told my mother that grandma was very ill. She had been in her hotel room and they were calling her but they never got an answer. Finally, they had the manager of the hotel to open her door. And there she was lying on the floor. They rushed her to the hospital. She had an aneurism. Her arteries are clogged, which caused this aneurism. My mother asked the doctor his prognosis and he said his only advice was to get there as fast as she could because she might not make it through the night. My mother immediately called Elsa. They didn't know what to do. After their conversation she called the airports, but there weren't any flights flying out going to that area. So, my mother decided she would drive down. She called my father and asked him to take her down, but he said no because he had better things to do. Then she asked could she take his van, because she would have to bring grandma home and she didn't want her to be uncomfortable. He said, "Hell no. you can't take my van down there." He is so selfish. He only thinks about himself and what he needs. Elsa called and my mother told her the situation, so she decided to go. She said, "I'm on my way down there." My mother decided to take me with her. Lawrence didn't want to go. He volunteered to watch Daphne and Tico, while Uncle Eugene and Elsa went down with us.

Elsa thought it would be best if my mother went around and told Whitney. So, we drove around the corner to give her the news. When we got around there the door was locked. We knocked and knocked, until finally she came to the door. My mother told her, "Look, Whitney, come outside for a minute, I have to tell you something about Mama." Before she could get anything out, Whitney jumped off the steps and started to scream. "Oh Lord, Mama's gone, Mama's gone, Mama's gone, Mama's gone." She wouldn't stop screaming. My mother was thinking maybe the hospital called her and gave her more details. So, she started to cry, too. Then she asked her, "Whitney, have you spoken to anyone?" She said, "No." So my mother's tears stopped and then she asked her, "Why in the hell are you saying ma is gone?" And she said, "Oh, isn't that what you were coming to tell me?"

My mother looked at her and walked away because after she said grandma was alive, Whitney showed no remorse. It was like she was upset grandma was still in the land of the living. I couldn't believe it. My mother told her we were going down to North Carolina to check on her mother because she was in the hospital. She asked did she want to ride with us and she said, "For what? But when you all come back, please make sure someone gets my check from her." My mother wanted to punch her but now definitely was not the time for that. She had to use all of her energy to focus on grandma. She just walked away. By the time we got back home, Elsa and Uncle Eugene were there. We piled into my mother's car and headed for North Carolina. My mother stayed up the entire ride. She is still fearful of highways since the accident. Uncle Eugene teased her the entire time were driving down there. She would tell him when he was going too fast or driving too crazy. He laughed at her but he understood. She is very apprehensive about driving on highways.

After a long drive, we were there. We went straight to the hospital. Grandma was in the intensive care unit. I couldn't believe it when I saw her. She was so helpless. She had tubes everywhere. All the hostility I felt towards her went away at that moment. That was my grandmother and she was dying. I walked out of there. I wanted to be alone so I could cry. I didn't want anyone to know this had hit me so hard. But somehow my mother knew what I was doing. She followed right behind me. And pulled me close to her and told me everything was going to be alright because God was in control. Then we went back into the room. Elsa just held her hand and rubbed her hair. The doctor came in and told my mother he needed to discuss some things with them. They left out of the room. He said, "Mrs. Hayes' condition is very bad but she has made it through today and we didn't think she would. So, we know she is a fighter. But she is not out of the woods yet. She is still a very sick lady. I have some news, though. I'm not sure if you know." At this point Elsa and my mother grabbed hands because they didn't know what to expect. They told the doctor they were ready to hear whatever he had to tell them. He said, "Well, I don't know exactly how to put it. Your mother had very high levels of marijuana in her system. Did you all know that she uses the substance?" Instantly they began to laugh. The doctor didn't get the joke. But he laughed anyway. I guess he was being polite.

We couldn't stay any longer. It was after hours, they only allowed us in so we could talk to the doctor. She made it over the first hurdle. Now the rest is in God's hands. When we got to the hotel, the manager was nice enough to let us stay in grandma's room. He asked did Elsa and my mother want grandma's things. They said yes. And when he brought it out there it was, her weed and the top paper. She was rolling joints in these people's hotel. My mother was so embarrassed. I just couldn't believe it. Elsa and Uncle Eugene made jokes about it. After all of the kidding around, they had to come up with a game plan. At this time ,we were still unsure about the outcome. She was still really sick and the doctors basically told us there was very little they could do. And the best thing would be to put it in God's hands. We didn't know if we were preparing for a funeral or preparing to take Mary home. Elsa and Uncle Eugene have already decided she is moving in with them. But she won't be able to smoke anymore. That right there is enough to kill her. I don't think grandma could survive without smoking a joint. So, we prayed again and went to bed.

When we woke up the next morning, Elsa called the hospital to check on grandma. I was in the bathroom at the time and I heard her shouting. Grandma is going to be alright. During the middle of the night she woke up and began speaking. It was a miracle. Those doctors really didn't think she was going to make it. But she proved them wrong. We rushed up to the hospital. When we got there, my mother and Elsa began to cry. Mary on the other hand wasn't at all emotional. The first thing that came out of her mouth was, "Where's my money? I had nine hundred dollars in that room and when I get out of here all of my money had better be there." I had to leave out of the room. When we got there, I was overcome with sadness seeing my grandmother laying there so helpless, and now she is back to being Mary. The tears stopped for my mother and Elsa. They were ready to kill her. How dare she? She was fighting for her life a few hours ago and now she is worried about nine hundred dollars. Elsa told her, "Oh, don't worry, you'll get your money. Nobody is going to take anything from you." The doctor told them they couldn't believe how she came out of it. They had never seen anything like it before. Instantly, my mother looked over and said, "That's what the power of prayer will do for you." The doctor nodded and went on his way. They were still upset with grandma and she did not care one bit.

We left the hospital. Then Uncle Eugene thought about it and said we didn't have enough room to get grandma home. We couldn't rent a car because they wouldn't allow someone from out of state to rent a car from them. So, Uncle Eugene and Elsa had to leave and go back to Leesburg to get a car. This is where the confusion started. Someone is going to have to tell grandma they needed to use some of her money. They elected Elsa to do the honors. We went into the room and Elsa said, "Mama we don't have enough room in Lola's car for all of us. Plus, the doctor said we should make you as comfortable as possible, since we have such a long ride. So, we have to rent a minivan." Grandma gave her a look as if to say, what are you telling me for? Then Elsa said, "We can't rent a van here because they don't allow people without credit cards to rent vehicles. So, we have to go home and come back." Then Grandma came out and asked, "What are you telling me all of this for Elsa?" Elsa said, "Because, Mama, we have to use your money to get home and to rent the minivan." That's when the shit hit the fan. Grandma rose up and told them off. She said, "I knew you all were going to try and take my money." My mother said, "Mama, we aren't trying to take anything. You are a blessed woman. God didn't have to spare your life. We could be preparing for your funeral but we aren't. We are preparing to take you home. You shouldn't be that way." Grandma looked at her and rolled her eyes. Then she told them, "I can call Herbert to come and get me. Blessings! I don't give a damn about no blessings. I want my money. You all aren't taking my money. You aren't doing a thing with it except bringing it to me." My mother walked out of the room because she can't deal with it when someone speaks ill of the Lord. Then she walked back in and told her, "Mama, you are being ungrateful. We didn't have to come down here. The kids are missing a week from school. Eugene and I are missing a week from work and all you can do is lay here and think about nine hundred dollars?" Then she told her, "You'd better be glad it's us instead of Whitney because you wouldn't have any of the money. And she could care less how you get home. She didn't even come down with us." After my mother lectured her, she still wouldn't budge, so we left the hospital.

Elsa and my mother were pissed off. Uncle Eugene went back to the hospital to talk with her. She finally gave in. But she still wasn't pleased about it one bit. But she was laying in a hospital bed. What could she do? Shortly after he got back we had to take them to the bus station. They were going to pick up a minivan, then they were going to swing back and pick up Lawrence, Daphne, and Tico. They were back at home having the time of their lives. They got to stay out of school for a week, plus they were seeing all our family and their friends. Me and my mother used this as a long overdue vacation. We shopped and shopped. Whitney wasn't worried about grandma, she was interested in knowing where her food stamps were. She didn't know grandma had the mail man give it to her nextdoor neighbor, Ms. Marie. Because if Whitney got her hands on it the children wouldn't eat. And since we had to stay down in Wilmington for the week, the trip to Chicago had been canceled. My mother wanted to go to see Albert get married, but making sure grandma was alright is top priority. We went to the hospital later on that night and grandma was in better spirits. She was still upset about her money. She apologized to my mother for acting that way. Then all was well. The doctor came in and said they would be moving her out of ICU and into a regular room. My mother was so thankful and appreciative. She was walking around blessing everybody's heart she came into contact with on the hospital staff.

They all had been pulling for Mary. And, of course, she did her bit using her name, Ms. Mary Magdalene. She says, "Now you can tell people that you met the real Mary Magdalene." It makes me sick whenever I hear it. I always tell her, "Grandma, what are you proud of that for? She was a prostitute, they were going to stone her to death until Jesus stepped in and saved her." Then she always goes on to say, "Well He saved me too." But the people are always tickled when she says it.

A couple days went by and grandma was doing extremely well. The doctor said she was doing better than any of them had ever expected, so she could go home in a day or two. Elsa and the crew would be down later on that afternoon. We were excited because we were away from Lawrence all week.

Boy, have we been through it. But this time God truly saw us out of it. When they got there the first thing Lawrence wanted to do was eat. We were in the Deep South and he wanted to find some soul food. He is so greedy. We took him to this all –you-can-eat buffet. The food there was excellent. He asked the lady could he take some food to go. Of course, her answer was no, because the meal was only five dollars. So, he gathered up all the napkins that he could find and piled food into those napkins. He had everything, chicken, rolls, ham, roast beef, turkey, and then for dessert he had cookies and cake. He placed it all in my mother's purse. We all laughed and laughed at him. He is such a clown.

We went back to the hotel and the next morning grandma's doctor called to say she was going to be released that afternoon. We packed up and went to the hospital. The adults allowed us to drive home with Lawrence in my mother's car, while they drove in the minivan. The plan was set and grandma was moving in with Elsa. My mother is going up to Leesburg every other weekend. And when she has to go to the doctor, Uncle Eugene is going to take off and bring her to her appointment.

Grandma thought this was a lovely idea. She was excited for the first time since all of this happened. Well, during the ride things changed. We were half-way home. We stopped at a gas station and grandma says she is moving in with a close friend. See ,Mary already had this planned; she just didn't want any mess from my mother and Elsa. They were pissed off. My mother came and got into the car with us. Elsa was cursing up a storm. She didn't want to move to Leesburg, because she knew Whitney couldn't come. So, before we went home we had to show Uncle Eugene where this friend of hers lived. After a nice, long, stressful ride, we made it to Aunt Frieda's house. She and grandma have been friends since forever. Grandma was shame-faced when we got there. She had very little to say to us because she knew she was wrong.

We said our goodbyes and everybody was so happy being home. Well, God was truly in the midst of it all. Grandma was alright and we made it home safe and sound. The next couple of weeks were crazy. Grandma was supposed to stay stress-free. That was the whole point of her moving in with Aunt Frieda. But she just can't stay away from Whitney. She went home to pick up the children. Whitney doesn't deserve them, because she is never home. Well Grandma had a relapse and ended right back up in the hospital. Whitney showed no emotion whatsoever. My mother and Elsa were ready to kill her at this point. My mother and I went around to grandma's house. There was Whitney lying on the couch. My mother asked, "Whitney, what happened to Mama?"

She said, "I don't understand you and Elsa. Damn, she is back in the hospital. What's the point in getting your nerves all upset? You need to chill." The next thing I know, my mother was whipping her ass again. She told my mother, "Go on and beat me, I understand. Your mother is in the hospital and you don't know what's wrong with her. You need to beat up on someone, so use me." The whole time her lips were smacking back and forth. I had to pull my mother off of her because she was so upset, she didn't know what she was doing.

We went back to the hospital. My mother didn't tell grandma about this encounter. She didn't want her to feel any worse then she already did. It's crazy. No matter what Whitney does to grandma she is always there pushing her on and never giving up on her. She never turns her back on her no matter what she does. She couldn't even walk two blocks to see grandma while she was in the hospital. But it is typical of Whitney. Everyone tries over and over to tell grandma she is no good, but she never listens. She always says Whitney is her child and she can't turn her back on her. Too bad the feelings aren't mutual. Whitney could careless about grandma's situation. Everyone can see it. It's just too bad grandma can't. After grandma's doctor from Wilmington sent the information about grandma's condition, the doctor gave her a prescription and she was allowed to go home. But he told her she should take it easy. She went back to Aunt Frieda and left Whitney back at the house to fend for herself.

Well, things in Leesburg were going good. The family was all in tact. Daphne was back to acting like a normal teenager. Things are so carefree up there. Not like at home, where you had to always be aware of your surroundings. My best friend came to school crying because her boyfriend got killed. He was only fifteen years old. Someone killed him over a bicycle. She was so upset. But this was beginning to be the norm for us. It was to the point where death didn't faze us anymore because it happened all the time. I went home from school and I immediately told Lawrence what happened. He felt bad for my friend. He told me, "All you can do is listen to her. You don't know any of the circumstances. And don't ask any questions." I listened to him because he is my older brother and he would never tell me anything that would hurt me.

Well, time seemed like it was flying by and it was already time for Spring break. Daphne and Tico were coming down. I couldn't wait to see them. It's been about a month since the ordeal with grandma, and even then we didn't spend any time together because I went with my mother while they stayed with Lawrence. We were going to have a house-full.

Randy's girlfriend was having a hard time with little Randy and she needed a break. Of course, my father said, "No." But my mother wasn't going to have it. She was in need. She agreed to take him and the baby, too. Little Randy is a disturbed boy. After Randy died we would bring him over to the house. At first, he was the sweetest little boy. But after we got to know him the devil came out in him. He told me he was going to kill me while I was sleeping. And he was serious. I pulled him by his ear and I told him, "Little boy, you don't mess with me. I have the same blood you have flowing in my veins. I could kill you right now." I scared the shit of him. After that, I didn't have to worry about him. We were going to have him for an entire week. My father told my mother not to call him if he showed off. Well, here we were, all piled up in the house for a whole week. My mother must have been crazy to agree to this. When Lawrence pulled up, Little Randy ran up the street to play with the neighborhood kids and before he got up the block, he came running down the street and ran into the house. He threw a soda bottle at Ms. Bertha. She was sitting on her porch. The children chased him down the street and into the house. He wouldn't tell Lawrence why he ran down the street so fast and why he didn't want to go back outside. So, Lawrence went up the street and asked the children. After they told him, Lawrence came back down the street and tore his ass up. Daphne and Tico couldn't believe how terrible he was. And that's saying something because he has to be terrible if he is worse than Tico.

Little Randy was driving everyone crazy. Daphne likes talking to him, so she is his only ally. He was confused about her. He told his mother,

"Mom, I have these cousins I met over here, but someone is telling a lie. I don't think they are brother and sister. Someone is lying." His mother asked him why he would say something like that. So, he told her, "Mom, the girl's name is Daphne and she is really black and the boy's name is Tico and he is white. So how could they be related?" She explained to him that their skin color has nothing to do with it. So, he didn't bring it up again. But the trouble started with him. He was upset with me because I punished him for cursing at Denise and so he told my mother he caught me having sex with Walter. My mother instantly panicked and assumed the worst without talking it over with me first. She quickly came back down to earth. She thought about it and apologized for thinking I would be that crazy. He started to drive my mother crazy. She had to take him to the doctor to get his medicine. She told him he needed to hurry up so they wouldn't be late and he told her, "Grandma, you need to get the hell out of the bathroom." She was dumbfounded. She couldn't believe him. She didn't want to hit him, because he is a troubled child.

When they got back from seeing the doctor my mother made dinner. Randy decided he would rather have dessert instead of what my mother cooked. She told him, "Randy, you can have ice cream but you have to eat your dinner. He stuffed the food in his mouth so he could get his ice cream. He swallowed the scoops of ice cream whole. Then he put fingers down his throat and made himself gag. The food went everywhere, over the walls and on the floor. My mother ran out of the house in the middle of a thunderstorm. She wanted to be a help to his mother but at this point she wanted him gone. I was terrified. I didn't have a clue where she went. I called Lawrence so he could find her. When he finally found her, she was standing in the middle of the street, two blocks from the house. He had to force her to come home. She begged and pleaded for him to just pack her a bag. She wanted to stay at her job until that devil child was out of there. It was like she was having a nervous breakdown. He finally got her to come home.

We were all tucked away in our rooms. And it happened. Tico started to scream. We didn't know what to think. We ran out of our rooms and there he was standing in front of the bathroom door with one hand over his mouth. We didn't know if someone was in there or not. He was frozen and wouldn't say a word. My mother ran down the stairs and then she began to scream. She told Tico to find Lawrence. Then she yelled for us to stay upstairs. She said, "You all don't need to see this." Daphne and I didn't know what to think. We kept on asking her to tell us what happened, but she wouldn't. She just stood there in disbelief. Finally, Lawrence came running into the house to see what Tico was talking about. Then he began screaming. I started running down the stairs but my mother stopped me. She wanted me and Daphne to stay upstairs. Tico came up and he told us what was going on. He was going downstairs to use the bathroom but when he got there he found the surprise of his life. Someone had been in there before and they left a present. It was shit everywhere. Whoever it was smeared it on the toilet seat, the walls and the sink. And that's why he screamed because he had never seen anything like it before in his life.

Lawrence saw Little Randy go in there before he left the house. So, he called him downstairs. When he got down there, he went back and forth with Lawrence for a few minutes. He said, "Uncle Lawrence, someone in this house set me up, I didn't do this. They all hate me, it's a conspiracy."

Lawrence told him, "Randy, don't lie to me, because when you lie it gets you in more trouble, so tell me the truth." After he lied a couple more times, he put up his hands and said, "Okay, you caught me. I smeared my butt on the wall." Lawrence lost it at this point. He ran out of the house into the rain. My mother went after him. It's safe to say that after this incident Little Randy was no longer allowed at our house. Daphne and Tico were ready to go home, because they didn't want to be bothered with Little Randy anymore.

After the chaos with spring break, things went back to normal. One night I was getting ready for bed and Denise was knocking on the door. She said, "Where is Aunt Lola?" I said, "She is upstairs. Why?" She said, "You all need to come quick, because some DEA agents have Lawrence and his friend Chucky." I ran upstairs and got my mother. We rushed outside to see what was going on. Lawrence was coming to meet us. The people let him go because he was clean. He didn't have anything on him. He was just standing out there with them and when he started quoting things from his law books, they got scared and let him go. But they were going to take Chucky to the police station.

Denise and Aunt Joanne were hysterical. The agents asked were they related and they said yes. Chucky had one-thousand dollars on him and the officers were about to turn the money over to them. Chucky screamed for my mother. He knew if Denise and Aunt Joanne got their hands on his money, he would never get it back. My mother walked over and the agents gave her his belongings. Then the agents gave my mother the information about where he'd be. So here it is one o'clock in the morning and we were on our way to the police station to pick up Chucky. Dwight was on his way home and he saw all of the police cars. He walked over to see what was going on. Lawrence filled him in and he said he wanted to go along for the ride. When we got to the station, Dwight told my mother, "When we get in there you don't have to say a word. I will handle everything." We all walked in and he walked up to the desk. The officer walked over and said, "Yes sir, may I help you?"

He pulled out his security badge and flashed it in the lady's face. He said, "Yes, special officer Carson. I'm here to check on a PR 7950. The name is Charles Grover." The police officer couldn't believe him. She walked away laughing. Then she sent another officer up to the front. He flipped his badge again. The officer said, "Is there anyone else here that knows what's happening because I don't know what in the hell he's talking about." My mother walked over to the desk and got the information straightened out. We got a memorable laugh that night. They didn't have any proof of anything on Chucky, so they had no other choice but to let him go. They beat him up pretty bad, though. But there was nothing he could do because they denied it. He was just happy to get out.

A few days after this mishap a lady from my church approached me. Her name is Mrs. Hillman. She said she was the chairperson for the Mother's Day committee. She said, "This year we want members in the church to nominate women. Why don't you write something up about your mother and enter it into the running for Mother of the Year." I told her I would consider it. I instantly ran and told Lawrence. He said, "Don't you write shit, those people at the church aren't going to pick our mother because it's all about politics with them."

I said, "Well, I am going to do it, because I think she more than deserves this honor. She is our mother and that is exactly what I am going to put when I write this letter."

He said, "Well good luck, but please don't tell Ma and please don't get your hopes up." I laughed at him. He has a hard time dealing with the church, since one of the members told them he saw Lawrence selling drugs and it was a lie. The people in the church believed him over my mother and Lawrence. He was really hurt by it. Since then he hasn't gone to church and he rarely speaks to the people. But I still wanted to write this for my mother. We have been through so much. She deserves something nice, and I am going to do my best to give it to her. A couple days after I turned in my nomination letter, Mrs. Hillman told me my mother had been chosen to be Mother of the Year.

I called everyone in the family. I wanted everyone to be there. My father was his sarcastic self. He wanted to know what she received for winning. I told him there wasn't a prize. But she would get a trophy and maybe flowers. He said, "Well there is no reason for me to be there. They aren't giving her anything." I couldn't believe him. I just ended the conversation. I didn't want to say anything that would provoke him. Then he would tell my mother and it would ruin the surprise. Elsa couldn't come up because Uncle Eugene had to work.

It was hard keeping a tight lip. I tell my mother everything and for the first time I had to be secretive. It was killing me. But I couldn't let on. I begged and begged and Lawrence agreed to come to church. But after my mother received her award he was leaving. He couldn't be around those hypocrites for an entire service. My mother just sat in the choir loft. Rev. Turnblad stood up and told the congregation that this year they were going to liven things up and they called up a few children to read theri nominations. When he called me up, I had tears in everybody's eyes. My family walked in and instantly my mother knew. She began to tear up. She couldn't believe I held something from her for this long. My grandmother was so proud. She was there in rare form. My mother was overwhelmed with emotions because it was just a couple of months ago; she was fighting for her life. Everyone in the church stood up to clap, because they had heard of her struggles.

But today was more important than the trophy. Today I gave myself to Christ. I joined church today. When I walked up to give Rev. Turnblad my hand, the church was on fire. My mother couldn't believe it. All of those years of her preaching and I finally heard her. But I always told her I had to want it for myself. And today I did. My mother was ecstatic. It was the best Mother's Day she ever had.

THE END OF AN ERA

We all figured things were on an even keel. Everyone was maintaining their situations. I joined the church and I was getting ready for my baptism. Everyone teased me because I was the last one in the family to get baptized, and because of my age. Everyone else did it at an early age. But I am different and always have been. Plus, Lawrence and Daphne cornered me one night and put the fear of the Lord in me. I was only five or six years old at the time. They teamed up on me in Lawrence's room. Lawrence sat me down in a chair. Then he cut the lights out and flashed this bright light on me like I was being questioned for a crime. And Daphne went along with it. He said, "When you join church, the preachers are going to take you into this room and they'll flash a light on you just like this one. Then they will ask you questions. If you get any of them wrong you are going to burn in hell. So, you'd better ask God before you go up there and give the preacher your hand." That stigmatized me for years. I would leave out of the church when the call to discipleship came up during the service. I was petrified. I would always get a knot in the pit of my stomach. All I could think of was burning in hell for all of eternity. Lawrence doesn't even remember and neither does Daphne. But I do.

After all of those years I finally gave it up. I knew God was and is the center of my life and I didn't want to spend my eternity burning in hell because I didn't acknowledge my beliefs. And today was the day. Lawrence said, "Man, I went to church around those people once this month. I can't go today. I am really happy you are getting baptized, though. And I am proud of you today." I wasn't mad at him. He was being true to himself. God knows his heart. Sometimes hurt can overpower you. So, it was just me and my mother. Twinkie never comes to anything. He only deals with his needs. He told my mother he couldn't make it. He said he had something work-related. I really didn't care. Truthfully, my mother is my mother and father. My mother went out and bought me swimming shoes. She said she wanted me to wear them because who knows what's on the floor of the baptismal pool. That made me really laugh, because my mother is so particular. She hates filth.

I was relieved. I finally overcame my fears. That morning when I woke up, I got dressed and everything was going smoothly. We lived across the street from our church, so I didn't have to go far. When I got there, one of the deaconesses was sitting near the entrance waiting for me. She told my mother she wasn't allowed to go with me. My mother looked at me with a tear in her eye and said, "I'm so proud of you. I love you. God Bless you." I felt emotional but I held it in. We went upstairs so I could get out of my clothes. For some reason when we got upstairs the lady turned into a task master. Normally, she is a sweet old lady, but today she is a mean old bitty. She said in a firm voice, "Take your things off and put on this robe." I told her, "I need to go into a room. I don't change clothes in front of anyone, not even my mother." She said, "Listen, you don't have anything I haven't seen before. Take those clothes off." I told her again, "I am uncomfortable changing clothes in front of people. I am not taking a thing off unless you allow me to go into the restroom or even a closet." She saw that I was serious, so she allowed me to go into a corner where no one could see me. When I finished undressing she asked, "Do you have on your under garments?" I said, "Yes ma'am." She said, "Well you need to take them off. I went and took off my underwear. Then she asked what did I have on my feet? And I told her these were my swim shoes and t my mother bought them so that my bare feet wouldn't touch the floor. She looked at me with a coldhearted look and told me, "This is not a swimming pool. Little girl, Jesus is with you. You don't need any swimming shoes. You are going to walk into the water, Rev. Turnblad is going to dunk your body and then you are going to walk out. It won't even be five minutes. Now you do as I say or you won't be getting baptized today." I took off the shoes but I rolled my eyes and gave her the nastiest look that I could give.

Then I heard it. Rev. Turnblad was calling my name. I couldn't wait to get out of there. But just as she said it wasn't even five minutes. After my baptism, I went and sat with my mother. She was overcome with emotion. I asked could we leave church. She agreed. She wanted to go out and celebrate. Lawrence came with us. He kept going on and on about me going in a dry devil and coming out a wet one. All and all it was a wonderful day.

The next couple of weeks were really crazy, though. I was getting ready to graduate Junior High School. They were only allowing three invitations, so that was only enough for my immediate family. This was the happiest day of my life. Lawrence tried to pretend like he wasn't proud of me. He looked at me that morning and said, "Don't think that you are grown. You have a long way to go." I said, "You know you are proud of me." He said, "Who me? I am not proud of you. You are only doing what you are supposed to do." Then he grabbed me and said that he was happy I was graduating and that I was doing so well. And he hoped I would keep up the good work once I got into high school because it was a total difference. Then I looked at him and said, "Well, if you are that proud then where in the hell is my gift?" He said, "I just gave it to you." I told him that he'd better have my gift after my graduation or else. He looked at me and laughed. It was really good having my brother back. For a time there, I never thought things would be like this again. And here we were laughing and joking again, like old times.

I didn't want them to drive me to the ceremony, so I walked to my school with my friends. We were so excited, we were growing up. As Al Green says, "For the good times." I never thought they were going to end. But as they say, eventually all things must come to an end. I just never realized the day was fast approaching. There I was walking across the stage. My brother looked at me with his chest sticking out. I thought it was going to be a repeat of my sixth-grade graduation when Twinkie acted like a stock raving lunatic. This time it was Lawrence. Who would've thought? He was running up to the stage, taking pictures and screaming my name. All of my friends knew him and they knew how funny he was so they just laughed at him.

After the ceremony, we took pictures. Lawrence told me to pick any restaurant I wanted to go to and it was his treat. Of course, my father had other pressing engagements. He would not be accompanying us. He did give me a card, though. I wasn't interested in it. I wanted to see what was inside. And to my shock, there was a one-hundred-dollar bill inside. So, there we were my mother, Lawrence, and I. We were on our way to this all-you-can-eat restaurant Lawrence had picked out. He said it was similar to the restaurant in North Carolina. He is such a liar. This place had the nastiest food ever. I asked him was he crazy bringing us to such a hole in the wall on my graduation day? Then to top it off, I had to wind up paying for our food. He didn't bring his money with him. But we were all together so I didn't care.

Things were finally starting to level off for us. My mother was finally getting my father out of her system and Lawrence and I were back to our old selves. Yes, we still argued but it was normal sibling rivalry. Well, back in Leesburg things were also leveled. Daphne had a little more freedom. Elsa felt if she didn't allow her to do something, she would just go off and do it anyway. And then she was about to start her senior year of high school. Everything was perfect.

Mary was still living with Aunt Frieda with the children. She stopped paying all of the bills in the house. She felt there were grown people living there and they were more than capable of paying the bills in the house that they were living in. Well, she was wrong. My mother was awakened by the telephone. It was Elsa. In a whisper she said, "Girl, the people have foreclosed on Mama's house. Did she call you yet?" My mother shouted, "WHAT? NO!" Elsa said, "Well when she does act like you don't know what's going on. Then call me back when she lets you know the deal." My mother said, "Okay."

A few hours later grandma called. She told my mother she couldn't afford to help maintain two households and she was tired of Whitney. "Whitney has been living off me and draining me since the day she came into this world and now I am tired. Somebody has to look after these children and that's my main focus." My mother agreed and they prayed and after that grandma felt a sense of peace. The bank foreclosed on the house. It was a really sad day, but grandma was okay with it. Therefore, we all had no other choice but be to be ok with it too.

But before you knew it, Aunt Frieda and grandma were at odds. Grandma wanted Whitney to move in with them and Aunt Frieda wasn't having it. She called my mother and said, "Mary is crazy. She wants Whitney to come out here and move in with us. I am not putting up with it. I have worked too hard for the little I have and I am not about to let her come in here and rob me blind." My mother agreed. She tried to talk some sense into grandma but it didn't work. The things she said about Whitney just a few days before were a total lie. She missed the drama Whitney brings to her life. She craves it. And before you knew it she was looking for her own place, because she had to have space for Whitney and she knew Aunt Frieda wasn't going to allow it. My mother and Elsa were livid. The one thing the doctors told her to stay clear of is the one thing she seems to be in pursuit of.

I have heard the saying, there's nothing like a mother's love, but damn sometimes you have to cut the cord and wrap it around yourself and allow your children to live their own lives. Yes, they'll make mistakes but grandma has never allowed Whitney to fall without her being the safety net that catches her. She is always there lending her a hand to pick her up when she falls. Elsa told her she needs to let Whitney fall flat on her face. Maybe then she'll grow up.

Whitney needs to stand on her own two feet. But grandma will never let her. And at this point my mother and Elsa are just about fed up. Well, the stupid Housewarming, Blessing shindig is fast approaching. My mother and father are still going back and forth. She wants all of us to be a happy family under one roof and he could care less about family. His main priority is sowing his wild oats. He may be married, but he enjoys the single life, living free and clear.

Well, all of the invitations have gone out and everyone has responded, but there is no family there to bless. The day before there was a knock at the door. It's this man. I instantly ran to get Lawrence. He asked the gentlemen, "How can we assist you?" The man says he was there to see

Mrs. Lola Hayes-Felder. So, we run upstairs to get our mother. We don't have the slightest clue what this man wants so we pull her to the side and ask her what's going on. Then she tells us. "After tomorrow, Twinkie is going to be out of our lives for good. I am finally leaving him. He doesn't want us, well we don't want him." Lawrence's and my faces lit up like little children at Christmas. It was just what we had always hoped and prayed for and now the day is finally here.

Then she went on to tell us the man was there to appraise our house. She was thinking of refinancing and getting a loan to get the house fixed up. This was everything we ever wanted. Lawrence and I couldn't believe she had finally come to her senses. After the man left, she went over the figures with Lawrence and me. We were all in the same mindframe. This was the right thing to do. I could hardly sleep that night. I just kept thinking over and over, after today we won't have to worry about him popping up and stopping us from enjoying ourselves in our own house. I went into Lawrence's room and he was wide eyed and bushytailed; and he felt the exact same way. He said, "Man, I am so proud of Ma. She is finally coming to her senses. I always told her she could do better than him. He has held us back in so many ways." Then for a split second I felt bad, because this is my father we are talking about. But then I thought about all the years of suffering and pain finally being over. My mother was with him all of those years, but in reality, he was never really with her. So, after that thought went out, so did the feelings of sadness.

The sun started to rise and the day began. There was a lot of running around that had to be done. We had to go and pick up food and drop things off. My mother stayed her distance from him today. And he felt it. He was trying to start conversations with her all day, but she wasn't falling for it. I just kept on calling Lawrence and telling him she was really serious this time. She won't even hold a conversation with him. Lawrence couldn't believe it. We were ecstatic. She had never been like this with him before. He asked her, "Do you need any help?" She turned and looked at him and said, "No, thank you, I am quite well doing it myself." He couldn't accept it. She has never talked to him in this tone, even when they argued. She has never been this forward.

Well, we finished putting everything together and the guests started to arrive. As always, grandma was the first to get there. She always says she is getting there to lend a helping hand. But she is actually there to help herself to some food. At the last function we had she actually ate a whole platter of shrimp. But that's Mary being herself. But not today, my mother was not having it. She made grandma sit downstairs in the basement. She put a movie on and told her to just sit back and relax. A little after that, Elsa and the crew arrived. My father was nicer than he'd ever been. He needed someone on his side. He is a great manipulator. He had them eating out of the palm of his hand.

The other guests strolled in bit by bit. Mary told Rev. Turnblad to come and sit by her. They have known each other all of their lives. So, she knew that if she got him to sit by her, my mother would bring the shrimp and crab balls down. She knew my mother would never refuse the Reverend. And she figured she could have a feast just for herself. But what she didn't know was that her plan was going to backfire. Rev. Turnblad can eat. He is a greedy little thing. He devoured those shrimp and crab balls. Mary couldn't believe it. She called me and Daphne over and said, "Baby, can the two of you go upstairs and get me something to eat?" I looked and said, "Grandma, didn't my mother just bring a platter down here for everybody?" She said, "Yes, she did but Rev. Turnblad ate it. The greedy little bastard, he didn't even offer me any of the shrimp or crab balls." Daphne and I couldn't help laughing. We told grandma we would see what we could do.

When I got upstairs, Lawrence came straggling into the house, and you could tell he didn't want to be there. But he knew we were getting rid of the no-good lame ass man. He pulled it together for my mother's sake and faked a smile so he could go down and greet everybody. I told Elsa about grandma and the reverend because she was in the kitchen. My mother was handling something. Elsa couldn't believe it. She gave me the extras from the shrimp platter so I could take them to grandma. Then Elsa had to run and tell my mother what happened. She said, "Now how long ago was it, when you took the platters downstairs for Rev. Turnblad?" My mother said, "It was about ten minutes ago. Why?" Then Elsa proceeded to tell her, "Rev. Turnblad is a greedy son of a bitch. He ate all of those damn shrimp. He is just a damn glutton. Isn't that a sin? I didn't know he could eat like that. Shit, he didn't even offer anything to anyone else. I know he is the Reverend but damn, right is right. That was at least fifty dollars worth of shrimp. I should go tell his ass he's going to have to pay for that. The little greedy asshole. He had better not ask for a plate when the food comes out." My mother was trying to get her attention to let her know that Rev. Turnblad was standing behind her the entire time. But she was too heated. She wasn't paying attention to my mother's signals. When she looked behind and saw him standing there, she was dumbfounded. She couldn't say one word. You could have bought her for a penny at that moment. He just smiled and said what a lovely house it was. He didn't even make mention of it. My mother couldn't help for laughing at the situation. Lawrence said he didn't say anything because he knew that he was wrong for eating like that. It really was a disgrace, but the reverend didn't seem to care. Then he asked my mother was she ready to begin.

We all gathered in the basement and formed a circle. Rev. Turnblad asked for the beautiful family to get into the center of the circle. He wanted to pray that my mother and father would grow together as a married couple and that the two of them along with Lawrence and me would grow as a family. The entire prayer was in vain in my opinion. How in the hell can we grow as a family when he didn't want us? He was doing this for show. He loves compliments. It wasn't about us as a family. He wanted people to rant and rave about his house. So, the whole time Rev. Turnblad stood there praying, Lawrence and I kept looking at each other shaking our heads and we were hoping our mother wasn't falling for it, because she seemed really into the prayer. She began to cry and it just didn't look good. After the prayer was over she had changed the script with my father. She was warming up to him, and that's when Lawrence left. He said he couldn't stand for her to go back on her word. And he couldn't watch if in fact she did. So, I was there to fight off the big bad wolf on my own. My mother was totally different. She was following him around like a lost puppy dog. She wasn't the same distant person towards him.

Then the lies started. He pulled Elsa, Uncle Eugene and Grandma into their bedroom and told them all of these lame brain stories about my mother, Lawrence and me. He said, "Elsa, would you please talk some sense in to your sister? I am trying to be the best husband I can be. But she acts really crazy. She gets jealous over crazy things and I would never do anything to hurt her. I have been faithful and I am trying to be a family man. I want my family to be together but she just keeps pushing me away." Elsa and grandma pulled my mother into the bathroom and told her, "This man really loves you. You shouldn't be this way. Give it a chance to work. You have nothing to lose but there is a lot to gain." My mother told them she was tired of him treating her any kind of way and that their marriage was over. Then they went back in to the room. Then he continued his accusations, but this time it was about Lawrence and me. He told them it was us that was holding my mother back. He said we didn't want her to be happy and we were feeding her head with lies about him. He actually turned them against us. Elsa and Uncle Eugene left out of the room so they could find me. Elsa told me she wanted to talk to me for a minute.

When I came upstairs, there was my aunt with this far-off look in her eyes. She said, "Why don't you and Lawrence want your mother to be happy?" I couldn't believe what I was hearing. I said, "Who told you something like that? That's all we want. But this is not going to make her happy." She said, "How do you know?" I said, "Because if this is what she wanted she would come to me and Lawrence. No one knows the type of person my father is. You all don't see how he makes her cry. You aren't there. All you can do is go off of what he says and what you don't know is he is such a big liar." Uncle Eugene jumped in and said, "Well, this is what your mother wants and you all need to support and be happy for her." I looked at the both of them with a coldhearted stare. My mother and father were walking into the room at this point. And I told all of them then and there in my firmest voice, "I will support her if this is what she wants, but I'm telling all of you all right here and right now. This shit is not going to last. And when it starts to get ugly, I don't want any of you coming to me and telling me that I was right. Because I already know it." My father just stared at me. Then he looked at Elsa and said, "I told you they were the main problem." I looked at him and walked out of the room. I instantly called Lawrence. He couldn't believe it. He said, "Hey the hell with all of them. We know what the situation is and none of them have to live with it. This is our life, so don't you worry about it."

I asked him could he come and pick me up. The longer I stayed in that house the sicker I got to my stomach. He said I should ask my mother if I could leave. I went and asked her but she told me no. So, I had to stay there with all of them and endure these false accusations. The saddest part of the entire day was the fact that my mother totally forgot the plans we had made just the day before. I was devastated. The happiest day in my life took a complete turn and it became the worst.

The day started to wind down and everyone was leaving. None of the other guests knew what was going on. They ranted and raved about how perfect the day was. Elsa and her crew were about to leave. I said goodbye to Daphne, Tico, and Ahmad but I didn't have anything to say to anybody else in the family. They all turned on me and I couldn't deal with them. I resented them for taking my father's side. I felt betrayed. I didn't even say goodbye to Elsa because my feelings were deeply hurt. After everyone left, I got my things together and I headed for the door. Then my mother said, "Oh, you can take your things and put them into your room. We are staying here for tonight." I said, "What room! My room is at 1600 Sixth Street, at my home. I am not staying here. Can I call my brother and ask him to come and get me?" She said, "No, you cannot, we are staying here. You can go home in the morning. It's not going to kill you to stay here for one night." I went up to the room that was supposed to be mine, but it was burning up. The air conditioner was not working. I went and told her that I was ready to go home. Then the asshole jumped in and said I was going to have to deal with the heat because I was not going home. I said well then I am sleeping downstairs in the family room. He didn't want me to sleep down there because he said that I was going to mess up the cushioning in his couch. My mother actually had to talk him into letting me sleep down there. I knew this could not be a good thing, us staying over there. But I dealt with it. I really couldn't do anything else but deal with it.

I prayed that night that God would allow my mother to see him for the slime he is, and that she would feel the same way she had been feeling about him in the days before the housewarming. I could hardly sleep. I called Lawrence and gave him the low down. He said he figured this was going to happen and we should prepare ourselves for what was about to go down. I tossed and turned all night. Not knowing was really having an affect on me. Then before I knew it the sun was coming up. I couldn't wait any longer. I had to get out of there. I went upstairs and knocked on the door. My father yelled, "Are you out of your damn mind? It's too early. Take your ass back to bed." I said, "I need to get home. I have cramps, so my menstrual cycle is probably about to start. So, unless you want blood everywhere I need to get home because I don't have any pads over here." He didn't say a damn word after that. A couple minutes later my mother came down the stairs. I was lying my socks off. I just needed to get the hell out of there. I think I would have suffocated if I had to stay in there another minute. We didn't say anything while we were riding home. Then as we were approaching Sixth Street she told me, "I need to sit down and have a talk with you and Lawrence. There is going to be a big change for all of us." And I knew it. He had suckered her into staying with him. Lawrence told me this was going to happen. He was used to it. So, when we got into the house she told me to go and wake Lawrence. I went up to the stairs and when I opened his door, he said, "What in the hell is your problem waking me up this early?" I said, "Your mother wants to talk to us. She said come down there right now." He said, "Oh shit, this must not be good because you said my mother. What is it?" I said, "Man, I don't know, but whatever it is, it's not good because she says she needs to talk to us about some changes." So, he put on some shorts and we headed downstairs.

She told us to sit down. Then she said, "We're moving. Start packing your things now. I plan on closing up the house by the end of the week." I couldn't believe her. Lawrence didn't say anything; He got up and went back upstairs. For a minute, a sense of hatred came over me. I just stared at my mother with a blank look. I couldn't believe she would do this to us. Especially since the man came and she filled our heads with those pipe dreams. She really let us down and she didn't even give us a say in our own lives. I couldn't even look at her anymore. I had no feelings whatsoever for her at this moment. I went upstairs so I could talk to Lawrence. He said, "Don't worry, before it's over, we'll be back here and she'll be begging for our forgiveness. This shit is not going to last. I give it six months, one year at the most and they won't be together. Twinkie is used to living the single life. How in the hell is he going to deal with all of us living over there? Believe me the walls are going to start closing in on him and when they do she's going to have to come back to us." Then I broke down. I couldn't believe this was happening. I just laid in my brother's arms and cried like a baby. He said, "Don't worry. We are in this together. You always have me, no matter what. I'll always be here." I knew he was right. For the first time, we were fighting this battle on our own. We were the rebels now. I did the only that I could do. I began to pack. When the news got out in the neighborhood, everyone on Sixth Street was sad. It was like some one had died. People were coming in the house with somber looks on their faces. They couldn't believe it. Our family had been in this neighborhood since my grandmother's father was a child. That's a lot of history and now we are leaving it all behind.

My mother was staying her distance from Lawrence and me. She knew she told us all of these things and out of the blue she shattered the dreams we had. We thought we were getting rid of the fool and instead she is inviting him back into our lives and we would be under his roof. This is his territory now that we are dealing with; we will be fighting a losing battle. This is all new. But this is what she wanted to do. And we have no other choice but to follow her lead. I prayed and prayed the whole day, hoping she would come to her senses. Lawrence said, "I don't know what he did to her or what he said last night, but whatever it was it had to have been worth it. Because I can't see Ma treating us like this, it's like she is under a spell." I didn't care. I hated the situation. Then we overheard her on the phone. She was talking to Elsa. She was crying at this point. She said we were treating her like shit and she wanted us to be happy for her. She was finally getting the chance to turn his house into our home. Then Elsa asked to speak to Lawrence and me. I told her I didn't have anything to say to any of them. I felt I said all I had to say at the housewarming. But she insisted that we talk. She said, "Now listen. I don't want you to be upset with me. I know this is hard for you all to get used to. But it's what your mother wants. Please just give it a try for her sake." I said, "Listen, I told you all before its not going to last. You see, you all are going off of his words. I'm going off of his actions. It's a major difference. You all don't know the hell he has put us through over the years. So, I'm telling you now don't come back to me in a few months trying to talk to me because he has shown his true colors. Because I am not going to listen." She told me to give it a chance and if it is not working in a month, I can come and stay with her. But that was something I knew they would have never allowed. So, I went along with the conversation and ended it by agreeing with her. Lawrence said, "Listen Elsa, there is nothing you or anyone else can say that is going to make me change my mind. I am not happy for her and I am not going to be happy for her. How can you expect me to smile when I know my mother is going to eventually cry? And she is going to cry sooner than later. And when she does, I'm still supposed to be happy and smiling, right?" Elsa couldn't say a word to him. She knew he was right but she still held her ground and stayed on my mother's side. I guess it was a thing that the adults had to stick together.

Lawrence and I decided we were on our own. There was no one we could listen to because we were the outcasts. We were making our mother miserable. When in actuality it was the other way around. She totally turned on us. But she wanted her marriage to work, so who could blame her? Even if her husband is a snake, in every sense of the word. Everybody in the family was focused on us. Even Daphne and Tico, Elsa had them call because maybe they could talk some sense into us since they had been through the same thing when they moved to Leesburg.

Grandma called and when I got on the phone with her, she said, "The two of you are selfish. You have the chance to finally get off of Sixth Street. Your father has fixed up the house for you all and you need to make the best of it. That man loves you all very much." So, I said, "Yeah, well if that was the case, he wouldn't have let three years pass by before we moved in with him. Grandma, I appreciate your concern but I am tired of people talking about things they obviously don't have any knowledge of." After that moment, she didn't say anything else to me regarding the situation. At this point I was really tired of everyone coming at me and my brother. It wasn't the same situation as Elsa and her kids. Uncle Eugene came down and got them from the beginning. He didn't marry Elsa and wait years before they became a family. He didn't treat them like shit and then still expect them to welcome him with open arms. Elsa didn't send them mixed signals about the whole ordeal.

Twinkie married my mother then kept her dangling on a string for three years before he stepped up to the plate to move us in. I just felt that the best thing that I could do was not say any thing to anybody. I was better off that way. Lawrence agreed with me. He said, "Let them feel however they want to feel. Just keep your mouth closed. If anyone says anything, tell them that I said you can no longer talk about it."

So, we moved in. Lawrence told my mother he was going to stay at the house for a few days, so he could clean up. He was trying to buy time. He didn't want to live there. My mother got rid of everything in the house. She gave all of the furniture to grandma, because she had finally found a place. And anything else she threw out. I was totally miserable. I didn't have much to say to her. At the time, I was working my summer job, so I would ride to work with her but I wouldn't say anything to her. I started writing poetry and I would leave suicide notes around the house. I wanted her to suffer the same way she was making Lawrence and me suffer. Lawrence knew I was really down, so he bought me tickets to see my favorite group in concert. He bought tickets for my mother, his girlfriend, me and himself. He thought that maybe if we got her alone she would tell us something. But she didn't say a word involving the whole ordeal with the move. We really enjoyed ourselves. After the concert was over, we noticed that someone had hit my mother's car. We drove the car to the police precinct and my mother called my father. He said, "I'm not coming to the damn police station. You shouldn't have parked your car on the damn street." My mother was so hurt. I just laughed. It was starting quicker than I ever imagined. After we got the police report we went home. But when we got there, he had made some changes. He had moved out of their bedroom and into the basement. When we walked in, he didn't speak to either of us. I couldn't believe it. When we left that afternoon, he was in good spirits. My mother cried. I felt bad for her but that's the decision she made when she moved in there. I was excited I was leaving for a whole week. I was going to a multicultural program at Georgetown University. It would be like going to school during my summer break. But we were getting paid and I would be out of his house for a whole week. Lawrence said, "Man, I am not staying in there this week. I couldn't possibly deal with their shit without you." So, he stayed out with one of his many girlfriends. I didn't even call home the entire time I was gone. I didn't see the need to. I felt betrayed by everyone. Lawrence was the only person I had. He was my rock during these hard times.

Grandma moved into her new place and was so excited. Whitney seemed to be on the right track. She was too far from the old neighborhood to hang out with her running buddies. She was taking care of grandma and her children. Grandma didn't have to worry about going to work and worrying about the children being alone because their mother was there with them. Things were running smoothly. If only grandma would stop smoking weed. The temptation is greater for Whitney because grandma is still getting high.

Elsa is Elsa. Everyone in the town knows her. She is famous in her own right. When we walk through the malls with her, everyone screams her name. Everyone wants to get close. That's just her personality. Even after all of these years it still brings tears to all of our eyes to see how far she has come. Daphne is doing a lot better. She is learning to deal with her emotions. Plus, she'll be out of there in a year so she is trying to be easy. She has never been this mellow. She hasn't been arguing with Elsa and Uncle Eugene at all. She did a total three hundred and sixty-degree turn for the better. Everyone was so proud of her. Tico works constantly. He never gets a break. He doesn't even come down to visit us with the rest of the family because he is always working. Moving there was the best thing that could've happened to him. It truly saved his life because all of his friends on Sixth Street are selling drugs. And that's one of the main reasons my mother gave us for wanting to get rid of the house and being away from there. It never bothered her before. Lawrence said it was just her way of trying to cover up the fact she knew how wrong she was when she changed her mind about staying with Twinkie and us moving in with him. But there was nothing we could do. She was our mother.

When I got back from the program, I didn't want to go back to his house. My mother took me to Sixth Street. That was my home. I told her I would sleep on the floor if I had to, but I couldn't face another day living in the house with that man. I couldn't deal with the mood swings. I asked if was he going through menopause because of the way that he was acting. She said Lawrence and I owed it to ourselves to make our family work. She was putting all of this pressure on us and we weren't the ones that kept her in limbo for three years. But now they are putting all of the blame on us. How could we possibly be comfortable with the situation when he kept us waiting for three years? We would have never had a problem if he did it right from the get go. We were fed up with the situation. But I had no other choice; I had to deal with it. Lawrence could leave at any minute because he is a grown man. But I can't because this is my mother and father. Who could I run to but Lawrence? We spent the day on Sixth Street. We had only been gone a couple of weeks but it seemed like an eternity. Everyone missed us. I didn't know how my mother felt, but I was missing them too. Lawrence still hadn't gotten all of his things together. He said he wasn't moving out until she made him. Well after spending the day at my real home, I wanted to go back to the dungeon. I was tired. I had been gone all week and I wanted to speak to Walter. Some girls had called and said he was flirting with them. I wanted to get down to the bottom of their story.

When I got into the house, everything was back to normal. The two of them were sickening. He had moved back into the room with her. He made an announcement. He was going to Pennsylvania for two days. I wanted to jump for joy, but I composed myself. I went up into my room so I could express my feelings. It may have only been two days, but it was enough. I wouldn't have to deal with him. The next morning, I got up and I could breathe knowing he wasn't going to be there. Lawrence came into my room and started to jump on my bed. I said, "Man, I don't know why you are acting like this. He is coming back." Then he said, "Yeah, I

know, but at least for a couple days we don't have to walk on egg shells."
I totally agreed with that.

My mother was a different person since he wasn't around but I couldn't
allow myself to feel anything for her. Lawrence felt the same way. She had
really done some serious damage this time. There was no way Lawrence
and I would let her back into our inner circle. Especially since Twinkie
was coming back, I don't think I could have taken it if she turned on us
again. So, I kept my distance. That night there was a knock at the door.
I should I say a bang at the door. It had to be about two in the morning.
I instantly ran to see where Lawrence was. I was afraid maybe something
had happened to my brother as the banging got louder and the doorbell
was ringing. My mother emerged from the bathroom that separates our
rooms. We went to the window to see who it was. It wasn't a police car,
therefore we knew everything was alright and it was just a visitor. We didn't
recognize the car so we decided to go down and peek out of the blinds.
And to our surprise it was my older sister, Twinkie's daughter and her
children – all six of them. She was drunk and decided to visit her father.
And bring the children over to see their deadbeat granddad. My mother
doesn't believe in turning family away so of course she let them in and
boy did we have a night ahead of us. She danced and danced. Lawrence
came strolling in the house at around three thirty and said his hellos
and went to bed. We weren't that lucky. They left at sunrise. My mother
told Twinkie about it when he called and of course he cursed her out.
He wasn't pleased she allowed them to come into his house. My mother
said, "Twinkie, you have to realize this is not just your house. This is *our*
house." Twinkie said, "No, I beg to differ. That is my house and if you
don't like it you can leave and go back to your house."

She hung up on him and decided when she got home she would start
to pack her things. When he returned home the next day her things were

packed and ready to go. She didn't really have any intentions of leaving, she just wanted to scare him when he came into the house and he saw her things all ready to be put in her car. So, when he walked in the door he saw her things and began to chase her around the house. It was some type of game to them. It was like they were running a marathon. She had this duffle bag on her back running through the house and she was tired. He would give her time to catch her breath and then when she was ready to go back at it he would give her a running start. They kept running past my room and I got sick of it so I closed my door and locked it.

Walter and I broke up. So, my little heart was broken. And that was my main focus. Lawrence took me up to Sixth Street for the day. I just laid on the floor and cried. Lawrence bought me a stereo thinking it would make me feel better but it didn't. As I laid there the phone started to ring. It was Walter. He asked, "What do you want?" I said, "I didn't call you. I don't want you. You called me so what do you want?" He said he had seen Lawrence and that Lawrence told him I was a wreck. I couldn't believe it. I went outside and I got Lawrence. He said, "With all that we have going on with Twinkie and Ma, you need someone other than me that's going to make you smile. I really like Walter, that's why I went and told him you were really upset. So please, for my sake make up with him." I couldn't believe him but I knew he had my best interest at heart so I couldn't be mad with him.

It was crazy. Everyone else seemed to have it together. For once it was my mother and her children that had all of the problems. Grandma and Whitney were doing so well. Whitney started dating this guy. He seemed to be a nice man but there was something about him I couldn't put my finger on. Grandma loved him. She always sings his praises. The children have adjusted to their new house. My mother decided to throw grandma a birthday party and she invited our immediate family and I got to invite some of my friends over to see the dungeon I had ranted and raved about over the course of the last few weeks. And what an embarrassment it turned out to be. My friends and I were sitting in the backyard while my family was in the house. And here comes Twinkie with a bucket and mop mopping the wooden deck. My friend David wanted to know who in the hell was this man. I just put my head down. He didn't have anything better to do than to harass me. I couldn't believe it. He is such an asshole. He wanted to see what my friends and I were talking about. I went and told my mother and instead of her saying he was wrong, she took his side and said maybe we were giving him a reason to suspect us of doing something. But I chose not to cause a scene because it was my grandmother's birthday and Elsa and all of the other family members were there and I just pushed my feelings aside and let it go for that moment. I called my brother and told him about it. He couldn't believe it. He asked did I want him to come and get us but I said no because my mother would have punished me later for it.

A few weeks passed and things were the same. My mother and I went over to see grandma, and while we were standing outside, Mary went looking through her car. She was trying to find some money. My mother said, "Mama, what are you doing? I don't have any money in there." And just as she said it grandma found six bucks inside of a secret compartment. My mother left that money for gas or emergency reasons. Grandma said, "Well, if you don't have any money this must not be yours. Thank you, Jesus. He must have left that in there just for me." My mother was so mad, but she let it slide. It was her mother. At least that's what she always says to me whenever I try to tell her grandma is just using her.

Well, Elsa and the gang are doing just fine. Daphne drives here every chance she gets. A lot of the time, I don't even think Elsa knows she is here. And now that we have moved, Elsa never knows where she is and what she is doing when she comes. Daphne has been hanging with a group of older girls and Elsa is always worried. She parties until the wee hours of the morning. Lawrence has seen her out a couple of times at cabarets he and a group of his friends throw. He chased her out because he caught her with a drink in her hand. Tico is Tico, he is such a dork. He is only worried about working and playing ball. But he won't grow. I don't get it. His mother and father are a nice height and he is so short. My mother always tells him he shouldn't worry because he is going to shoot up overnight, just like Lawrence did. But he is not interested in hearing it. He wants to be in the NBA and it's not going to happen if he is four feet tall. He would be turning thirteen in a few weeks and still looks like he is about eight.

Things haven't changed in our household either. We are still a house divided. Lawrence and I stick together and my mother is still the same. She acts like we are the enemy. But the enemy is in the room lying next to her every night. Lawrence said, "Hey don't worry she'll find out for herself. I just hope we're still around when she does."

DISASTER STRIKES

Well, things were a little better. Lawrence and I were dealing with the situation as best we could. My mother and father decided it was best they go ahead and sell the house on Sixth Street. That way it would give us no reason to hang around there anymore. He was trying to make us forget our past. How in the hell could we just bypass a whole lifetime? Sixth Street was in our family forever. My great grandparents grew up in the neighborhood, so how could we just forget? But in the end, it was going to be my mother's decision and she went along with it. Twinkie got one of his sons to come up and do the necessary work to the house to get it ready for the realtors. They boarded the windows and put padlocks on the doors. This was so Lawrence and I couldn't get in unless they were there.

Lawrence had a stand across the street. He sold clothes and shoes. I racked up for school. I wanted to be a nice dresser since I was going to high school this year. But Lawrence treated me like any other customer. I paid full price for everything. He said he was teaching me how to deal with business. We may have been family but the two just didn't mix. I didn't mind. I knew on the back end I was going to get all of my money back.

It was really good having my brother to depend on. He is a good brother. If I could choose, I would say he is the best brother anyone could have.

We laughed and joked all of the time now because we were considered the outcasts no one wanted to be bothered with because they figured we were treating our mother wrong. But it's just as Lawrence says, "The hell with them. When the bastard turns on them they will see. Then they'll be coming back to us wanting to express their regret. But by then it will be too late."

Time was flying by with all that was going on I didn't realize I would be going to school in a few days. Then as I was preparing for church. Lawrence called and left out of the house early that morning so that he could go and set up his stand. He drove past our house and noticed that the boards on one of the windows was down. He got out of the car and went in the yard and he saw someone had broken into the house. They stole most of his things he had left in there. He was furious. He couldn't believe someone would do something like this to him. He told my mother he needed her to get up there and soon because he couldn't get into the house without the key to the padlock. He didn't want to upset her over the phone, so he told her he couldn't set up his stand without some of the things he had left in the house the night before. We rushed up to the house and when we got there we realized that it was all a lie. The front window was broken and you could tell someone had forced their way into the house. When my mother opened the door, we saw that everything was gone. Lawrence had a lot of things in there and someone took everything. You could tell it was someone who knew what was in there because they went straight for his things and got out of there. They didn't touch my father's tools or anything else that was lying around. When my father got there, we thought he was going to go off but for the first time he was civilized. He was interested in Lawrence. He wanted to make sure Lawrence was alright. But our brother Clarence, on the other hand was craving blood. He wanted to go out and whip the hell out of the person that was responsible for taking all of Lawrence's things. Lawrence wanted to go around the neighborhood to see if anyone had seen or heard anything. After walking around for a couple hours and no one had any information concerning the incident, Lawrence decided he was going to get a haircut. When he sat down in the barber's chair he noticed this guy holding a new VCR and it looked familiar. He said, "Hey that is a really nice VCR, where did you get it from." The guy said, "Oh, I just bought this from this crack-head. I think his name is Melvin. I only gave him twenty dollars and I think it's brand new."

Lawrence jumped up out of the seat. He couldn't believe it. Melvin was his mechanic. He was someone that had been in our house and knew where Lawrence kept all of his things. Lawrence looked over at the man and said, "It is brand new. Melvin broke into my house and stole it from me." The guy asked, "Do you want it back?" Lawrence told him, "Man, just keep it you paid your money for it but thank you for asking and thank you for buying it because now I know I have someone to blame. It has been driving me crazy all day and now I know who to deal with." He told his barber that he would wait for the haircut because he had to handle the situation with Melvin.

He came back to the house and when he got there he told my mother and father what he had just found out. Immediately, Clarence stopped what he was doing and he was ready to go and find Melvin. He said, "Lawrence, just point me in the right direction because I am going to set this punk straight." Lawrence didn't want to involve anyone but it was too late. He said, "Clarence, just stay here. I can handle it." Clarence said, "Listen, Lawrence, either you are going to let me deal with this guy or I am going to deal with you." Lawrence stepped aside and let Clarence do his thing. They went down the street to the apartments where Melvin lived. Lawrence went and knocked on Melvin's door. This little old lady came to the door. Lawrence said, "Hello, ma'am, I am a friend of Melvin's. Could you tell him to come outside for a moment?"

Melvin had seen them coming and told his mother to tell them he wasn't home. She said, "I'm sorry, baby, Melvin is gone out of town. He went down south to visit some family." Lawrence said, "Oh really, well when did he leave if I can ask?" She said, "Oh, I don't mind, baby. He left about three days ago."

Lawrence said, "I find that surprising because he just fixed my car the day before yesterday." She said, "Well, he must have left right after he fixed your car sweetheart." Lawrence said, "Well thank you and sorry for troubling you. If you talk to him can you tell him that Lawrence came by and that he really needs to see him in reference to his car?" The little old woman nodded her head and closed the door.

Clarence said, "Lawrence, you know she was lying. Why didn't you tell her the truth? You should have told her he broke into your house and that you wanted your things back." Lawrence said, "Clarence, no. I couldn't do that to her. Something like that could have given her a heart attack. I have grandmothers and a mother. I wouldn't want someone doing that to any of them.

Clarence said, "I guess you have a point, but hey she was lying and that means that she is an accessory. Where did he take the stuff? In that apartment and she knows where he got it from and that's why she was lying for him. Lawrence said, "Man, do not worry about it. I have a plan. We will just wait. He is going to come out of there eventually. And they waited. We were back in the house wondering what was taking them so long. My mother was frantic. All she could see was Clarence whipping him to death and the two of them being carted off to prison. My father said, "Well, whatever they do to him he is deserving of it. He had no damn business coming in here." My mother said, "Twinkie don't say that. That isn't right." I just stood in the door way praying to God everything was alright. Lawrence and Clarence waited and waited until finally the door opened up. It was the little old woman. She said, "You young men are still out here. Now I told you that Melvin wasn't here and I don't know when he'll be back. Now either you move your black asses away from my door or I am calling the damn police."

Lawrence said, "Well then call the police because I am not moving. And when they get here I am going to tell them how Melvin broke into my house last night and when they go in there and search for fingerprints it will be the two of you going to jail." The old woman got scared at this point. She said, "Oh I have something for you. She went into the house and when she came back she had a butcher's knife and she chased them out of the building. She was yelling, "Don't ever let me catch the two of you lurking around my door way again, because if I do then you will be leaving with extra assholes." I was still standing in the doorway and I saw Lawrence and Clarence running down the street. I said, "Ma, something happened because here they come." My mother and father came rushing to the door. By this time, they were entering the yard laughing. We were trying to figure out what the hell was so funny. But we waited until they got themselves together before we asked.

Clarence said, "Don't worry, he will have to come out of that house sometime and when he does he will get it." Lawrence said, "Man, I know." We were holding onto their every word because we still had no clue what they were talking about. Then they began to give us the chain of events. My father said, "Well, you should have taken the knife and scared the hell out of the both of them." My mother, being her normal self said, "Twinkie that is so wrong." He said, "Hey, she is an accessory. And she was the one with the knife." My mother thought about it and she left it alone. My father had a point. But there was nothing we could do because Melvin was not coming out of that house and that old woman was guarding her doorway like a hawk. So, we all went back to doing our usual thing.

I was getting ready for school. Lawrence and I stayed up the entire night talking about his high school days. He told me what teachers to watch out for and all of the areas to hide out in if I wanted to ditch a class. We went up to Sixth Street for Labor Day. We hung around while Lawrence and Clarence were on looout for Melvin. No one in the neighborhood had seen him. After a few hours of hanging out and playing catch-up to see what was going on in the hood, we decided we would go home. On the way there my mother started to get really sick. She ate some Chinese food and she was having pains in her stomach. We rushed home.

I couldn't sleep the whole night. It was really crazy because I was starting high school the next day. It seemed like the time just flew by. I had just recently started Junior High and now I was going to the tenth grade. I couldn't sleep at all I kept thinking about how much of a difference it would be. When I finally dozed off it was time to wake up. My mother woke me up. She said, "Lana, I can't take you to your orientation today because I still feel terrible, so Lawrence said since he knows all of the teachers he will take you. Is that okay? That was fine with me.

We got to the school late. Lawrence was being his normal comedic self. People were looking at us and he would turn around and under his breath he would say, "What in the hell are you looking at? Turn around and pay attention." A couple of people who heard him just laughed. When we sat down the principal was up giving her speech. She looked over in our section and she looked directly at the two of us. She said, "We do not and will not tolerate students chewing gum in our auditorium. There are two young people in here right now in that section. I will not point them out. They know exactly who they are. Lawrence stood up and shouted, "She was talking to me in case any of you wanted to know." I was so embarrassed but it was funny and everyone got a kick out of it, even the parents. He sat down and allowed the principal to finish her speech. Once the orientation was over he wanted to walk around with me until I was settled. We got my schedule and we were off to my homeroom class. On our way there was a table of refreshments for the parents and guardians. Lawrence said he wanted a donut. The security guard rushed over to the table and said, "Hey, young man what do you think you are doing? That table is strictly for parents and guardians. Put that donut back and you won't get into any trouble." Lawrence looked around and saw the man who was talking to him. He said, "Do you know who I am? I am not a student." At this point, people were starting to crowd around him and the guard was getting agitated. He said, "Listen, boy, take yourself to class or you will be going home to stay on the first day." Lawrence laughed at him and said, "Listen, I am not a student. Do you see that young lady over there? I am her guardian. Our mother died and I am here to see that she gets around the school. So, would you please go and harass somebody else." The man said, "Okay, now I see I am going to have to call for back up." The next thing that we knew, the police were coming around the corner. Luckily, Lawrence knew one of the officers from his high school days and he got everything under control. The security guard said, "Sir, I am so sorry. I didn't mean any disrespect." Lawrence said, "Oh, now you want to be humble? Just a couple of minutes ago I was a low-life." The man apologized and that was that.

We walked around the school and he introduced me to all of his former teachers and when I got to my first class he said, "I will be back to pick you up this evening, so be outside." I said, "Okay, and thanks for bringing me up here." He left and I went on about my day.

Later on that afternoon I saw a girl I knew from Sixth Street. She said, "Lana, your crazy brother is in the auditorium registering students for their classes. I said, "Yeah, whatever. Lawrence left hours ago." She said, "Honestly, he is in there with Mr. Franks." I didn't have my last class, so I went into the auditorium. Low and behold this fool was sitting there with the counselors giving students their schedules. I couldn't believe it. He had been there the whole day. I walked up to him and he thought he was so important. He said, "Young lady, do you have a pass?" I said, "Lawrence, I don't need a pass. I don't have my last class today." He said, "I just stayed around in the event you needed me." I said, "Need you for what? I am in high school now. He asked the security guard if it was alright for him to take me home since my last class was canceled. And because of the incident that morning he was more that willing to let me leave. I had to go to the bathroom so he waited outside the door. A girl came in behind me and she just stared at me. I felt uncomfortable so I left out of there as quick as I could. When I got out my crazy brother was standing in the corner biting his nails. I was trying to figure out what was going on. He said, "What did she say to you?" I didn't know what in the hell he was talking about. He said, "The girl that came into the bathroom behind you, what did she say to you?" I said, "She didn't say anything. Why? Was she supposed too?" He said, "That chick is nuts. I was involved with her but she went psycho on me. And when I saw her I tried to walk in the other direction but she saw me. I told her my girlfriend was in the bathroom. She said she was going to stab you."

I said, "Man, are you crazy? I am telling Ma on you." So when the girl came out of the bathroom, he started to hug on me like I was his woman. I couldn't help but laugh at him, he is such a joker. But he is my brother; I couldn't allow the girl to think that he was a liar. So me with my dumb self I went along with it. He took me home and we laughed and laughed about it. The next day when I got to school, I found out that my brother was infamous. All of the teachers adored him, all the guys wanted to be like him, and all of the girls were in love with him. I couldn't see what all of the hoopla was about. To me he was just Lawrence. I couldn't wait to get home to tell him what was going on.

As I was leaving school and heading back to Sixth Street to tell him about my day, I saw Clarence's little car speeding down the street. Then I saw Chucky's car speeding behind him. I instantly thought something was wrong with my brother. I dropped my book bag and ran down the street. Then when I got to the corner, the cars were speeding down the street in the opposite direction. Denise walked over to me and told me that they had found Melvin and that Lawrence and Clarence were going to catch him. I stayed outside the entire time waiting for him to come back. About an hour later the two cars came riding down the street. Lawrence and Chucky got out and Clarence followed shortly after them. None of them said a word. They were all just standing there. I thought of the worst thing possible. I said, "Lawrence, you all didn't beat him to death, did you?" He said, "Girl, shut the hell up." I said, "Well, the way you all are acting, what is a person suppose to think?" He said, "No, what you need to do is stay in a child's place." I just walked away because I didn't want to get into anything with him. I knew he was upset and he was all I had. So, I just let it go.

Then Clarence came in and told everything. He looked over at Lawrence and said, "Man, I can't believe you." Lawrence walked out. Clarence began to tell us what had happened. He said, "When we finally caught him I started to beat on him. I was whipping him good and this fool started to cry." So, I jumped in and said, "Well what do you expect? You were whipping on him." Clarence said, "Girl, didn't Lawrence just tell you to stay in your place." I rolled my eyes and walked into the other room. He said, "It wasn't Melvin crying. It was Lawrence." I fell on the floor laughing. Clarence said, "He told me it was enough. He had suffered enough and we needed to let him go." Clarence was livid. But Lawrence didn't seem to care much. Lawrence is soft-hearted, he cared more about Melvin being hurt than he did his things being stolen. In the midst of all this we never realized that this was the beginning of a long spiral that was only falling deeper and deeper into the pits of hell.

The next day everything went back to normal, or so we thought. Lawrence got his revenge on Melvin and everything was good. Then the phone bill came in. For some reason this month it seemed a little heavier than normal. My mother usually pays the bill without opening it but today things were different. When she opened it, BAM! It hit her; there was a long-distance phone call that was eighty five dollars. She approached my father instantly, because he was the only one in the house during the day. And, of course, he put the blame on us. He said, "Why are you accusing me of that. I don't even use the phone. I don't know anyone outside of DC. It was probably Lawrence or Lana. You need to be checking with them instead of harassing me." So, she took him at his word and she decided to come to Lawrence and me. Naturally we had no idea what she was talking about. Then she threatened us. She said, "You all are denying it. Okay, but if I find out it was either of you I am going to be very upset." She said something about calling the phone company thinking it was going to make one of us crack, but how in the world could we or would we confess to something we didn't do? She ranted and raved about one of us doing it and making us pay for our calls but it didn't matter. Lawrence and I looked at her like she was out of her damn mind and thought no more about it.

The next morning, she went to work and called the phone company. The lady said, "Ma'am, this call came from your house and someone there had to make it. My advice to you would be to call the number to see if the people know someone in your house." My mother thought that was an excellent idea and she took the lady's advice. And when she called she got more that an earful. She didn't speak to anyone but she found out who made the phone call. It was Twinkie. And his shit had finally hit the fan. There was a woman on the answering machine and she was leaving a message for him that they needed to talk. The message said, "Hello this is Martha. I am not in right now but Gavin if this is you I really need to speak with you." She hung the phone up. She couldn't believe her ears. What in the hell is going on? This dude has been stepping out on her. Now she knew the reason he stopped speaking to us before he went out of town. And now she knew it wasn't a business trip. He never thought his ass was going to get caught but now the roosters had finally come home to nest. And she could finally see him for the dog everyone else knew he was. She instantly called the house, but he was already gone. He was at the house on Sixth Street doing some work thinking that he was going to get the big pay-off when the place was sold.

She couldn't wait until five o'clock because his ass never thought she was going to go through with calling. When she got there, she confronted him. She asked him, "Who in the hell is Martha and why is she leaving messages for you to call her." He looked like he had just seen the ghost of his dead mother. He looked over and said, "I don't know what you are talking about." She was outraged. How dare he stand there in her face and lie like this. She said, "It's funny you would say that because this bitch knows what I am talking about. And she knows you oh too well. You didn't think that your shit was going to surface. Well I guess you are just too old and to stupid to be up on it like you used to. Do you remember that phone call I asked you about and you gave me that long drawn out speech? Well, you no good son of a bitch, you've been found out. I just want you to know I called the number and it was you she wanted to speak to. She had a message on her phone specifically for you. She says that the two of you really need to talk."

He looked at her with this cold stare. He stood there for a moment. He was trying to gather his thoughts. He knew he needed a good comeback but this time he had none. This caught him by surprise. He never thought she would follow through with calling the phone company and he had no idea where in the hell she got the notion about calling the number. She said, "You old decrepit bastard you had better be thinking of a good one because there is nothing you could say to make me forgive your ass." He said, "Don't you think we should discuss this when we get home? The people in the neighborhood will hear you and then they'll think I am doing something to you." She looked over at him and said, "They will only be thinking to themselves I told you so, because no one thought we should be together in the first place. I was the stupid naïve one because I never thought I would have to put up with you cheating. That was my stupidity. I hate your ass and I am leaving you. So be prepared."

He said, "Well if you are leaving me then why in the hell am I fixing up this raggedy ass place. I am going to pack up my shit and I am going home. I don't have to put up with this shit. And don't come back crying to me when you realize you were wrong."

She couldn't believe him. She stormed out and told me to get my things. Clarence said he would ride back to the house with us because he didn't want to ride with dad. Everyone was furious with him. Lawrence said he would be home late because he didn't want to be involved in the nonsense. The three of us got into the car and the whole ride was centered on my father's adulterous ass. And Clarence let out a mouthful. He apologized to my mother because he knew all along what was going on. Come to find out this woman has been in the picture the entire time.

Oh, dear Clarence let the cat out of the bag. He told her everything that he knew. He said, "Lola, you have been like a mother to me and I can't see you going out like that. My father is so wrong and I am sorry for being a part of the deception all of these years." This woman has been coming down every weekend from Philly playing the role of the woman of the house on those weekends when he made something up to keep my mother away. We stopped at a stoplight close to the house and my father was in the lane right next to us. You could see the terror in his eyes. My mother beeped the horn. They both rolled down their windows and she shouted to him, "Worry, you son of a bitch! Worry, because I am going to whip your ass. I am going to make you feel the pain that I feel. You have broken my heart and I am going to break you." His look only intensified then the light turned and he sped off. He was trying to get the hell away from us as fast as he could.

Clarence was like a little songbird. He was singing the entire time. I looked over at him and said, "No disrespect to you. I am sure my mother is glad you are telling her all of this, but why are you speaking up now? You knew this all along and you said nothing. Why are you confessing everything to her now?"

He said I had nothing to do with it. That I should stay a little girl because I had no business in what was going on. And I told him that as long as this situation involved my mother and father, I didn't care how old I was in some way or another I had a lot to do with it. My mother intervened and said I had a point. Why didn't he speak up before now? He was just as guilty as my father because he knew and he was probably smiling up in this woman's face, eating her cooking and playing a role. The same way he does my mother like everything was alright. He wasn't being fair to either of them because he knew the story, that his father was a married man. Even if he didn't want to tell my mother he could have told this woman to spare her feelings, and my mother would be none the wiser. But it would have helped to save his marriage. He agreed and apologized for the role he played in all of it and that was the end of that. Well, until we got home. Clarence didn't come in. He felt that he had done enough in the situation and his presence would only make things worse. He got his things, got in his car and got the hell out of there before my father knew he ratted him out.

We pulled up at about the same time. He drove around to the back so he wouldn't have to go into the house with us. He didn't know what my mother was going to say. He saw the rage in her eyes and it was never a good time to mess with her. She would have all of his neighbors knowing what a low-life son of a bitch his really is. They all thought he was the perfect man. And he didn't want that image of him to be tainted. But boy, when we got into the house, all hell broke loose. I have never seen my mother in such a rage. She was saying all types of things to him and before I knew it she was jumping on his back. She told me to go upstairs to my room and close the door. I did, but I could still hear everything that was going on. They were on the other side of the house and it was as if they were standing outside of my door. She told him that out of everything they had been through she never expected to hear he had cheated on her. He was still holding onto the mistake theory. That this woman didn't know him and it was all a mistake and when she found out she would have to come back to him on her knees and beg for his forgiveness.

She said, "Okay, maybe you are right. But we are going to find out right now. I am going to give you the benefit of the doubt. I am going to call this woman back and if she tells me she doesn't know you, all is forgiven and I will owe you my deepest apology. But if she tells me what I already know, first I am going to whip the living shit out of you and then I am leaving you. He agreed and then he went up to their room and locked the door. She picked up the phone to call this mystery woman. Ring, Ring, Ring, and someone picks up the phone. "Hello?"

"Hello, may I please speak to Martha."

"This is she, how may I help you?"

"I hate to disturb you. But by any chance do you know a Twinkie or Gavin Felder."

"Know him? Yes I do. I have been involved with him on and off for over thirty-five years. Is he alright? Is something wrong?"

"Well, I don't know where to begin. First things first. The son of a bitch is fine. I don't know for how much longer I'll be able to say that, though."

"I hate to be rude miss, but who are you?"

"Oh, I am so sorry. I am his wife."

"HIS WIFE?" The phone drops on Martha's end. My mother could hear the lady screaming on the other end and when she came back to the phone her voice was cracking the entire time. "Please excuse me; this has really taken me for a loop. I always felt in my spirit he was married but whenever I brought it up he always told me I was trying to find something. He never wanted me to be a part of anything that went on in his life. I broke it off with him when his father died because I saw the obituary and it had your name in it and he beat me down that it was a typo. Then when his son died the same thing took place. But this time he said it was his mother's name."

"Well we did have the same name but why would they be saying anything about his mother in that section of the obituary when his mother passed away months before he did."

"Yes, I know. That is the same thing I told him. But he didn't want to listen. Then out of the blue he told me he didn't want me to come down anymore on the weekends. He said something about his daughter moving in because her mother couldn't control her anymore and he didn't want to upset her by having his woman over. But it never set right in my spirit. And when he came up the last time a couple of weeks ago I ended it. He called me a few days ago and we talked and I admit he had me going for a while, but after I talked it over with my family they told me it was time to leave him alone. No one in my family wanted me to be with him. My mother hated his guts and my kids can't stand him. They always felt I could do a lot better."

"Girl, tell me about it. I know how you feel but at least after all of this you have closure and you can leave it alone. I don't have that luxury. I am married to the bastard."

"Yes, you have a point but I have a lot of issues to deal with because he has done a true number on me. I actually embezzled money from my job for him. I would do purchase orders and say that he did tens of thousands of dollars worth of work at a time. He would come up to here and do a little work and he would get the check. I can't believe this. So, I can't just sweep this under the rug like nothing ever happened."

Of course, my mother forgot about her hurt and ministered to this woman. I mean they both had no idea about the other. Why should they hold ill feelings about each other? He did both of them wrong. So after an hour of Twinkie bashing, my mother got off of the phone and the war of the roses commenced. She ran up those stairs so fast she should've won a medal. But he had locked the doors. He knew he was caught. His excuse was he was involved only in business with this woman and she found out he was married and she was only trying to break up his marriage. He had no idea his son had already given us the low-down and this was before the run-down of the relationship with this woman.

My mother told him they were going to talk everything out, so he should open the door. But when he opened the door, she gave him the surprise of his life. She punched him right in his face and the she jumped on his back again and proceeded to beat on him. She went berserk. I was really scared. I called Lawrence and told him what was going on. He said, "Look. I am not going to have you in the middle of all of that confusion. Pack some clothes and we will just stay in a hotel for the night and I will leave a note for Ma, alright?"

I told him I would be waiting by the door. But when he got there he wanted to come in so he could hear what was going on. He wanted to be nosey. He said, "Come in and listen." But I didn't want to hear that nonsense. I had been listening all night. And I was tired of it. I told him I would be waiting by the door. My mother could hear someone walking back and forth. She had no idea Lawrence had come in and was being nosey. She thought it was me so she told my father she needed some space and she was coming downstairs to get a cigarette. She thought she was going to scare me but it wasn't me. When she got downstairs and saw that it was Lawrence she told him she deserved an Oscar for her performance and both of them fell out laughing. I ran in to see what was going on and she told us she was leaving him but she would need some time and she wanted us to bear with her. Lawrence said he would take me to a hotel for the night if she didn't want me around the situation. She said, "No, I need the two of you here tonight." Lawrence withdrew his offer and we had to stay in that hell-hole for the night.

For the rest of the evening they went back and forth I got tired of listening to them so I told Lawrence I was going to bed. The next morning, I was awakened to the sound of the phone ringing. It was Elsa and Uncle Eugene. And boy did they get an earful. My mother came into my room and wanted me to give them the run-down of the night's events. Before I opened my mouth, I demanded an apology on behalf of me and my brother. Elsa said they were deeply sorry for the way they had treated us. But now she wanted to hear the low-down. I told them all that happened. But I had no idea what was next to come. The next morning Uncle Eugene called the house. The same way he had been calling there every morning to check on my mother and to tell her to have a nice day and then it happened. This morning Twinkie answered the phone. He was that nice guy that needed their support. He had been found out and everyone knew he was no damn good. So this morning he turned on them. What we didn't know is that the day before when I was telling them what transpired between them. He was down in the basement listening to the entire conversation and he was going to get back at them for laughing and making fun of him. So when Uncle Eugene said hello, Twinkie told him not to call our house anymore and that he no longer needed to call his wife every morning. He said, "Listen, you have a wife, you don't see me calling her every damn morning. So don't call my damn house anymore." Then he hung up without giving Uncle Eugene a word in edgewise. The phone rung again, this time it was Elsa. He picked up the phone again, this time he hears her voice. She said, "Twinkie what's wrong? It's Elsa." He said, "Bitch, you don't have to tell me who it is I know who you are. I just told your punk ass husband not to call my damn house and the same thing applies to you. Don't call my got damn house anymore. You all are not welcomed here." Then he hangs up again. The phone began to ring for a third and final time. It was Uncle Eugene again. He told my father he was not going to disrespect him or his wife and they were not calling to speak to him. He said they were calling for my mother and they would not allow him to come between them and my mother. He said that he would kick his ass.

My father thought it was funny. He told Uncle Eugene all he would have to do is come down the highway so they could meet up and he would show him he meant business. He didn't want them calling the house anymore. Uncle Eugene heard my mother in the background crying so they decided to just give up and talk to my mother when she got to work. I couldn't help but feel somewhat vindicated. They all had turned their backs on me and my brother and now they had fallen right into his hole. And now they would all have to run back and beg for our forgiveness. Lawrence woke up. He couldn't believe his ears that Elsa and Uncle Eugene had finally seen the light at the end of the tunnel and that he wasn't the man they thought he was.

This had been a very busy week, but the thing is it was only going to get worse. We had no idea what was in store for us. My mother decided she was tired of arguing and she didn't want to go back to the house on Sixth Street. That would mean she would have to admit that she failed and that couldn't happen. She never told Twinkie all of the things Clarence told us. The two of them just kept working side by side to fix up the house. Lawrence kept his distance. I joined a choir so I could relieve some stress. And no one knew what in the hell my mother was doing. And we kept our distance from her. She was like a ticking time bomb. She was liable to go off at any time. She was hurting so much. She didn't want anyone to see just how much.

After my rehearsal, I walked back over to Sixth Street and I saw this guy with this dog. He had been abusing the dog and Lawrence walked over. He hated to see any person or animal in pain. The guy was kicking and hitting on the dog. Lawrence asked him what he wanted for the dog. The guy said two hundred dollars and Lawrence gave it to him. And now he had the cutest bull dog. Lawrence named him Remi, because he was the color of the liquor. He was fat and lazy. I was so proud of my brother at that moment. And I was so happy. We had never had a dog before and I always wanted one but my mother was persuaded by my father not to allow us to have one. But we were much older now and maybe he would have a change of heart, especially since he could relate. He is a dog himself and he is in the dog house. Lawrence told me not to worry about it. Remi was going to be a part of our family. Lawrence didn't have any children but I swear Remi took over that role. The first thing he did was take Remi to the vet. He got all the necessary shots and things. Then he started taking him around to all of our family members and friends. He hid him in the house on Sixth Street until he could smooth things over with my mother. But that didn't work because Twinkie's ass went up to the house and found Remi in there and accused my mother of knowing the whole time and he told my mother he wouldn't allow us to have this beast in his house. He wanted to hurt Lawrence and me to get back at my mother. And it worked. She told us we couldn't keep the dog so we had to get rid of him. Lawrence kept Remi at the house on Sixth Street as long as he could. They eventually shut off the gas in the house and he couldn't stay there because it was starting to get cold at night. Lawrence gave him away to Elmo's kids. Their mother had just moved into a big house and they had the space. He still picked him up and took him to the vet like a good father. One night, Lawrence was taking me home from school, he had Remi in the car and he told me to go and sit in there with my nephew. I looked at him and I knew my brother was losing it. I told him that he needed to go out and have some children because Remi was a dog. He laughed and when we got in the car there was Remi doing something that he shouldn't have been doing. He was scratching the seats. Lawrence looked at him and said, "Didn't I tell you about that?" The dog put his paw over his eyes. He was ashamed. I had never seen anything like it in my life. At that point I could see his paternal instincts kicking in and I couldn't wait to see him as a real father.

A couple of weeks went by and things actually started to settle. Lawrence and I relied a lot on each other. He came into the house every night and he would wake me up so that we could watch TV together and talk about the day's events. We were closer than ever before. The family couldn't believe what had transpired. We couldn't talk to Elsa unless we were up at my mother's job. She was infuriated with my father. My mother was so embarrassed; she tried to keep her distance from everyone. Lawrence and I just laughed about the situation; we knew eventually it was going to happen. We had no idea that it was going to be this soon. Lawrence and I would sit up and just talk about the way our lives had changed in such a short period. I would get down a lot because my life was ruined. Lawrence could come and go as he pleased but I had to follow the rules of the warden.

This one night in particular he came home earlier than usual. He had a bag with a Coogi sweater in it and a pair of Timberlands. And he was asking me for my opinion. I was so mad at him. I said, "Man, how can you ask me to look at something you bought for some dusty ass girl." I didn't care, I was so mad at him for throwing this sweater in my face. He said, "Man, just try on the damn sweater and see how it fits. I bought this stuff for my friend and she is about your size." I tried the stuff on only because I knew it would make him happy. And this girl, whoever she was, must be very special. The sweater was a little big but it fit. Then I tried on the boots and they fit too. I put the things back on his bench and I stormed out of his room. A part of me wanted the stuff, but he always told me I was a spoiled brat so I didn't want to ask him for it. Then about fifteen minutes later he came into my room and threw the stuff on the bed and said, "Man, you are such a punk. You knew that the stuff was yours. I just want to make sure you are as happy as you can be under the situation. I can't move us out of here but I can make it as comfortable as possible." I jumped up on my bed and screamed. Of course, my mother ran out of her room to see what the confusion was all about. And that jackass of a father of mine just yelled to keep it down. But when my mother went in there to tell him the nice thing Lawrence had just done his reply was, "He didn't bring one in here for me." That was always his way. He is never happy for anyone except himself. He would have been happy if Lawrence would have given it to him. But it really made my day. It made my whole year. Lawrence's birthday was fast approaching and he said he needed a break. He wanted to go away, so a group of his friends surprised him and took him to Atlantic City. He was so excited. He was turning twenty-two and it was a far cry from the year before when he was arrested for improperly sitting in a parked vehicle.

He called the house in the middle of the night. My mother was frantic. She thought something was wrong. But he wanted to let her know he won so much money the hotel decided to give him a suite. He was so excited, and my mother was so happy for him. It had been months since she heard the jovial Lawrence. My father, on the other hand, was anxiously awaiting his return so he could see what kind of money he won. So he could get my mother to try her hardest to get him to give some of it to them to put away. But he would have total control over it. But boy was he shocked when Lawrence walked in the door the next day and he was empty-handed. Lawrence let a friend borrow his earnings so he could get on his feet, because he had just come home from prison. But they didn't know it yet. My mother said, "Okay, what was the damage." Lawrence said, "Damage? What are you talking about?" My mother said, "Lawrence, don't be funny. You know exactly what I am talking about."

He said, "Oh, the money that I won, well I won 15,000 but I let Bunny borrow it." She said, "Bunny who?" He said, "The Bunny that you went to school with. He just came home and was down on his luck so I let him borrow the money until he gets on his feet." Twinkie's face soon dropped to the floor. I looked over at him and said, "I guess that changes your mind about getting your hands on that money." He just looked over at me like he wanted to do something, but I knew he wouldn't as long as Lawrence was there. My mother thought it was noble but Twinkie was livid. Of course, he was going to have words for her when they were alone. Lawrence said, "But don't worry I didn't come home empty-handed. Let me go and get my things out of the car." And when he came back in the house he had a big bag. Twinkie's eye lit up but he wasn't prepared for what Lawrence was about to pull out. The casino sent him on a shopping spree. He brought back two pairs of sneakers for himself and these hand-made glasses for the three of us with our names engraved in them. My mother said, "Well, Lawrence where is yours?" He said, "Well I didn't see the purpose of buying one for myself." Then my mother began to cry. She started talking about him not being there and if we were all a family then why wouldn't he get a glass for himself. He laughed and walked away. But my mother was dead serious. I didn't want to hear her acting like that and I didn't want my glass in a cabinet with theirs because I didn't think of us as being a family. I love my mother but she considers him a part of her family and I don't. But I didn't say anything because it would only breed more confusion.

The holidays were slowly coming around again, but I never thought I had anything to be happy for this year. Lawrence was the only thing I was glad to have in my life. My mother and I barely spoke two words to each other and I really hated my father's guts. Then it happened. My mother and I were leaving a concert that she and her group were singing in and while sitting at a stoplight, bullets started to fly. A bullet flew through the lady's back car window where I was sitting. My mother's friend saved my life. She pushed my head down and when I got up there was glass everywhere. I cried and cried. My whole life flashed before my eyes. All I wanted to do was hug my mother. When we got back to the church's parking lot there was my brother. He saw the state we were in so he ran over to the car. The police came shortly after to get our accounts of the incident. I was really hurt when my mother looked at me and instead of her asking me how I felt, she said, "Well, you know God is trying to get your attention and show you that you should apologize for the way that you have been treating me and your father." I just walked away from her. I could have been killed but I agreed with her. Right now was not the time for me to argue with her or have any ill feelings in my heart toward her. I was overly emotional at this point. Lawrence came and he just held me in his arms and told me if I needed to cry just let it out and I did. The police told my mother she should take me home and make sure I was alright. When we got into the car she looked over at me and told me God spoke to her and told her I should go into the house and apologize to my father because it was like God was giving me a second chance to get my life together. So when I got home that is what I did. I went into their room and I pleaded with him and begged for his forgiveness for the way that I had acted over the course of the couple months I had been there. He looked over at me and said, "God should have done a little more to you because I don't think you mean it. Get the hell out of my room and don't come back to apologize unless you mean it." I couldn't believe it. I told my mother never to expect me to say another word to him. He was a jerk and I couldn't believe I allowed her feelings to fall on me. I went upstairs to my cell and got ready for bed. When Lawrence came into the room he asked could he stay in there with me because he could not sleep. He said while he was driving home all he could see was me laying on the ground shot and there was nothing he could do. So that night my big brother and I slept side by side. We were all that we had.

The next couple of weeks are a blur. And then the shit hit the fan. Lawrence and I were driving back up to Sixth Street from one of my rehearsals. When we pulled up to the house you could hear the commotion from outside even with Lawrence's stereo pumping out in the car. My mother finally brought up the things Clarence had told her and Twinkie was not happy about it. Clarence was standing on the front porch, we were supposed to be going roller skating that evening. But with the new situation coming to a head it didn't seem like that was going to happen. He said he didn't know if he was going to be coming around us much anymore. Lawrence told him to just walk around for a while and he would see if he could work things out. Lawrence went into the house and told me to stay outside. He was in there for a while. When he finally came out he was very upset, he looked over at me and said, "That's your mother and your father. I don't want to have any part of that situation. He went to talk to Clarence and when they finished both of them walked far away from that house. So I decided to take matters into my own hands. I went into the living room where my father was and I told him he shouldn't be mad at Clarence because he was only telling the truth. He told me I should shut the hell up and go back outside. He said, "This is between your mother and me." I said, "Well I am going to tell you like this: Clarence is my brother and I am going to stand by him." The next thing I know this bastard gets up in my face and tells me that he will not stand for me taking my brother's side. I just laughed at him and walked out of the house. Then he said, "Clarence was supposed to be taking you out tonight, right?" I said yes. Then he looked at me with this happy look and told me, "Well you can cancel that because you are not going." I ran out of the house and told Lawrence what had just transpired. He told me not to worry about it. He gave me some money and told me to get on the train and go to the movies. But when I got back the situation had only escalated and it was so much worse than I could have ever imagined. My father took a garden tool and hit Clarence in his mouth. Clarence was running around like a crazy person hitting himself telling my father to hit him again, and there was my mother in the middle of it. She said she didn't care she was leaving my father for good this time. He told her he didn't care. I ran and got Lawrence. He couldn't believe what was going on. He got in the middle of my father and Clarence, but Clarence picked him up and pushed him to the other side and the two of them started to fight. My mother started screaming at the top of her lungs. Lights in the neighborhood started to come on and people were looking out of their windows. And the two of them stopped the rumbling. My mother told me to get my things from the car. My father jumped in and told my mother she could stay around there but I wasn't staying there with her. When I heard this I got the hell out of there. I ran away. When I looked up I was downtown. Lawrence came looking for me. I was in Chinatown just wandering around. He told me to get in the car. I was not going over to that house, especially if my mother wasn't there. I didn't feel right going over there to sleep in a bed and my mother was up at our home on the floor. If my mother was leaving then so was I. When we got back around there Clarence was gone and my father was waiting for me. I told him I was not going anywhere with him. He jumped up like he was about to slap me and Lawrence jumped in. He told my father he was going to bring me back over to the house. He just had to make sure our mother was alright first. He was so scared of Lawrence he backed down. Lawrence and I went over to talk to my mother. She told us it was best that we go back over to the house and that she was going to be alright. So, Lawrence and I went back over to that hell hole. I didn't do much sleeping that night. I had to get up for rehearsal the next morning and I would have much rathered preferred sleeping on the floor on Sixth Street. Our performance was the next week so we were practicing almost every day.

When we left out of the house that morning, there was Twinkie. He wanted to talk to Lawrence and me. He said he wanted to apologize for what happened the night before. Lawrence seemed a little more understanding but I know he was just pretending so we could get out of the house, where I was more verbal. I told him I was not going to accept his apology and I was tired of him treating my mother like dirt. Because Lawrence was there he didn't say anything to me. We left and Lawrence dropped me off at my rehearsal. Once the rehearsal was over Lawrence was out there to pick me up. We went back around to Sixth Street to be with our mother. She was very apologetic about everything that went on over the course of the last couple of months and said we were going to get our lives together. We just needed to give her some time to get back on her feet. She asked us did we mind sleeping on the floor. My dear brother said, "Hell yeah, you all can stay here if you want but I am going back over there to sleep in my warm bed. Even if I hate it, I can't see myself sleeping on the floor." So, he was out until we got some furniture. But we didn't care. I know I didn't.

Things for the other family members were okay. Daphne was working and counting down the months until she graduated and would finally be free to move back home. Tico was into some real strange things and was nothing like he was back at home. He was involved in skateboarding, bike riding and collecting sports cards. Finally, for once, it wasn't them involved in a dysfunctional family setting and for the first time it was us. Who would have ever thought? Daphne and I teased about it all of the time when she would come down and spend time with us. Elsa and Uncle Eugene were doing better than anyone ever expected. People were actually taking bets to see how long it was going to last, but they proved them wrong. They were really living their happily ever after. And we were living out our worst nightmare. It's funny how the tables turn.

Grandma and Whitney were doing okay, too. Whitney has been trying to get herself together and she is taking care of grandma and the kids,

which was great. Things were starting to fall into place and my mother
was going to kick Twinkie to the curb. Lawrence decided it was best that
he come back to Sixth Street with us. I asked him what was he doing
there and he said, "Man, I didn't feel right being there with out the two
of you." So, there we all were laying on the floor eating takeout every
night, but we didn't care. We were together and finally our mother was
talking some sense. Or, so we thought.

The night of my big concert things changed and we were headed
straight back to the path of no return. Somewhere between the car that
morning when my mother dropped me off and the concert, things took
a lousy turn for the worse. When the last song was sung and I was on
my way back to Sixth Street, she broke the news. She said, "Your father
believes we all deserve a better life and the only way we can have it is if
we are all together under one roof and we need to go through some type
of counseling to get over all of this."

My poor little heart broke into a million pieces and I couldn't believe
I was hearing those words come out of her mouth for a second time. I
was thinking to myself, why in two hells is she doing this? Does she have
stupid written on her damn forehead? But this time I showed no emotion
I just looked over to her and said, "Hey, if that's what you feel we have to
do then so be it. But I'll tell you this: He isn't going to anybody's therapy
session; you can cancel that. That is just him trying to reel you back in
and once you get there the talk about counseling is going to be kicked
right out of that back door as you are heading for the front."

She just gave me one of those stares and kept on driving. She knew I
was right. He isn't the type that wants someone giving him advice. But
deep down somewhere she was holding onto a dream that they would
go to counseling and they would work things out. But I knew it was a
lie. I was over the idea really fast. I was so tired of her falling for his shit.

And I wasn't even going to allow her issues with him to become mine. We went back to Sixth Street to get our things for the second time and all of my dreams were shattered. I had a feeling in the back of my mind it was a temporary state anyway. But hey, I was getting closer and closer to eighteen. Only two more years to go and I will be free of the madness.

Lawrence wasn't surprised in the least. He said he was waiting to get the memo she was going back. In fact, he had already started to direct his girls back to the Prison. He wanted to make me laugh our first night back, so he said to me, "Watch this." One of his oh too many women fell for anything he dropped on her plate. He hadn't spoken to her for a few days since we were up on Sixth Street and he couldn't invite anyone over. But during their last conversation he told her to meet him over at my father's house and like a fool she did, but he never showed up. He called her up knowing he could get her to fall for anything. He asked her where she was that night because he was waiting for her all night and his feelings were so hurt that she would lead him on only to drop him. She began to cry and ask him where was he. He called her a liar and said he couldn't deal with anyone that would blatantly lie about something that small. She began to grovel and plead with him. He told her if she didn't tell the truth, she would be cut out of his life forever.

Then her story changed. She did come over that night but he didn't show up. But because she was scared to lose him she went right along with his story. He then told her it was too late and now he really knew how much of a liar she was and that he couldn't deal with someone like her. And then he hung up. She begged and pleaded and called back time and time again but he wouldn't answer the phone and when he did he would just hang up on her.

Thanksgiving rolled around. Lawrence stayed away as long as he could. He didn't want to be there for the festivities, just me and my mother sitting in front of a bird. Because of course Twinkie had my mother believing he was going to the cemetery to put flowers down on my grandparent's grave. I often wanted her to follow him to the cemetery because it doesn't take but five minutes to put flowers down on a grave. And he would be gone for hours at a time. I didn't mind too much, though, as long as he was out of the house and I had some peace.

It was crazy. My mother cooked all this food like we were still on Sixth Street and people were coming over. But that was the last thing that was going to happen. People didn't want to be bothered with his mess. They would rather go hungry than be exposed to the jail we were being forced to rot in.

LAWRENCE'S EXIT

Thanksgiving passed and for the most part things were starting to settle down. Lawrence and I made amends with our mother. It was all his idea. He didn't see any point in holding a grudge. "What was is the point?" he said. My mother was very happy that we were accepting the life she picked for us. She decided to invite the entire family over for a big Christmas celebration. I didn't see the point. It really wasn't as happy as they were trying to make it seem, but hey, who am I? Then, to top it off, Elsa and her family weren't going to be invited because Twinkie still had something against them for what happened when we were talking to them over the phone months back. They were his strongest supporters and now they hated him and the feelings went both ways. They didn't care they weren't invited because Uncle Eugene said he wouldn't be caught dead in his house. So, the festivities wouldn't be complete without the entire family, but, I wasn't trying to rock the boat because I didn't want to participate anyway.

Things were strolling along so well. Lawrence and I were closer than ever. We found ourselves deep into our childhood again. We were like little kids fighting and staying up all night talking. He would sleep in my room just like he did when we were little children. He would come into the house every night and wake me so I would know he was alright, then he would make me go downstairs with him while he cooked his favorite food, Oscar Mayer Cheese Hotdogs and Oodles of Noodles. Then he would come back upstairs and try his hardest to kick me out of my own bed. It was the best times for us. I believe in my heart that moving over there to the dungeon was causing us to lean on each other again. It was like the few years that had passed never took place. He was my touchstone again, and I was his.

During that week leading up to Christmas my mother decided to invite people over. She had a party for the people at her job as well as a get-together for the members in her choir. Everyone seemed to rant and rave over this place like it was a castle or something. I made cracks under my breath, saying, "Castle? Yeah, right. More like the dungeon."

Twinkie is so into himself. He wanted people to walk around the house like he was giving them a tour of some museum. I said to my cousin Denise (she was there because of the choir), "This is a *house*, not a *home*." She said, "Yeah, I know. It doesn't even look lived in. Everything has a place and everything in its place. It's creeping me out being in here." He walked around with his chest poked out not knowing that people were going around talking about him. But hey, that was his ignorance.

Christmas Eve was the absolute worst. My mother and father sat down in the basement and got drunk. They wanted to be our best friends. Lawrence wasn't there; he was out partying with some friends. But when he got in, boy was he in for a treat. There they were, calling our names. They wanted us to be in on their dance card. He came into my room and said, "What in the hell is their problem?" I said, "Alcohol." We both laughed and my mother began to scream our names at the top of her lungs. Lawrence said, "Oh, so I see why your TV is up so loud. Let's just go down there to see what the hell she wants." I said, "I don't have to see, I already know. They want someone to dance with them. I don't want to be bothered tonight. It's the alcohol speaking and that's not real." He grabbed my arm and made me go down there.

There she was crying and dancing in the middle of the floor. She had her arms open wide asking one of us to just come and dance with her. I laughed and walked right back up the stairs. By this time she had walked over to Lawrence and grabbed his arm. She was dancing but he was just standing there. I went straight to bed. I didn't feel the need to be around them. Christmas morning came and I was in the worst mood ever. I couldn't see Walter and I couldn't be around my family members because she was too afraid to put her foot down and tell him they were welcome in her house. My father didn't believe I was old enough to have a boyfriend. And even though my mother allowed me to see him on very few occasions, she went along with the stuff my father said. But I wasn't going to allow that to get the best of me.

The first thing I decided to do was find Lawrence and give him his gift. My mother gave me the money to buy it, since the jerk wouldn't allow me to get a job. But it was cool. I understood he wanted me to depend on them. Lawrence was appreciative of the gift. It was a cologne set. He liked the fragrance. But my present was nowhere to be found. I wanted to kick his ass. But he gave me the lame excuse he wanted to take me shopping so I could get whatever I wanted. And like a little fool I went along with it. But I let him know I was on tohim. That would end up being the joke for the entire day.

I made my calls to my family members and friends. I was hurt to find out Elsa and her family were on their way to grandma's house and they didn't let us know. But grandma told me they couldn't call our house and she wasn't trying to get cursed out for calling and mentioning Elsa and

Eugene. She knew what happened between them and my father and she just wanted to stay out of it. So, I went and told Lawrence and he got our mother's attention. She was downstairs in the kitchen cooking breakfast. Twinkie wanted to showboat in front of some of his family and friends. I didn't care too much for them. I was fifteen years old I didn't know any of them. Don't come around me for the first time and expect me to act like a little girl. One guy gave me a dollar and wanted me to act like it was a hundred. I looked at him and said, "Thank you, but no thank you." My father said, "We are still working with her. She is something." I looked over at him and said, "Well, whatever I am it's not any fault of my own. If you keep any animal locked up, they rebel." My mother then walked in and asked me to go to my room. I went upstairs to put on my clothes because Lawrence and I were heading to grandma's house so Lawrence could see her new place and we could see Elsa and the gang. My mother came in and asked what my problem was. I looked at her and told her this just wasn't working for me. I didn't like my father and I didn't want to be around him. He wasn't my family. She asked where Lawrence and I were going and I told her. She decided to go with us since Twinkie had to take these people home and go to the cemetery to put more flowers down on his parent's grave.

I looked over at Lawrence and said, "Damn, didn't that fool just put flowers down a few of weeks ago? He doesn't put real flowers down so shouldn't the flowers he put down still be there?" Lawrence popped me and said, "Shut up, but you are absolutely right." My mother couldn't have believed he was out at the cemetery every time. But hey, I was fifteen, and still a child. But I had more sense than they were giving me credit for.

So. we were off to see our family. I wanted to ride with Lawrence but my mother wanted the company because it was Christmas. I wasn't trying to start any confusion today. When we got to grandma's house, there was Daphne. She was upset with Elsa and didn't want to be around her. Lawrence, Daphne and I had a lot in common at this time. We stayed outside for a minute, plotting to take off somewhere they would never find us, but what good would that do? Lawrence finally talked us into going in to see old Mary. She began to cry when Lawrence walked in the door. He looked over at her and said, "Woman, what in the world is wrong with you?" She said, "You being here is the best Christmas present I could have ever asked for." He said, "Well, Merry Christmas and Happy New Year." She laughed and we all sat down and had a good visit.

Daphne didn't want to go back home so Lawrence told Elsa that if she let Daphne stay down here for her Christmas break then he would be responsible for her and he would bring her home in time to go back to school. She said she would have to check to see if it was okay with Eugene. Daphne stormed out of the house for the second time. Lawrence said he had to leave, so if they were going to let her stay she could ride home with me and my mother. Of course, when Elsa got to talk with Uncle Eugene he was against it and Daphne was not too happy about that. She decided she would run away and come back down here on her own.

My mother was ready to go home because she had a lot of cooking to do and time was ticking away. I asked could I stay and Uncle Eugene and Elsa drop me off, but my mother said my father may be against it plus she needed my help in the kitchen. I wasn't at all happy about that, but what could I do? After they heard that, Elsa told me I should follow directions and go home with my mother and I did. When we got there, naturally Twinkie wasn't there. She headed for the door. I asked for a minute. I walked over to Elsa and said, "I told you so." She looked and said I was right but it was best I go on so I wouldn't get into any trouble. I told her how I hated that man I don't want to go back. I told them before and no one believed me that he wasn't shit but now they all saw I was speaking the truth.

Elsa said, "Your mother is calling you, don't keep her waiting. I don't want you get into any trouble. So, like a good little girl I gave my hugs and told my family goodbye. While riding home my mother didn't say much and I was upset again. I was just praying that his ass wasn't back yet. And this time God truly answered my prayer. There was no sign of him being there. Lawrence hadn't returned yet either. He had to make his rounds. He had girlfriends and other family members to see, and my mother didn't want me to go – only because I might talk Lawrence into taking me to see Walter and my father wouldn't approve. So, there we were in the house alone. I went to my room. She wanted my help but I didn't see the point in helping her prepare for people to come over and it was all fake.

Deep down inside Twinkie didn't like any of our family members and he didn't want them in his house. He said they weren't use to anything and they were destructive. He makes me so sick. His family is a lot worse than ours. They were all from the projects. But hey, that is his opinion and he wanted to make my mother happy, though after they left, it was like clockwork, he was going to curse her out because some family member didn't use a coaster, or someone sat in the living room, or someone ate too much. He is just an ass and isn't use to family and people getting along and loving each other. And he hated the fact we had that with one another. But hey, that's him.

Eventually I went down to lend a helping hand. But shortly after, he came in and I couldn't stomach him. He started to criticize me and I couldn't deal with him. Not today, anyway, so before I said something that was going to get me into trouble, I went back upstairs to my room.

The people started to stroll in about an hour or so later and I had a sense of home. Not because of where I was but because I was around some of my family members and friends from Sixth Street. Everyone was longing to see my brother who wouldn't be there for a while. He called and wanted to trade sweaters with my father so he could give it to one of his girlfriends. She was the one he was falling for. I'm not sure if it was her so much or her family. Her mom was a doctor and her dad a judge. And my brother is very status-conscious. He asked could he get one of the Coogi sweaters back in order to impress her dad. Of course, Twinkie went along with it. Only because Lawrence told him he would get him some more. So, he was still only looking out for his best interest.

Back at the party my mother was having the time of her life. She was so happy. Everyone was laughing and drinking and eating, but hey, it was free, so who wouldn't? I went upstairs to call Daphne only to hear from Elsa she had run away. I said, "Well, at least this time you know where she ran too." Elsa said, "Yeah, but this time I am too tired to come after her. Tell Lawrence if he sees her to make sure she gets back here in time for school next week. I only have a few more months and she will be out of here and on her own." I felt really bad for my aunt, but what could I do? Daphne does what she wants to do when she wants to do it. I called and let Lawrence know if he saw her to please have her call her mother. He said he would look out for her. Then I called Walter. only to be interrupted by Twinkie. He was listening on the other end of the phone and after I realized he was on the phone I told Walter we would have to talk later. The relationship between the two of us was drifting further and further apart. And there was nothing that I could do because my father had total control of my life. I went and told my mother what was going on and he told her it was his damn phone and he would listen to anyone's phone calls. And, of course, she said and did nothing. I wasn't even bothered by it. I couldn't be. Things were happening like this all of the time.

I just waited for my brother to get there and when he walked through the door, boy was he heated. He had just come from Grandma Maggie's house (His biological father's mother) and she was a little under the influence. He said she was so drunk he had to make her go to bed. He called to check on her when he walked in the door and then he told my mother she needed to talk to her. Grandma Maggie was tickled that he cared so much. He hadn't been down there to see her in a few months and she understood he was getting older and he had a life. But boy was she laughing on that phone. Lawrence didn't think it was funny at all. He was still steaming mad. But he was starting to come around and joke about it. He said, "Man, my grandmother was twisted and I couldn't believe her. She was joking and acting crazy, so I told her, 'Grandma, I am not playing with you, get yourself together and go to bed.'" Then he said she began to laugh at him and he walked her in her room put her in bed and closed the door. Then he told another one of his cousins to make sure she didn't get out of bed. We all laughed about it.

I tried to change the subject by telling him I wanted my gift. I said, "Look, man, you can just give me the money and I can go and get my own gift." He said, "Listen, didn't I tell you this morning I was taking you shopping." I said, "Yes, but when you didn't say when and I know how you are." His friend Fran just laughed and said, "Why don't you give her the money?" He said, "Because she is a spoiled brat. She knows I am going to give her a gift but I am not going to give it to her now."

Then things started to get very interesting. Right there in the middle of the floor, Grandma slapped the hell out of Whitney. For the life of me I don't know why, but they were going at it. It was no different than any other gathering. Whenever there is an audience, they show off. And boy was Twinkie going to have a reason to go off tonight. Lawrence said, "Whitney, what did you do?" Grandma said, "She is acting a damn fool. But don't worry about it." Whitney was angry. She wanted to go home and Grandma was enjoying herself far too much to allow Whitney to ruin her Christmas. Grandma said she had ruined too many of her holidays and she wasn't going to allow it this year. My mother came in and calmed the situation down. But people were tired and decided they would leave before anything else kicked off, meaning that Twinkie would throw them out. He had done it before when we lived on Sixth Street, and I wouldn't have put it past him to do it again. So, people called it a night and that was it.

Our first Christmas in the prison of all prisons, and boy was it something. All in all, it was a nice day, though, for what it was. But after all of the people left I was feeling homesick again. While they were there it was like having a part of Sixth Street being there and now all of a sudden it was all gone again. And there I was in this foreign place again, all alone. Lawrence went out with some friends and my mother went into the room with Twinkie. I couldn't do anything but sit and look stupid. I have gotten really good with that over the course of the last few months. As I sat there, I thought about what I could do to pass the time since I was going to be out of school for the week and I didn't want to be in this place. So, I decided to ask my mother and father if I could have a sleepover with my friends. And to my surprise, they were in total agreement and I was ecstatic. I called all of my friends and they were all in. And Daphne called. I told her about the party and she said she would be there, too. She needed Lawrence to take her home and she was coming so she could meet up with him. My mother and I went shopping for all of the things that girls need for a sleepover and my father was being very generous with his money and his time. For once he was being very decent. And I truly appreciated it. The only thing they asked of me was to make sure the basement was cleaned. I had to vacuum and put away some of the Christmas decorations. But I was cool with that. I was going to have a party and for this I was grateful.

We picked up my friends and it was just as I thought it was going to be. Daphne was there when we returned. We stayed up all night laughing and joking around. Then when Lawrence got home, the party really started. He was one of the girls. He brought a movie for us to watch and he stayed down there with us. My friends all had a crush on him, so they didn't mind him being there. The next morning my mother cooked a smorgasbord for us to eat and we decided to check out the area, since I would be living here and we wanted to see what kind of guys lived in the area. Come to find out the area was just as dead as my house. But I didn't mind much. I still had Walter and I was just happy my friends were there.

Lawrence decided to take Daphne home early and he said he was going to surprise Elsa and stay with her for a couple days. A couple hours had gone by and the phone started to ring. It was Elsa and she was so happy Lawrence was going to stay with her for a few days and she was so tickled by it.

I couldn't believe it – the week had gone by so fast and the New Year would ring in new beginnings, and with those new beginnings maybe our family could reconcile and things would somehow change between us. My mother decided we would go to church to ring in the New Year and of course Twinkie decided he was not up for church about an hour before we were going to leave. Lawrence was not in either. He had a party to go to and he said he would meet us outside the church.

As he promised, there he was waiting for us. My big brother and his friend. He said he wasn't going to come in and asked that we pray for him. Then he told me to come to him. He said, "Man, make sure you tape Def Comedy Jam. It's a marathon starting at one o'clock." I promised him I would and he hugged us and said Happy New Year. And as always, he ran off in a hurry and that was it.

My mother and I went into the church, and just as the New Year arrived and we were on our knees praying, the gun shots rang out so loud and so many that it was like we were in the middle of a full-on war. My mother and I both prayed that God would protect my brother while he was out there and that was that. We hugged everyone in the church and wished everyone a Happy New Year and that was it. We were on our way home and as soon as I hit the door I instantly ran into the house so we could tape the show as my brother told me. I was in a really good mood. The best mood I had been in for long time. I was so happy and I knew things were somehow, some way going to turn around. I even made peace with my father. I was sixteen and I only had two more years to go. Life couldn't get any better.

Lawrence came into the house early the next morning. He and his friend Chucky had been in the hospital with their friend Steve. He had been shot while coming out of a party and no one in his family would come and show any support for him. Lawrence and Chucky felt a sense of responsibility for Steve. He was a couple of years younger than them and our families all grew up with each other. So, he didn't have such a good night. My mother was upset with him that he involved himself in this confusion, but she knew this was just how she raised us so she couldn't do anything but feel proud. But she also warned him and he laughed at her and called her paranoid.

That New Year's Day we sat and watched Def Comedy Jams and laughed until we couldn't laugh anymore. The next day it was back to school for me. Lawrence took me to school and the night before I had a really strange dream. These guys were following my brother and they killed him in front of our house. I told him about it and he laughed and told me I was trying to jinx him. He made more jokes about it and then told me to get the hell out of his truck and have a good day.

While walking home I had a wild conversation with my friends. We were talking about the closest person in our lives and if something happened to them how would we feel. The closest person for me was Lawrence and I couldn't imagine my life with out him. And just for that brief moment, trying to envision my life and him not being there made me begin to lose my breath.

Things were settling at my house. We were all beginning to have fun with one another. We were starting to act like a family. It wasn't like Lawrence and I against our parents. We were all one unit. Then it happened. One of the worst snowstorms was heading straight for the city. So, we went up to Sixth Street so we could get some things done because we knew that if we got snowed in we wouldn't be able to get up there for a while. While I was in the living room I saw my grandfather's obituary and for the first time I saw the resemblance between he and Lawrence, so I went over to my brother and put the picture up next to his face and I called for my mother to come and look. I said, "Ma, doesn't Lawrence look a lot like granddaddy and Lawrence turned around and looked he said, "Girl, have you lost your damn mind? You have been trying to jinx me all week. Don't ever put an obituary up to someone's face." I had never heard that before and I was so apologetic. He laughed it off and said, "Girl, you know I am not going anywhere." Then he left and went on about his day.

My mother and I went grocery shopping because the news was calling for the worst storm to hit the city in decades and we weren't going to take any chances. When Lawrence came home, he was really shook up. The guys that shot Steve came around Sixth Street and shot up the house where Denise lived. One of the bullets almost hit her and the children. The guys were driving through and Rufus thought that they had some type of beef with him. He decided to go on the roof and be a sniper. He shot at them and they came back and retaliated. Lawrence had just walked out of there. By the grace of God his life was spared.

My mother was in tears. She begged and pleaded for him to stay his ass away from Sixth Street and from any of them that were involved in this mess. He told her this was the last straw and he wasn't going around there anymore. He then looked her in her eyes and said, "Ma, nothing is going to happen to me." He could see the tears well in her eyes and he got up, hugged her and rubbed her shoulders and came upstairs. That night we were all in the house together. I really didn't want to believe the snow was going to be as bad as they were saying, so after about an hour waiting to see some flakes fall, I went to bed.

To my surprise the next morning, snow covered the ground. It was so much snow that the cars were almost covered completely. I couldn't believe it. Instantly I ran into my brother's room to wake him so he could see what was going on and he couldn't believe it either. He said, "Well, you know it's time to put some clothes on because they are going to tell us to go and shovel. I said, "Man, I am not shoveling anything. If they want something shoveled they had better come out there and shovel it themselves. I will help, but all that snow we will be out there all day." He laughed and said, "Man, go and wake your mother up so she can see all of this snow." I was shocked to find she was already awake and knew what was going on outside. She was downstairs in the kitchen cooking. She wanted to make sure we had a home-cooked meal and were comfortable seeing as we wouldn't be going anywhere for a while. She was making fried chicken, her famous cheese potatoes, greens, corn bread and a homemade cake.

She called the church and to her surprise Reverend Turnblad answered the phone. She said, "Hey Reverend, you know there is a storm out there. Why are you at the church? Are you having service today?" Then he said, "I showed up because sometimes people will still show up for service on days like this and I didn't want someone to feel that if they were in trouble they couldn't come to the church, but you know not one nigga showed up. I am about to head home." They ended the conversation and that was that. She then called for Lawrence and me telling us we needed to get a head start on the shoveling. I hollered down the stairs, "What about you and Dad? You all need to help us because we can't shovel all of that snow on our own!" Lawrence came into my room and threw a pillow at me. He was laughing because he couldn't believe I said it. He told me to put on my clothes and we could go out there and start. Then he told me not to say a word about them. My mother knew it wasn't right, them trying to get us to shovel, so she decided to come out there with us. My father stayed his happy ass in the house; like we were his slaves and we were supposed to be out there shoveling all of this massive snow.

My mother tried to change the subject when I asked why he couldn't come out there and help us. But Lawrence hit me with a snow ball and I forgot all about him. Then Lawrence came and told me to distract our mother so he could get her. I went over and started asking her about the most snow she had ever seen and Lawrence crept up from behind and knocked her face down into the snow. We laughed and laughed because she got stuck and the more she tried to dig herself out the harder it was for her to get up. Lawrence and I finally helped her up and when we finally finished we had a heater and cups of hot coco waiting for us inside.

Just as we were going inside gun shots rang out. Someone a few blocks away was shooting in the snow. Lawrence just shook his head and said, "I guess those fools have nothing better to do." Then he told us to make our way in the house. For the rest of the day Lawrence played superhero to many people in the neighborhood. He was shoveling snow for the elderly and helping people get down the street. He was just being his normal self.

This storm was titled as the worst in the city's history. It wasn't a storm anymore, it was a full-out blizzard. The snow was so high it came to my waste. It was hard trying to make your way through it. They city was calling for people to stay inside unless they had to leave. But that meant nothing to my brother. He was starting to get cabin fever. The next morning, Lawrence got a call from two of his friends. They didn't have any food in their house and they had three young children. Lawrence got up and made his way through all of the snow and got to them so he could take them to the store. I asked him, "Why in the hell do you have to leave out and take them anywhere?" He looked at me and laughed and told me to stay in a child's place. He said he had to help them because he couldn't allow the children to go hungry.

When he came home that evening, he had bags and bags of groceries. We didn't need any food so he went knocking on doors to see if any of the elderly people needed anything and passed out some of the food. The two of us stayed up that night, playing games and talking. When we woke up the next morning and he spent the entire day with me. We just had a good time, it was something he hadn't done with me since I was a very little girl and he had no other choice because he was punished. He said he knew I was getting cabin fever and he was going to take me out in the morning. I was so happy. It seemed as if things were finally falling into place and I didn't care what our residence was because I had my brother.

That night I snuck on the phone and Chucky called. I told him he would have to call back because I was busy and Lawrence was sleep. Lawrence was covering for me downstairs in the event my mother and father woke up and heard me on the phone, but I knew if he got on the phone with Chucky then I wouldn't be able to get back on the phone. The two of them were worse than two females when they got to talking. They talked about women and all of the issues that came with that territory. Chucky continued to call and I continued to tell him Lawrence was sleeping. Then I got tired of him calling so I cursed him out. He called Lawrence on the cell phone and also the pager. When they talked, Chucky told him I had been hanging up on him and that I said he was asleep. Lawrence picked up the phone and asked me about the things Chucky told him and I denied it. Then he said, "I know he is not lying because I heard you say it." I believed him so I thought that I was caught. I then started to curse him out and he told me he was going to beat my ass. I knew he was only joking but I still locked my door and tried to use myself as a weight so he couldn't push his way through. Lawrence ran up the stairs and pushed my door open. I thought my door was locked but I instead I unlocked the door. He beat my ass that night but I wasn't mad at him. I knew that I was wrong. He then told my friend I would have to speak with him in the morning. I asked him, "Are you still taking me out tomorrow." He said, "Yes, I promised and I wouldn't break a promise to you. But it felt good to beat you up. I haven't done that in a long time. You still need to know I am the boss." We both laughed and he told me that it was getting late and I needed to go to sleep because we were leaving early.

I woke up especially early so that I could get dressed and be ready because Lawrence would sneak out on me and I wanted to have one up on him. When he got up I was all dressed and ready to go. He told me to make his bed and he was going to pay me. I did and then I went and sat by the door and waited for him. He came down the stairs in his bath robe and said he wanted us to play some more games because it was too early for us to be leaving out of the house. I went along with it. I asked him for my money and he said he would give it to me while we were out. We played the game for a few minutes then he told me he was going to get something from his room. He said, "Go ahead and play my game for me and I will be right back." He went upstairs and told my mother he was leaving and not to tell me. He went out and then he came back. My mother said, "Boy, you aren't gone yet." He said, "I'm leaving now." After a few minutes, I went upstairs to the kitchen and called for him. There was no answer, then I asked my mother where he was and she said he left a while ago. I was so angry with him. I paged him and called his phone but he didn't answer. I knew that he knew I was going to fire him up. So, I said I would just wait for him to come home. I played the game for most of the day and then I went to bother my parents. They put me out of their room after about an hour. Then the phone began to ring. It was Lawrence. he wanted to speak to his mother. But she was sleeping. I told him I had something for him when he came into the house. He told me to get the hell off the phone and to get our mother. She was sleeping so he told me to tell her to make him some spaghetti and he would be home in a little while and to make sure his food was ready. I told him to get out of my face and to stop playing with me and to get his ass home. He hung up on me. When my mother woke up I told her what he said and my father told her she had better go and make Lawrence's food.

The two of us went downstairs and began to play cards. Usually, my mother sucks at playing cards but tonight she was whipping my tail. The phone started ringing; I thought it was Lawrence so I answered the phone. And surprisingly, it was Keith, Lawrence's best friend. I told him Lawrence wasn't home and he should be back in a few minutes. He said he wasn't calling for Lawrence and he needed to speak to my mother. I asked what for and he began to yell and told me I needed to put my mother on the damn phone. It took me by surprise because Keith was usually in a playful mood, so I handed her the phone.

She had this puzzled look on her face and asked where her baby was. My heart instantly fell to the ground all I wanted was my brother and she wasn't telling me anything and I needed to know just where he was.

She ran to other side of the house to find my father and she told him what Keith had just said. She said Keith told her that Chucky had just been killed and that someone else was with him that got shot and that they didn't know where Lawrence was and that we needed to get to the crime scene immediately. She wanted to know why they wanted her to come up there for Chucky if they already knew he was gone. If they didn't know for certain why would they want her to come up there? My father came into my room to find me in tears. I was hysterical. I wanted answers. Where was my brother and why was mother crying and why weren't they telling me anything? My father just held me in his arms and told me everything was going to be alright. I immediately started to page my brother and call his phone. Normally he would call back within a couple of minutes but the phone never rang. My mother made a call to one of our cousins, Mark. He worked at the hospital and he could make some calls to see if they had brought in any victims that had been shot. He was Lawrence's other mother. So, the news to him was devastating but he wanted to be there for my mother. He told her not to worry and to go handle whatever she had to do and he would call around to make sure that everything was alright.

My father said that we needed to head up there. I grabbed my bible and prayed the entire way. When we arrived at the crime scene there was Chucky's truck and police officers and a lot of people that just looked at us as if we were foreigners. Denise and Little Bits' sister Tiny were there. My mother went to speak with the detectives that were on the scene and they were very rude. I asked Denise and Tiny did they know where my brother was and they ignored me and told me to wait for my mother.

The detective was very rude to my mother. She said she couldn't give out any information to anyone until the two murder victims were identified. My mother said, "So both of the victims were killed?" The detective said,

"Ma'am, that is just what I said. One of the victims had an ID and the other had to be identified." My mother said, "Well, I know my son carried ID on him at all times." The detective just gave her a callous look. She was being overly nasty until my mother blurted out my brother's name then this woman's disposition totally turned around she became overly nice.

At that point, my mother's worse nightmare was starting to unravel into a reality. My mother then went to speak to the owner of the store and he began to describe my brother to a tee. He was so heartless, standing there talking to them while he was mopping up all of the blood. My mother then looked over at me and shook her head in a way to tell me my brother was gone. I totally lost it. I couldn't believe my father got to me so fast. I was about to take off. I was running away from it all. I didn't want to live if Lawrence was not standing by my side. And my father caught me. He just held me in hopes he could take the pain away. But it was too late, all of the life in me swept away at that very moment. I was numb. I couldn't feel the cold air rushing or the wind blowing the snow on my face. I couldn't do anything but see my brother walking away. And at that moment the only instinct I had left was to yell out for him, as if yelling for him would make God change his mind and allow him to breathe again and bring him back to me. Like he was going to walk up and push my father aside so he could hold me like he did so many times before and tell me everything was going to be alright. It was too late, he would never be there for me again and now I was standing there all alone. My touchstone was gone and my world was tumbling down slowly in front of my face.

By this time, I was finally coming to and I was realizing that this was not a nightmare. It was all truth. The detective walked my mother back over to us and she wanted to offer her condolences to our family and before she got out what she wanted to say, my mother fainted in the middle of the street and in the middle of all of the snow. The detective lost it. She said, "Oh Lord, call the Ambulance. This poor woman, her son was just murdered and now she's had a heart attack." The detective who had just been so cruel to us was standing there hysterically crying and asking God to have mercy on this poor woman. My father told them to step back. He slapped my mother and then she came to. She didn't know where she was, neither did she know what was going on. When she got up she realized what had just happened. No one could give us any information and we didn't know what was going on. All we knew is that Lawrence was gone and he was never coming back.

A DIFFERENT WORLD

W e all just sat there in the car, driving. I am not even sure my father knew where he was going. All our minds were on one thing. Their son and my brother was gone. Now we had to break the news to all of our family members and friends. How would we tell them? I'm not even sure how real it was to us. I know for myself I didn't believe it. I felt as if I was in a nightmare I couldn't quite wake up from. My brother was going to be in the house waiting for me like he always is. But when I got into the house there was a calm peace over that place – no laughter, no talking, just shattered memories and shattered dreams that would never be.

I went into his room and just cried and cried because he wasn't there and I knew my nightmare was really my reality. He wasn't supposed to leave me. We were supposed to be together forever. We always had longs talks about us being old and telling our children and grandchildren about Sixth Street and all of our memories and now all of that in one quick second was gone. When I got myself together the phone began to ring. It was Lawrence's friend Bam from prison. They always say word travels fast when you are locked up, but man I didn't think it was like a lightning bolt. He knew before anyone in our family. He wanted us to know how sad he was and he told me he loved Lawrence as if they we brothers, and that his love for him would transfer to me. He said I was the only connection to Lawrence he had left and now he was my big brother. I was so grateful that someone cared.

When the call ended I got the phonebook and started to make calls for my mother. She was in no shape to call people. The first person I called was Walter. He had already heard on the news and tried to comfort me as much as he could. He was breaking down himself. Lawrence was like a big brother to him also. Next, I called Elsa. Daphne answered the phone and I told her what happened. She started to scream, and it was a piercing sound. Elsa came and got the phone. She didn't have any idea what was going on and when she heard Daphne screaming out for Lawrence she knew and her tears became evident. She had to get off of the phone because Daphne began to shave all of her hair off. Tico was in a daze and Uncle Eugene tried to console them all at one time and little Ahmad was oblivious to everything that was going on. It was a call I will forever regret I had to make.

My mother took over and called Mary. I think my grandmother and Whitney were both high when she called. Grandma said," Ok, baby, I will give you a call in the morning." My mother just looked at the phone in disbelief, but she didn't let that stop her. She didn't miss a beat. She made calls and the both of us let people know what had just happened. Everyone had the same reaction. Not Lawrence. What could he have possibly done to deserve this? Denise and Tiny got a ride over with some of Lawrence's friends and Reverend Holmes walked six miles in the snow to console my mother. My mother asked, "Why my baby?" And the next thing I knew the whole room was in tears.

The news traveled really fast. The phone began to ring off of the hook and people were knocking at the door. The two friends he had helped out of the snow were the next ones at the door. The snow still fresh on the hood of their car, "It was a struggle getting here but we had to come," one of the girls said as she held my mother's hand.

The phone began to ring. It was a calm peace over the phone; no one said anything. I kept saying hello and then finally you could hear someone sobbing. It was one of Lawrence's girlfriends. She said, "Lana, someone just called my mother and I know they were lying and just wanted to play games. I cursed them out and I know it's not true. Please, just put him on the phone so I can hear his voice. If he wants me to leave him alone after this I will but I just need to hear him."

I told her I wished that I could but I couldn't, and that it was in fact all truth. My brother and the man she was hopelessly in love with was gone. I hated saying the words myself but I had to. There we were all sitting in the basement. As I sat in the corner I could hear all the laughs we had just a day ago. And a pain went through me. I would never hear that laugh again. I would never hear that voice again or feel those hands again that woke me up on so many nights so I could come downstairs with him.

One of the girls looked at me and said, "Well, Lana, even though you all fought your brother really loved and cherished you. He was always talking about doing this for my little sister and doing that for you." But that wasn't making me feel any better. I didn't want to hear that. All I wanted was my big brother. He was the one person I depended on my entire life, especially over the course of the last few months and now I felt empty and alone. After a few hours, everyone started to leave. There were no more words that could be said.

Denise and Tiny decided to stay the night so they could help us make more calls if my mother needed them to. My father made up the basement for them and my mother and I went upstairs. As we were walking up the steps my mother stopped dead in the middle of her tracks and said, "I know you are, baby." I stopped for a minute and looked at her because I knew I didn't say anything. I said, "Ma, you know I didn't say anything to you. Maybe you should go and lay down for a while because that was a hard fall." She looked over at me and laughed. She said it was funny as we began to start walking up the steps. Then she said, "I heard you brother, and he was apologizing to me for having to leave us and he told me he was alright. And I told him that I knew that he was." Then the tears began to pour again.

At this point, all we could do was lean on each other. Lawrence was no longer there to lend his shoulder. I couldn't go on the other side of the house and sleep in my room. I had this overwhelming feeling and I couldn't describe it. I wasn't afraid; I just think if I would have walked through that door and glanced over at his room I would have lost it. How was I going to go into that room? My last and fondest memories of the two of us together were with him in those rooms. And at that point it was too much for me to deal with. I would go and sleep in his bed and wait for him to come home when he went partying with his friends. If I went in there I don't think I would have ever come out because I would be there waiting for him. I couldn't go into my own room because he would come into my room and kick me out when it was starting to get extra cold. He didn't have heat in his room and he would say I was going to suffer with him. What was I going to do? I couldn't allow myself to do it. At this point I wasn't strong enough to do it. I was going to have to begin my life at fifteen. I was like a newborn baby and I would have to learn to do everything all over again on my own with out my brother.

My mother understood so she said I could sleep in the bed with her and my father would have to just sleep on the floor. When he came up into the room he looked and he just gave a smile and went into the bathroom. He was in there for so long I was starting to get worried about him. So I went over and I knocked on the door. You could hear him sobbing but when he heard my voice he tried to cover it up. He flushed the toilet and started running water as if he'd been in there using the bathroom. When he came out I noticed his hands were dry. I just patted him on the back and told him he would have to get it out and that I understood. He said, "Yeah, okay, I don't know what you are talking about. I wasn't crying. My allergies are acting up." I just smiled at him because it was all too obvious his eyes were bright red and they were puffy like he had just been in a fight with Mike Tyson or something. He told me to lie down and try and get some sleep but I knew that would be like asking a drug addict to not use drugs. It wasn't going to happen. Every time I closed my eyes I could see his face and that only made me cry more so I just sat up in the bed and let my mind drift to a far-off place, like I was in this nightmare and I was fighting myself to wake up. In the morning, he will be here and all will be back to normal is what I tried to tell myself.

My mother just laid there in the dark with her eyes open. I can't imagine the pain she was feeling. This creature she carried in her womb for nine months, that she went through the pain and agony to bring into this world, that she loved and nurtured and cared for and raised for twenty-two years and three months to the exact day, was gone. Someone had taken away the very life she called her own.

When the sun started to rise the three of us were still in a complete daze. My father was sitting on the couch like he was waiting for something to happen. He was still fully dressed and my poor mother was lying on the bed with a broken heart. I got out of the bed and I needed to see him, and for a brief moment I thought he was in the bed waiting for me as always to come and wake his sorry behind up. But when I got to the room, Lawrence was not there and I just began to scream, for my soul and spirit were being snatched from under me. I yelled his name to the top of my lungs. I wanted him to hear me. I wanted him to feel the pain that I felt. Why did he leave me? He knew beyond any and everything and everyone in this world how I needed him. We were a pair and now I was all by myself, and I wanted him to feel the same way I did. I didn't care about anything else that was going on in that house; all I wanted was my brother. I wanted him to walk and hold my hand, tell me it was just a bad dream and everything was going to be alright. My father was only a substitution and it was only making matters worse for me. I walked out of the room and ran down the stairs. I had to go outside for awhile to get some air.

I got myself together and went to check on my mother. Denise and Tiny woke up shortly after and came upstairs to make sure I was alright. I was feeling a little better I just didn't want to talk to anyone or hear anyone talking about him. The phone began to ring off of the hook again. One call was from Aunt Hanna. She is Lawrence's aunt, his father's sister. My mother had briefly talked to them the night before. My mother told her as much as she could and now she was calling to get the information. She told my mother no one had the heart to tell Grandma Maggie. My mother asked if they wanted her to come and do it. They said no, but they wanted to ask was it alright to leave out the way in which it happened. They didn't think her heart could take it. She loved Lawrence more than life itself and they felt it may be too much for her to handle. My mother told them they should let her know because someone may slip up and say something and then she will have to deal with it and then she will deal with them for not letting her know the truth up front. She said no matter how much we want to protect the ones we love, the truth is always the best thing for them in the end. Aunt Hanna agreed but the decision was already made and she said they would make sure there weren't any slip-ups. They were going to tell her Lawrence died in his sleep of a heart attack. My mother was very troubled about it but there was nothing she could do, plus she had to deal with her own pain.

Shortly after that my parents got a call from the police saying they had to identify the body and pick up my brother's belongings. I wanted to see what the paper had to say about all of this. I put on some clothes and took a stroll across the street to the store. My cousin Skip was driving down the street. He beeped the horn and I noticed him so I stopped. He said, "Man, I knew if I drove up this block long enough I would see one of you all coming out of the house. I heard the news but man, please tell me that it isn't true." I didn't know what to say. I just put my head down and he knew I wasn't in a place where I could handle all of this. He took me by the hand and told me how sorry he was. He began to break down. I didn't know what to say. I don't think there's anything harder than seeing a grown man cry. I told him I would be right back. I went to the store and got the paper and when I returned Skip was outside his car talking to Tiny and Denise. He had pulled it together. He said he couldn't stay around much longer because he didn't want to see my mother. He said he didn't know how to face her.

When I got back into the house, my Uncle Ned was sitting in the living room. He was going to stay with us for the day to show some support to my father. He said, "Hey little lady, how are you holding it together?" I could feel the tears well up in my eyes and I just shrugged my shoulders. He got the hint that it wasn't a good time to talk about it. My mother and father came down shortly after. They were dressed and ready to go. My mother asked me did I want to go into the morgue to view my brother's body with my father because she didn't want him to do it on his own, but I wasn't ready to see him like that. Uncle Ned said he would handle the job of being there for my father. Tiny and Denise said they would go in there with him, too. He said, "I'm a big boy, I can handle myself." We all laughed it off but he knew he needed someone to go in there with him.

But boy were we in for a rude awakening when we got there. As we were pulling up, there he was Lawrence's deadbeat dad, Lance. How much nerve did he have showing up? How in the hell did he find out, and how did he know we would be there at that time? It was like he was waiting there forever for us. When he walked over to the car my father began to ball up his fist but my mother told him it was neither the time nor place for any of this mess. And regardless of anything we maybe feeling, he had just as much right to be there as any of us because he was still Lawrence's father. When he walked over to the car he went toward the passenger side where my mother was. My mother asked him had he been to see his mother and if he knew of the story they were telling her about Lawrence's death. He said, "Now you know I can't go down there." Lance and Grandma Maggie have been on the outs since Lawrence was a little boy because of some money he owed her. She always made Lawrence promise he wouldn't allow Lance into her funeral. He said he wasn't going to involve himself in the decisions concerning her and how they dealt with telling her. He didn't agree with it, but he didn't want to be the one to tell her the truth either. She would have hated his guts even more. He didn't seem to care much about it, either. He was talking all of this crap about finding out who did this and killing the people who were responsible for it. My mother said, "Lance, obviously right now you are a little under the influence and I am not in a place right now where I can deal with your bullshit. I have to get things cleared up with my son. He said, "Your son? He was my son, too. And right now, I want some answers." My mother said, "And you think that I don't? But right now I have to put all of that aside and handle the business at hand. Have you been in there yet?" He said that he hadn't been in there yet because he wanted the two of them to go in there together. He said, "I mean, it is our son, right? We made him together so we need to do this together." My mother said, "I'm not going in there. Twinkie is going in there. He is more of his father than you are or have ever been." He just gave her this look of total disgust, but he didn't say anything because he knew that deep down she was telling the truth. He walked alongside my father but neither of them said a word. They always had a competitive spirit when it came to the other. Lance despised Twinkie and always felt he got my mother by way of default because they broke up and somehow in his warped mind he felt she married Twinkie out of spite. And Twinkie always hated him because he had Lola first and he always threw it up in his face indirectly.

So, as they walked into the place my mother felt at ease thinking his two fathers would handle the situation appropriately. But boy when they got in there did Lance's attitude totally change. He got really indignant. When they walked in the lady brought out all of the paperwork. She handed everything over to my father. Lance started yelling, saying he was Lawrence's father and that this man was only his mother's husband, referring to my father. But what Lance didn't know was that our next door neighbor was the medical examiner and he was on duty. When he saw my father in there he wanted to know what in the hell was going on. The first person he asked about was Lawrence. He said, "Man, make sure you tell that boy of yours thanks for helping me out of the snow yesterday morning. Without him I don't know how I would have gotten to work." My father just put his head down and told him Lawrence was the reason for him being there. Our neighbor lost it right there on the spot. He wanted to know all of the details – the when, where, and how. My father began telling him bits of information and immediately he stopped my father. He said he was in the van that picked Lawrence up but his head was spinning so fast one of his subordinates took the call. Lance interrupted them. He said, "Listen, I understand your pain and everything but I am here to let you know if you didn't already. Lawrence is my son and I am running this show. His mother is unable to handle this and that leaves me his next of kin. This man, your neighbor, is only his mother's husband." My father interjected by saying, "Stepfather then. Where in the hell have you been over the course of the last 22 years? That boy was my son. I have been there since he was nine months old." Lance just stood there. They began to tone things down when security was called.

Vincent, our neighbor, told the guards they wouldn't be needed and he would handle this heated situation. He then told Lance it was fine, however he wanted to handle it. Lance said, "Yes, I know it is. This man shouldn't even be in here." Vincent could see the fire building in Twinkie's eyes so he quickly interrupted Lance and let him know, "If you sign these papers for the body you are responsible for it. You have to pay for the funeral arrangements and everything." His demeanor totally changed. It went from him trying his hardest to humiliate Twinkie to almost having to kiss his butt. He quickly slid the papers over to Twinkie and said, "Man, I am just in shock right now. You all have to handle this. I didn't know what I was saying at the time." Twinkie said, "Yes, I thought you would have a change of heart. Just as you always do. You want to be his father for show but when it comes down to handling business you always find a way out." Twinkie signed the papers and they allowed the two of them to see Lawrence.

They no longer allowed you to see the actual body they just brought out a picture and when my father saw it he couldn't believe it. At that moment, it was reality for him. When the two of them came out of the building my father was speechless. He was quiet the whole ride back to Sixth Street. We had to take Tiny and Denise home. When we got into the neighborhood everything seemed dull. The sun was shining, the snow was still piled a mile high on the ground but it was something different. It no longer had that radiant glow we had always seen. The light and the life was taken away. We got out of the car for a minute because people wanted to pay their respects to my mother.

As I walked down the street there it was a beautiful red bird. It seemed as though this bird was following me and when I arrived at our house it flew to the window sill of my mother's window. I yelled for someone to come and see and when Uncle Ned walked over the bird flew away out of sight. No one else saw it. When I told my mother she just said that it was my brother's spirit coming to tell me goodbye and that he was alright. And it was only meant for me to see it. It was just like when he told her he was sorry. I just laid my head in her lap and cried.

One of the guys in the neighborhood asked my mother what she was going to do with Lawrence's car. We didn't even know where the car was. He was driving around in Chucky's car when it happened. Then the boy let us know his car was parked across the street in front of the store and we would probably have to move it. Uncle Ned said he would drive it home if we had the keys. My father had keys to all of Lawrence's cars that he kept for him. He gave Uncle Ned the keys and told him to follow us to the police station so we could pick up his belongings. When we got to the station my mother didn't want to go in, but this time she had no other choice. She was Lawrence's next of kin and she had to be the one to sign off on everything. When the officer brought out the things, I didn't notice anything. My brother always had a rubber band around his wrist, napkins in his pocket, and his pager. The pager that was inside the bag wasn't his. I tried telling my father but he began to act like an ass. He told me it didn't matter and I should just shut up because I was upsetting my mother. But here she was holding onto this bag for dear life and these things didn't belong to my brother. No one knew my brother the way

I did and I was hurt that he would even question me about it. I went over and whispered into my mother's ears that those things belonged to Chucky. She asked the officer but he said that he would have to check and it would take a couple of days. But in the meantime take what they had and if it wasn't his things they could bring them back when they came for the switch. My father was so angry I did that, but I wanted to make sure we walked away with a part of my brother.

I was feeling that overwhelming feeling again about Twinkie. How dare he accuse me of trying to hurt my mother? I just went into the room and laid my head on my brother's pillow and held on to his picture because that's all I had left of him and now when I needed protection I would have to protect myself. I stayed in the basement for the rest of the day. I just stared at his picture and remembered the day before when we were there playing video games. I felt like he knew he was going to leave me, and I was happy we had those couple of days together.

My mother came down and asked if I wanted to help them plan the funeral. She didn't feel like she was up to it. I pulled myself together and walked up the stairs. My brother would want me to do this. I didn't know the funeral director was there. I didn't even hear her come in. She had all of the information laid out on the couch. I had the honor of picking out his casket. My mother didn't care about the cost as long as I was happy with the decision. My father, on the other hand, said that maybe my tastes were a little too extreme and I needed to pick something else out. My mother looked over at me and said, "Is that the one that you want for your brother?" The tears began to fall down my face like a river and I nodded my head because I couldn't quite get any words out. She said, "Then that's what we are going with."

I didn't want my brother in a regular suit. He wouldn't have looked right. He had this checkered black and white Versace suit he only had for a few months. He bought it to wear to one of his presentations at school. I wanted him to wear that. My mother agreed. In the process of planning everything the phone started to ring. It was Bertha and she wanted to contribute to the process of planning a wonderful service. I told her my mother was in no shape and that whatever she wanted to do was fine. She picked out some of my mother's favorite songs for the service.

My father was in and out. He was supportive one minute and then the next he was being an ass. My mother said he didn't know how to deal with his pain and I should just understand and walk away when he starts up. When the lady from the funeral home left, some of our cousins came over to bring food and see how we were doing. Our cousin Mark was with them. I led them down to the basement so they could wait for my mother to come down. They were all asking a lot of questions about what happened. I told them as much as I could, but when the word funeral was brought up, Mark wanted to know who died. There was a calm silence that came over the room. He didn't know. My mother never called him back to tell him the awful news. One of his sisters said, "Mark, baby, I don't know how to tell you this." He began to scream NO! He ran up the stairs back to the kitchen and I told them I would go and see about him. I just rubbed his back to make sure he was alright. And then he went off. He said, "My son, my son. That was my son. I was the one that took care of him when he was a baby because your mother was nothing but a Harrington's hostess." I just continued to rub his back and tell him everything was going to be alright. Though he didn't want to hear it at the time, he eventually went back downstairs. He just thought Lawrence was shot and my mother hadn't called back because we had been at the hospital. And when they were on there way over to the house no one said anything about him being dead, they just said they needed to see my mother to make sure that she was alright. When my mother finally got downstairs she was so apologetic to him. She knew how much he loved Lawrence and she would have never intentionally hurt him.

The next morning people were stopping by, dropping off buckets of Popeyes and Kentucky fried Chicken and even some homemade soul food. But we couldn't eat. Just looking at that food was beginning to make me sick to my stomach.

Then the phone started to ring. Grandma was finally about to make her way over to see her heartbroken daughter two days after her son was killed. And when they got there they weren't at all concerned about us. They wanted to know why we weren't eating all this food. Whitney's little twins went into fits because they saw food. They even started to do a chicken dance. Their eyes lit up like it was Christmas morning. I couldn't believe it. After they were there for a few minutes and each had a couple pieces of chicken, Mary made her way downstairs to see my mother. She is such an actress. When she got to the bottom step she opened out her arms and said, "Release it. Come to mama, baby, and tell me all about it." My mother looked up at her and said, "Mama, come and sit down."

Whitney said, "How are you holding up?" My mother said, "I am holding it together the best that I can." She said, "Okay, that's good. I'm going to get me another piece of chicken." Of course, her kids followed and Grandma wasn't too far behind. It went from her coming over there to see my mother into an all-you-can-eat buffet. My mother just looked at me and shook her head. She didn't mind, though, and it didn't surprise her. That was just how Mary was. She hollered down the steps to us that she had to run but she would be back before the week was out. They didn't know my father was standing in the doorway and could see them sneaking the chicken out.

When my mother and I walked up the steps all of the food was gone. We thought my father may have thrown it out. My mother said, "Thank

God he threw it out because I was tired of looking at it." He walked in the kitchen and said, "I didn't throw anything out. Your mother and sister stole it." That was the laugh we all needed. He began to tell us how they were acting when they saw all of that food. And he said when they were leaving, Whitney asked grandma, "Do you think they want this food?" And grandma said, "No, take it. They probably don't have an appetite and it would be a shame for all of that food to go to waste. Go ahead and get it. And pull me a leg out while you are at it." My father couldn't say anything because he was too busy laughing.

We all went upstairs to just chill out for a minute. A couple of hours passed and my mother told me to go downstairs because someone was coming to stay with us. Lawrence's long-time friend, Hope, came over. She and Lawrence had been friends since they were in the seventh grade. Everyone always had hopes of them finally getting together but the two of them claimed they were more like brother and sister, but whenever Lawrence got with another female, Hope was very jealous and upset with him. But now no one will ever know. She felt the same as I did. She couldn't go into his room. She said she was so tired of him bragging to her and all of the other girls about his wallpaper being made of fabric. So, there we were, the four of us in my parent's room. My father on the floor and my mother, Hope and I bunched up in their bed. The next day we got a call from the officer at the precinct stating there had been a mix up with Lawrence and Chucky's belonging and that because my father took Chucky's things if we weren't there by the time his family got there they were entitled to take Lawrence's property and he said Lawrence had about six hundred bucks and if they got it they wouldn't have to give back.

Twinkie jumped up off the floor and woke all of us up. He said, "Don't wash nothing, just throw on your clothes so we can get to the precinct and pick up Lawrence's things. You all have to get up right now. I just looked at him and laughed. I said, "Didn't I tell you those things weren't my brother's? if you had only listened then." He said, "I will apologize when we get there and get your brother's stuff. Right now we are working on a deadline." We got there and gave them Chucky's belongings and we got my brother's.

When we got back to the house, Dwight was at the door. He was drunk and just out of it. He didn't want to believe this was the truth. My mother grabbed him and they went outside to talk. He told my mother he was prepared to go to jail. He said something about getting his boys from Philly to come down here and take care of whoever did this. My mother told him you don't fight fire with fire. He said, "But you don't understand. They killed my cousin." My mother said, "No I don't, he was only my son." She told him he needed to come inside and take a seat. Then there was another knock at the door. It was Lawrence's friend Kyle and Twinkie's other son. They were coming to check on me. Kyle always called me his little sister and he said he wouldn't feel right if he didn't step in and take over the role Lawrence couldn't fill anymore. He said I had been on his mind all night and all day because he knew I was probably the one missing his presence the most. Everyone knew I idolized my brother and I was going to be hopeless without him. He said, "The one person in his life that mattered most was his little sister. You wouldn't believe just how much he talked about you. He wanted to see you do big things in your life and I know wherever he is right now he is sorry he won't be with you to carry those things out."

I couldn't believe he was telling me this. Lawrence and I talked all of the time but he never actually seemed like he was listening to me when we talked and it didn't seem like his love for me was that real. Kyle began to cry. He said, "I am really going to miss him. You don't find true friends like him. He was only person in my life who told me I was better than standing on the street corner hustling. He pushed me to go out and do something better for myself and for my son. And through his example I decided to go back to school. When I got stuck on something all I had to do was call him and he would be right there to push me. A lot of my friends thought I was crazy for going back to school, but he said in the end when they are all in jail or dead for the decisions they are making, you will have a since of peace because you don't have to look over your shoulder because you are living your life right for your sake and your son's." He just sat at the kitchen table and cried. When my mother walked in he just grabbed her and told her how sorry he was and how much he loved Lawrence. He wrote his number down and told me if I ever needed anything, someone to talk to or someone to hold my hand through all of this pain, he would be right there.

Twinkie's son knew Lawrence and really felt a connection with him as brothers but he never really got to know him and he began to cry for the loss and what he would never have. My mother had called our doctor because she didn't think we would be able to sleep so they called in prescriptions for us . I didn't think it was a good idea. I didn't want to sleep. I wanted to be up so I could *feel*. If I fell asleep, when I woke up I would have to face this harsh reality all over again and I didn't want that pain to be there every time I wake up, so I didn't want to do it. But my parents felt if I didn't sleep then I would be making myself sick. So, I decided to take the pills for my mother's sake.

When they left to go to the store, Sonny, another friend of Lawrence's, was at the door. He was a lot older and the two of them met at work. He was close to our cousin Head and when Lawrence and Sonny linked up years later they clicked. Lawrence was the only family Sonny had. He had lost all of his family in a violent way. They were either killed or died from drug abuse. When he met Lawrence and was introduced to our family he fit like a perfect glove and Lawrence completed him on many levels. He came into the house staggering. He was drunk. He couldn't even make it into the chair. We were glad to see him. We didn't know how we were going to find him in order to let him know. He hadn't heard from Lawrence in a couple days and he knew it was out of the norm. Before he went to work he went around Sixth Street to see if he was around there but no one was outside. When he got to work there was a note on his desk that said I'm sorry to hear about Lawrence, he was a really good guy and he will be greatly missed. Sonny lost it. He couldn't take it. He said he had to leave. He didn't say a word to anyone. And from then until the moment that he ended up on our doorstep is all a blur to him.

He told my mother, "Lawrence was the only family I had left. When I met him, I started to have a reason to live again. He helped me cope with all of my loss. And now that he is gone I don't have a reason to live anymore." My mother held his hand and said, "Sonny, Lawrence wouldn't want you to feel like this. He would want you to carry on and remember all of the things he told you. And so would the rest of your family." He just laid in the chair and cried. At this point I was all cried out. I couldn't handle the pressure anymore, seeing all of these guys I looked up to and admired for so long breaking down like this. My brother never realized just how much he was loved. He never knew his own worth.

When my father and Dwight got back from the store my mother got the pills and my father stayed downstairs talking to Sonny and another friend that came over. My mother brought the pills up to me and said we had to take them. I did and by the time my head hit the pillow I was asleep. I didn't dream. My body was just getting its rest. When I woke up the next morning I could hear Mariah Carey and Boyz II Men singing One Sweet Day. The tears began to flow, but I was starting to accept it.

Lance called later in the day to check on the arrangements and to see how my mother was doing. My father told him she was unable to talk at that moment but he appreciated the call and he would let her know. He said, "Yeah, I just wanted to see how things were coming along because I have to go and take my daughter out for her birthday because we need to be having a good time, if you know what I mean." Twinkie said, "No, I don't know what you mean. My son was just killed so regardless if it was my birthday, my daughter's or even God himself, I wouldn't be speaking of having a good time because at this moment all I feel is hurt." Lance got quiet after that and said, "Well, just tell Lola that I called and to let me know when everything is settled." Twinkie said, "Well everything is settled, no thanks to you. But hey, you have to be going so you can have a good time with your daughter." He didn't allow him to get any words in. He just hung up the phone. He couldn't believe Lance had that much nerve. He had always thrown that girl in Lawrence's face and the saddest part is that he was still trying to do it in death. My brother was never fond of that girl. My father told my mother and she just laughed. She said, "He was never there for him in life, what made you think he would be there for him in death." At that moment Twinkie let it go because he knew she was right.

The next few days are all a blur to me. I can't quite remember how we made it through. One moment we all sat around laughing at the crazy things he did and the next we were all crying our eyes out trying to make some type of sense of it all. Then I woke up and it was the day before the funeral. The day I had been dreading for a week, the day it would all become a harsh reality because today I would see him. We had to go to the viewing at the funeral home. Before we left the house, Tanya the undertaker called. She asked to either speak with my mother or father. I gave my dad the phone and all of a sudden, he started yelling and cursing.

He said, "Whatever you do don't let the son of a bitch back inside." Quickly my mother and Hope ran into the kitchen to see what all of the hoopla was about. When he finally got off the phone he told us what was going on. Lance had gone up to the funeral home before anyone got there and told Tanya and her staff that he was Lawrence's real father and he didn't want anyone else to be able to come and view the body. She told him that she couldn't honor his wishes because she had no knowledge of who he was and he wasn't the one paying her. He then said he needed an extra car for his family and he would have to get it on credit and he would bring the money to her after the funeral. She told him he would have to take that up with Twinkie and Lola because they were the ones paying the tab. If not, then she could only accept cash right then on the spot. He wasn't at all pleased and said he was going to stand outside and block anyone from trying to get through those doors because he didn't want anyone standing over his son. Tanya thought he was a crazy man and sent one of her brothers out to speak with him. She said if that didn't work would it be alright if she called the police? My father told her she should've called them right there on the spot. She said he isn't allowed back in there. Yes, that was his biological father but that was all. And right now, he was making a complete fool of himself. He never did a thing for Lawrence except change his name when he was born and didn't tell my mother. And run his credit through the roof.

Elsa and her gang would be meeting us there. My father and Uncle Eugene had to put aside whatever ill feelings they may or may not have been carrying over from the incident of that unforgettable morning. When we got there, Lance was gone and Elsa's crew had already gone in. Daphne was standing on the side of the car bawling her eyes out. Grandma and Whitney were there. too. They were standing on the steps of the funeral home, wanting to show support to my mother. But she chose to stay outside. Hope couldn't go in either. But I had to, I couldn't let him leave me without me saying goodbye to him and I just had to see him for myself. I had to be able to touch him in order to know he was really gone. If I didn't I would never be able to accept his death. In the back of my mind I would always think he was going to come home. So, I took a deep breath and I walked straight into the building.

There he was, lying there looking just as peaceful as he does when he is asleep. The closer that I got to him I thought he was going to jump up and scare me like he had done so many times when he was asleep in his room. I took baby steps in the beginning. But the closer I got the more anxious I got, but when I got up there nothing happened. There was no movement, no laughing, and no cursing me out telling me to leave him alone. There was just peace. And I couldn't take it; I felt the air literally leaving my body. I couldn't breathe. I was beginning to suffocate. I immediately ran to the door. I wanted to be free. I wanted to be with my brother. I don't know where I was going but before I could get out of the door that damn Whitney jumped in front of me and slammed it shut. I stopped for a minute and asked her what in the hell was she doing. She said, "I will not let you run from this." I said, "Whitney, I am telling you now I can't breathe so either you get the hell out of my damn way or I will beat all of the holy shit out of you right now." She said, "Oh my," and opened the door for me.

I just screamed out hoping that someone would hear me and rescue me, hoping someone would take the pain away. But as the people walked by they all stopped and looked at me like I was a crazy person, not knowing someone had come and stolen the only person I had in this world. He was gone and he was never coming back. After a few sad looks, I pulled it together and walked back in with the rest of my family. By this time my mother and Hope had come in but they were sitting in another room. My mother couldn't do it. I understood, but I needed to go back. I knew it was the truth now and it was time for me to face up to it. I walked back up there and this time I was calm. When I finally reached the casket, I just rubbed his hand and his head. Then I began to have a conversation with him. There were a few things I had to get off of my chest. So first I said, "Lawrence, I just want to thank you for being my brother and always being there for me. I love you so much and I never thought you would leave me. I know this is not your fault, but I am still angry. I am going to miss you and my life will never be the same. I will watch over and protect our mother." Then I laid my head on his chest, like I had done so many times before. I knew this would be the last time I would ever be able to do this so I had to make the moment last forever. I didn't kiss him because that was something we never did. For the rest of the time I just sat there holding his hand until they were ready to go. I didn't want to leave him lying there all alone but I had to, and it killed me to do it. The closer I got to the door the more the tears fell and the more pain I felt in my heart. But I knew my mother had an appointment she had to keep. She was doing an interview with one of the reporters from channel 9 news. He had done several pieces on Lawrence over the course of his life and he wanted to be there for the end.

When we got home there was the news van waiting for us. The entire family was there to show support, even Uncle Dole, Lance's brother. He was very close to Lawrence. Lawrence thought of him as more of a father than he did his own. Uncle Dole had been there for every part of his life. It's crazy because he even looked just like him. Grandma Maggie would always tease my mother, saying that Uncle Dole was his father. She would always say, "Now, baby, tell me the truth. You know it won't make me any difference because either way he is still my grandson and I am still going to love him more than anything." My mother would turn red and she would tell her, "Grandma, I don't know if Dole is a man or woman under his clothes. That boy is Lance's son. You all just have some strong genes." They would both fall out to laughing.

Uncle Dole wanted a drink. He just cried his eye out. He had gone up to the funeral home shortly after we left and he saw him. That night reality came knocking on all of our doors and we were all in the same place. When Glen Patterson walked in, there was Whitney acting a damn fool. She said, "Man, look at you. You must think you are something sharp. I did too, until now, that is. You are a puny little thing." My mother grabbed her by the arm and pulled her out of the living room. My mom asked me if I wanted to be with her but I decided not to. They had a big picture of him sitting in the middle of the floor so they could give close ups. I couldn't sit there and look at that picture and talk about him, just standing there watching my mother made me feel so bad. My mother asked me to go and get Twinkie because they needed to do this together as a mother and father desperate for answers. When he walked into the room my mother introduced him to the crew and Mr. Patterson. He asked if my father wanted to be a part of the process and he said, "No thank you. I am alright standing over here watching."

I don't know what happened at that moment, but my mother went off. She said, "What do you mean, no? Our son was murdered and these people are nice enough to come into our home and do a segment on him and you turn them down? What are you afraid of? What, do you think one of your women might be watching?" He just walked out of the room. Mr. Patterson didn't know what to think. He apologized for causing any family disputes. My mother told him no need to be sorry for him because he was a low-life, rotten, son of a bitch. Mr. Patterson was trying to avoid any confrontations, so he quickly said, "Okay, let's get started." They did the interview and my mother was totally out of it. But she pressed her way through like the trooper she is.

I couldn't take seeing my mother talk about the man that was. I just kept hearing him laugh at me. He was the only person I went to with my problems. We understood each other and now I didn't have that. No one would be able to understand all of my issues and my pain. So, I just walked around the house. My father and Uncle Dole were sitting in the family room getting drunk. Twinkie told him about how Lance had been acting over the course of the last few days. Uncle Dole said, "Well, that is my brother, but if I were you I would have kicked his ass at the morgue. He had better not start any mess tomorrow because I will kick his ass." The two of them began to laugh. They have always had a great relationship and Lance couldn't deal with that. But his family had a certain respect for Twinkie because he was there for Lawrence when he needed a strong male role model to look after him, and Lance wasn't there.

Elsa, her gang, Mary and Whitney were in the basement with Aunt Annie and Baby Jay, Uncle Dole's wife and little son. Daphne was in my room making calls. Hope was gone to get her some things from her apartment. My mother was still upset about the interview, so she didn't want to talk to anyone. So, there I was all alone. I just went into Lawrence's room. This was the first time that I had been in there all week but today I needed to go in there. I laid down on his bed and smelled his pillow and the clothes he left on his bed. My mother didn't want us to touch anything in the room so everything was the same way he left it. Just being in there for those minutes made me feel better; I was close to him. I could feel his presence with me. So, I laughed and asked him to please be there with me at the funeral and to hold all of our hands. I decided I needed to turn in early. The day had been rough and tomorrow would only be worse. I needed to prepare myself for the task that was in front of me. I took one of those pills and it was like clockwork. Before my head hit the pillow it was bye bye birdie.

THE FUNERAL

When I woke up, it was early in the morning and I was in a sad state. I knew the moment was coming for me to say goodbye and I knew I was going to lose it. I didn't want to tell anyone because I knew it would be hard for everyone. No one spoke a single word. Everyone was just in a far-off place. My mother must have stayed in the bathroom for about an hour. She looked as if she was drugged. My father was up and dressed. He knew it would take us awhile. Elsa and her bunch just laid around like we didn't have anyplace place to be. There was no noise, no talking or laughing. None of us wanted to be in the place where we were but we all knew it was something we had to do.

An hour or so had passed and there was a knock at the door. The limo was there to pick us up. At that moment, I felt this knot in the pit of my stomach. I ran and told my mother I didn't think I was going to make it through the day. I didn't want to go. How could I say goodbye to my hero? The one person I emulated my entire life, the one person I could tell my deepest and darkest feelings and never had to worry about a look of judgment, he just listened. She looked at me and said, "Think about tomorrow. How will you be able to deal with yourself if you don't go?

Think about the regret you will face for the rest of your life if you don't go. How do you think he would feel if out of everyone *you* weren't there?"

I did exactly what she said and I got my coat and headed for door. We were about to take one of the longest rides of my life. Elsa and her bunch drove in the car with Uncle Eugene because they were going to leave from the church, to head back home. Grandma and Whitney were going to meet us there, because as always, they were late. That car was as silent and still as a cemetery. We all just stared out the windows.

When we finally arrived at the church, there was a line that went down two blocks. When my mother saw this, she was in total amazement. We knew he was well liked, loved and respected, but you never know the true measure until something like this happens. She began to break down. The nurses and other people crowded around her. They said the family needed to go in and take our seats. They knew this was going to be an emotional day. They blocked off the lines so we could get down the center aisle to see him. My mother still wouldn't go up there. She said it was not in our best interest for her to go up to that casket because someone would probably have to come and pry her fingers off him. Everyone understood and agreed it was best if she just took her seat.

My father just stood there for a while I don't know exactly what he was saying or doing. It was like he was trying to dress him, but that was just his nervous energy kicking in. Then it happened. Grandma Maggie walked through those doors and when her eyes met with my mother's it was like a bolt of lightning had hit that place. She gave my mother the release that should've come from her own mother. Grandma Maggie just held my mother in her arms and told her to just let it all out. She whispered in her ear that God makes no mistakes in what he does. She said, "I know we will miss him but now we have got an angel up there on our side and he is watching us right now." And then she began to lose it herself.

Grandma looked overwhelmed with emotion. It was like she was happy my mother had an outlet but she wished it was with her. Lance walked in with his freak of a daughter. You could tell by the look on her face it was more trouble than it was worth being there. I just stared her down. He was *my* brother. They just shared the same sperm donor. She sat down and began to pick at her finger nails. When I saw that, I had to leave because I wasn't trying to add more drama to the situation. I walked outside and it was like I was in a display case; everyone was looking at me. It was like they were waiting to see if I was going to crack. I spoke to a few of them and then I headed back for my seat.

The church was really starting to fill up and I knew they were going to have to extend the viewing because it was so many people and the line just got longer and longer. We were still in the middle of a lot of snow. But he was just that kind of person. He had a heart of gold and it showed at that moment. When I got back to my seat my mother was being he normal self. Here it was, her son lying there in a casket and she was consoling everybody else. She glanced over at the casket and for a minute the tears filled her eyes and our cousin Relly leaned over and said, "Now, Lola, get yourself together. You have to set the tone for the entire service. When people see you cry they are going to cry. You need to be strong and try your hardest to hold it together, alright?" She nodded her head in agreement and wiped her tears away and started consoling people again.

The next thing you knew she heard someone hysterically crying and when she looked over it was Relly. And now she had to console him. I began to laugh at people because it was taking my mind off of what was really going on. I looked up and there was Quinton, the neighborhood drunk. He was crying his eyes out and when he reached the casket he just hung over it. He began kissing Lawrence on the head and I told my father and he kindly walked over and helped him to his seat. I knew if Lawrence could feel that he would have kicked my tail again for letting it happen. The undertakers came and told my mother they would have to close the casket and get things started because we had to be at the cemetery at a certain time. It was okay with her because she was ready to get things started before her emotions totally took over.

And then I saw them coming down the aisle. Reverend Turnblad and the rest of the ministers in the church started walking towards us. I felt my knees buckling and I knew it was the end. I glanced over at him as the undertakers walked over to ask if anyone in the family needed to see him one last time. My father was first in line. He kneeled down and kissed his head and told him goodnight. Whitney was next. I'm not sure what she was doing. Next came Elsa, and she broke down before she reached the casket. An overwhelming feeling came over me I had to go up there and ask him one simple question. I stood behind Elsa and when she was through I leaned toward him and ask him, "Why did he have to leave me?" And just as my words began to flow Reverend Turnblad began to speak. He started off saying, "The Lord is my shepherd, the twenty-third chapter of Psalms, but I guess God put it in his heart to lead from the fourteenth Chapter of John. He quickly changed it, "Let not your heart be troubled." And because this was my favorite verse in the bible, even though none of them knew it, I began to break down even more. He began speaking to only me. He said, "In my father's house are many mansions. I go to prepare a place, Lana, for you." At this point, it was really emotional and everyone began crying. There wasn't a dry eye in the place.

My mother thought it was best to get me out of there before I did something really drastic. She walked over to me and said maybe we should go outside and get a little air. I didn't want to go. I couldn't let them close that casket. I couldn't let him leave me. It was all too much for me to handle. I was beginning to lose it. But when I turned around and saw that every eye in the place was on me, I changed my mind real quick. I just wanted to sit down. I tried to squirm my way into the pew but I kept looking at him lying there. I kept yelling to him he wasn't supposed to leave me. He always promised me he would always be there for me and he broke his promise. I know it wasn't his fault but he broke my heart. And I yelled so loud I just wanted him to hear me in heaven and I wanted him to feel my pain.

At this point, other members in the family walked over to assist my mother so they could take me out. I just wanted my brother back. Dwight lifted me up and they walked me out of the church. When we got outside of the church I twisted and turned thinking I could get loose but they had a tight grip on me. I had to get back in there to him. And then out of the blue, Uncle Eugene slapped me in my face. I couldn't believe he had done this to me. Who in the hell did he think he was? My emotions drifted for a minute and now I wanted to fight. I said, "You have lost your damn mind." But that was the only way for them to get my attention. While we were outside my father thought it was best for the undertakers to close the casket. But he wanted to be the one to do it. Elsa said he tucked him in, kissed his forehead and said goodnight.

When we got back in the sanctuary and I saw he was gone, the tears ran like a river. I didn't want to cause a big scene again so I took my seat. I was so angry, and I just cried. They wouldn't allow me to have one last moment with him. Who cares if I caused a scene? He was the love of my life and they knew it, and didn't let me say goodbye for the last time. The music began to play and the service started. There wasn't a seat in the church; people were coming in having to sit in the choir area and in the pulpit. The service was long but it went by really fast. Reverend Turnblad's eulogy was the best I had ever heard him do. He started asking the question, why? Then he even referred to my brother, the one who cursed me and kicked my butt, as being just like Jesus. I couldn't believe what I was hearing. He started off by saying my mother should compare her pain with the same pain Mary felt. My mother had told him in the days before the service how she always hated him hanging with the guys on Sixth Street. So, he summed it up by saying Jesus hung around with people Mary didn't approve of, but Lawrence was not uppity and he was trying to get those guys to better themselves, the same as Jesus did with the twelve disciples. I never looked at my brother that way, none of us did. But I could truly see him standing there with his chest puffed out. He wanted to let my mother know she was a good mother and she had raised a good son and he encouraged her to do the same with his beloved little sister. When he concluded his sermon, there was that knot again at the pit of my stomach. As the congregation began to sing and the undertakers began to roll the casket down the aisle, I could feel myself a about to lose it again. This time I was in total control. I just had to get away from the crowd. I felt like the walls were caving in on me and I couldn't breathe. My mother and father were on both sides of me and Elsa was behind. I got away from them and the next thing I knew I heard someone whispering saying they had to keep an eye on me because they feared me doing harm to myself. I looked over and it was one of my mother's friends from the church. I made my way through the crowd and headed for the bathroom. And there she was right there behind me. I said, "Look, lady, I loved my brother but I don't think it's to the point I would do any harm to myself." She said, "Who said that?" I looked at her and I wanted to slap the shit out of her but I knew they would have blamed that on Lawrence's death. I looked at her and said, "There are a lot of people going to hell by way of the church. So get your life right. If I have learned anything through all of this, I have learned that. Godly folks don't tell lies in His house. I heard you and that other so-called saint." She looked at me and stormed out. She had some nerve lying to me and I was standing right there.

When I was through I walked outside. All of those people crowded around. It's a crazy thing, they all had the same look in their eyes. He meant so much too so many people. A guy walked over to my mother and he just held on to her. We had never seen him before and my father was a little irritated because he wouldn't let her go. Then finally, he said, "Ma'am you don't me. I haven't been living in the neighborhood that long but I had to come and pay my respects to one of the nicest people I have ever met in my life. What the pastor said about your son was all truth. He was an angel on this earth and God had more work for him to do. I met your son about nine months ago, while I was in the liquor store. He was in there buying some lottery tickets and I was behind him talking to my friend. I had lost my job and didn't have enough money to buy my children clothes for Easter. I was devastated and he must have been listening the entire time. He got his lottery tickets and walked out of the store. When I walked out there he was. He called out for me and when I turned around there he was with this money in his hand. I said, "That's not mine." He said, "I know that you don't know me, and I apologize for eavesdropping but I overheard what you are going through and I know it must be rough. Here is the money for your children's Easter clothes, shoes, and a little extra." I began to cry and told him I couldn't take his money. He didn't know me and I didn't know him. He then introduced himself. He told me everyone in the neighborhood was like a family and if I lived in the neighborhood then I was family, too. I said, "Okay, I will take the money but I have to pay you back somehow." He said, "Kiss your kids for me and bring them around to meet me." And after that moment he became their honorary godfather. He would talk to my little ones and he always treated me like I was somebody. He didn't look down on me.

We were equals and you don't find that much in areas like this. It's every man for himself. I didn't know him that long but he touched my life and I will truly miss him.

My mother had tears rolling down the side of her face after she heard his story. Lawrence never acted like a hero around us. He was just Lawrence. But to the many people in that area, even ones we had no clue about, he was a modern-day hero. The driver said it was time to leave and go to the cemetery. That was the longest ride. But he got a chance to ride through Sixth Street for the last time. There were so many people just standing there as the hearse rolled down the street. It was like they were giving him a chance to say goodbye. Everyone was standing out there; even the police officers that harassed him all of those years were there. I didn't have anything to say. We all just kind of sat there. I didn't want to go to the grave site. I felt like it was going to be too much, but I thought about what my mother had said to me earlier in the day and I knew as much as I didn't want to go, the regret would be much harder to deal with.

When we finally arrived, the driver had to throw down salt because of all of the snow and ice. He opened up the doors on both sides, one behind the other we climbed out but my mother just sat there. My father walked over to her side and reached out for her. She said, "No, I can't go. I couldn't possibly leave my baby out there. I will just sit in the car and wait for you all." I asked did she want me to stay with her. She shook her head and asked to just be alone. When I got over there I took a seat in front of the casket and waited for Reverend Turnblad to begin the the ceremony. He must have really loved Lawrence because he never comes to the cemetery. Then he began, "Everyone repeat after me: Our father who art in heaven…" I just sat there as cold as it was, people were shivering but I didn't feel a thing. My body was numb. I longed to hear his voice or see his smiling face. When he finished I couldn't get up. My father told me it was too cold and I needed to come to the car. I didn't budge. Clarence walked over next. "Come on," he said. I couldn't get up. It was like I was paralyzed. I couldn't just leave him. My dad told Walter to see if he could talk to me. I didn't want to hear anything that anyone had to say. I just wanted my brother. I finally got up and I picked up a rose they had painted black and I put it in my pocket. I kneeled down and I kissed both ends of the casket. I didn't know which one was his head and I definitely wasn't trying to kiss his nasty, crusty, stinking feet. When I thought about that, I began to laugh, and the crazy part of it all is that I could hear him laughing too. I knew he was with me. He just wasn't there in the flesh anymore. I started walking toward the car. But it was like I could feel him looking at me and I couldn't go. I had to walk back over there. I didn't want to cause yet another scene but I had to go back. I said a small prayer for him, asking God to keep my brother and thanking him for allowing us to be paired together. Then I walked away again. But as I walked to the car for the second time, I felt him calling me back again, but this time as I walked over there it was like he was standing right there and he said, "Get your ass in that car." It scared me and I hauled my tail back to the car.

We went back to the church for the repast, but none of us could eat. I couldn't believe all of the people there. My father said, "It's a free meal isn't it?" I laughed and when we got into the fellowship hall of the church the real shit hit the fan. One of Lola's friends wanted to start some shit up in there. She had spoken with my mother earlier in the week and she wanted to come over and pray with my mother. Lola told her it was fine whenever she got there. But she was taking so long that Lola started going through the motions and felt she needed to get out of there. My father explained this to her when she got there and everything was fine, but it was another story when she got to the repast and saw my mother face to face. She told her that if Lola didn't want her in the house then she shouldn't have given her the invite. I looked at her and had to ask for God's forgiveness before I did anything. I said, "Bitch, my brother just got put into the ground if you don't get the hell away from my mother with all of that foolishness, I am going to take matters into my own hands and beat all of the living shit out of you." She looked and just stormed out of there. I guess she thought one of my parents would correct me. My mother was out of it and my father was proud of me at that moment for taking up for my mother.

And in the middle of all of this there was Mary up to her same old antics. She had the nerve to be walking around the room with a busted up five-dollar check asking for someone to cash it. She knew the damn thing wasn't any good and she also knew everyone in there knew what she was up to. This had become a routine for her at funerals or other family events. It was really embarrassing. When she got to the side of the room where we were, my father and Uncle Eugene were standing side by side. My father went on and gave her the money and said he didn't want her check. Uncle Eugene said, "Don't look over here Ma, I don't have any money." And he walked the other way. Grandma is like a little puppy, she is loyal to whoever is feeding her. So when he walked off, she said to my father, "The broke bitch. He walked off because he knows he owes me money. Just look at him over there being the bull shitter he is. It doesn't make any sense, does it?" My father couldn't believe she was saying this to him, but he knew that it was typical of Mary so he just shrugged his shoulders, shook his head and walked away.

The people were starting to fade out. It was getting very late. It was turning more into a social hour than a repast. It didn't seem like everything was as long as it was. But that was just the type of person Lawrence was. He brought out the dignitaries as well as the drunks on the street corner. The limo driver was nice enough to stay around to take us home.

When we got into the car it was just in time to see the segment they had done on the news. We didn't even know they had been there at the service. Then we saw him. That curly haired, pretty eyed little boy in one of the earlier segments that Mr. Patterson had done on him, he was the cutest thing. My mother instantly started up again, as she kept repeating over and over again, "My baby, my baby." My father thought it was best they cut it off, but she wanted to continue watching. She said, "Wow, look at how good I look." That lightened the mood and we just sat there laughing and talking and remembering all of the fun times we all had shared together. We were about to begin the healing process. All of the work was over, the funeral was over and he was placed in the ground. And now we can begin to grieve. I couldn't imagine how my life was going to be without him, but at this moment I felt safe, even with all of the issues between my parents and me.

When I got home, though, the pain intensified. All of the preparations were over and all of the people were gone. And the reality of it all began to set in and now I had to figure out just what to do with my life. I was barely sixteen. But up until that moment I was still a little girl. I was Lawrence's little sister and now I am just Lana. Now I have to look at things as me being alone.

My mother and I have mended some of those fences but she is still the enemy and my father has his moments where I'm not even sure how he feels about me. I always felt he looked at Lawrence and me as baggage and a part of me felt like he was happy Lawrence was out of the picture because now he could run wild and be free to do whatever, because now my mother didn't have this grown son to protect her. And when it comes to me and my father, he only dreams of the day when I am out of his hair. Lawrence was the balance in a shaky situation. Now everything is uneven. I told my mother I no longer wanted to take those pills. They were just a means to an end. Tonight, I just wanted to feel everything.

I wanted to see him laying there and think about the last time I would ever see that face in front of me and the last time I could reach out and touch him. I wanted to think about just how much I loved him and how much I depended on him and just how much I was going to miss him. My life would never be the same.

Hope stayed with us one last night. We sat in my room and talked about all of the things we had been through with Lawrence. We talked about our fondest memories of the greatest love in both our lives. She told me he had given her money to hold for him because he was planning to get a place for the two of us and she wanted to buy some things for me because she felt he would want her to do it. She said she wanted me to have a nice birthday in spite of him not being there in the physical. I told her she didn't have to do it. I would just much rather her give the money to my parents. At that moment, she just stared into space. I never understood why she told me she had money that belonged to my brother, but she never spoke a word to my mother about it.

When I woke up the next morning, she was gone. She left me one hundred dollars and a note that said this is your Christmas and birthday present from Lawrence. I know he loved you and that you must do whatever it takes to make him proud because he will always be watching from the clouds.

I told my parents she had some money that belonged to my brother. I felt it was only fair she give it up, but they wouldn't believe me because of how good she had been during the whole ordeal, staying with us and all. I couldn't believe they didn't believe me, but that just showed me things hadn't changed much between us. My feelings were a little hurt, but I brushed it off as always. I knew at this point I could only depend on me. So, at that moment I became a woman, because the little girl no longer had a superhero.

Later on that day my parents called me into their room. I had no idea what was exactly going on but they felt it was in my best interest to leave my school. They didn't want the person or persons to come looking for me because we had been on TV and they didn't know what was going on. I looked at the pain in my mother's eyes and though I didn't agree with it, I said okay. They had already gotten in touch with Reverend Turnblad to see if he could pull some strings at one of the private schools in the city. I really started turning red, but what could I do? I had to play their game. I no longer had the protection of my brother anymore. I had to learn how to grin and bear it and fast.

I needed an outlet. I knew if I didn't have someone or something to take my mind off it all, I would lose it. I began to write, and it was my only therapy. I wrote poems about Lawrence leaving me, and once I started I couldn't stop. My mother came in and told me I didn't have to go back to school until they found a placement for me. I was happy about that. I loved school and I always got good grades but who wouldn't want to be out of school? She said they had made arrangements with my guidance counselor so I wouldn't fall behind and I would be prepared when I got to my new school. However, we had to go up to the school in order to get the work. She asked if I was up to the task. I said, "No." I wanted to wait until the next morning. I didn't want to go up there at the end of the day and see all of those people, staring and feeling sorry for me. She understood and left me alone to finish my writing.

For the rest of the afternoon I just sat there writing and allowing my emotions to come across on that paper. My tears began to run down my face and I let it all go. I put on my favorite sad music and took out all of the pictures Lawrence and I had ever taken and I cried and cried until I felt a little better. I knew it wasn't his fault he left me, but I started to feel resentment. I resented him for getting out of the situation and leaving me here to fend for myself. I would have been with him if he didn't leave me that morning or he would have made it home because he had me with him. I resented my parents for the situation they had placed us in. The last six months of my brother's life we were in hell.

I was lost and I didn't know how I was going to find my way. The next morning, we went to the school. All of my teachers and friends told me how sorry they were for my loss. And then I had to do it. I had to go to my locker and see all of those pictures. It had only been a couple of weeks since I last opened it, and my brother was still alive. My father went with me and held my hand as I took the pictures down. When we got home there was a message on the machine from Reverend Turnblad. He had made contact with a representative from a few of the private schools in the area. She spoke with my guidance counselor at school and she wanted to meet with me and my parents over the weekend. Of course, my father said no, he wasn't going. He left the decision up to my mother. When I heard this, I asked the wrong question, "Well, if you aren't going to be a part of the process then why can't I just go back to Dunbar?" Instantly my mother began to cry. She said, "We don't know who killed your brother. That maniac is still out there and they could find out you go to that school and come looking for you and my heart can't go through losing my only living child. I already lost your brother and I can't lose you." I just looked at her. I wasn't going to fall for this guilt trip. The person who murdered my brother wasn't looking for me. Everyone knew he was just in the wrong place at the wrong time. Why in the hell would the person or people come looking for me? But for argument's sake I just agreed and left the room.

Things were starting to go back to the way they had been all along. I knew I would have to face this dark road alone. For the next few days I just stayed in my room. I cut myself off from everyone. I didn't want to speak with them. They were ruining my life and they knew it. Everyone else began to go through their own turmoil. Daphne couldn't handle the pressure of her senior year. It was to rough trying to concentrate on school and deal with the pain of losing another cousin/brother/role model/ friend. The last two years haven't been peachy keen. We lost Elmo and now Lawrence. She really went crazy. Cutting off all of her hair was only the beginning for her. She ran away again but this time she went to New York City. Elsa was a nervous wreck. Daphne was almost legal, so there was nothing the police could do because she was old enough to know exactly what she was doing. She was all over the place hanging with God knows who and doing God knows what. And with all that was going on, Elsa was tired. She didn't know what to do. She knew her child was in pain but what could she do about it, if she didn't know where her child was? Daphne had to be the one to ask for the help. Elsa had other things to worry about. Tico and Ahmad were young impressionable minds and she refused to allow Daphne's constant mishaps to affect her little boys. She just prayed Daphne would get it together for her sake and to honor Lawrence and Elmo's memory. Really, they would be the last one's wanting any of us to fall apart over them. If anything, they would want us to do something positive with our lives. Elsa prayed every day and night that Daphne would wake up and straighten up. But she would have to want that for herself. This was a really shaky time for all of us. Lawrence was the stronghold in most of our lives and it was hard trying to face another day knowing he wasn't going to see it.

Now let us put our focus on the real Queen Bee, Ms. Mary Magdalene and that wacky child of hers, Whitney. The two of them together are the funniest duo of all times. Mary is still trying to break out either through her blues or becoming an actress. She goes on more auditions than the law allows. That's one of the things we respect most about old Mary. She will get up and go in a heartbeat and not give a damn about how any of us feel about it. It's just a sad thing that she is in her second coming with motherhood. Whitney gets up and leaves whenever she gets the urge of getting high. I am so sick and tired of her calling my mother asking for food and a babysitter. Mary called and when she asked I had no other choice but to tell her exactly how I felt. I told her "Grandma, I am not their mother and I can't watch them. You should take them to whatever hideout their mother is in and drop them off." She was outraged. You could hear her anger through the phone. "What do you mean? I am not taking these kids anywhere but right here." I said, "Well, I guess it's either that or miss your audition. I am not watching them." She said, "Wel,l I guess I will just tell your mother." I laughed, "Grandma, no offense, but we barely speak, and neither she nor my father can make me do anything. So, go ahead and try to say something to them. They will be babysitting them theirselves, and we both know that's not going to happen." She slammed the phone down on me. I laughed and called Elsa to tell her, just how sick her crazy ass mother was. We laughed about it and that was the end of that.

Then a call came in on Elsa's end. She told me she had to go because it was Daphne and she seemed to be in some kind of trouble. "Ma, is Eugene home?" Daphne said, while she was sobbing profusely. "What is wrong with you? Where are you? Where have you been? What's going on?" Elsa was a nervous wreck with this phone call. She knew something was really wrong with her baby girl and she had no idea how to get to her, where she was and if she was she alright. Daphne was trying to explain but the more she tried to cut into the conversation, Elsa just went on and on. Then finally Daphne yelled, "Ma, can I talk please? I know you are upset but let me get a word in." The phone was beginning to break up, Daphne managed to get out what she had to say. "Ma, I am in Front Royal and these girls beat me up. I am hurt really bad. If Eugene is home can he come and pick me up or can you come and get me, I want to come home. Ma, I am so sorry for putting you all through this. Please come and get me. I don't want to be here anymore."

Elsa began screaming, and instantly Eugene ran down the stairs. With our family's track record, he just knew someone else had kicked the bucket. But when he finally got her calmed down she explained the conversation and he quickly grabbed his keys and headed straight for the door. He wasn't thinking that he didn't have a clue where he was going until he got clear down the street. Then he drove back and beeped the horn. Elsa came racing out of the house to give him the address to where she was. He raced all of the way there. They had never been able to build a relationship, but whenever she needed him he tried to be a father and come running to her rescue.

When he got there, she was lurking behind the building. At first, he thought maybe Elsa had given him the wrong address, but when he turned the lights on he saw her peeking from around the corner on the side of the building. She had been badly beaten. He got out of the car to help her. For the first time in almost four years there was no sign of her rough exterior. She was humbled by the experience of having those girls whip the hell out of her. At first, there was total silence, but the both of them knew a barrier had been broken and a new-found respect had formed. Then out of no where she began to cry again. "I know I haven't been the best child to be around and to even love and I am sorry. Thank you for rescuing my mother and making us a family, and thank you for rescuing me." He didn't want to seem as though he was softened by her comments. He didn't want her to think any less of him, because there was so much animosity between them over the course of these four years. So, he just said, "That's what a father is here for." He wanted to break down but he held it in, but there was crying on the inside and he knew the tears would flow once he got home and was able to tell Elsa about their touching conversation and he knew she would break down.

Finally, something happened that made Daphne's true feelings come out. The next morning when she woke up, she went to her mother and really made amends for the time she was gone. She had missed everything she had worked so hard to accomplish. She was months shy of graduation and now she would have to relive her entire senior year over again. So, there would be no prom, no graduation. She pretended as if she wasn't bothered by it but deep down inside it was killing her. So, after she lied to her mother and said she really didn't plan on participating in the activities, Elsa promised not to bring it up anymore. Daphne said, "Ma, while I was away I made a decision that I do want something out of my life. I just regret the fact I screwed up so close to my graduation. But hey, death is a reason for not caring and giving up. But I know Lawrence and Elmo would want more for me."

Elsa asked what she was going to do in order to make these things happen. She said she looked into the opportunity of going into Job Corps. Elsa thought the idea was great as long as the placement wasn't back in DC. She knew Daphne would be eighteen in a couple months but she was still in control until then. So, the two of them had a long talk about the mistakes Daphne had made and how she could clear things up. Elsa was no longer upset in at situation because Daphne was allowing her in and that was something she hadn't done in a very long time. They began doing research on Job Corps and were able to narrow the search down to three choices. There was a place not to far from Front Royal, but Elsa was against that because it was still too close and if things got too hard for Daphne then she may just run off again. Then there was a place in New Jersey, but Daphne didn't want to be too close to the misfits she had been running with over the course of the last few months. They finally decided on Pittsburgh, Pennsylvania. They knew if she went there then there would be no way of her running home or back to DC when things got a little shaky. To her shock and amazement, Daphne was in total agreement with what Elsa was saying. She said for the first time she realized just how screwed up she was and it took Lawrence's death for her to wake up. So, Elsa and Eugene took her down to the office in order for her to sign the papers. They were only giving her a few days to get her things together. She was going to be gone for at least a year. The good thing was she would be able to come home on weekends after being there for at least three months. Daphne was finally being the responsible person we all knew that she could be. We promised each other that we would write every week so she wouldn't feel this was ever a mistake. She needed to be prayed for and encouraged because she made the right decision in all of this. Elsa was so happy. Finally, things were coming together and Elsa had her daughter back and the family was starting to fall into place. Its' just sad it took Lawrence and Elmo leaving for things to turn out this way.

But back at our house, on the other hand, things were just about to liven up. For some reason, everyone was under the impression Lawrence's death had changed everyone or because of divine intervention it was going to change them. But no matter what, Twinkie was going to be Twinkie. He couldn't deal with the pressure of my mother and I being upset all the time. But no one expected him to take the stance he did. I was laying in my room, and even though I finally talked them into letting me go back to my school, I still had my issues involving my brother leaving me. I was in a depressed state. The girl everyone laughs at and laughs with, but deep down inside my heart is breaking and I am slowly dying a painful death. He walked past the door and when he peaked into my room the tears were flowing from my eyes. And then he said it, "What in the hell is wrong with you?" I tried to ignore him but he kept picking, and when

I answered I said, "I don't want to be bothered right now, can you please get out of my room and leave me alone?" He said, "I know you aren't still crying about Lawrence." I jumped up off of the bed at this point because by now the smoke was starting to blow from my ears. I said, "Would you please go away? I don't want to talk about it." He said, "Well I know that's what you are upset about and just to let you know, I am getting sick of this Lawrence shit. You and your mother should be over this shit by now." Then he walked out of the room as if he had just done something good. I couldn't believe I heard what I heard. I had to stop what I was doing because my adrenaline started to pump and something came over me. I ran down the stairs in the kitchen and headed straight for the butcher knife. How dare he speak of my brother's death as if it was a piece of cake or a game we were playing and lost? Those are the types of things a person gets tired of hearing after a period of time. But he was speaking of my brother. It hadn't even been that long for him to say he was sick of it. I wanted him to feel the same pain I was feeling. My mother ran behind me and grabbed the knife and pulled me from behind and sat me down so we could talk things out. I didn't want to hear anything she had to say because the end result was that she was going to take his side in the end so it really didn't matter. It was at that moment that my mother told me she felt that she couldn't handle her pain and mine, so she was going to send me to a psychologist. I didn't know why she wanted me to do this. I was just interested in seeing him hurt. So, I agreed with her for the moment, all the while I was plotting. But then I thought about my brother and what he would want me to do, I just went back upstairs to my room and blasted the sad music louder than it was before just to irritate his ass.

The next day when my mother came to pick me up from school I was informed I had an appointment with a therapist. At first, I was a little nervous but in the end it was like a sense of release came over me because I was going to be able to talk out my emotions with someone who didn't have direct contact with the situation. Everyone else I spoke with wanted to tell their feelings about Lawrence and how their lives were shattered because of his death and then there was me just sitting there like I was an afterthought. No one cared that he was my brother and that I was the closest person to him. No one seemed to understand that my life would never be the same and that I would never get over him leaving me. In a sense, everyone else (other than my mother) could put the pieces of the puzzle back together. Their family unit was still intact but mine was minus one, and to top it off, he was the most important piece of the puzzle you need for completion. Lawrence completed me, and with him dead, my life was at a standstill, and whoever this therapist was they would be able to help me work through the issues I was facing. I was drowning in my own sorrow.

When we arrived at the office, I was shocked. It was in a row house not too far from my school. I covered up so none of my peers would notice me if they lived in the area. I didn't want anyone to think I was crazy. When we walked into the house the receptionist pointed me upstairs my mother said, "Go. It will be alright once you talk to someone else." The layout of the house was similar to our house on Sixth Street, so that was a good sign for me. I had a comfortable feeling walking into the room. It wasn't like I thought it was going to be. It wasn't like on TV and in movies when you lie on a couch and tell someone your innermost feelings. When I opened the door there she was this tiny little woman with a persona that was so big it over took the room. "Come in! I won't bite," she said, lightening the load.

I walked in and sat down in a lounge chair and she asked me to tell her a little about myself. I told her some things and then I went straight to the point, my life without Lawrence. I had my poetry in hand and I let her read some of the thoughts I had since he'd been gone. When she finished reading my poem entitled *Life Without You*, she had tears in her eyes and she couldn't go on reading. She stepped out for a minute. I guess she had to gather her thoughts and wipe her eyes. When she returned she began by saying, "You are an amazing young woman and I know you are going to make something of yourself." Then she started to tell me her thoughts surrounding the whole ordeal. She said, "Do you know what I think that your problem is?"

I said, "My brother died and I am living in a total nightmare that I can't seem to wake up from."

She said, "No, not that. Of course, your life is forever changed and unfortunately there is nothing anyone can do about it. Everyone has an appointed time in life to leave this earth. Your main problem with all of this is you were never able to see him for the last time and able to tell him goodbye. It would have been hard for you regardless, but the fact he wasn't able to see you and vice versa is painful."

I never thought about it from that aspect. I said, "I guess you have a point. It does bother me. I feel abandoned. He knew he was the only person beyond everything I could rely on and he left me and he didn't say goodbye. Even down to when he left out of the house that morning, he snuck out. I had no idea he was gone and that is the same way he left my life. So yes, I am hurt so much by that. And I hate the way he died and I hate the fact my brother died alone. I hate to think he was scared. And I often wonder what the last thoughts in his mind were when he just gave up. And then I am angry because I feel he should have fought a little harder to hold on for me. I needed him. He knew what our situation was and he got out and I have to face this dark road alone and now with him gone it's even darker. I am all by myself now."

She said, "You are not alone. You have your mother. And she loves you." I began to laugh. I said, "I know she loves me but she is not on my side right now. She is with my father. They never mentioned me coming to a therapist until I tried to kill him last night because he made a very hurtful comment about him being tired of me crying over my brother."

She couldn't believe it. She just shook her head and said sometimes men don't know how to overcome their emotions. She said, "Enough of that, we will get into that later. I want you to do me a favor. Close your eyes and envision yourself in a room with your brother right now. If God gave you five minutes alone with your brother in order to say goodbye to him, what would you say to him?"

I closed my eyes and I could see him there and I began to cry. It was like my emotions were purging themselves. I couldn't stop crying and I began to talk to him. "Why did you leave me? I needed you and I loved you more than anything in this whole wide world. I am lost. I have to learn to live on my own. How can I live without you? I know it wasn't your fault and I know I must say goodbye, so goodbye, Lawrence. I loved you then and I love you now." The tears were like an endless river. I couldn't stop crying.

She said, "Okay, open your eyes." When I did I felt better. I felt as if a weight had been lifted off of my shoulders. Then she began asking me about Twinkie and the role he played in my unhappiness. When I began to tell her about the horrible things he had done and how he treated me and my mother she wanted my mother to come in and be apart of the session.

My mother walked in and when she did it was no longer my session. She took it over. I was like, "Hello, you could have just made the appointment for yourself." She laughed and the therapist said, "Girl, hush your mouth. You will have plenty time to get your feelings out. I just wanted to see your mother's point of view." A couple more minutes went by and my hour was up. I went to visit her a few more times but I was noticing a pattern. My mother was now coming into each session and I was not being allowed my therapy time because she was taking it up talking about her issues, so I decided not to go back. If I am in need of therapy let me have therapy and you set up your own appointments and don't waste my time. My mother was a little disturbed by my decision, but she knew she was taking my sessions for herself. There was no denying it.

Once she realized therapy wouldn't do the trick for me, my mother just let it go and said well two years will go by fast and then I would not have to deal with the issues with my father unless I wanted to because I would be in college. Though it didn't help me, I felt a little better. I mean, two years wasn't that long. I just tried my hardest to put my issues aside. I was already unhappy in my situation, so there was no point in making my problems have problems.

One of Lawrence's friends made these special shirts and I was proud to wear it, but as always Twinkie had something to say about it. "I don't have any problems with you wearing that shirt just as long as you wear it in the house," he said. I laughed and agreed for argument's sake. He painted some picture to my mother that if someone saw me wearing that shirt then I would be considered a target. So she begged and pleaded for me not to wear the shirt outside of the house. So, the next morning I folded up my shirt and went to school. I put it on when I got there and wore it proudly. He was my brother and I wanted everyone to know just how much I missed him.

Toward the end of the day I knew I had to take the shirt off because my mother would be coming to pick me up and I didn't want her to see it. I went to my locker and to my surprise I had someone there waiting for me. "Little girl, I don't know who you are but you need to take that shirt off," the person said as they stood behind me. All of these crazy thoughts filled my head, and all I could do was think, Oh Lord, Twinkie was right. I turned around and said, "Excuse me, who are you?"

He then said, "There is no need to know who I am, just take off the damn shirt. That is my cousin Lawrence and I am tired of you females walking around this school wearing shirts of people they don't know like it's a badge of honor. Take off the shirt or I will take it off for you."

I began to laugh hysterically. At this point, and I could see it was frustrating for him and he was dead serious. I said, "So this is your cousin? Lawrence is your cousin?" as I pointed down to his picture.

"Yes," he said, "you heard me, my cousin. Is that a problem?"

I said, "No, it's no problem. So how is he your cousin? Do you know all of his family?"

He said, "Yes I do, he is my cousin isn't he."

"You know all of his family, mother, father, sister and everybody else." I said in amazement.

"Are you deaf? did you hear what I said? Yes, that's my family, of course I know all of them. His mother is my aunt," he said.

"Okay, I apologize since this is your family and obviously I don't know him but I'm not taking off my shirt."

By this time one of his friends had walked over, but little did he know his friend knew my family very well and he was like a brother to me. "Bern," he said, "Can you please tell this chick to take off my cousin's shirt?"

Bern walked over and gave me a hug and when he saw the shirt he instantly began to laugh. "Are you sick or something? Do you know who this is?" Bern said as he still laughed in disbelief.

"Yeah, that's my cousin."

"Not him, the girl wearing the shirt."

"I don't know who she is but she needs to come up out of that shirt."

Bern said, "Dummy, that's her damn brother." As black as he was he started to turn purple. I looked at him, shook my head closed my locker, and went on about the rest of my day.

When my mother came she saw I had the shirt on but she wasn't upset. I told her the story and we had a good laugh. That's how I knew part of her was still the same, but she had to play a role in front of Twinkie.

Things were the best they could be, I guess. But then, before we knew it, more drama was right there smacking us in the face. We got home from work and school and Twinkie was nowhere in sight. His truck was parked outside, but he wasn't in the house anywhere. Then when we got upstairs the bed was not made up. And that is not Twinkie. He will make the bed when you are still laying there sleeping. Instantly, my mother knew there was something seriously wrong with the picture. She picked up the phone and before she called she pushed redial to see who the person he called was. The phone rang and when the person on the other end said hello, things got really shaky. "Who is this?" the voice shouted on the other end. My mother kind of stood there baffled for a few seconds. "Who wants to know?" she said in response to this unidentified person's rude tone. "Whoever you are, what are you doing calling from my man's house?" this woman was screaming now on the other end. My mother just laughed and said, "Your man, who is this man that you are speaking of?" She said, "Twinkie Felder, that's who. And again, I ask, what in the hell are you doing calling me from his phone? What in the hell are you doing in his house?"

My mother said, "First, I will say you are not the first and sweetheart, you won't be the last. I am Mrs. Gavin Felder, Twinkie's wife for four years and we have been together for twenty-one years. Now it's my turn to ask the damn questions. Who in the hell are you? I am calling from my own damn house looking for my damn husband. So now you start answering the questions."

The lady became irate by this time. "His wife? You must be on something. He is not married."

"Sweetheart, I beg to differ. I have the marriage license and the photo album to prove it."

She then said, "Well. I need to see them. I need proof. Women always lie to try to take what you have. And I refuse to allow someone I don't know to steal my man away from me."

My mother just laughed and then said, "Well, since you are so familiar with him then I know you know where I live. I will be here and you can come over at any given time to see me." When she hung the phone up she had a dazed look on her face. I wasn't sure what was going on and I really didn't want to know. Things were too crazy as they were and I wasn't trying to get caught up in any more of their drama.

My mother told me to stay upstairs because she didn't know what was about to go down. A few minutes later there was a knock at the door. My mother had just come from getting her hair done and had on a nice suit she wore to work that day for a meeting. It's funny, a woman always wants to look her best when she is being approached by another woman. She invited this lady in and they sat and talked for awhile. This poor woman was just an innocent victim in Twinkie's scheme. He had this poor crippled woman thinking he was going to marry her. She was the one that had done all of the work in the house. He was only giving her a couple hundred dollars here and there and she accepted it because she had been in love with him all of the years she had known him. My mother was there consoling her. Yes, that was the Christian thing to do, but when a man changes his number out of the blue and all of a sudden has a curfew and can only speak to you during the day then you should get a light bulb over your head.

She should have been cursing her ass out and throwing her out of the house. But that's not the type of person my mother is. You have to accept her and love her for who and what she is or leave her alone. She consoled the woman and then the lady asked to take the wedding album with her to show her mother. Her family had been so fond of him. Her sister was married to one of his dear friends. My mother told her she couldn't allow her to take the whole album but she would let her take a few pictures, but she had to promise to bring them back. The woman was so hurt. She stood at the door and laid her head on my mother's shoulder and cried like a little baby. I looked down the stairs in disbelief. I couldn't believe my ears and eyes. Another woman had surfaced. I didn't want to say it out loud, but "I told you so" began running through my head a thousand miles a minute.

As the lady was leaving, my mother said, "I know you probably know where he is, so when you get to wherever you are going, tell him his wife and daughter are at home waiting for him."

Then about ten minutes after the woman left, he came straggling through the door as if he didn't know what had just taken place. He was calling my mother honey and baby like it was something he did on a regular basis. He even offered to take us out for dinner, which was a dead give away all on its own. Why is it that men always make matters worse when they get caught? All he had to do was act normal. But no, he wanted to play a knight in shining armor all of a sudden.

My mother looked over at him and said, "You know what? You disgust me. But hey, now I know the truth, which I suspected all along when you refused to get on camera with me when Lawrence died."

He interrupted, "Oh, here we go with that again. I have told you before and I will tell you again you are talking reckless and you need to stop." And the words went back and forth until there was a knock at the door. He began biting his nails and stuttering. He had to have known his lie was going to catch up to him.

My mother answered the door and called out, "Twinkie it's for you. There is a Barbara at the door." He just stood there. And when he glanced over at me I just laughed at him. He looked like a child before they get a spanking. He knew he couldn't run and he had to face the music. My mother walked into the room and said, "Honey, did you hear what I said? You have company, or would you like me to bring her in there? Lana, you need to go upstairs. You don't need to see any of this." As I was walking up the stairs my mother showed the lady into the room. And before any words were spoken she smacked the living shit out of Twinkie.

I cried laughing as I ran up the stairs. He was screaming at this woman, accusing her of trying to ruin his marriage. The lady just cried. She said how he had used her for all of those years and he took her love for granted. She apologized to my mother and asked for her forgiveness. My mother told her she had nothing to be ashamed of. She was just as much a victim as she was. Twinkie just sat there. He didn't say anything and he didn't move. My mother then asked the lady for her wedding pictures and then showed her out. As she was getting up to leave she walked over to where Twinkie was and then she kicked him in his bad knee. My mother didn't say anything when she hit him the first time, but this time she had to speak up. She then told the lady to get out. She stood at the door and begged my mother to keep in contact with her. My mother said, "Miss, I feel nothing but sorry for this whole ordeal. The pain both of us feel, I would do anything to take it away, but it isn't that easy and I took a vow before God to stay through the good or the bad and right now it's a test of my faith. So, I have to be with my husband. I am sorry, but now that you know he is in fact married, I would appreciate it if you left him alone." Then she closed the door.

I ran down the stairs to see if my mother was alright. When I saw she was holding it together I just told her my emotions on the whole situation.

Judging by the way the woman left, I knew it was far from over and I let my mother in on how I was feeling. My mother in all of her infinite wisdom said, "Baby, I'm no fool. I know it is just beginning with that nut." Neither of us knew just how nutty she actually was. Neither of my parents said a word to each other that night. My father slept on the couch.

The next morning we found out just how nutty this woman really was. The phone began to ring at six o'clock the next morning. I was just rolling over for the last time. I picked up and then placed the phone back down. And after that it continuously rang until my mother got up and took the call. All of a sudden, I was awakened by my mother. She said, "Well, you were right. She is a sick one. I made plans to meet with her sometime tomorrow. She says she has some things she wants to get off of her chest." I looked at her as if she was crazy. What else did she need to hear? He was having yet another affair and this woman didn't have any knowledge of him being married, just like the first. This is his pattern. What else did this woman need to say? But that was my mother, always trying to help someone out of the situation, but who was going to help her? I didn't say a word. I let her make her own decision. She was the mother and she had to have reason to be meeting this lady.

Then a few minutes later she ran in my room and said she had changed her mind. She said as she was sitting there in the bathroom that God gave her a vision of this woman having a gun and trying to kill her. Then she had a vision of me alone in a house with my father. And she knew it was the wrong thing. I was so happy to hear she had changed her mind. I didn't have a good feeling about this woman. Then the phone calls started again. My mother came into my room to answer. It was Barbara. My mother asked her if she would stop calling and she let her know that meeting her was out of the question. Barbara became outraged. She said, "Why don't you want to meet me? I have so much I need to get off of my chest about the whole ordeal with Twinkie." My mother said, "Well, I heard all I need to hear. You all had an affair and it's obvious. And I said you have no reason to be sorry. He deceived you, just as he did me."

Barbara was not going to take no for an answer. You could hear the desperation in her voice. She said, "You don't understand. I need to talk to you." My mother told her, "Look ,I am sorry. I cannot and I will not meet with you, not today, not tomorrow, not ever."

Then Barbara went on to say, "Well, I need to know if Twinkie still taking me to the doctor." Then my mother said, "Let me tell you something. I have tried to be nice to you. But now I feel you are taking my kindness for weakness. My husband is not taking you any damn where. So, you need to stop calling here."

Barbara hung the phone up. But my mother knew it was far from over. She went downstairs to where Twinkie was and lit into him. He needed to hear what was going on. This situation was only going to get worse. This time he had met a force to reckon with and he was going to have to be the one to deal with it.

NEW BEGINNINGS

The pain of losing Lawrence was starting to settle and things were finally starting to mellow out. My parents were getting along very well. Twinkie was being a perfect angel. He was barely leaving the house. But then the fear of crazy ass Barbara doing some harm to him helped put things into perspective for him. She was now stalking us and every morning we got a wake-up call like we were living in a damn hotel.

Every morning one of my parents told her not to call, but she refused to listen. I had enough drama on my plate at home, making school my only refuge. My guidance counselor called me to the office and showed me a copy of my transcripts. "Do you know what you are looking at?" he asked.

"I'm not quite sure, but it looks like a copy of all my grades," I said.

He said "Yes, but this is a key to your future. What would you do if I told you that you could get out of this place a year early?"

I smiled and said, "I would jump on it!"

He said, "Well, you are only a few credits shy of graduating. So, next year if we put you in Government and Senior English, then you will be out of here. You just need your mother's permission." I knew she would go along with it because she saw just how unhappy I had been. But I would have to sell Twinkie on the idea. Things had been running smoothly, but that could change at any given moment. This was a great opportunity, but it also meant I would have to work like crazy to do all of the things I was planning on doing the following year, like the SAT and sending out college applications. But I was up for the task.

Before I left his office, he looked at me and smiled as he said something I needed to hear; that I longed to hear, "Your brother would be so proud of you. Through all of your pain you could have given up, but you are fighting. I can see Lawrence right now smiling down on you." I smiled as the tears began to fall heavy from my face, because that was my main concern for the way my life would turn out. Lawrence was the only person whose approval I sought. He was the only person I wanted acceptance from and when he died, I felt empty. It felt as if I had no purpose. And now someone was acknowledging my pain and putting it into perspective.

During this time, everything was going wonderful for everyone in the family. My mother and father were working out whatever issues they had in regards to his affairs and she accepted it and forgave him. He was staying on the straight and narrow. The family up in them there hills were doing fabulous. Tico was about to go to high school, Little Ahmad was growing up and would soon have a playmate. Elsa and Lola's half sister Aretha contacted Elsa after many years to let her know she was dying. She had gotten herself together around the same time as Elsa, and their lives sort of imitated each other. They had done most of the same things in the streets, the both of them suddenly realized at the same time that the lives they were leading would only bring hurt and pain to themselves and others, and now the both of them started their second phase of motherhood. Aretha had a little boy a year older than Ahmad. When Elsa heard the news that Aretha was ill, she made a promise to be with her every step of the way. She came down to visit every week. She wanted to be there with her as they had been there for each other all of their lives. During their visits, Ahmad and her son Montique became very fond of each other. One day while Elsa had the boys outside, Aretha broke down and discussed her pain with Eugene. She was disturbed by the uncertainty of her little boy's future. She had two daughters with children his age but didn't think they would be willing or capable of bringing him up. And without discussing it with Elsa, Eugene offered to take Montique and raise him as their own and they would never let him forget his mother. She felt a sense of relief after knowing this. When Elsa returned she had no idea of what the conversation was, but felt an eerie feeling the way Aretha was hugging her when they were leaving. Aretha felt a sense of gratitude, but Elsa not knowing thought this was possibly the end. While they were riding home, Elsa cried the majority of the way. She just kept saying over and over, "Please don't take her now. We need to find someone to take Montique. Lord please don't take her now."

Eugene intercepted her prayer and said, "Well, I am glad you brought that up. We found a place for Montique while you were outside with the boys."

"Thank God for Jesus," Elsa quickly responded. "Who is taking him? Is it one of the girls? I don't want him to go to foster care. I would take him myself before I allowed that to happen."

"Wow, we think so much alike," Eugene said nervously.

"What are you talking about Eugene?" Elsa said now with a very puzzled look on her face.

"Well, I see how much Ahmad and Montique love each other and I don't want that poor boy to end up in the wrong environment, so I told Aretha we would take Montique and raise him as our own. That's why she was crying and so sincere when we were leaving; not because she got news her time is up."

Elsa was happy and disturbed at the same time. She loved Montique and she was grateful to Eugene, she just wished he would have discussed it with her first. But Aretha was her sister and she knew if her little boy was safe, then Aretha could go in peace, and that mattered more than anything. Eugene and Elsa wanted to give the little boy a little more time with his mother before they took him away. He was so young and he didn't understand any of the things that were going on. They wanted him to be around her for as long as he could because they were unsure if he would have any real memories of her as he got older.

It was so sad because Aretha was so full of life when we were children. She and Elsa together were like two peas in a pod. She was the other Aunt we never had and now she was dying and there was nothing any of us could do about it. At this time, we could only wait. When things started to get really bad for her, Elsa and Eugene came and packed Montique's things and headed back for the hills. A couple weeks later, Aretha said her last goodbye, took her final bow and headed for the skies. Yet another funeral, but this time it wasn't as sad. More than anything, our hearts went out to this poor little boy. Her daughters knew the joys of their mother, the smell of her hair, her laugh that was so contagious you couldn't help but laugh even if you didn't get the joke. And there sits this little boy that will never know her. He will only be able to go off of stories told by someone else.

There we were all in full force. The only piece of the puzzle missing was Daphne. She was doing to well in Job Corps and didn't want to sabotage her own growth by coming home. Whitney was even there. She had been doing great. She had a new boyfriend and he seemed to be what was missing for her. She had even been interviewing for jobs. Time marched on, even without some of the major players in our lives. But somehow things were taking a turn for the better. We were all getting older and we now understood life a little better.

The next few months went by like a flash and before I knew it, I was about to start what would be my junior *and* senior years in high school. I had been able to sell Twinkie on the whole graduating early idea. My mother was only concerned with my happiness at this point. Lawrence's death seemed to be the only thing that pushes me to get up in the morning. After my episode with Twinkie, I promised myself I wouldn't cry and show my emotions until I got out of that house. I was just biding my time.

If everything went according to my plans I would only be there for the school year, and after my graduation I was never sleeping in that house again. Little did I know his shit had only begun to come up to the surface. My mother and I were talking again like old times. She still had her moments where she would fall back under his spells, but it wouldn't last as long. She was even willing to do whatever possible to speed up the process in order to get me out of school. She was my number one supporter. "As long as you are happy with the choice you are making, then I am happy." She said over and over again. Twinkie was just happy I would be out of his house. He would walk around saying stupid shit like, "I'll be glad when you walk across that stage because you are getting out of here. You will have a diploma in one hand and suitcase in the other." And I would say right back to him, "You got that right. I am not coming back in here ever unless it's to visit my mother. Not for Christmas break or summer break. I hate this place. So that's something you don't have to worry about."

My mother was so hurt by both of our words but we were both being truthful. That's how I felt about him and that house and obviously that's how he felt about me. It was cool, though. I was just trying to get my things in order. Unfortunately, as with everything in my life, forks in the road always seem to pop up and try to detour me. But on this I was not going to allow any obstacle to stop me.

Since I was considered to be the mascot for the guys at my school, all of the girls seemed to hate me. I was a tom boy and all of the guys looked at me as their little sister and they all felt a need to protect me. I only had Lawrence to look up to growing up and there was no female presence. Daphne was always gone and the other females in the family were too old, too tired, and too much for me to deal with. The females in the senior class despised the fact I was being allowed to graduate early, and even went to the extreme of writing a petition to try and stop me. But little did they know there was nothing they nor the principal could do about it. I had just as many if not more credits than any of them. But the principal and the senior advisor did call me in for a meeting, which felt more like an interrogation. "Why are you in so much of a rush to graduate? Don't you know how much responsibility there is out there in the world? What are you going to do about college? Isn't it a little late to be filling out applications?" The fat bald-headed bitch, Ms. Williams, the senior advisor said. And Ms. Robinson agreed. I just sat there for a minute and stared at the wall. Then I felt the lump come up to my throat and I had to speak. "Do either of you know what my situation is? No, you don't. Therefore I don't think you should be allowed to tell someone they can't do something that will potentially help them. I have all of my credits. I get straight A's, so how can you tell me I can't graduate?"

"Well, Ms. Haynes we need to look at your files and see where you are before we approve anything," Ms. Robinson said.

"That's fine with me, Ms. Robinson. I know I have everything I need and if there is a problem, my mother can call downtown and speak to someone at the School Board. The student body doesn't run this school.

You are supposed to run this school, so if they have a problem that's on them, but I am graduating in June of 1997." After I shared my thoughts with them I kindly picked up my books and walked out of Ms. Robinson's office. I just knew there was going to be some trouble, but I said I will wait until everything comes about.

After all of the paperwork was signed by my mother, there was no way either of them, Ms. Robinson or Ms. Williams, could do anything about it. I went to my counselor's office and let him know what was going on. He laughed and said, "Now do you really think they want bad press? If your mother goes to the superintendent with your records and he sees your grades and credits, he will walk you across the stage himself. They will be the ones looking like fools. You are a bright young lady and it would behoove them to let you go through this. It is not often that you have a young lady like yourself in an environment like this, with all of your trials and tribulations and yet still you press on. So, don't worry about those old hags. They are just trying to feed into the issues of these envious girls." He made me feel better knowing I had someone on my side in that building. He told me to just wait it out for a few days and if I hadn't heard anything by then, then I should have my mother set up a meeting or go and speak with them again. In the meantime, he enrolled me in all of my senior classes.

It was so amusing seeing the faces of the girls that totally tried to harm any chances that I had of graduating. But I wasn't going to allow them to get the best of me. I just enjoyed watching them sweat. It was so obvious they were bothered just by my mere presence. I did as I was told and I waited a few days. There I was sitting in my government class and another student brought in a note for my teacher. I could tell it was about me. She said thank you to the student and then told him he could leave the room after she finished. She then got out of her seat and sat on the edge of the desk in front of me. She said, "For all of you that have a problem with this young lady being in this class, please raise your hand." They all looked around to see who would be bold enough to say how they really felt. No one was strong enough to do it. The saddest part is that the ring leader was sitting right there in the middle of the class. She then went on to say, "This young lady has as much right to be here as any of you. As a matter of fact, I think she may have more of a right because she has gotten an A on every homework assignment and pop quiz. And if any one has a problem with it, then tell them to come and speak with me."

I felt so relieved by her words and when I looked around the class everyone's eyes were on their work. The next day, I was in my English class and I got a call to the front office. When I got down there, it was Ms. Williams waiting for me with a smile on her face. "I knew there was going to be something that would hold you back and I found it. Last school year you had 31 absences. Can you explain?" I looked at her and I began to laugh. I said, "No disrespect, intended when I say this to you, Ms. Williams, but I feel as though I am being picked on by my peers as well as you adults and leaders of this school. Apparently, when you did your research, you didn't dig deep enough because if you did when you saw that many absences you would have seen they were all excused. My brother was killed a year ago and that's the cause for me being out of school that long. And even though I was out that long, I still had a 4.0 grade point average. You really have some nerve to call me out of class and make me rehash the most devastating incident in my entire life."

"Oh my, I am so sorry. I didn't know. Please forgive me." She said. But I didn't feel I should forgive her at that moment. She had played such a major role in my unbearable surroundings over the course of the last few weeks. When I saw that she was in such a state of shock, I began to milk it for everything it was worth. I wanted her to feel sorry for harassing me. "May I be excused now? I am missing out on my class time."

"Yes, and again please accept my apologies." I went to Mr. Buford's office and told him everything that went on. He told me I should have my mother come speak with them, that way they would know I meant serious business when I said I was going to graduate. I my mother and she said she would get on it. The next day she was called in for a meeting with Ms. Robinson to discuss the matter of whether or not I would be able to walk across the stage in June. They called me out of class to participate in the meeting. Ms. Robinson started by saying she felt it would be in my best interest to stay in school another year and have them to enroll me into a college bound program where I would take college courses and still graduate with my class. But I would be in a five-year college program instead of four. I was shocked to hear these words coming out of her mouth.

My mother looked at her and said, "That doesn't make any logical sense to me. My daughter has all of her credits now. Why in the world would I agree to her going to college but still be in high school? What if she fails next year? She wouldn't be failing her first year in college, she would be held back in the twelfth grade. If it was your child would you honestly agree to something this ludicrous?"

Ms. Robinson looked with total disgust on her face. "Mrs. Felder, I am only looking out for Lana's best interest. College is very expensive and by doing this she will have the chances at getting into one of the top schools."

My mother smiled and told her how much she appreciated her concern, but when it came down to it, it didn't matter about all of the scholarships because my education was already paid for. Ms. Robinson's face turned beet read. "Mrs. Felder, let me be frank. If you take her out this year, you will be messing up my quota. Each year we get funding and it is based on how many of our children graduated and go on to continue their education. We have already met our quota for this year. So, if Lana walks this year, that's a number missing from next year. I just have to be honest."

My mother said, "So, you are telling me you would prefer to hold this child back in order to meet a silly quota? Ms. Robinson that is a damn shame and thank you for your honesty, but no thank you for your help, my daughter will be walking across that stage in June." She picked up her things and walked out of the office. I quickly followed behind her. Although they had been making things very difficult for me, I couldn't help but feel sorry for Ms. Robinson, but she had been very harsh and cruel. So as quick as the feeling came that's how quick it left.

By this time, I had become attached to my surrogate brothers and sister, Lawrence's friends, Charles, Kim, and Bam. Just as I told my parents, Hope was only in it for what she could get out of him. She hated the fact he and Kim started hanging out with each other. But they were childhood friends. And she was genuine with her feelings for him. It wasn't about what she could get out of him. After the services and things were over, we barely saw or spoke to Hope, and truthfully that's when we needed her the most. But the three of them were there every step of the way. Unfortunately, Bam was incarcerated, but we wrote each other weekly. Kim would come by and pick me up and I saw Charles every day. He had become the second-best thing next to Lawrence. He would listen to my problems and he would make fun of my clothes and he would run guys away. Because of him I started to see the light at the end of that lonely dark tunnel. He was so excited when I told him that I was going to be graduating. He was opening a pager shop right up the street from my mother's job and I could go there whenever I wanted and see him and that was a great thing for me. I didn't have Lawrence and I was dealing with that as best as I could, but he made sure he left me in the most capable hands. Charles would always joke around and say he had to take care of me because I was Lawrence's most prized possession, so he had to make sure I was alright.

For me, life was as normal at this point as it was ever going to be. Daphne and I had been keeping in touch and we were rekindling our relationship. It was like we were children again playing on Sixth Street. She was really getting things together and she met a guy she seemed to really like. The only thing is, he was a little person. That's the one thing she has in common with her mother – they have a thing for the physically challenged. But she really liked him and the feelings seemed to be mutual. My mother was glad that the both of us were making the best of the situations in our lives, especially with all that we had lost. But we couldn't just let this life swallow us whole. We had to keep pressing on and keep fighting because Lawrence and Elmo would have kicked our asses if we had done otherwise.

Things at school settled and the issues I had were all in the past. I ran for homecoming queen and since I was still considered a junior they wouldn't allow me to win, but I sold more tickets and got more votes than any other girl there. I didn't care. I was just doing it for my brother. He always said he wanted me to run and I did, and for all intents and purposes, I won.

The next thing you know the holidays were rolling around again, the first Thanksgiving and Christmas without Lawrence. I had no idea how in the world we would ever get through it, but we did. We went to the cemetery and talked and laughed and cried. My parents and I shopped every day for Christmas. They bought everyone from the nextdoor neighbors to the elevator man at the hospital gifts. They say for some people, shopping is therapy, but for them that therapy session cost them every bit of ten thousand dollars. I wasn't going to question it, though, because Santa was very good to me.

My father for once seemed normal. We laughed and joked with one another. He even went down in the basement and played Christmas Carols while my mother and I sang. He started directing us and everything. It made the holidays seem bearable. I made sure I got him a very nice present and not the pair of socks I was thinking of getting him. I got him a nice robe and slippers to match. He was very appreciative.

And then the New Year rolled in. We had to say goodbye to all of the bad things that had transpired, from Lawrence's death to the adultery Twinkie had committed. It was a New Year and with the New Year came numerous possibilities. I was graduating from High School in a few months. There was so much to look forward to. We decided against going to church because we didn't feel the need to be reminded of what we didn't have going into the New Year. And Reverend Turnblad would be the one to bring it up in his year-end prayer. And none of us were capable of hearing him mention Lawrence's untimely death.

With time moving on and things being so perfect for everyone, I could only sit and wonder what would be next. There we were sitting a few days into the year and days away from the first anniversary of Lawrence's death and Grandma called. Whitney's new man was Chester, and turned out to be Chester the child molester. He had been raping one of the twins and Whitney didn't want to believe it. Grandma was irate but Whitney believed his cock and bull story that the little girl was imagining things. She wouldn't even take the girl to the hospital. My mother and Elsa decided if they didn't take her to get checked out they were going to call the authorities. Of course, with the fire from Elsa and Lola burning under her, Whitney flew to the emergency room. And low and behold her visit to the hospital proved that Elsa and Lola's worse nightmare was true Chester had been messing around with her. Grandma was ready to spit bullets. It was like she had to re-live her experience as a child a second time. For the first time, I could see the pain in her. It has to be a hard thing to deal with, especially when it's a person you trusted. My poor grandmother and little cousin, it's sad they had to be subjected to that. What a horrific incident for anyone to go through. My mother was now on this therapy kick. That was the first thing that she suggested. Eugene and Elsa wanted to come down but Grandma talked them out of it. Everyone, including Twinkie, wanted to teach this guy a lesson, especially since Whitney refused to press charges.

My father told me, "Boy this ass hole had better be glad that you are older and able to fight for yourself. Because if you were younger and he was around you, I would kick his ass just off of GP, it's no telling the thoughts he had running through his sick head. The sick bastard." When I heard him say it, I felt like I was dreaming or he wasn't talking to me about me. I just hugged him. Every so often the evidence that he loves us comes shining through. It seemed the New Year was going to be a good one and my thoughts were maybe my father is changing.

On the anniversary of Lawrence's death, he took me and my mother out for dinner after we left the cemetery and he even asked my mother to pray. I couldn't believe it. All of the prayers for him were finally being answered. He was even speaking to Elsa and Eugene again. God was truly working a miracle in his life. It was good to finally see my parents loving each other.

My mother and I were on our way home from church and she noticed one of her bracelets was missing. She cried and cried the entire way home. When we got there, she cried to Twinkie the entire night. When we got home the next day there was a box sitting on their bed. It was nicely gift-wrapped and the card on top said, "Thanks for being the greatest mother and wife a child and man could ever ask for." That was the nicest thing he had ever done for her. And he was even open to me having guys over and going out on dates. My mother said, "Maybe he is realizing, now that you are about to leave, what he has in our family unit and wants us to stay together. I almost fell for it. A few days before my seventeenth birthday he became very withdrawn, he wouldn't speak to any of us. I told him that whatever he was going through, it was going to be alright. The next morning, I went into their bedroom and I joked with him as usual. "Hey old man, can I get two dollars so I can catch the bus to my mother's job when I get out of school?" I said that to him thinking he was over whatever had been bothering him the night before.

"Hell no, I am not giving you anything. You need to walk to her job. I am tired of giving you money. How do I know you are actually spending it on the bus?" he said back to me in a very condescending tone. It really hurt my feelings because we had really been bonding over the course of the last few months.

"Why would I lie about two dollars? You know what, never mind I will just ask someone else."

Before I could complete my statement he had jumped clear across the room and was now confronting me in my face. "I am so sick and fucking tired of your mother fucking mouth. I should bust you in the lip for talking back to me," he said now in a very aggressive manner as he had his fist in my face. My mother jumped in the middle and pushed me back into the bathroom. "What in hell is wrong with you? I will not allow you to disrespect this girl like that. She was not being rude. She just asked a simple question to you and now you are taking whatever issues you have with someone else out on us. I was just waiting for the real Twinkie to come forward. I knew it was only a matter of time before you showed your face around here again. If you ever threaten to punch my baby in the face again, I will kill you."

He began to call the both of us all kinds of bitches and said he wished we would just leave his house. My mother told him that was the last time he was going to tell us to get out of his house. We left for work and school. While we were riding neither of us said a word. When I got to school my mother asked was I alright and I nodded my head. I think I was more in shock, because for the first time since I was a little girl I thought I had my father back. But I was quickly brought back into reality. And unfortunately, that was only the beginning.

I started spending more and more time at Charles' shop. He was my saving grace. He started throwing bowling parties and since I was known now as his little sister I had to be there by his side. He made me feel so special. It was like Lawrence had taken form in his body. Charles couldn't believe Twinkie had turned on us. He asked my mother was it alright for him to keep me up at the shop some evenings until they had the chance to work things out. My mother agreed, but what I didn't know was that this time she was really tired of him and she wanted out. She just needed real proof this time that he was still doing his dirt in the street so she could leave for good and never go back. A friend of hers had been caught up in a very similar situation and when she wanted to kick her old man to the curb she put a taping device on her telephone. And with that idea in mind Lola became inspector gadget.

She put that bug on our phone and found out that while the cat's away the mouse does more than play. She decided she would no longer perform her wifely duties and if he wanted to eat he would have to go out and buy food. We ate out every night. The first time she checked the tape we were in the mall shopping. I went into the dollar store in order to get some school supplies. When I got to the register a nice little old lady grabbed my attention. "Excuse me, baby, but are you with that lady in the silver car?" She said to me as I looked out the window. I said, "Yes ma'am, I am." She said, "Well if you are you had better decide on getting these things or getting a ride home because she is about to leave you."

Just as she was finishing I looked out the window and saw my mother speeding off. I dropped everything and ran for the door. I had to literally chase the car down. It was like she forgot she was waiting for me. When I caught her she was at a stoplight. I was huffing and puffing all out of breath. "Why were you trying to leave me?"

She said, "I'm sorry I was going to come back after I kick your father's ass."

"Why?" I said, because I had no clue what she had found out. She said, "Did you know your father has another child that's younger than you?" I instantly felt a lump come in the pit of my stomach. I couldn't believe my ears. I wanted to know what proof she had. And before I could ask her she popped in the tape and there was my father's voice and he was speaking with some woman. The woman started yelling at this little boy in the back ground. Then Twinkie asked to speak with the little boy. He was acting macho and trying to scare the little boy. The little boy said, "You aren't my father." And Twinkie said back to him as if he was offended, "Oh, so I'm not your daddy anymore?" Then the little boy apologized. I told my mother I wasn't sure if he was just saying it or if he really was the little boy's father. With Twinkie, one never knows.

When we went into the house she went into the room, closed the door and went to war. "I need to speak to you upstairs and right now. I don't give a damn what you are doing right now because I am going to kick your ass." She didn't flinch once. I was shocked usually when she was cursing him out; she would break under the pressure of it all. But this time she was calm cool and collected. Twinkie didn't know whether to run out of his fear or take whatever he had done like a man and follow her as she walked up the stairs. He turned and looked at me trying to figure out what was going on but I shrugged my shoulders and walked away. I went up to my room. I wasn't sure what was going on but I knew that it wasn't going to be pretty.

Then all of a sudden, I heard screams. I ran down the stairs and grabbed my knife and went charging into their room. "Get your hands off of my mother." But to my dismay, it was the other way around. It was Twinkie screaming. I was confused by the whole situation. She was really whipping his ass. He looked at me and said, "Get my hands off of her? She is beating on me! What about that? Tell her to leave me alone."

She said to him she was sick of the entire situation. It wasn't worth it. He had disrespected her far too many times and if she was to find out this little boy was his, then she was going to kill him and cut his thing off. I couldn't take it anymore. I was going to explode because my insides were dying to laugh. But I just looked at him and I began to shake my head.

He denied everything and told her wherever she was getting this information from then the person needed to be a man or woman about it and come and confront him and not try to break up his marriage and take his family away. I really died inside because his bullshit was so thick, I could smell it. He was the biggest con artist I had ever seen. But for the first time my mother stuck to her guns and refused to fall for it. I had no idea how serious she was when she told him it was over for them.

When I got to her job the next day she was on the phone with a realtor and we had an interview with him to see a house. She had finally reached her breaking point with him. I half-way believed her sincerity when she spoke about leaving this time for good. I wasn't able to put my total trust in her because I wasn't able to go through the process of having my hopes crushed if she fell back under his trance. So, I just let her do what she was doing and if it panned out, then I would show my emotions then and only then.

We didn't like the house we went to go see, so we went home in hopes the agent would find something else. But boy when we got there we were in for a bigger surprise than we ever expected. I went into the room to get the tape and we drove around the block so she could listen to it. "Did Kita enjoy her day in school? There was a bad accident on Silver Hill Road this morning and I didn't think that we would ever get there on time. I had a rough night so I am going to get some sleep. I will talk to you later. If I don't call it's because this bitch is calling me to nag me," he said to the same woman he had been conversing with the day before. She just laughed and asked him how in the world he put up with it. And his response to her was he had to do it for the sake of his daughter. When my mother heard this, she immediately cut through the alley way and ran to the house. He wasn't there so she patiently waited in the living room and this time she was going to draw blood. I tried calming her down. I asked did she want to talk to anyone but she refused every one of my suggestions and told me it was best that I go to my room and stay there until she told me it was cool to come out.

About an hour later I heard the key in the door. I almost felt sorry for him. I knew she was going to kick his ass and bad because of all of the times he would refuse to take me to school when my mother was ill. He had some nerve, his own flesh and blood. My mother would have to get out of her bed and then turn around and go back home whatever the situation was she may have been going through. Because he told her it wasn't his job to make sure I got there and if need be then I could just take the bus, but I wasn't allowed to ride the bus any other time. But here it is he could leave the house and pretend that he was going to the cemetery because that was the only place he would go early in the morning and he would take this woman's daughter to school with no problem.

So, when the door opened he was startled to see her sitting there in the living room. He told her it reminded him of his mother when he had done something wrong. She asked him, "Where did you go this morning?"

He said, "Oh shit, I knew it wasn't over last night. Look, I told your ass where I went this morning. I am not about to sit here and let you accuse me of something else."

"Accuse you of something else?" she said. "Then what in the hell were you doing on Silver Hill Road this morning and your black ass saying you were going to the cemetery. See, you never know who is watching you. And you always end up getting caught." He looked like he was staring at his mother's dead ghost. He stormed off and went into the family room. She sat there for a while. I went down there to check on her. She just sat there in a daze as the tears formed in her eyes and gently ran down her face. I had seen that face on numerous occasions and I knew the outcome was going to be good.

Then out of the blue she jumped up and went after him like a predator hunting for its prey. She was after blood. She ran into the family room but he wasn't there. He had gone upstairs. She slowly walked up the stairs because she trying to surprise. And when she got to that top step, she charged into the room and she jumped on his back. "Why do you have to lie? Just tell me the truth. Who in the hell is this woman this time? I am so sick and tired of you lying all of the fucking time. I have been there for you time and time again and I am so tired. Who in the fuck did you have in the car this time?"

He then told her that it was one of his daughter's kids that he was taking to school. So she called Charlene and asked did he take her daughter to school. You could tell by the conversation she was caught of- guard it was a long hesitation, but she then said yes, he did in fact take her daughter to school. The only thing about that was the little girl's school wasn't even in the direction in which he was going. But she felt bad enough putting someone else into the equation. So, when she got off of the phone with her she told him about himself and his lying ass daughter.

"Oh, so she is a part of your scams to, I see. It doesn't matter, though, because you are a fucking liar and so are your dysfunctional ass children. That stupid bitch didn't even know where you were or anything and she still lied. Too bad for her and too bad for you, maybe the two of you will meet up in hell together."

He still denied everything she was talking about so Lola walked away. She knew the story had only begun to unfold and she was anxious about him getting on the phone the next day. She played it off like nothing was wrong and nothing happened. But all in all, she was planning the greatest move yet. It was like a soap opera. I had no idea this storyline was going to be so hot. It was the biggest news to hit the airwaves since Lawrence's death.

So, there we were on our way home and he was home and when we opened the door he was in the kitchen just sitting there. "I'm hungry and there is no food in here. Don't you think you should stop all this foolishness and go to the grocery store and be the wife that loves and forgives whatever wrongdoing you think I have done to you and cook me some damn food?"

She just looked at him. Then she leaned over, smiled, and said, "I am not cooking anything else in this mother fucking house. If you want food, do as I do and go buy it. You said I should be a wife then mother fucker you should have been a decent husband and not out here trying to fuck everything in sight. Blind, cripple, and crazy, eight to eighty, your ass needs business cards with that on it.

"Oh, so you want to be a comedian now? Well you don't have to cook, I will go and buy me some food but I just want you to know you are not being a good role model to my daughter. She shouldn't be seeing this. And I don't think it's good that you are taking her out to restaurants every night," he said in a plea, thinking he could use me as bait to get her back in.

She laughed so hard I thought she was going to bust a gut. "Your daughter, oh please, the same daughter you refuse to take to school for me but you can get up and take this bitch's kid to school? Oh, and then lie and say it was your granddaughter? For future reference, don't use my daughter as a pawn in your game." She told me to go upstairs and get my purse, which was code for go and get the tape. When I got back there he was still standing in the kitchen and my mother was waiting by the door. He looked like a sad little puppy dog – he has this thing with his eyes. He can make them fall like a little puppy and you can't help but feel bad for him. He looked so sad, but I didn't allow myself to feel anything for him. He had hurt my mother too many times and I was tired of caring about his emotions when he had made it so very clear he could give a shit about ours.

So, there we were in the restaurant and the both of us were dying to know what was on that tape. We finally let the curiosity get the best of us so we cut our meal short and headed for the car. "Hey what's going on, you may have to get Kita out of school early today. I am not sure where this bitch is getting her information from but she knows what school she goes to and I don't want to add any more fuel to the fire," he told the lady nervously as he spoke so harshly about my mother.

"Do you think that she would do something to my daughter? Should I call the school and put them on alert?" the lady said back, now fearful for her daughter's safety. "No, you don't have to call them. She wouldn't do anything to her. She is not that type of person, but she would go up there and try and start something with me. Did you tell your mother what was going on?"

"No, I don't want her involved in this bullshit."

"Well that's good. I wouldn't want to upset your mother. I keep telling her it's over but she refuses to listen. She just keeps using my daughter as a crutch, knowing I would never just kick my daughter out in the streets." When I looked over to see what my mother's reaction was, I swear you could see the smoke flying out of her ears. The nerve of this dude, my father was really something. So, this time she was really going to get rough and rowdy with him. When we got home he was laying on the bed as if he was reclaiming his territory. I went in the room and I told him, "Man, you are going to get it this time."

He said, "Girl, you had better leave me the hell alone and go in your room and get ready for school." I paid him no attention. I went into my room and waited to hear the fireworks go off. And then like a firecracker bursting, my mother began to go off on him. "I am a bitch now, and you are trying to figure out where I am getting my information from. Well then, bitch, look into the mirror and you will see where I am getting my information from. Who in the hell is this woman?"

"Ok I will admit that I did see my friend's old lady the other day and I haven't seen him in a while and that was his daughter I took to school because they got put out and lost everything. So, I have been trying to help them out and if you don't believe me you can call the girl right now. Damn, are you satisfied now? I didn't want to say anything because I know how jealous you can be, like right now."

She looked at him like the fool he was. He didn't know she had him on tape and the sad thing was he was still lying and he didn't get it when she told him to look in the mirror and he would find out who the snitch was. So then and there he picked up the phone and he called the lady and the dummy she was she went along with his whole story. She told my mother all of these lies about her looking for a job and how Twinkie had been helping them out by taking her little girl to school because she and her boyfriend were put out and she had to move in with her mother but the school was clear across town. But the tape didn't lie. No mention was ever made of this imaginary person who was supposedly her boyfriend. Then she told my mother she had done work for my father cleaning the house. My mother laughed and told the lady that in no way shape or form was she stupid. The lady claimed how sad she was and she never meant any harm and that from that day on she would never have any contact with Twinkie. What kind of fool were they taking her for? Even in a messy situation Lola still put the emotions of others in place of her own. She told the woman she would help her in any way and that she would pass her information on to one of the supervisors in house keeping at her job. She knew Twinkie would never admit to the truth so she had to just go along with her plan and get the hell away from him.

As the days went by we found more and more information and no matter how much more we heard, he still denied every bit of it. Until one day he figured it out. And he played along with the game. I was so afraid. He followed me around the entire house. And when I finally found myself alone there was a knock on the bathroom door. I had to pretend as if I was in there throwing up. My mother and I started staying out later and later. We went looking at more houses and more furniture than the law should have allowed. But she was determined this time to show him just how serious she was.

By this time everyone knew what was going on. Grandma and everyone were so happy. They finally could see through Twinkie. And now everyone wanted forgiveness for treating Lawrence and me so badly over the course of the years. But none of that mattered to me; I was excited to see my mother finally waking up from the nightmare that he had placed her in for all of those years. Daphne and I wrote each other more and more. At this point she was the only person I allowed in my circle. I told her everything, from my fears about graduating to whether or not my mother was sincere about leaving. I had a lot going on in my head and she was my shoulder to lean on as I became hers. She would be home soon and from her idea on it all she had no place to go. She didn't want to live in the house with her mother and Eugene again. Their relationship seemed to be doing very well and it would be hard for her to have so much freedom and then go back to the way things had been. So, I came up with the idea of her moving in with me and my mother once we moved into our new house. She liked the idea a lot. We decided she would come home and we would bring up the conversation in front of my mother and let the magic happen. Lola was never going to see her niece/almost daughter out on the streets.

Charles was having a bowling party in a couple weeks so Daphne got a furlough from Job Corps so she could come home for the weekend. By the time Daphne got there we had already found a house. Kim came by to pick Daphne and me up and we went to look at the new place. For the first time in years I was ecstatic. Lawrence was in the midst of all that was going on. He couldn't give our mother the strength in life to leave Twinkie but he surely gave it to her in his death. When we got to the new house and Daphne saw it, it gave her the strength to ask my mother if she could move in with us. And when the conversation came up that night, my mother already knew what we were doing as we all laid across her bed. She said she wouldn't have it any other way.

Things were finally coming together. A few weeks later my mother got up the nerve to tell Twinkie we were leaving. To him it was just a ploy to scare him, but she was so serious. She asked him if he wanted to accompany us to the house but he blew her off. He was in denial about it all. I don't think he ever thought she would leave him. A few days later my mother was on the phone with Grandma, she wanted her to be with us when we did the contracts and the final walk-through before settlement and our nosy neighbor was listening to the entire conversation.

Ms. Lucy had to be one of the nosiest people in the world. She knew my mother and father had issues but she wanted to know everything and my mother refused to tell her anything because all of her business would have been around the neighborhood. So, she became a good lip reader and wrote down all of my mother's information as she gave it to grandma over the phone.

That evening while we were sitting in the realtor's office we had to wait for grandma to get there. Mary had reached the age where her driving got slower and slower. Then Mr. Albert, the man that worked for the developers said, "Okay, I think we can get started now because I see your mother and father coming now." My mother looked puzzled and I began to laugh. My mother then said, "Albert, my father is dead and has been dead for ten years. Maybe that's not my mother."

Then the door opened and Mary walked in and she was accompanied by Frank, Ms. Lucy's husband. My mother was all choked up we could hardly get through her signing the papers or the walk-through because she kept laughing and Frank kept on butting in trying to get information.

Frank and Ms. Lucy had a lot of nerve. How in the hell did he know where we were moving and how in the hell did they know we would be there at this moment? My mother just focused on the bigger picture. We were finally moving on with our lives and Twinkie was no longer a part of the equation. My mother was finally growing up.

I, on the other hand, wanted answers, but my mother said she would have a talk with Lucy in the morning before she went to work. . When we got home that night, Twinkie was in the family room, which had now become his bedroom. He was asleep on the couch. I went over to greet him and when I got close to him he turned his face into the couch so I could not see him. I pretended as if I had walked into the kitchen and when he turned around I walked over to the couch. Someone had kicked his ass.

I said, "Man, what in the heck happened to you?" He lied and said he had been running in the rain and he slipped and fell into a pothole. He must have thought I was stupid, as if a pothole was that big and would do that much damage to his face. I ran up the stairs and told my mother so she could help him. He was beat up pretty bad. She got the things she needed so she could clean him up. In the middle of her bandaging him up he grabbed her hands and told her, "I never meant to hurt you. That is the last thing I ever wanted to do to you." She accepted his apology and told him she hoped he was going to be alright.

During this time when my mother was gathering her strength, Whitney was losing hers. She had been doing so well. I guess the pressure from her boyfriend hurting her child got the best of her. She was back on the streets getting high again. And it was killing Mary, slowly seeing her child spiral downhill like that. Elsa refused to allow the situations involving her family members to rock her world. Things were great in the hills and that's how she planned on keeping them. On numerous occasions my mother and Elsa offered to let Mary move in with either of them or even get her a place close to Elsa and they would pay the rent but, she declined all such offers. She was and is always more worried about Whitney than she is about herself. So, in Elsa and Lola's case there was nothing they could do. Whitney will always be Mary's top priority, and Elsa and Lola come in second every time.

My mother wasn't that worried about the situation. Whitney was a grown woman and she was going to have to find her own way. No one could want it for her if she didn't want it for herself. She had made it painfully obvious our prayers were in vain. She needs to be the one to pray for herself. Things were already crazy enough with us moving and me getting ready for all my graduation activities. On the day of the settlement, Twinkie went along for the ride because he was going to help my mother decorate the house. Even though Lola was going to settlement, Twinkie still didn't believe her when she said she was leaving. But when we pulled up in front of that house and she had the key, the truth smacked him dead in his face. I stayed with him while my mother went to the settlement. He just stared out the window and tried to hide the fact he was hurt. He had tears running down the side of his face. And when I asked was he alright he just put his head down and said, "I never thought she was really going to leave me."

I felt really bad for him and I didn't know what to say. But he brought it on himself. My mother had been the greatest wife to him and no matter how much she gave it was never enough. And now that he had finally lost her, he wants to sit there and cry. I wanted to tell him not to cry because he brought it on himself, but you never kick a man when he is down. I just put my hand on his shoulder and told him everything would work out the way it was supposed to. He wanted to play macho man and act as if the sun was shining in his eyes but we both knew the truth.

When the settlement was over my mother came running across the street and she was ecstatic. She didn't know what had transpired and I didn't want to tell her. She still had a soft spot for him. He told her how proud he was of her and then he got in his truck and drove off.

Over the course of the next few weeks things were so hectic. Daphne finished up Job Corps and was about to come home and I was finishing up with school getting ready for prom and all of the rest of the activities. I couldn't believe all of this transpired at the same time. I was graduating from high school and my mother was finally waking up from the nightmare that she had been in for far too long. She became a grownup. Everyone was so proud of her. But none of them could top me and my brother. It had been a long journey, but at last she got the point. As much as you love a person, sometimes you just can't be together. It doesn't mean you can't still hold onto your feelings. It doesn't mean you failed at anything. Sometimes being with someone can be toxic for you. And that love is killing you painfully and slow. But Lola finally got up and got out of that messy situation.

The next few months went by so fast. I was a high school graduate! I was finally coming into my own. I could just see Lawrence smiling from the clouds. With all that had transpired, I knew my brother had to die. It still hurts, but sometimes God tries to wake us up and we can't see or we won't allow ourselves to see the message he has placed in front of us. God tried time and time again to grab my mother's attention. And it wasn't until Lawrence's death that she took heed to His message. Through Lawrence's death she finally muscled up enough courage to get out.

The time passed fast as things changed and it felt as if we were finally starting our lives. Things were close enough for us to grab hold of. Daphne took a job at a local hotel and my mother was happier than I had ever seen her in my entire life, even in Lawrence's absence. Twinkie was still Twinkie – he thought he was going to have his cake and eat it, too. Now that we no longer lived under the same roof, he thought he had free reign over two households. But it didn't matter to any of us, we were just happy.

I was starting my freshman year of college, the first day of the rest of my life. When we drove up to campus, Twinkie was as crazy as he normally was, cursing people out and never trying to let on just how proud he was. My mother cried the entire time. She cried for my accomplishments, she cried for all that we had, and all we had lost. We put all of my things away and headed over to main campus for the pinning ceremony. Twinkie talked about everything from the grass to the suit that the President of the University had on. I tried not to laugh. My mother was still crying, but I understood her tears of sorrow and joy. And there I was standing on the lawn of my new school waiting for my father to pin me. I couldn't believe this day had finally come. The sun was shining bright, as if the heavens were looking down on me and there was my brother standing tall and proud. I knew then that Lawrence would be so pleased. I was beginning a new phase of my life. I am going to college. That light at the end of the long, cold, dark tunnel was finally here, and it took a lot to finally get to this point. I lost so much and in actuality, heartache was all I gained. But I know in the end it will make me a better person. I may have gone through hell and high water but som how I made my way out. And I passed each of the tests that were placed in front of me with flying colors. My brother didn't raise me to be a quitter.

My mother had finally grown up. She realized that through her son's death God allowed her the opportunity to live, and though she lost everything, she had her self respect and peace of mind she could build on from there. Daphne was a new person. Leaving us all for that timeframe really matured her and made her a better person. Elsa was and is a walking miracle. God could have taken her life a long time ago but she had to go through the process in order to become the beautiful butterfly we all knew she was from the start. She just had to realize it. Whitney is just Whitney. We pray to God to keep her safe. She has a habit and until she wants to get clean we have to keep her in prayer. And Mary, while we were growing up, we all thought of her as being the begging, nasty-mouthed, weed-smoking grandmother, but deep down inside we have to finally face reality and realize because of her we have life. She was the tool God used to bring all of us into this world, no matter what her faults may be. With all of her flaws, she is still their mother and our grandmother.

What people don't realize is that it doesn't matter how you start in life, it is how you finish. You never let the bad things turn you in to a bad person. Take the negative and somehow turn it into a positive. Everyone had turned over a new leaf and decided to start anew. Over the course of these five years, so much had changed, some things for the better, but a lot for the worse. But we all made it through with flying colors. We are all very different in our own right, but we all fit together like the pieces of a puzzle. And when all of the pieces are finally connected together ,it will be a masterpiece that tells a wonderful story.

ABOUT THE AUTHOR

Tiffanye R. Paige is a native of Washington, DC. Tiffanye attended Howard University where she received a Bachelor of Music and a Master's Degree in Social Work. Her love for writing began at an early age. When she was 15 years old, she lost the most important person in the world to her, her older brother, who was tragically murdered. From the pain of her loss, *We All Have a Story* was born.